Memories of the Heart

A River Falls Novel

Valerie M. Bodden

River Falls Series

Pieces of Forever
Songs of Home
Memories of the Heart
Whispers of Truth
Promises of Mercy

River Falls Christmas Romances

Christmas of Joy

Hope Springs Series

Not Until Forever
Not Until This Moment
Not Until You
Not Until Us
Not Until Christmas Morning
Not Until This Day
Not Until Someday
Not Until Now
Not Until Then
Not Until The End

A Gift for You

Members of my Reader's Club get a FREE book, available exclusively to my subscribers. When you sign up, you'll also be the first to know about new releases, book deals, and giveaways.

Visit www.valeriembodden.com/freebook to join!

But one thing I do: Forgetting what is behind and straining toward what is ahead, I press on toward the goal to win the prize for which God has called me heavenward in Christ Jesus.

Philippians 3:13-14

Chapter 1

Abigail made sure to keep her eyes closed lightly—not scrunched—and her breathing deep and even as she heard Simeon drop his toothbrush back into the holder. She knew his routine well. Next he'd spritz on a dash of the light, earthy wild sage cologne she loved so much, pat the spot where his hair stuck up in a perpetual cowlick on the right side of his head, then reappear in the bedroom to say goodbye to her before heading off to work.

Only she wouldn't say it back.

Because she was still sleeping.

The soft swish of the cologne spray was followed two beats later by the bathroom door creaking open. Then a sigh, deep and long, that tore at Abigail's insides. It was her fault, that sigh.

All of it was her fault.

Simeon's footsteps shuffled across the hardwood floor to her side of the bed.

Abigail let out a slow, even breath, careful not to let her eyelids flutter as Simeon brushed a lock of hair off her forehead. His scent drifted over her as his lips pressed to her skin, his breath breezing across her cheek with a whispered, "I love you."

She forced herself to inhale, slow and even, eyes still closed, as he pulled away. It was a moment before she heard his footsteps retreat and the bedroom door click softly closed.

A tear trickled slowly from the corner of her eye, following the line of her nose until it reached her lips. Still she didn't open her eyes. Getting out of bed would be too much work.

She crunched the pillow under her head, scooting toward Simeon's side of the bed to soak up any warmth he may have left behind. But it had grown cold.

The sound of Simeon moving around the kitchen drifted up the stairs, and Abigail let herself remember the days when she used to get up with him, when they'd laugh as they got in each other's way in the small bathroom, when they'd linger over a kiss or two in the kitchen, even if it made them late for work.

It hadn't been that long ago. They hadn't even been married for five years yet.

So why did it feel like a lifetime stood between them?

You know why.

Abigail punched at the pillow as the front door opened and closed, its sound echoing up the stairs even though Simeon hadn't slammed it—he would never slam it. His dress shoes clicked across the driveway, followed by the rumble of his SUV's engine. She pictured him buckling his seatbelt, adjusting the mirror—he did it every time even though no one else drove the vehicle—and turning down the volume of the radio so he could use his short morning drive time for prayer. She wondered briefly if those prayers included her.

She had tried to work up the energy for her own prayers, but her mind was one big blank when she tried to think about God these days. Well, not so much a blank as cluttered with all the lies and accusations and blame. With all the things she'd done wrong. All the lies she'd told. All the reasons she deserved this punishment he was putting her through.

With a groan, she pressed her fists to her eyes, then opened them. The only thing harder than getting up was lying here and letting her thoughts continue down this path. She peeled herself off her pillow and ran a hand through her tangled hair. Though it was May, the chill of the hardwood bit at her feet as she dragged herself to the bathroom.

The scent of Simeon's cologne still lingered in the air, and she sucked in a big breath of it. If she closed her eyes, she could probably imagine his arms around her, imagine burying her nose in his shirt and drowning in the comfort of his embrace.

She shook her head and turned on the shower, cranking the temperature to maximum. Steam quickly filled the room, blocking her view of the mirror. Good. She peeled off the sweats she'd slept in, trying hard to avoid looking at the body that had let her down so many times. It didn't even seem to belong to her anymore, soft and spongy in places that used to be firm and toned. A mom body. Only she wasn't a mom.

With a sigh, she stepped into the shower, wincing as the scalding water stabbed her shoulders. But even the heat couldn't drive the thoughts away.

She flipped the water to cold, showered quickly, pulled on a new pair of sweatpants and a t-shirt, and brushed her teeth, then headed for the kitchen. Simeon had left her favorite mug next to the full coffee carafe. A bright yellow sticky note clung to the front of the mug, and curiosity pulled Abigail forward to read it.

I'll be home early for our doctor appointment. I love you.

She ran her fingers over the letters. *I love you.* She'd always teased Simeon that his handwriting was way too neat to be a doctor. To which he'd always reminded her that he wasn't a *doctor*, he was a counselor.

It was one of the things that had drawn her to him. He'd been so easy to talk to.

And all you told him was lies.

Abigail set the note down, the *I love you* still seared against her fingertips, joined by the prickle of guilt. She loved him too. But she was starting to wonder if that was enough. He was such a good man. And she was . . . not who he thought she was. She'd thought she could leave that behind. That she could be someone new. But instead she'd only dragged him into her mess.

She poured herself a cup of coffee and moved to the kitchen table, which overlooked the spacious backyard. The outdoor space was the whole reason they'd bought this house. There was supposed to be a tire swing back there by now. And a sand box. And maybe even a tree house. Instead, it was immaculate. And empty. There was no reason to have all those things when there were no children to use them.

Chapter 2

Simeon tipped his coffee cup back, grimacing as the lukewarm liquid coated his tongue. With a sigh, he plunked the mug on the corner of his desk, resisting the urge to venture into the small reception area to refill it. He'd already had three cups, and he needed to save some for his clients. He glanced at the time on his computer screen. Eleven o'clock. Three more hours until Abigail's doctor appointment. He scrubbed a hand down his freshly shaved cheek, wondering if he should call to make sure she'd gotten out of bed.

Not that she'd been sleeping when he'd left. They'd been married long enough that he could tell the difference between her fake sleep, with its deep, even breaths, and her real sleep, with its uneven, soft half-snores. But he hadn't had the energy to call her out. And even if he had, it wouldn't have changed anything. She would have said everything was fine, just as she always did, then rolled over and gone back to sleep for real.

He tried not to take it personally. It was the depression. Diagnosing it wasn't the problem. Neither was discerning the cause. The losses they'd experienced over the last two years would leave anyone reeling.

No, the problem was that she wouldn't let him—or anyone else—help her.

So he went on, day after day, acting like he knew exactly how to help other people sort out their lives, how to help couples renew their marriages, when his own was unraveling. It felt like there were only a few stitches left.

And once those let go, he wasn't sure there'd be any way to mend their relationship.

He picked up the framed photo of the two of them in Ecuador that adorned his desk, rubbing at a smudge that marred the glass over Abigail's smile. Maybe they'd rushed into things too quickly. He certainly hadn't planned to meet anyone on that mission trip—let alone propose marriage to her. But she'd upturned all his carefully laid plans with that smile. And he'd known almost immediately that it was a smile he wanted to wake up to every day for the rest of his life.

He tried to remember the last time he'd seen it—a real, genuine smile—rather than the strained "everything's fine" smile she'd put on for months now. Maybe his own certainty that they were right for each other hadn't been enough. Maybe he should have given her more time . . .

A bell jingled as the exterior door out in the waiting area opened, and Simeon set the picture down, giving a quick glance at his schedule. Wendy Storm. Good. He needed a relatively "easy" client right now, and Wendy was always more than willing to talk—and eager to hear his suggestions and report on her progress. He only wished he could have helped her and her husband Jeff more—but Simeon had only met with them a few times before Jeff had decided he'd had enough and left her. The day she'd walked into his office alone, crying, Simeon had been devastated. It wasn't his first failure as a counselor, but he'd really thought they'd been making progress.

Wendy's depression after the divorce had been hard, but she'd been willing to seek help. Willing to talk. Willing to do all the things Abigail refused to do.

Simeon shook his head and closed the file of notes he'd been making. That wasn't fair. It wasn't that Abigail refused. It was that she was so far down, she couldn't see the way out. That was what he needed to help her with—no matter how long it took. He wouldn't give up on her.

Simeon blew out a breath and tried to refocus his attention on the client he was about to counsel. He closed his eyes and bowed his head to pray as he did before every session. *Dear Lord, give me wisdom and guidance as I counsel Wendy. Help her to see that even when the love of people fails, your love never will. Help my love for my wife never to fail. Help me figure out how to reach her, Lord.* He cut himself off. This prayer was supposed to be for Wendy. *Help Wendy continue to heal, Lord. Amen.*

Simeon opened his eyes and got up slowly, still working to let go of thoughts of Abigail. Being a counselor meant he had to put his personal life aside, even when it was hard.

He opened the door that led from his office to the small waiting area.

"Good morning." Wendy jumped up from one of the cozy armchairs Abigail had helped him pick out a few years ago to replace the stiff chairs he'd had before.

"It's a beautiful day, isn't it?" Wendy smiled broadly, flipping her dark hair over her shoulder.

"I— Uh." Simeon glanced toward the large windows that looked over the small parking lot and the Serenity River beyond it. He hadn't even noticed the weather when he left home this morning, but the sky was a bright, cloudless blue, the mountains that skirted the town carpeted in the green of late spring. "Yes, it is. Come on in."

He stood aside to let her pass through the doorway into his office, then followed her to the leather chairs arranged around a small coffee table. The furniture made the space feel more like a living room than an office. That was Abigail's doing too.

Wendy dropped into what had become "her" chair, and Simeon sat across from her.

"So, how are you today?" Wendy slid off her shoes and folded her bare feet under her.

Simeon laughed. "I think that's supposed to be my question to you."

"Who asks you then?" Wendy peered shrewdly at him.

Simeon swallowed. It used to be Abigail. But it had been a long time since she had asked anything about him—how was work, how was he. None of that seemed to matter to her anymore.

"I'm fine, thanks," he answered Wendy's first question, skipping the second.

He was always fine. That was his job. To be fine so he could help others who weren't fine. "And how are you doing?"

"Really great." Wendy leaned forward, as if the momentum of her happiness might pull her out of her chair. "You know that job I applied for? At Zelensky and Baker? I got it!"

"That's great." Simeon felt his own lips lift into a smile. He spent so much time listening to clients' troubles that it made him extra joyful when he had cause to celebrate good news with them. "Congratulations."

"Thanks." Wendy's cheeks flushed. "And that's not my only good news."

"No? What else?"

"I'm in love." Wendy pressed her palms together in front of her heart.

Simeon had years of practice in not registering surprise or skepticism at clients' revelations. And this certainly wasn't the wildest he'd ever heard. But it still tested his ability to retain a neutral expression. "That's rather sudden, don't you think?" he asked.

Wendy shook her head. "Actually, I think it's been coming on for a long time now. I was just too caught up in everything with the divorce to recognize it at first. But he was there for me through all of that, and now—" She pressed a hand to her heart. "I think I'm finally ready."

Simeon considered his next words. He didn't want to put a damper on her enthusiasm, and yet he had a responsibility to make sure she wasn't being taken advantage of. "You said he was there for you through the divorce. You were very vulnerable during that time. Is there a chance he took advantage of that fact?"

Wendy shook her head emphatically. "It's not like that. He has no idea I feel this way. I didn't even realize it myself until I was journaling like you told me to. I was kind of daydreaming, I guess, about the ideal man, and it hit me—" She slapped herself on the forehead. "I already know him."

"Okay. I feel like there are a few things to unpack there." Simeon made a quick list in his head.

"I knew you would." Wendy's smile lit up her whole face. Maybe she really was in love.

Simeon thought wistfully of Abigail's smile but pushed the image out. This wasn't about him and his wife.

"Let's start with this." He directed his attention back to Wendy. "What were some of the things you wrote about this ideal man you're looking for?" Simeon could only hope her answer wouldn't be too wildly unrealistic.

"Well, a good listener. Someone who really hears me, you know? Who doesn't just nod and smile when I talk."

Simeon found himself nodding with relief. Those were realistic expectations. "And you feel like this guy is a good listener?"

"Oh yes," Wendy gushed. "We've talked for *hours*, and he never tires of listening to me. And I can tell he really cares what I think."

You're a really good listener, do you know that? Abigail had said that to Simeon moments before their first kiss.

He forced his thoughts back to the present. "How can you tell that?" he asked Wendy.

She tapped her lip, then leaned forward. "He asks questions, like he wants to understand me better. And he remembers what I say, even weeks later."

"That's good. But you said he doesn't know how you feel?" Simeon asked carefully. The last thing Wendy needed was to have her heart broken by some guy who didn't reciprocate her feelings.

"No." Wendy bit her lip. "Not yet."

"So you're thinking about telling him?"

Wendy shrugged, looking uncertain. "Do you think I should?"

Simeon hesitated. This wasn't a matter of right or wrong, so he couldn't really give her a yes or no answer. What he could do, though, was give her some things to consider.

"Do you think he reciprocates your feelings?"

Wendy nodded slowly. "I think he might."

"And if he doesn't?" Simeon asked gently. "Are you ready to deal with that?"

Wendy's head stopped bobbing. "I'm not sure," she said quietly. "I don't want him to hate me."

"I'm sure he wouldn't hate you," Simeon reassured her. "But it might change your relationship. You need to be prepared for that."

"So you don't think I should tell him?" Wendy's face fell.

"I'm not saying that." Simeon considered how to phrase it. "I'm saying there's a risk. But some things are worth the risk." He happened to believe love was one of them. After all, that was how he'd ended up proposing to Abigail after only three months.

But then, given the current state of their relationship, maybe that wasn't the best example. "It's just something to think about," he told Wendy. "Before you move forward."

Wendy chewed her lip. "Okay, I'll think about it."

"Good." Their talk turned to other topics Wendy had journaled about, including her childhood trauma in the foster care system. Every time she talked about it, Simeon wondered if this was what Abigail's experience in the system had been like too. But unlike Wendy, who talked about it openly, Abigail had said she'd rather forget the past. But maybe, if he—

"So anyway—"

Simeon startled as he realized he had no idea what Wendy had just said. How long had he tuned her out?

"I think maybe that's why I was drawn to Jeff, don't you?" Wendy continued.

"It could be," Simeon answered hesitantly.

"You don't think so?" Wendy leaned forward.

Simeon kicked himself. He couldn't agree or disagree with something he hadn't heard—but he couldn't really explain to Wendy that he hadn't been listening to her.

"There are probably a lot of reasons." Simeon tried to cover his lapse. "It's rarely one simple answer." He glanced at the clock on the wall behind her. "Oops. It looks like we went over our time."

Wendy giggled. "That's nothing new."

"True." Simeon stood and waited for her to do the same.

He escorted her toward the door, but halfway there, she stopped and turned toward him so abruptly that he nearly plowed her over. She grabbed his arm to steady herself.

"Sorry." Though she was wearing heels, she came up only to his chin, and she tipped her head back to meet his eyes. "Thank you."

"You're welcome."

"No, I mean, for everything. For listening. For not laughing me out of here when I said I was in love. I know it sounds crazy, but . . ."

"It's not crazy." Simeon subtly maneuvered his arm out from under her hand and started toward the door again. "I just want you to be careful, that's all. So you don't end up getting hurt."

"That's sweet of you."

Simeon shrugged uncomfortably. He hadn't said it to be sweet; this was his *job*.

"Can I ask you one more favor?" Wendy paused in the doorway to the waiting area. "Would you pray for me?"

"I always do." Simeon opened the office door and ushered her out.

"Thank you," she said with another wide smile. "I always feel so much better after talking to you."

Simeon waited until she was outside to close his office door. He let out a breath and rubbed at his temples. He was fortunate Wendy hadn't noticed how much his mind had wandered during their session. He had better get it together before his next client showed up. It was his job to help them with their problems. Regardless of his own.

Chapter 3

Abigail reached for the remote to click the TV off. She'd been staring at it for the past hour, but she had no idea what she'd even been watching. Just as her finger hit the power button, a familiar face flashed on the screen. The TV went black, but Abigail pressed the power button again, leaning forward as she waited for the image to reappear.

"Senator Harris announces bid for Illinois governor," the caption on the bottom of the screen read, though the camera was focused on the interviewer, who was asking how the candidate proposed to lower taxes. The camera panned to a man with silver hair and a politician's smile, and Abigail caught her breath.

She hadn't seen her father in over five years, and now there he was, staring at her through the screen.

"I'm glad you asked, Walt." The voice was deep and resonant with a practiced empathetic pitch.

Abigail fumbled with the remote, jabbing her finger to the power button before she could hear more. She threw the remote onto the coffee table and wrapped her arms around herself.

It was good to know her mistakes hadn't cost her father his career, as her parents had said would happen. But then, she supposed they had plenty of people to help them spin the story. And banishing her to Ecuador on that mission trip had probably helped too. All it had cost them was one daughter. A small price to pay for her dad's political position, she was sure.

She hadn't called them, visited them—had any contact with them—since the day they'd sent her away. They'd made it perfectly clear that they had no room for her in their lives.

She wondered once in a while if they knew where she was now. It wasn't like she was hidden away. And they had the resources to find her—if they wanted to.

Which they clearly didn't.

And that was fine with her. She certainly didn't need them.

She'd never even told Simeon about them, instead letting him believe her parents were dead.

It wasn't entirely a lie. They were dead to her.

It is a lie, her conscience argued. *You told him you grew up in the foster system.*

Okay, that part had been a lie. But it didn't hurt anyone.

And what about the rest of your lies? her conscience persisted.

Abigail jumped to her feet. She couldn't sit here and think about this.

She pulled on a sweatshirt and headed for the front door. Heat hit her the moment she stepped outside, and she looked around in surprise. Big white blossoms clung to the magnolia tree Simeon had planted their first year in the house. Tulips and snapdragons poked up from the flowerbeds that lined the porch. And the sky was a blinding blue that made her squint.

When had spring arrived?

She pulled out her phone to check the date. May 1.

Which meant it had been spring for a while.

How had she not noticed? She left the house almost every day for work. But she could have sworn that every day for the past she-didn't-know-how-long had been gray and gloomy.

She drew in a deep breath, the scent of fresh-cut grass tickling her nose. Simeon must have mowed the lawn yesterday after he'd gotten home from church. She'd spent the morning watching TV, then retreated to bed for a nap when he got home.

Tears poked at her eyelids. Simeon didn't deserve to be treated like this. But being around him—pretending everything was fine—was too hard.

But she could change. She *would* change. Starting now, with a walk. Already, she could feel the fresh air reviving her.

She set off down the sidewalk at a brisk pace, making herself take notice of the flowers in the neighbors' yards, of the gentle swishing sound of the leaves in the breeze and the call of the birds flitting overhead and the . . .

She stopped, listening, her heart jammed up against her ribs.

Children.

That was the sound of children. Shrieking. Laughing. Playing.

It must be coming from the school around the corner. She and Simeon had chosen this house because it was so close to the school. They'd talked about how they'd walk their children there every day. About how when the kids were too old to want them along, they'd just "happen" to take a morning walk in that direction. About how it would be so convenient for going to the plays and sporting events and other activities their children would be involved in.

Abigail knew she shouldn't, but she let her feet pull her in the direction of the noise.

Despite the slamming in her chest and the churning in her middle, she walked right to the green space where a group of children chased each other in what looked like a game of tag. She kept walking, her eyes going to the jungle gym and then to the swings. She paused a moment, her gaze lingering on a little girl with dark pigtails that rose and fell around her head in time to the swing's movements.

Abigail wrapped her arms around her middle. She wanted to be here thinking about how quickly the years had passed. Wondering how her baby was in school already. But instead, she and Simeon had three babies who had never made it beyond the womb.

After the first miscarriage, she'd told herself it was normal—sad, yes, but it happened to lots of women. After the second, she'd thought maybe she'd done something wrong. But the doctor had reassured her it wasn't her fault. But after the third, she knew better.

It was her fault.

God was punishing her.

She'd tried so hard to make up for her past. To be the perfect wife. To be worthy of Simeon's love.

But God knew better.

And the worst part was, her past sins were hurting Simeon, and he didn't even know it.

"Hello." A small voice pulled Abigail's attention to a little girl in front of her. The girl gave her a bright-eyed smile and waved. "Hello," she said again.

Abigail opened her mouth to reply, but all that came out was a strangled gasp for air.

She spun away, dashed across the road, and sprinted home. Inside, she slammed the door, then leaned against it, panting heavily.

No more walks, she scolded herself.

When her breathing had finally slowed, she pushed off the door and dragged herself up the stairs. She could try to take a nap, but she knew that little girl's face would haunt her. Instead, she grabbed her laptop out of the bottom drawer of her dresser and carried it to the bed.

She stacked the pillows behind her back, then settled the computer on her lap and opened the document she'd been working on for the past few weeks.

She wasn't sure what made her think she could write a book. Maybe it was working at the Book Den, surrounded by all those words every day. Or maybe it was the woman who came in regularly and sat at one of their tables for an hour or two, her fingers clicking away on the keyboard.

At any rate, one day Abigail had come home from work and just started writing.

She had no idea if what she had written was any good. And it didn't matter. She never intended for anyone else to read it.

All she knew was that maybe if she got everything down on paper, she could leave it in the past and truly move forward with Simeon.

She skimmed the words she'd written a few days ago, letting herself get caught up in pretending these things had happened to someone else. That this woman wasn't her. That the real *her* was the woman she was now, not the woman she'd been then.

Garrick leered at me. "What, you thought the cars drove themselves across the state? Come on, it'll be like a road trip. I'll even let you drive."

I eyed the Porsche. It would be fun to drive. And it wasn't like the owner was going to miss it. I'd seen his outrageous car collection.

"Yeah. All right." I held out a hand for the keys, and Garrick dropped them into it, their heft much greater than the actual weight of the metal. I swallowed. Was I really capable of this?

"That's right, baby. Road trip time." Garrick grinned and slapped a hard kiss onto my mouth, then jumped into the passenger seat.

With one quick glance over my shoulder, I giggled, hoping it sounded carefree rather than terrified. I opened the driver's door. This was so far from anything I'd ever done before. So far from anything my parents would approve of.

And it felt exhilarating.

Abigail's stomach turned over, and she wished she could forget everything. But there were so many more terrible scenes to write before she got to the part she truly wanted to remember. The part where she'd met Simeon. The part where it felt like she'd gotten a do-over. A chance to start a new life.

This life.

So why did it feel like that old life still held her captive?

Abigail resolutely brought her fingers back to the keyboard. She may not be able to forget the past. But maybe once she finished this, she could leave it behind.

Chapter 4

Simeon glanced surreptitiously at the clock. He needed to leave for Abigail's doctor appointment, but there was something Adam was holding back from him. His usually candid client had seemed preoccupied, not saying much about anything today.

"Is there anything else you want to talk about?" Simeon tried one more time.

"What? Ah, no." Adam stood. "Thanks."

"Of course," Simeon answered, though the man may as well have said, *thanks for nothing*, for all the good Simeon had done him today.

"Can I ask you something?" Adam didn't look at Simeon as he asked.

"Of course." Simeon got to his feet as well.

"Do you think— I mean, it's not wrong to talk to someone online, right?"

Simeon kept his groan to himself. Whenever someone started a sentence with *it's not wrong*, it usually meant they were looking for his permission to do something they already knew they shouldn't. "I suppose that depends. What do you mean by talking? And by someone?"

Adam looked sheepish. "I mean, I met this woman—well, reconnected actually. We went to high school together. And we've been talking a lot online. And she just makes me feel . . . I don't know . . . Good about myself, you know. Like Sheila used to make me feel."

Simeon waited to see if Adam would pick up on what he'd just said on his own.

"I mean, that's not cheating, right?" Adam held his hands out. "She's in Canada. So it's not like we'd ever *do* anything. We're just talking."

"Like you used to talk to Sheila?"

Adam nodded. "Yeah. Like that."

"And is there a reason you don't talk to Sheila like that anymore?"

Adam laughed. "Let's see. Three kids might have something to do with it."

Simeon winced internally. Three times, he and Abigail had thought . . .

"Plus she just got this promotion," Adam added, "so she's working long hours. It's not like she has a moment to spare for me."

"So you feel like your wife doesn't have time for you. And you're seeking intimacy somewhere else."

"What?" Adam crossed his arms in front of him. "No. I told you, Lisa lives in Canada. It's not like I'm going to fly up there to sleep with her or something."

"There are other kinds of intimacy." Simeon managed to keep his voice even, though it felt like it'd been months since he'd experienced any kind of intimacy with his own wife. "Talking is one of the deepest forms of intimacy. And the basis for all other kinds of intimacy."

"I don't—" Adam uncrossed his arms and dropped back into the chair. "So you're saying I can't talk to Lisa anymore?"

Simeon retook his seat as well. "I'm not making rules here. I'm saying, you need to think about what it means to be faithful to your wife. And right now, it sounds like talking to Lisa is hurting your relationship with Sheila. She's the one you need to be talking to. I really think it would be beneficial if she came to an appointment with you at some point. Have you told her yet that you're coming?"

Adam shook his head.

"It's nothing to be ashamed of, you know." Ah, those words. How many times had he said them to Abigail about the miscarriages she was so determined to hide from everyone else?

"I know." Adam crossed and uncrossed his leg. "But I'm not sure I'm ready to tell her everything about my past yet."

"I understand." Simeon adjusted his position in his seat. "We can work into that slowly. But I want you to think about this: if you want to have true intimacy with her, holding back the truth isn't going to help."

"And if your wife told you she had a past like mine?" Adam stared him down, crossing his arms again. "What would you do?"

Simeon nearly laughed at the thought of his sweet wife having a secret past. But even if she did, it wouldn't change how he felt about her. "I'd remind her God has forgiven her," Simeon said. "Just like he's forgiven you. He's made you a new creation. You aren't that old man anymore."

Adam sighed and dragged a hand through his closely shaved hair. "Yeah. I know. It's just hard to believe sometimes."

"That's the thing about grace." Simeon smiled. "It seems unbelievable, but it's true nonetheless."

Adam nodded, his expression pensive.

"Just think about bringing her," Simeon said. "Not talking to each other is about the worst thing you can do for your marriage." He should know.

Adam stood. "I didn't bring this up earlier because I knew this was what you were going to say. But it was what I needed to hear. Thank you." He held out a hand, and Simeon shook it.

"That's what I'm here for." He ushered Adam out, then rushed back to his desk to shut down his computer and grab his keys. If he hurried, he should make it home just in time to pick Abigail up for her doctor appointment.

Outside, he jumped into his SUV and rolled down the windows, both so he could enjoy the warm May air and so he could clear his head after Adam's bombshell. As much as he and Abigail were struggling right now, he couldn't imagine wanting to find comfort in another woman. Even on their hardest days, she was still his wife, and as long as he had anything to say about it, that would never change.

He blew out a breath, steering through the quaint downtown, past his brother Joseph's veterinary clinic, Daisy's Pie Shop, Henderson's Art Gallery, the Book Den—where Abigail worked several days a week. As he pulled up to a stop sign, his eyes went to the river flowing behind the stores. The early May warmth had drawn people to the riverwalk, and Simeon's lips lifted as he caught sight of a couple swinging a young boy between them. The boy's squealing giggle reached through Simeon's open window, and he chuckled. He remembered his own parents swinging him like that as a kid.

Behind him, a car honked, and Simeon jumped, pressing his foot to the accelerator with an apologetic wave over his shoulder. The boy's giggle followed him down the block, and Simeon wondered if he and Abigail would ever have that experience.

If it is your will, Lord, he prayed for what felt like the millionth time. *Please bless us with a child.*

He let out a breath as he turned onto their street and pulled into the driveway of the two-story home they'd purchased because it had enough room to start a family.

He left the SUV running and jumped out to collect Abigail. If she was ready to go, they'd make it to the doctor just in time.

But she wasn't waiting for him in the living room off the small entryway.

"Abigail," he called. "Sorry I'm late."

When there was no answer, he strode to the kitchen at the back of the house. But she wasn't there or in the dining room either.

"Abigail?" He jogged back to the entry and took the stairs two at a time. If she was still in bed, they'd never make it to the appointment, and it would probably be at least another couple of months before they could get on the schedule again.

He passed the two smaller bedrooms—one of which they'd painted a light green when they'd first decided to start trying so it'd be one less thing they had to worry about once they had a baby on the way. The other served as a home office for him for now, although the plan had always been to eventually turn it into a second child's bedroom and maybe convert their one-car garage into an office.

He continued past the home's single full bathroom—the real estate agent had joked that they'd better have boys if they were going to live in a house with only one bathroom, but they'd both dismissed the concern. Everything else about the house made it the perfect place to raise their family, and they weren't going to let a lack of bathrooms stop them.

"Abigail?" Simeon stopped in the doorway to their bedroom.

Abigail sat propped in the bed, her computer on her lap, staring at the screen with her brow furrowed, fingers flying across the keys. She didn't look up.

He took a step into the room. "Are you ready to—"

Her head jerked up, and her eyes landed on him a split second before she looked back to her screen and then slammed the computer shut. "You scared me." Her voice shook a little, and her eyes were too wide. She clutched the computer to her chest as if it held state secrets.

Simeon knew guilt when he saw it.

But guilt over what?

"What were you doing?" He nodded to the computer.

"I— Nothing. Shopping."

Acid rose in the back of Simeon's throat at the obvious lie. No one typed like that when they were shopping.

It's not wrong to talk to someone online, right? Adam's question flashed in front of Simeon's eyes like a fluorescent sign.

"What are you doing home?" Abigail asked.

"Doctor appointment, remember?" he answered dully. He couldn't take his eyes off that computer.

"I texted you." Abigail dropped her gaze to the blankets balled at the bottom of the bed. "The appointment got canceled."

"Oh." Simeon pulled out his phone. He hadn't had time to check his messages all day. "Sure enough, there it is. When is it rescheduled for?" He tapped on the calendar on his phone.

Abigail was silent, and he looked up. She had dropped the computer back onto her lap and was running a hand back and forth over the cover.

"Abigail?"

She looked up at him, her eyes tortured. "I can't," she whispered.

"Can't what?" He moved to the bed and sat carefully on his side. Although they slept together in it every night, it had been months since she'd welcomed so much as a kiss from him. He couldn't even remember the last time they'd held hands.

"I can't go to the doctor." A tear trickled down Abigail's cheek, and Simeon moved closer. Whatever she had been doing on the computer, she was his wife, and he couldn't bear to see her hurt.

"Why not?" he asked gently, lifting one hand off her computer and cradling it in his. She let it lie there limply, but at least she didn't pull away.

"Because." Abigail sighed, and he was pretty sure that was all she was going to say. But he waited anyway.

"Because," she finally started again. "Either she's going to say we can't have children." Tears splatted against her cheeks like raindrops on sand. "Or she's going to say everything is fine and we can try again. And—" She gulped in a shuddering breath. "And I don't know if I can go through that again."

"Oh, Abigail." Simeon reached for her, but she stood and paced to the window.

He tamped down his frustration. Why would she never let him comfort her?

He forced himself to push aside the hurt and go to her. She kept her back to him, running her finger over a trail of dust on the windowsill.

"We don't have to go to the doctor," he said, resting his hands gently on her shoulders.

She nodded stiffly. "Thank you." She shrugged out of his hold. "I'm going to go shower."

She sped toward the hallway, leaving her computer on the bed. Simeon eyed it.

Had she been talking to someone? Someone who wasn't him?

He took a step toward the bed but then stopped himself. He trusted his wife.

And anyway, he had a vehicle to turn off.

⸙

Abigail cracked her eyes open. The room was dark, but something had woken her. She readjusted her pillow and closed her eyes again. But something was different—missing.

She didn't hear Simeon's breaths.

She reached behind her, toward his side of the bed. But her hand didn't bump into his back. She opened her eyes again and rolled over. Simeon's side of the bed was empty.

Maybe he'd gotten up to use the bathroom.

But the bedroom door was closed, and he always left it open when he used the bathroom in the middle of the night—ever since the time he'd run smack into it in the dark and broken his toe.

She rolled back to her side of the bed and picked up her phone to check the time. 3:20 a.m. Simeon was an early bird—but not that early.

Abigail closed her eyes again. Whatever he was doing, he probably didn't want to see her right now anyhow. Not after the way she'd pushed him away earlier when he'd been so sweet and understanding. She had longed to fall into his arms and cling to him and never let go. But that would have been unfair to him. After spending the day writing about all of her sins—all of the reasons God was punishing them now—she couldn't just let Simeon hold her and tell her everything would be okay.

She could only be thankful that he hadn't read what she'd been writing when he got home. She was usually so careful not to let him see her working on it, but she hadn't heard him come in.

She reached for her nightstand to reassure herself that her computer was still there. She'd shut it down before bed but had been too tired to stash it in her dresser drawer.

Her hand hit bare wood, and she slid it a little farther. Still nothing.

She propped herself onto an elbow and turned on the small lamp at the back of the nightstand. She blinked against the glare. But even through her bleary vision, she could see the computer was no longer there.

Her heart wedged itself against her throat, but she told herself to calm down. Maybe she had put it in her drawer after all.

It wasn't like it could have walked away on its own.

And Simeon wouldn't have . . .

She flung herself out of bed and dropped to the floor in front of her dresser, yanking open the bottom drawer. She rifled through the pile of jeans, but the computer wasn't there.

The way Simeon had been looking at it when she'd closed it earlier . . . like he thought she was doing something wrong. And her lie about shopping had been so thin.

But he wouldn't really snoop on her, would he?

She sprang to her feet, suddenly wide awake. If he read it . . .

Her feet slapped against the hardwood floor as she launched herself toward the door.

No, no, no. Please don't let him read it.

Simeon's office door was closed, but soft light trickled out from under it.

That doesn't mean anything, she tried to reassure herself. It wasn't terribly unusual for Simeon to get emergency calls from clients who needed to talk in the middle of the night. She paused to listen at the door, struggling to hear over the sound of her own choppy breaths.

Silence.

Abigail lifted a shaky hand to the doorknob, easing it slowly open. The door glided silently for a few inches before it let out a loud squawk that made her jump.

Across the room, Simeon sprang up from the old recliner next to the window, lifting her laptop as if it were a shield.

In the dim light, Abigail couldn't make out his expression. Was it guilt? Or revulsion?

"What are you doing?" Abigail's cry was too shrill, and she rushed across the room to grab the computer out of his hands, spinning it toward herself.

It only took one glance to confirm that it was her manuscript on the screen. "Did you read this?"

"Is it a book?" Simeon asked. "Did you write it?"

Abigail swallowed. "Simeon, I can explain."

"Man alive, Abigail." Simeon shoved a hand through his hair, his laugh incredulous. "I thought you were having an affair or something."

"It's not what—" Abigail cut off as the full impact of his words hit her. "You thought what?" She closed the computer slowly and clutched it to her chest.

He let out a shaky breath. "I'm sorry. I shouldn't have— It's just— The way things have been between us lately. And then you seemed so secretive about your computer earlier. And I had a client who—" He shook his head. "The point is, I'm sorry."

"You thought I would cheat on you?" she asked dully.

"I know it was stupid." Simeon took a hesitant step closer. "I shouldn't have doubted you. Please forgive me." He reached for her, but she stepped backwards.

It was easier to let him think she was upset with him than to stay here and risk him asking about what he'd read.

"I'm tired," she mumbled. "I'm going back to bed."

"Abigail—"

But she spun on her heel and scurried back to the bedroom. When she reached it, she waited for a moment to listen for his footsteps following her.

When she didn't hear them, she yanked open her dresser drawer and buried the computer under a stack of jeans at the back.

Then she climbed into bed, pulling the covers up to her chin.

But she couldn't stop shivering.

Her secret was out now. And it was only a matter of time before Simeon sent her packing.

Chapter 5

Simeon tapped his fingers impatiently on the counter at the flower shop. The cashier who was ringing up his purchase—a giant bouquet of soft tangerine-colored hibiscus—gave him a quelling look, and he stopped tapping with a mumbled sorry.

"Apology or special occasion?" the cashier asked.

"Uh." A fresh wave of shame went through Simeon.

The flowers were an apology for last night. He still couldn't believe he'd taken Abigail's computer and read her book without her permission. If a client had ever come to him, asking if they should snoop on their spouse's computer, he would have told them in no uncertain terms that it was a terrible idea. And he'd told himself the same thing, over and over again, lying in bed next to his wife.

But he'd had to know. And she refused to talk to him.

It had seemed like the only way.

In the light of day, he could see that statement for what it was—a baseless excuse for his actions. But somehow, last night, it had seemed justifiable.

He realized suddenly that the cashier was still waiting for an answer.

"Something like that," he said as he passed her his credit card.

She raised an eyebrow, as if waiting for him to elaborate. But he couldn't.

Yes, the flowers were an apology, first and foremost. But he also hoped they'd mark a brand-new special occasion. A chance for them to move forward. He'd met with new clients today who had just embarked on the adoption process, and the longer he'd talked to them, the more convinced Simeon had become that this could be the right path for him and Abigail too.

Now all he had to do was convince her.

He'd broached the topic a few times before, in passing, but she'd always blown him off.

But he hadn't had information then. Hadn't had a plan. Now he did.

Ideally, he'd wait a little longer to talk to her about it—give her a little more time to forgive him for last night—but the adoption agency was having an orientation meeting in two days, and he didn't want them to miss it. This was just what Abigail needed to pull her out of her depression, just what their marriage needed to move forward.

What would you tell a client who thought bringing a child into the equation would solve all their problems?

Simeon ignored the question as he took his credit card back, thanked the cashier, and headed for the door. In most cases, adding a child wouldn't solve the problem—but when the lack of a child *was* the problem . . . Well, maybe it would.

And if there are other problems? Deeper problems?

Again, Simeon ignored the counseling questions that were always rolling through his brain. He and Abigail had been fine until the first miscarriage. And they would be fine again once they'd gotten past all of this.

He jumped into the SUV and tucked the flowers carefully into the passenger seat, then started toward home. As he passed the Book Den, he considered stopping and surprising Abigail with the flowers.

But he'd left work early so he could make her a nice dinner. He wanted everything to be perfect. So he kept driving.

⁓

"What are you still doing here?" Ruth's sleek white hair swished around her shoulders as she bustled to the counter where Abigail was dusting the bookmark display. "Your shift ended twenty minutes ago."

Abigail concentrated on the bookmarks, not meeting her boss's eyes. "You were busy in the back, and we had a few customers come in, so I thought I'd stay until they were done."

Ruth glanced around the empty store and raised an eyebrow. "I didn't realize we had invisible customers today."

"Don't worry. I clocked out already."

Ruth waved a hand covered in rings at her. "I'm not worried about paying you, dear. I just don't think a dusty, musty bookshop is the place for a young person like you to spend her evenings. Especially a young person with such a handsome and charming husband waiting for her at home."

Abigail smiled tightly. She wasn't sure if she was more amused that Ruth had called the bright, cheerful bookstore musty and dusty or that she'd called Abigail young when she was almost thirty-three.

One thing Ruth was right about, though—her husband *was* handsome and charming. But Abigail highly doubted he was waiting at home for her. As far as she knew, he'd never come to bed last night—and he'd been gone when she woke. This time he hadn't left a note.

She couldn't imagine what he must be thinking after what he'd read last night. Or, actually, she *could* imagine, but every time she did, it made her feel like she was going to throw up.

She fully expected him to hand her divorce papers the moment she walked in the door.

"All right. No more stalling." Ruth plucked the dust rag out of Abigail's hand. "Off you go. I'll see you tomorrow."

Abigail nodded and moved behind the counter to collect her purse. There was no point in arguing with Ruth. She may be the kindest woman Abigail had ever met. But she was also the stubbornest.

Abigail made her way through the back room lined in boxes and boxes of books. Curse this place for giving her the notion that she could—that she should—write her own story. She kicked at a box, not hard enough to do any damage but just hard enough to remind herself of the pain words could inflict.

She pushed the back door open, her eyes accidentally going to the riverwalk crowded with couples and families. She averted her gaze, concentrating on her shoes as she strode toward her car.

The last time she and Simeon had strolled here was a few weeks after they'd learned they were expecting for the first time. They'd walked along, making giddy plans for the nursery, for the baby's name, even for the tire swing Simeon would hang and the sandbox they'd make. But as they'd walked, she'd started to feel cramping. She hadn't said anything, and by the time they got home, she'd felt better. Until she'd woken up the next morning to find she was bleeding.

Simeon had been wonderful. He'd kept her calm, taken her to the doctor. He'd held her hand through the appointment and stroked her back through the tears. He'd brought her home and tucked her into bed and gotten her pie from Daisy's.

And all she'd given him was more grief and heartache.

The sweet scent of pastry drifted toward her on the light breeze, but she dropped into her car with a heavy sigh. Even pie wouldn't fix what she'd broken now.

She made the short drive home on autopilot, not snapping out of it until she pulled onto their street and spotted Simeon's car parked on the road.

Because he didn't plan to stay?

Abigail's heart started to whomp against her chest, and she gripped the steering wheel tighter as she turned into the driveway. She tried to order herself to relax. He had probably parked there so she could put her car in the garage, just like he always did when he got home before her.

Only that didn't explain what he was doing home early. He was supposed to have appointments until six tonight.

Maybe his clients had canceled.

Or maybe he was packing up her stuff even now.

Abigail pulled into the garage and turned off her car. But she couldn't bring herself to go inside. Nausea turned her stomach upside-down, and she pressed both hands to it. She forced herself to take a few deep breaths, until she could at least stand without feeling like she was going to vomit, then made her way slowly to the door that led to the kitchen.

"Hey, there." Simeon looked up from the stove with a smile the moment she stepped through the laundry room that doubled as a mudroom—which they'd thought would be such a perfect place for kids to take off their dirty shoes—and into the kitchen.

Abigail blinked as her heart shifted from a painful thrum to a surprised one. She wasn't sure which was harder to bear.

"What are you doing?" She inhaled as the scent of the food hit her. "Is that enchiladas verdes?" She took a step into the room, her stomach suddenly rumbling.

"It sure is." He scooped the enchiladas onto a serving platter, then stirred the sauce that was still on the stove and wiped his hands on the "Hot Stuff Coming Through" apron she'd bought him their first Christmas.

He pulled the apron off and laid it on the counter, then swept a big bouquet of flowers she hadn't noticed off the table and into his arms. He crossed the room and held them out to her.

"What are these for?" She must have been in shock because she couldn't even lift her arms to take them.

Simeon's face fell. "Please, Abigail. You have to know how sorry I am about last night. Checking your computer was absolutely unacceptable. No excuse. It was the worst thing I've ever done."

Abigail rubbed at her forehead, not sure if she should laugh or cry. Because she was absolutely certain it really *was* the worst thing he'd ever done. And in comparison to the things she'd done . . .

"Can you forgive me?" Simeon was still holding out the flowers, his expression torn between hope and fear.

"I forgive you." Abigail took the flowers, and Simeon let out a breath.

Abigail's stomach started up its anxious churning again as she turned around and retreated into the laundry room to hunt down a vase big enough to hold the bouquet. She buried her nose in the flowers, which were the same exact shade as the first flowers he'd ever bought her from the market in Ecuador. Their sweet scent brought a sudden prickle of tears to her eyes. Simeon shouldn't be the one apologizing. She should.

"About what you read," she called as she reached for a vase on the top shelf of the cabinet over the dryer. She half hoped he wouldn't hear her from the other room.

"Yeah?" Simeon called back.

Abigail's fingers closed around the lip of the vase, but her arm jerked before she could get a good grip on it. She tried to catch it on its way down, but she only managed to bobble it twice before it hit the floor with a crash.

"Are you all right?" Simeon was at her side before she could fully register the field of shattered glass that surrounded her.

"I'm sorry," she whispered, the tears that had prickled now falling openly.

"Hey, it's okay." Simeon took her arm and steered her through the glass into the kitchen. "It's only a vase."

She shook her head, but she couldn't bring herself to say that wasn't what she was sorry for.

"I'll clean it up," she choked out, swiping at the ridiculous tears she couldn't seem to go a day without shedding.

"I've got this," Simeon soothed. "You go sit down. I'll be right there."

Numbly, Abigail made her way to the dining room table. Simeon had set it with the china his parents had given them for their wedding. Two unlit candles stood in the center of the table, and soft music played in the background. Simeon had really gone all out for this apology.

She sniffed.

She had to tell him. He'd read it all anyway. It was only a matter of time before he confronted her. She couldn't fathom why he hadn't already—except maybe that he felt guilty for the way he'd learned about it. But even that was her fault. She was the one who'd kept her past a secret from the beginning.

"All better." Simeon smiled as he hurried back into the room. He washed his hands, then moved to the stove. He stirred the sauce once more, then turned the burner off and poured the sauce over the enchiladas. He carried the platter to the table and scooped a large serving onto her plate. "I hope you're hungry."

Abigail pushed her cheeks into a smile, though her appetite had completely fled.

Simeon added an enchilada to his own plate. "Oh. I forgot to light the candles." He pushed his chair back to get up.

"Simeon." His name came out as more of a gasp.

He paused, half standing. "What's wrong?"

"Why aren't you saying anything about what you read last night?"

Now it was out there. They'd get this over with. He'd say he couldn't be with her anymore, and she'd—

Well, she had no idea what she would do.

He sat back down. "I wasn't sure if you wanted me to."

She stared at her food, nausea swimming up her throat. Of course she didn't want him to. But there was no point in avoiding it any longer.

"Do you hate me?" She barely pushed the whisper out.

"Hate you?" Simeon sounded shocked, and Abigail had to look up. "Why would I hate you?"

He looked so sincere that Abigail almost couldn't make herself say the next words. "Because I never told you. Because I—"

"I admit I was a little hurt that you never told me. But I understand why you didn't."

"You do?" Abigail took a sip of water. It didn't even seem possible. She knew he counseled people who probably told him big, devastating things about their past every day. But she was his *wife*. Was he really okay with her having a past like that?

"Of course I do. Writing a novel is a pretty big thing. You probably wanted to wait until you were done to tell me, right?" Simeon smiled, as if his conclusion was the only possibility.

Abigail nodded mutely. He understood why she hadn't told him she was writing a *novel*. He thought she'd made the whole story up.

A strange mix of relief and dread went through her. He didn't know the truth. Her secret was safe. But also, *he didn't know the truth*. Which meant she still had to hold onto this secret all on her own.

"So—" Simeon passed her a basket of tortilla chips she hadn't noticed. "How long have you been working on this book?"

"A few weeks," she mumbled as she picked up her fork. "It was a silly thing to start."

"It's not silly." Simeon reached across the table, touching his hand to the back of hers. The contact was like a thousand daggers, reminding her of her lies.

"It's actually really good," Simeon added. "I was impressed by your psychological insights into your characters. Where did you get the idea?"

Abigail pulled her hand back, pretending to be interested in cutting her enchilada. Now was her chance to tell him. To break free of this lie once and for all. "Uh. Books, movies. You know."

"Well, it's very realistic. I can tell you did your research."

Abigail shrugged. "Should we pray?" Not that she had any appetite. Or any desire to talk to God. But it was the only way to get out of this conversation.

"Of course." Simeon's smile was so hopeful that Abigail had to bow her head and close her eyes.

"Dear Lord," Simeon started. But Abigail's thoughts drifted to the words of her story. The words Simeon thought she had made up from some deep creative well. Not from her own life.

"In Jesus' name we pray, Amen."

Abigail startled as Simeon ended the prayer. "Amen," she mumbled, though she had no idea what he'd prayed for. Hopefully nothing that had anything to do with her. Because there was no way God would listen now.

⚬⚬⚬

Simeon's food was almost gone and still he hadn't brought up adoption.

Although Abigail had said she forgave him, she still seemed rather subdued. She'd hardly touched her enchilada, and every time he brought up a topic, she seemed to barely notice what he was talking about, only mumbling a word or two here and there.

The worst part was, he couldn't blame her for still being upset. What he'd suspected her of—it was terrible.

So maybe he should wait. Give her time to get over this. The adoption agency's website had said they held orientation meetings every three months. That wasn't terribly long to wait. But something told Simeon it was too long. He couldn't guarantee their marriage would make it another three months if something didn't change.

He pushed his plate to the side. "Ready for dessert?"

Abigail looked up from her half-eaten enchilada with what might have been the closest thing he'd seen to a real smile from her in months. "Is it chocolate?"

"Of course." He stood and cleared their plates, then pulled the French silk pie out of the refrigerator.

He cut them each a large slice and returned to the table, watching as Abigail slid her fork through the fluffy filling and lifted it to her mouth.

"It's good." This time her smile was *really* real, and it gave Simeon courage.

"There's something I wanted to talk to you about." He cut off his own bite of pie, mostly to give himself something to concentrate on, other than the nerves suddenly flaring through his chest.

Abigail stopped with her fork halfway to her mouth, her eyes going wide and scared.

"Relax." Simeon laughed, though he couldn't keep himself from sounding as terrified as she looked. "It's something good."

But her expression didn't change, and she didn't bring the pie to her lips.

Well, he'd made the opening. Now he had to go for it. "I think we should consider adopting." The words came out in a rush, sucking all the air right out with them, but he couldn't seem to breathe back in.

Abigail's expression shifted from fear to surprise, and it struck Simeon how similar the two expressions could be. She set down her fork with its uneaten piece of pie. "Adopting?" she finally asked.

At last Simeon could inhale again. She hadn't flat-out refused. At least not yet.

"I have some clients who just started the process. It begins with an orientation meeting. It's purely informational. No obligation." He reached across the table for her hand that still clutched the fork, wrapping his fingers around hers. "It's this Thursday, which I know is short notice. But it can't hurt to go, right? Just to find out what the process involves?"

Abigail stared at their joined hands but didn't say anything.

"Please, Abigail." He reached to take her other hand as well. "This could be the answer to our prayers."

Abigail kept her head bowed, and Simeon's heart sank slowly through his middle, down his legs, into his feet.

He'd been so sure this was the answer to saving their marriage. But if she wasn't willing to at least go to the meeting . . .

"Will you at least think about it?" he whispered.

She looked up slowly. "I'll go."

"You'll . . ." Before he could even finish the thought, he'd pulled his hands back and jumped up so fast his chair hit the wall. But he didn't care.

He raced around the table and engulfed her in his arms. She gasped, and he was afraid for a second that she was going to pull away. But then her arms were around his back, and she was crying into his shirt.

"Shh." He held her tighter and stroked her hair. "It's going to be okay. We're going to be okay." For the first time in a long time, he felt like it was true.

After a few moments, he loosened his grip and gently leaned back so he could wipe the tears off her face.

"These are good tears, right? You're happy?"

She nodded.

"Good. Me too." His fingers stilled on her face, and his eyes went to her lips. Slowly, he leaned closer, keeping his eyes on hers. Instead of turning away and offering her cheek as she had so many times over the past months, she leaned into him.

Simeon closed his eyes and brought his lips to hers, gently, questioningly. Abigail sighed as her lips responded and her arms wrapped around his neck. Simeon pulled her in closer, soaking up her fruity-floral scent. It had been so very long since they'd shared a real kiss, and he wanted to keep her here, wrapped up in his arms, forever.

But after a few minutes, he eased himself out of her embrace. Since the last miscarriage, she hadn't been ready for more—and he was willing to wait as long as she needed.

"That was nice," he murmured, stroking a hand over her cheek.

She nodded, and Simeon smiled to see that he'd left her breathless.

"I'm going to go register us for the orientation, to make sure we get a spot." He brought her hand to his lips and pressed a kiss to it, then stood and headed for the stairs.

"Man alive." He stopped and grinned over his shoulder at her. "This is going to be great."

Chapter 6

Abigail clutched the armrest of the SUV as Simeon steered them into Brampton. The hour-long drive from River Falls hadn't been nearly long enough to prepare her for this.

"I think the adoption agency is around the next corner," Simeon said. "My client said it was right by the hospital."

Abigail nodded tightly. She never should have said yes to this. It was clear God was determined not to let her be a mother. But she'd already given Simeon more than enough reasons to reject her—it was a miracle he hadn't already. If she gave him one more, maybe he would finally give up on her for good. Just like her parents had. Just like Garrick had. Losing them had been painful. But losing Simeon—that would be unbearable.

"It's okay to be nervous, you know." Simeon touched her hand, and her heart jumped as she realized he was turning into the parking lot of the adoption agency. The sign out front said *Hope for Tomorrow* and showed a smiling couple holding a grinning, curly haired toddler between them. Abigail peered at it more closely. A tiny grain of hope tried to poke its way into her heart. Could she and Simeon really have that?

Please, Lord. I know I don't deserve this. But Simeon does. It was the first prayer she'd uttered in months.

Simeon pulled the vehicle into a parking spot and took off his seatbelt but didn't get out. Instead, he turned toward her, wrapping both of his hands around hers. "Whatever they say, whatever we decide, we're in this together, okay?"

She swallowed through the dryness of her throat and made herself nod.

"Good. I love you." He leaned forward and brushed a soft kiss over her lips. Abigail closed her eyes. How had she never realized how much she missed his kisses? How much she needed them?

"I love you too," she whispered past the painful lump in her throat. This had to work out. She couldn't lose him.

He kissed her once more, then jumped out of the vehicle and jogged to open her door. He slid his hand into hers as they started toward the building, and she was grateful for the solidity, the dependability of his presence.

Inside, a bubbly receptionist gave them a folder and directed them down a brightly lit hallway to a large meeting room. At least a dozen couples filled the space with laughter and small talk. Abigail clutched Simeon's hand tighter. These people all looked like they were completely at ease. Like they were ready for someone to plop a baby in their arms and take a picture of them for the sign out front.

Abigail tried to smile. To look like she belonged.

"If everyone could please take a seat, we'll go ahead and get started." A woman with silver hair and an energetic stride made her way through the crowd, smiling warmly as she passed.

Abigail let Simeon usher her to a spot near the back. He kept his hand around hers as they took their seats, and she allowed herself to lean a little closer so that her shoulder grazed his. Simeon looked to her with a smile and dusted a kiss over her forehead. Abigail closed her eyes, the contact whispering through every nerve.

Maybe Simeon had been right. Maybe this was what their marriage needed.

The silver-haired woman reached the front of the room and introduced herself as Brenda, then started her presentation with story after story of successful adoptions. As she spoke, Abigail became more and more excited. More and more sure.

Next to her, she could tell Simeon felt the same way. They kept looking at each other and grinning, and she felt a trace of the energy that had pulsed between them when they'd met in Ecuador.

She leaned closer to him. "I'm glad we came."

"Me too."

"So these stories are the end of the process, of course," Brenda was saying. "Let's talk about how to get there." She held up a folder that matched the one Abigail and Simeon had received when they'd arrived. "In here, you'll find a stack of forms. Don't be alarmed. Most of them are pretty easy to fill out. You'll need to collect some paperwork too. I'll go over all of that with you in a minute so you'll know what's needed. But filling out these forms will start the home study process, which also includes home visits and interviews. It all sounds a lot more daunting than it is, trust me."

Abigail let out a breath. That was good. Because it suddenly sounded almost impossible.

"We've got this," Simeon whispered.

Abigail nodded, opening the folder and paging absently through the forms. It looked like they wanted tax records, medical records, income information, social security numbers, and—

Abigail stared at the large words at the top of the last sheet: *Consent for Criminal Background Check.*

No.

No. No. No.

How had it never occurred to her that before someone gave her their baby, they'd want to know she didn't have a criminal record?

"Can I see the folder?" Simeon whispered.

She passed it to him, watching as he thumbed through the sheets until he came to the one about medical records, which Brenda was apparently explaining now, although her voice had gone all warbly and incomprehensible in Abigail's ears.

The grain of hope she'd dared to let sprout as Brenda shared other families' happily-ever-afters let go of its hold on her heart and blew away.

This wasn't going to happen for her and Simeon.

She dared to glance at him, but he was listening to Brenda, nodding along to something she'd said.

He turned her way with a wide smile, and she forced herself to return it.

She managed to hold the smile in place for the rest of the orientation, through Simeon's insistence that they talk to Brenda afterward, through his enthusiastic chatter all the way home about how easy the process was going to be since all their records were organized already.

By the time he pulled into their driveway, her cheeks hurt and her head pounded.

"We should celebrate," Simeon said as he unlocked the front door. "I think we have some French silk pie left."

"No thanks." Abigail toed off her shoes. "I think I'm going to go to bed."

Simeon's smile slid off his face. "Is something wrong? You've been quiet. Do you not want to . . ."

She shook her head. "I just have a headache. Information overload." She attempted a light laugh. "You get some pie, though."

He studied her closely, and she had to work hard to keep her smile in place.

"Okay," he finally relented. "Goodnight." He brushed a sweet kiss over her lips.

"Goodnight." She managed to keep her grip on the smile until she reached their bedroom. Then she dropped onto the bed and let herself cry silently.

But after a few minutes, she swiped at her cheeks and sat up. She'd spent months crying, and it hadn't done any good. She'd just have to tell Simeon that she didn't think she could handle adoption. If need be, she could blame it on her past experience with foster care.

Simeon would be disappointed. But she also knew he wouldn't push her.

She pulled up the covers and laid back in the bed, trying not to picture the brave face he'd put on to hide how much she was hurting him.

Tomorrow.

She'd tell him tomorrow.

Chapter 7

Sunlight streamed into the room by the time Abigail opened her eyes. She hadn't expected to be able to sleep, but she must have slept deeply since she hadn't heard Simeon come to bed last night or get up this morning.

She reached for her phone to check the time. Nine o'clock.

That meant Simeon had already left for work. And she needed to get up and get ready. Her shift started at ten.

Which meant she didn't have time to lie here and think about the adoption paperwork and what she'd tell Simeon. Hopefully the answer would magically come to her by the time they both got home from work.

She grabbed a flowy green dress that didn't hug her curves too tightly and headed for the bathroom.

A scraping sound from down the hallway drew her up short.

She knew the sound well. It was the sound of Simeon's office chair sliding against the floor. But he should have left for work at least an hour ago.

Was someone else in there?

Abigail tiptoed down the hallway, careful to avoid the floorboard in front of the bathroom that creaked. Simeon's office door was ajar, and Abigail carefully poked her head around it.

Simeon stood hunched over his desk, his arm moving as if he were writing something.

Abigail let out a breath. "You scared me. I thought someone broke in."

Simeon didn't even jump at her voice. He turned to her with a smile. "Good morning. I was just writing you a note."

"What are you still doing home?"

"I didn't have a client first thing this morning, and I wanted to finish these up." He held up a stack of papers and waved them in the air with a grin. "I was just marking the spots where you need to sign."

"I— Sign?" She stared at the papers. She couldn't read them from across the room. But she could make out the logo of the adoption agency. "Are those the papers we got last night?"

Simeon nodded proudly. "All done."

Abigail blinked at him. "Done? Did you sleep at all?"

"A little." Simeon ran a hand over his slightly mussed hair. "I figure it's good practice for when we get a baby."

"Simeon." She couldn't let him keep hoping like this.

He glanced at his watch. "I have to fly. I have a client in twenty minutes. All you have to do is sign in the spots where I left a sticky note." He crossed the room and set the papers into her hands, which she didn't remember lifting to take them.

"There's an envelope on my desk," Simeon continued. "Just stick them in there when you're done and pop them in the mail."

He bent to give her a quick kiss. "See you tonight."

Before she could even say his name, he was out the office door. She could only stare at the spot where he'd been standing a moment ago.

"Hey, Abigail?" Simeon's voice sounded like it was coming from the stairs.

"Yeah?" She stepped into the hallway, the papers still clutched in her hands.

"This is really happening." His grin was boyish and charming and hopeful and all the things Abigail had fallen in love with. "We could have a baby *soon*. I mean, I know the home study will take a few months, but after that . . . Man alive." He shook his head in wonder. "We could be parents."

Abigail nodded dumbly, incapable of opening her mouth and puncturing his happiness.

He turned and bounded down the stairs, his "I love you" drifting up behind him as the front door opened and closed.

"Love you too," she whispered.

The adoption papers seared against her fingers, and she carried them back into the office and spread them out on Simeon's desk. He had marked all the spots she needed to sign with efficient little sticky notes.

Most of the forms, it would be no big deal to sign. But that one piece of paper stared up at her. *Consent for Criminal Background Check.*

She scanned the desk for a pen. Maybe she could sign it. After all, the charges against her had been dropped in return for her testimony, so maybe they wouldn't even show up on her record. She'd never asked. She'd never realized it would be an issue.

There. A black pen peeked out at her from under the papers. Abigail fished it out.

Simeon wanted a child so badly. And she wanted him to have one. He deserved a family. If it turned out that her crimes didn't show up on a background check, then he would never have to know there was any question.

She set her pen to the paper and scribbled her name before she could change her mind.

She gathered the papers up, tapping their edges against the desk to make a neat stack. Then she grabbed the pre-addressed envelope and stuffed the papers inside so she wouldn't have to see them anymore.

She hurried to get ready for work. On her way out the door, she slipped back into Simeon's office and grabbed the envelope. There was a mailbox a couple of blocks from the Book Den.

The drive downtown was much too short. All the way there, she was too aware of the envelope, sitting on the passenger seat. Accusing her.

She parked her car behind the Book Den, then started on the short walk to the mailbox. But the closer she got, the harder it was to move her feet.

If those charges against her did show up . . .

Simeon will leave.

By the time she reached the mailbox, her breath heaved in and out as if she'd just been involved in a foot chase, and she stared at the envelope clutched in her hands. It stared back at her, taunting her. Was she really going to do this?

She lifted the envelope to the slot.

But her fingers refused to let it go.

She yanked it back and tucked it under her arm. Sprinting now, she raced back toward the Book Den, to the dumpster that sat squished between two storefronts.

Guilt pulsed from the papers into her skin, and she glanced over her shoulder like a criminal.

Then, with a quick, decisive movement, she lifted the lid of the dumpster and tossed the envelope inside.

Nausea overtook her as the envelope thudded on the empty bottom, and she had to bend over and rest her hands on her knees to keep from throwing up.

What have you done? her heart cried. *Climb in there and get those papers back.*

She shook her head. She'd done what she had to do. With any luck, it would be a few weeks before Simeon even realized the adoption agency hadn't gotten the papers. She could claim they must have gotten lost in the mail—and maybe it was a sign they weren't meant to adopt.

A fresh bout of queasiness rolled over her, but she straightened and smoothed her dress. Then she sped away from the dumpster before she could change her mind.

Chapter 8

"Good morning." Simeon set a steaming mug of coffee on Abigail's nightstand and slid a hand along her shoulder. A wave of optimism and gratitude rolled over him. After months of not knowing how to help her—how to fix their marriage—things were finally looking up.

Just starting the adoption process had seemed to lift her spirits, and though he could see that things were still weighing on her, he felt like she was at last willing to move forward now. Yesterday, she'd even gone for a hike with him. And she'd agreed to go to church and lunch at Dad's today—for the first time in months.

"Do I smell coffee?" Abigail opened her eyes slowly.

"You do." Simeon bent and kissed her cheek. "Are you still up for going to church?"

"Oh." Abigail closed her eyes, and for a moment Simeon worried that she was going to change her mind. But she opened them again and gave him a weak smile. "Of course."

"Good." He stroked her arm again. "Because we have a lot to thank God for."

Her smile drifted, but she nodded. "We do." She reached for the coffee and brought it to her lips. "Perfect."

"Yes, you are." He bent again, this time kissing the top of her head.

"Simeon, don't—"

"Don't what? Kiss your head?" He would be more than happy to kiss her lips instead—he just didn't want to make her spill coffee on herself.

"Don't call me perfect," she whispered.

"All right, fine." He kissed her head again. "You're not perfect. But you *are* perfect for me." He strode toward the door. "You have plenty of time to shower and get ready. I'm going to go take some measurements in the baby's room. I thought we could go furniture shopping this week. Start getting everything ready for the home visit."

"Wait. Simeon—" Abigail's voice carried into the hallway.

"What's up?" He turned and poked his head back into the room.

She was facing the window on the other side of the room but staring at her coffee cup.

"Abigail?" He stepped into the room. "Is something wrong?"

She shook her head and looked at him over her shoulder. "No. I just wanted to say thanks for the coffee."

"Oh. You're welcome." He studied her for a moment, trying to figure out if there was something more.

But her smile looked genuine, and she waved him off. "Go. Do your measuring. I'll be ready for church in a little bit."

An hour later, Simeon was just finishing a rough drawing of a potential layout for the baby's room when Abigail came in. He stopped with his pencil hovering over the paper. She was wearing a creamy white shirt with a floor-length floral skirt. It reminded him of something she would have worn when they'd first met.

"You look beautiful." He crossed the room and pulled her into his arms, letting the pencil and paper fall out of his hands as he brought his lips to hers and tangled his fingers in her hair.

"Hey." She pulled back with a protest, but she was laughing. "You're going to mess up my hair. I thought we were going to church."

"Right." Simeon dropped his hands from around her and worked to catch his breath as he picked up the paper and pencil. "Let's go." He stashed the drawing in his desk drawer and escorted her out to their vehicle.

"We'll have to get a car seat," he said as he opened her door.

"Simeon." Abigail turned to him with worried eyes.

"I know. I know." Simeon kissed her cheek. "I shouldn't get ahead of myself. I'm just excited. For us."

Abigail nodded and got into the vehicle. Simeon forced himself to rein in his enthusiasm on the drive to church. As excited as he was about the possibility, it wasn't going to do any good to get Abigail's hopes up that the process would go quickly when their caseworker Janice had warned that it could take months or even years to be chosen by a birth mother. From now on, he'd do a better job of showing restraint. Of helping her manage expectations—even if he couldn't manage his own.

A sigh came from Abigail's side of the vehicle as he pulled into the parking lot at Beautiful Savior, and he glanced at her. She was gazing out the window at the big brick church.

"It's going to be okay," he said. "Everyone will be happy to see you."

She nodded, but her smile held a thousand nerves.

He pulled into a parking spot and got out to open her door, grasping her hand in his as they walked toward the church. Inside, he spotted his best friend Liam standing with his arms around Lydia—the half-sister Simeon and his siblings had only learned about a year ago. She'd quickly become one of the family, though—and as soon as she and Liam married this summer, Liam would officially be family too.

"Good morning, you two." Lydia stepped away from Liam to offer Abigail a huge smile and an even bigger hug. "It's so good to see you."

Liam held out a hand to Simeon. "Hey, man." His raised eyebrow said what his words didn't. Simeon nodded in response to the unasked question. He knew Liam had been worried about him and Abigail—he was the only one in the family who knew about their miscarriages and troubles—but now he didn't have to worry anymore.

Simeon wrapped an arm around Abigail's back as they followed Liam and Lydia into the sanctuary. They made their way to the front of the church, where his brothers Joseph, Asher, and Zeb already sat with their wives Ava, Ireland, and Carly. His youngest brother, Benjamin, was still away at school but would be graduating in a couple of weeks. His sister Grace and her husband Levi would be here for that too. Maybe that would be a good time for him and Abigail to share their good news.

There wasn't enough room in the pew to fit four more, so they slid in behind the rest of the crew. The others all turned to greet Abigail, and Simeon's heart filled. He was so grateful that his own family had embraced her the moment he'd brought her with him from Ecuador. She'd had no family or belongings of her own to return to, so she'd rented a small apartment in River Falls until their wedding.

He slipped an arm around her shoulders, sighing in contentment as she leaned into him. When they'd said their vows in this church, he couldn't have imagined what the next few years would put them through. But it felt like they were finally coming out on the other side, and he trusted their marriage would only be stronger for it.

Thank you, Lord, he prayed silently as Dad stepped to the front of the church to begin the service.

⟡

"Good morning." The deep, warm voice drew Abigail's eyes to the front of the church. Her father-in-law, Abe Calvano, was smiling out at the congregation. His eyes landed on her, and she was pretty sure his smile grew.

Abigail tried not to tense her muscles. He wouldn't be smiling at her if he knew what she'd done.

Then again, Simeon wouldn't be sitting here with his arm around her either. He'd been so happy the past two days—and Abigail had forced herself to act happy too. To act like she expected that any day now they'd get a child. Even though she knew better.

"I'm glad you came," Simeon leaned closer to whisper in her ear, his warm, comforting scent cocooning her.

She nodded as he handed her a hymnal. "Me too."

It'd been months since she'd been to church, and the truth was, she didn't even know if she shared her husband's faith anymore. If she ever really had.

She certainly hadn't been a believer when her parents had shipped her off on that mission trip to Ecuador. She'd been plenty good at putting on an act, though—at least at first. Somehow, as she'd heard the pastor there, as she'd listened to Simeon talk with passion about God's love and what Jesus had done to save sinners, she'd wanted to know more.

She'd believed it was true. She'd believed Jesus had died for her sins.

Or at least she thought she'd believed it.

But maybe that had all been part of the act. Maybe she'd been so good at pretending that she'd convinced herself.

Whether she'd once believed or not, it was getting harder and harder to believe now.

The hymn ended, and Pastor Calvano invited the congregation to stand. Abigail had to bite back a gasp as her eyes fell on her sister-in-law Carly at the end of the pew in front of them. Simeon had told her a few weeks ago that Zeb and Carly had announced they were expecting. But Abigail hadn't been prepared for Carly to be showing already. Zeb looked down at his wife, the hardened police officer's expression all mushy and adoring.

Abigail averted her eyes, but the room seemed to spin a little, and Simeon's hand pressed to the small of her back.

"Are you okay?" he asked quietly, shooting her a concerned look.

"Yeah. Fine," she whispered.

His eyes remained on her as they retook their seats, and she concentrated on looking interested in Pastor Calvano's reading.

After a moment, Simeon's eyes shifted off her, and her gaze went back to Carly. But now that they were sitting, she couldn't see the baby bump.

She covered her own stomach with her hand, aching for the little lives it had held and lost. One more sign that God hadn't forgiven her after all.

She lost track of the service until Pastor Calvano moved to the pulpit to deliver his sermon. For some reason she couldn't explain, Abigail felt her attention zero in on him.

"Y'all ever had jury duty?" he asked. Somewhere in the back of the church, someone groaned, and Pastor Calvano laughed. "My thoughts exactly." The congregation chuckled, but Abigail's fingers curled in on themselves until her nails sliced into her palms. She'd never had jury duty before, but she'd sat in front of a jury . . .

"Oh, I tried to get out of it," Pastor Calvano continued. "But nothing worked, so on the day of the trial, I found myself at the courthouse. Now, if you've never been in a courtroom, let me tell you, it can be a pretty intimidating place."

The whole room went blurry, and Abigail was suddenly back there. In that courtroom. On that stand. Seeing the way the members of the jury were looking at her. The man who had frowned the entire time she'd testified. The woman who had curled her lip in disgust. The white-haired grandmotherly type who had given her a gentle smile but also shaken her head every few minutes.

Pressure on her shoulder brought Abigail's attention back to the church. She shifted forward, so that Simeon's hand fell off her shoulder. He let it rest on her back.

"And if I was just a juror and felt that intimidated," Pastor Calvano was saying. "Imagine being the defendant. Sitting on the stand. The judge looking down on you from the bench. The prosecutors staring you down from their table. The jury sitting in the jury box, dissecting everything you say." Pastor Calvano shook his head. "Truth be told, I actually felt a little sorry for the defendant. Not because he was innocent. But because the prosecution kept piling on the evidence of his guilt. You know those pictures of the scales of justice? It was like I could see one side getting heavier and heavier. Kind of reminded me of a teeter-totter. Remember those? Fun, unless you got on with a kid who was bigger than you and wouldn't let you down. Well, this guy might as well have had an elephant on the other side of his teeter-totter for the weight of all that guilt."

Abigail felt her past pressing against her, cinching tight around her lungs until she wasn't sure how she was going to take another breath. *The weight of all that guilt.*

"And no one asked how sorry the defendant was for what he'd done," Pastor Calvano continued. "No one asked what he'd done to make up for it. Because it didn't matter. It didn't change anything he had done. Justice had to be served. But as I sat there, listening to the district attorney hurling all these accusations at the defendant, I couldn't help but picture a different accuser and a different defendant. And the defendant was me."

Abigail's head jerked up. There was no way Pastor Calvano had ever stood trial.

"And it was you," he continued. Abigail's stomach turned in on itself. But Pastor Calvano kept going. "And the accuser was Satan."

Abigail dropped her head, staring at her lap. She didn't need Satan to accuse her. She already knew the charges against her were valid.

"The thing is," Pastor Calvano said. "There might as well be an elephant on the other side of our teeter-totter too because we have committed the sins Satan accuses us of. We are guilty."

Abigail's chest squeezed so tight she didn't know how her heart was still beating, but somehow it was—so loudly that she couldn't hear Pastor Calvano's words any longer. She was guilty.

Guilty.

Guilty.

Guilty.

Pastor Calvano paused, looking thoughtful. "We found him guilty. And the judge sentenced him to be punished. Because that's how justice works. When someone breaks the law, they have to be held accountable. They have to pay their debt to society for their crime."

Abigail thought she *had* paid. She'd testified. She'd changed her life. She'd become a different person, a better person. But maybe that didn't matter. Maybe she was just as guilty today as she had been then.

"We already know we're guilty, right?" Pastor Calvano picked up his Bible. "God commands us to be holy as he is holy. But we fall so far short of that: 'all have sinned and fall short of the glory of God.' And for that, we deserve to die: 'the wages of sin is death.'"

Pastor Calvano shook his head, looking grim. "That's a lot of law, isn't it? It hurts, doesn't it? Makes us quiver in our boots. Because when we hear it spelled out like that, we can see what we deserve. See where we're headed. See the punishment that belongs to us: hell."

He paused for only a beat. "But here's the thing the accuser doesn't want you to know—the end of the verses I just read: 'The wages of sin is death, but the gift of God is eternal life in Christ Jesus our Lord.'"

He beamed a smile around the church, then added, "And the verse that starts, 'All have sinned and fall short of the glory of God,' ends with, 'all are justified freely by his grace through the redemption that came by Christ Jesus.' Justified. As in, declared not guilty. Not because we've kept the law perfectly. Not because we've paid our debt for our sins. But because Jesus has done both of those things in our place. We get on the stand in God's courtroom, and Jesus says, 'All these things you're accusing them of? *I'll* take those on myself. *I'll* pay for them. Punish me.' He lifts that elephant right off our teeter-totter. And he replaces our sin with his righteousness. So when God looks at us, he doesn't see a lawbreaker. Instead, he sees a lawkeeper. Not an enemy but his child. Not our old self with all its corrupt and deceitful desires but 'the new self, created after the likeness of God in true righteousness and holiness.' Amen."

Abigail stood with the rest of the congregation, trying to focus on Pastor Calvano's prayer, but all she could think of was that elephant sitting on the other end of her teeter-totter. And she doubted that even Jesus could remove it.

Chapter 9

"Abigail didn't go home after church, did she?" Lydia asked as Simeon entered Dad's kitchen, waving the spoon she'd been using to stir a big bowl of potato salad.

"She's in the restroom." Simeon zigzagged around Zeb and Carly to grab a deviled egg.

Lydia swatted at his hand. "Wait for lunch."

"Oh, is it lunchtime?" Liam came up behind Lydia and reached around her for an egg.

"You two." Lydia shook her head. "Just for that, you can be last in line."

Simeon grabbed at his heart. "You wouldn't do that to your own brother?"

"And your fiancé?" Liam added, nuzzling his face into her hair.

Lydia laughed but scooted away from him. "Oh, I would." She turned to Simeon. "It was good to see Abigail in church."

"I know." Simeon's heart felt lighter than it had in months. It was like a giant weight—as heavy as that elephant Dad had been talking about in church—had been lifted off his chest, just to have his wife in worship with him again. And she'd been so intensely focused on Dad's sermon. He prayed it had touched her with the reassurance of God's forgiveness the way it had him.

"So everything's good?" Liam asked in a low voice.

Simeon nodded. "Things are really good." He almost went ahead and told them about the adoption but stopped himself just in time. That was for him and Abigail to share together. When she was ready.

"There she is." Lydia smiled over his shoulder, and Simeon turned, his heart flipping at the sight of his wife the same way it had the first time he'd seen her. He held out a hand to her, and she took it without hesitation. Simeon's heart flipped two more times. He would never take holding hands with her for granted again.

"Hey, Abigail." Lydia slid the potato salad over to make room for a bowl of Jell-o. "You don't work Mondays, right? Because I found this really cute dress shop in Cypresswood, and I thought maybe we could all go check it out tomorrow."

"Um." Abigail sounded hesitant, and Simeon squeezed her hand to encourage her. It would be good for her to spend time with her sisters-in-law. Plus, Lydia and Liam's wedding was coming up fast, so they probably did need to get the dresses soon.

"Yeah. Sure," Abigail answered.

"Oh good. One o'clock? It works for Carly and Ava too. I just have to ask Ireland yet. And we'll have to do a video call with Grace or something. She can send her measurements once we find something everyone likes."

"I vote for an empire waist." Carly joined them at the counter. "I can only imagine how big this little one will be by then."

Simeon watched the way Abigail's eyes went directly to the hand Carly held over her tiny baby bump. He wrapped an arm around his wife's back and snugged her in closer, kissing her hair.

"Hey, can I get a ride with you?" Carly turned to Abigail. "Zeb scheduled my car to get new brakes tomorrow, and Lydia and Liam are going to Brampton first to pick out a cake. I'd go with them, but my morning sickness says that would be a bad idea."

"Oh, um, sure." Abigail's voice was a little strained, but she smiled dutifully. "I can pick you up at noon."

"Perfect. Thank you."

"All right. I think everything is ready," Lydia called loudly.

Simeon chuckled. She was definitely a Calvano. If the fact that she'd inherited Mama's gift for singing wasn't enough proof, her ability to yell over the cacophony of this lively group certainly was.

The kitchen grew louder as the rest of the family filled the room. But after a few minutes, everyone quieted. They all knew the drill. Dad would lead them in prayer, and then it would be a free-for-all to get to the food first.

"Before we pray." Asher cleared his throat, and everyone looked to him in surprise. Though he wasn't exactly shy, their park ranger brother also wasn't generally the most outspoken of the group. "Ireland and I have an announcement." He looked to his wife, who was grinning radiantly. Simeon tightened his grip on Abigail's hand. He had a feeling he knew what the announcement was.

"Don't tell me you're having a baby," Joseph called from his spot next to the French doors.

Both Asher's and Ireland's mouths opened, and Asher scooped a deviled egg off the counter and chucked it in Joseph's direction. "Are you kidding me right now?"

The egg hit the glass door with an ugly splat.

"What?" Joseph looked chagrined. "Is that really what it is?" His eyes widened. "Dude, I'm sorry. I didn't mean to— Oh man. Seriously. It's just that we're expecting too."

"Joseph!" Now it was Ava whose eyes were huge. "We said we were going to wait to tell."

"Sorry." But this time Joseph looked much less apologetic as his face broke into a giant grin. "I told you. I had to wait so long for you to finally come to your senses and marry me that I couldn't wait for this too."

Ava rolled her eyes but laughed as the room broke into an explosion of congratulations and hugs for all four of the newly expectant parents.

Simeon turned to Abigail. She was smiling bravely. But the moment her eyes met his, she gasped and pulled her hand away, shoving past the others to get out of the room.

Simeon tried to follow her.

"What? No congratulations?" Joseph stepped into his path with a playful shove.

"Not now," Simeon growled, pushing past his brother.

"Simeon, what—" But Joseph's voice faded as Simeon burst into the living room. Abigail wasn't there. He flew down the hallway, checking bedrooms and bathrooms. All empty.

As he returned to the living room, his eyes fell on the picture window that overlooked the front yard. Movement near the end of the row of cars lining the long driveway caught his eye.

He shot out the front door. "Abigail!"

But she was already at their vehicle, climbing into the driver's seat. He patted his pocket. He still had the keys. So at least she couldn't—

He gasped at the sound of an engine turning over. She must have had her set of keys in her purse. But she wouldn't really leave without him, would she?

The sight of the SUV backing up and turning around answered his question. He stared after the vehicle, kicking himself. He'd gotten so caught up in his own excitement about the adoption process that he hadn't taken the time to acknowledge that she was still mourning the loss of the dream of having a child themselves. What kind of counselor was he? What kind of husband?

"Hey." A hand fell on his shoulder. "Is she okay?"

Simeon rubbed at his forehead, not looking at Joseph. "Not really." He sighed. "Let's go inside. There's something I have to tell you all."

Abigail kept herself curled around Simeon's pillow, shuddering as she heard the front door open.

"Abigail?" Simeon's voice carried up the stairs, sounding worried and compassionate. But not angry. He never got angry.

Even when she wished he would.

His footsteps pounded up the stairs.

Fresh tears coursed down her face.

"Oh, sweetheart." His voice came from the doorway, but the next thing she knew, he was in the bed with his arms around her. "I'm so sorry." He stroked her hair. "They didn't mean to hurt you."

She tried to hold it back, but a sharp sob escaped from her core. Why did he have to be so understanding? She didn't deserve it. Didn't deserve him.

She fought to get her tears under control, but Simeon kept rubbing her back and her hair, kept whispering that everything was all right. And every time he said it, she only cried harder.

Everything was *not* all right. And she could never make it all right.

When she finally managed to stop crying, she sucked in a rough breath and slid out of his arms to sit up. "I'm sorry. I didn't mean to . . ."

What? What hadn't she meant to do?

Any of it.

But there was no way to explain that.

"You have nothing to be sorry for." Simeon's smile was gentle, but he ducked his head. "I had to tell them."

Abigail froze. "Tell them what?"

Simeon sat up and reached for her hand. "About the miscarriages. And that we're adopting." He brushed a tear off her cheek. "They're all happy for us."

Abigail's lip quivered, but she made herself say it. "I can't, Simeon."

He gave her a quizzical smile, his thumb still circling on her cheek. "Can't what?"

She swallowed. "I can't adopt."

His hand stilled. "What do you mean, you can't? You don't want to?" The hurt in his eyes clawed at Abigail's heart.

But she wheezed out an answer. "I just can't."

His hand fell from her cheek to the bed between them, and he let out a hard breath. "I'm sorry if I rushed you. We should have talked about it more. Do you need more time?"

She shook her head. "More time won't help. I can't ever adopt."

"Why not?"

"Because . . . all of this is my fault."

"All of what is your fault?" He looked genuinely perplexed.

"Everything we've been going through."

"Of course it's not your fault." Simeon let out a breath, sounding slightly relieved. He probably thought she was just being dramatic. "These things happen. You didn't do anything wrong."

"Yes," she whispered. "I did."

Simeon blinked at her. "What do you mean?"

This was her chance. She should tell him everything. Get it over with.

"I mean . . ." She let out a breath. "I threw the adoption papers away." She slapped a hand over her mouth, horrified. That wasn't what she'd meant to tell him.

Simeon stared at her. "You threw them away?" His voice was strangled, and it almost cut off all of Abigail's air.

"I threw them away, Simeon. I can't adopt."

"Help me understand, Abigail. Why would you do that?"

"I'm not who you think I am," she choked out.

"What does that even mean?" It was the closest to frustrated she'd ever heard him.

She shook her head, and a tear zigzagged down her cheek.

Simeon lifted a hand to wipe it away, but she turned her head so he couldn't.

She didn't deserve his comfort. Not when she was the one inflicting the pain on him.

Simeon jerked to his feet. The shift of weight in the bed was so abrupt that Abigail nearly tipped over.

"You want to push me away, Abigail? Fine. I'll consider myself pushed."

"Simeon, no. Wait."

He paused and turned toward her.

But the look of hope on his face was too much.

"I want to help you," Simeon said wearily. "But I can't. Not if you won't talk to me."

Abigail dropped her head. There was nothing she could say that would make the situation better.

After a moment, Simeon sighed roughly. And then his footsteps retreated out the door.

Abigail lifted the pillow to her face. She'd finally succeeded in making him angry.

And there was nothing she could do to fix it.

Chapter 10

Simeon closed his Bible and stared out his office window at the sunrise hues of muted gold reflecting off the Serenity River. It was a peaceful scene, the Bible passages he'd read had been about peace, and yet all he felt was turmoil.

He had messed up. Massively. He had pushed too hard and fast for adoption. He'd assumed it was what Abigail wanted—what she needed—but he should have made sure. He should have given her time to think about it, should have taken the time to talk to her more.

And now, because he hadn't, she didn't want to adopt at all.

Worse than that, the rift between them felt larger than ever.

It didn't matter to him if they never had kids—adopted or biological. If being parents wasn't God's will for them, that was fine. What wasn't fine was losing her in the pursuit of them.

Lord, give us healing, he prayed, still watching the slow current of the golden river. *Lead us back to each other. Help us connect with each other over our shared love of you. Like we did in Ecuador.*

Simeon blinked at the water. Maybe that was the answer. They could go back to Ecuador.

Yes, for their anniversary. He sat up straighter, excitement taking over.

He wasn't naive enough to think the trip was going to solve everything. But at least it would give them a chance to get away from all the heartache here and rediscover the relationship that had started there.

Simeon punched the power button on his computer. He'd come to the office way earlier than necessary this morning, so he still had a couple of hours before his first clients arrived.

Plenty of time to plan a trip.

⁓

"Can I help you?"

Abigail blinked, trying to make sense of the voice. But all she could see was the giant letters behind the receptionist's desk: Zelensky and Baker. Attorneys at Law."

"Ma'am?" the woman repeated. "Can I help you?"

"Oh, uh." Abigail stepped forward, wiping the rainwater off her face. Though it had been a short dash from the parking lot into the building, it was pouring outside, and she was completely soaked. She glanced at the placard on the desk. The woman's name was Wendy, apparently. Abigail didn't think that was who she'd talked to on the phone earlier this morning, but it didn't matter. "I have an appointment. Abigail Calvano."

The woman's perfectly lipsticked mouth seemed to form a small O, but before Abigail could worry about what it meant, she had replaced it with a smile. "Yes. I'll let Debbie know you're here."

"Thank you."

Abigail took a seat in the posh-looking lobby. She clutched her purse in her lap, taking in the wood paneling and the slight leathery scent, the tasteful but bland landscapes on the wall, the soft music. All designed to make a client feel comfortable and at ease, Abigail imagined. And all failing miserably.

"Abigail? I'll take you back to see Debbie now." Wendy appeared in front of her, her slim skirt and tailored blouse a sharp contrast to Abigail's sweats. "If you'll follow me."

Mutely, Abigail obeyed. Was she really here? Was she really going to do this?

"Here we are." Wendy opened a frosted glass door and motioned for Abigail to step inside.

Abigail licked her lips. It wasn't too late to turn around and march right out of here.

But that would only delay the inevitable.

With a mumbled thanks, she stepped past Wendy into the attorney's office.

Forty minutes later, she emerged, clutching a thin packet of papers.

Keeping her head down, she plodded toward the lobby.

"Have a nice day," Wendy called cheerfully as Abigail passed her.

Abigail's stomach tightened. Didn't the receptionist know what people came here to do?

But the woman was just doing her job. "You too," she mumbled, stuffing the papers into her purse, then pushing the door open.

It's still raining. The thought registered dully as drops of water splatted on her head. But she couldn't make her feet move any faster toward her car. She shivered as a raindrop hit her neck and made its way down her spine. Finally, she got to the car and opened the door.

But even in here, out of the rain, she couldn't stop shivering. She turned on the ignition and cranked up the heat, but that didn't help either. She wrapped her arms around her middle, rocking back and forth for a second. But after a moment, she stopped, taking a deep breath. She had to get herself together. She was supposed to pick Carly up in ten minutes.

She moved her purse to the floor. But the paperwork from the attorney poked from it. She snatched at the papers, reaching across the seats to open the glove box and shove them inside.

She slammed the glove box shut. There. Now no one would see them. Until she gave them to Simeon. The thought nearly made her pass out. But she had no choice. She'd tell him everything tonight—give him the papers. And pray he wouldn't sign them.

That last part was selfish—and unrealistic—but she couldn't help it.

She forced herself to shift the car into gear and steer toward Zeb and Carly's house. The whole way there, she focused on breathing and not thinking about anything.

The rain fell harder, the drops making a racket against the roof of the car. She turned the windshield wipers on full blast, grateful for the distraction of driving.

By the time she pulled into Zeb and Carly's driveway, she'd almost managed to forget the papers searing a hole right through the glove box and into her heart.

Carly popped out the door and dashed through the rain toward the car, holding a jacket closed over her belly.

"Hi." She dropped breathlessly into the passenger seat, sliding a water bottle into the cupholder between them. Abigail's eyes went instantly to her sister-in-law's stomach. Her own pregnancies had never made it to the point of showing.

Resolutely, she drew her gaze away, grabbing her phone and typing in the address Lydia had given her for the dress shop.

"Whew! Are you trying to turn your car into a sauna?" Carly fanned herself.

"Sorry." Abigail turned the heat down and backed out of the driveway. "I was trying to dry off."

"Don't you have a garage?" Carly teased.

"I had some errands to do." Abigail's eyes went involuntarily to the glove box, but she pulled them back to the road.

"Anything fun?" Carly shifted in her seat, sliding the seatbelt below her belly.

"Not really." Abigail swallowed painfully. She was not going to cry with her sister-in-law in the car.

"Oh." Carly took a long drink of her water, and Abigail took the turn the GPS instructed her to make into the hills outside of town.

For a while, the only sound was the rain lashing at the car, and Abigail focused on the unfamiliar curvy road.

"Why didn't you tell us?" Carly broke into the silence.

Abigail jumped, though her sister-in-law's voice had been barely audible over the rain. "Tell you what?"

"About the babies." Carly's hand landed on her arm. "We're all so sorry. If we'd known . . ."

"I know." Abigail shrugged, turning up the wipers to full speed as she navigated a sharp curve. "I'm fine."

Carly pulled her hand back, but Abigail could still feel her gaze. "I'm glad y'all have decided to adopt though."

Abigail pressed her lips together, but it wasn't enough to stop the tears from falling.

"Oh no. Abigail, what is it?" Concern coated Carly's words, making Abigail cry harder.

"Nothing." She sniffed and leaned forward, trying to see through the rain and her tears.

"Abigail, really . . ." Carly leaned toward her.

"It's nothing." Abigail wiped her eyes. "I don't want to talk about it."

Carly fell silent and sat back in her seat, reaching for her water bottle. Abigail squinted out the windshield. Too late, she noticed a deep pothole in the road. There was a car coming in the other direction, so she couldn't swerve.

She hit the pothole harder than she intended, gripping the wheel as the car hydroplaned for a moment.

"Sorry about that," she murmured, glancing toward Carly.

Her sister-in-law held her water bottle out in front of her but was staring at her lap. "Bad time to take a drink." She laughed. "Are there napkins in the glove box?" She had it open before Abigail could react.

"No." The delayed cry finally came out.

But Carly had already moved the papers out of the way so she could dig under them. Abigail held her breath. Maybe Carly wouldn't look at them.

She flicked her eyes back and forth from the road to Carly.

"Here they are." Carly pulled out a wad of napkins and slid the papers back into the glove box, then pressed it closed.

Abigail let out a ragged breath as she maneuvered around a hairpin turn. That had been much too close. Her sister-in-law—Simeon's whole family—would find out soon enough. But not today. Not like this.

"Oops. Must not have latched it tightly." Carly's words pulled Abigail's eyes off the road. Carly was trying to readjust the papers in the glove box.

"It's okay. I can get it later," Abigail said quickly.

"That's all right. I think I've got— What's this?"

Abigail's head jerked toward Carly. Her sister-in-law was holding the bundle of papers in front of her, reading.

Abigail's mouth went Sahara-dry, and her vision glitched. She blinked and turned back to the road. "It's— Uh—"

"Are you and Simeon getting divorced?" Carly sounded disbelieving.

"We're— I don't know." Her own words turned around and slammed right into her chest. She gasped for breath.

"But why? I know y'all have had a hard time lately, but you're adopting now and—"

"We're not," Abigail said flatly.

"Not what?"

"Not adopting."

"But Simeon just said yesterday . . ." Carly sounded near tears, and Abigail hated herself for hurting yet another person.

"We can't." She might as well tell Carly the truth. "*I* can't."

"What on earth? Abigail, that doesn't even make sense. Everyone can adopt."

"Not—" She let out a breath. Once she said this, she couldn't take it back. She'd have to go forward with telling Simeon tonight. "Not me. Not after the things I've done."

"The things you've done? What kinds of things?"

Rain trounced the window, and Abigail leaned forward, trying to follow the yellow lines as they crested a hill. She tapped the brakes to round a curve, eyeing the terrain that fell away sharply on the right.

"Things like—"

"Watch out!" Carly gasped.

Abigail swerved sharply as a pickup truck in the other lane crossed the center line. The guardrail loomed in front of them, and Abigail stomped her foot to the brake and yanked the wheel in the other direction. The car spun, and there was a deafening crunch of metal on metal. Something white burst in Abigail's face. The car was still moving—much too fast. Abigail pressed her foot harder to the brake. But there was nothing she could do to stop it.

Chapter 11

Simeon's phone dinged with an email, and he scooped it off his desk. He had two minutes before his next appointment, and he'd already heard the bell on the outer door jingle, but he was hoping this was a response from Pastor Mateo in Ecuador.

He smiled as he glimpsed the sender's name and the first few words of the email: "Yes!!! You are welcome here anytime."

That was the last detail he'd been working on securing. He'd already bought the plane tickets, and he'd figured he and Abigail could always find somewhere else to stay if Pastor Mateo didn't have room.

But this would be perfect.

Simeon tucked his phone into his pocket as he stood and opened his office door.

"Good morning, Wendy."

She immediately jumped to her feet and crossed the small space. "Oh good. You're here."

Simeon laughed, ushering her into the office. "Of course I'm here. Where else would I be?"

Wendy took her seat but seemed to be studying him. "So you're okay?" She tilted her head to the side, as if to show sympathy. But for what, Simeon didn't know.

"Yes, I'm okay." Simeon bit back the urge to tell her about his surprise for Abigail. That would be totally inappropriate. He just wanted to tell *someone*.

You can tell Abigail. Tonight.

Right. Maybe he'd get her flowers again. He'd noticed a beautiful orchid at the flower shop the other day—just like the ones they'd seen growing in Ecuador.

"How are you doing?" Simeon brought his focus back to his client. "You started your new job."

Wendy nodded, still tilting her head. "I did. I was there this morning, actually, and I could hardly believe—"

Simeon's phone rang sharply, and he grabbed at his pocket. "I'm so sorry. I usually have my sound turned off . . ." In all the flurry of planning the trip this morning, he must have forgotten. He gave a quick glance at the name on his screen. Zeb.

His brother had never once called him during the workday.

It was probably nothing. Simeon declined the call, then silenced the phone. But before he could put it away, it lit up with Zeb's name again.

His gut clenched. Something could have happened to Dad. Or Asher, working out in the national park in this rain.

"I'm so sorry. I just need to . . ."

"Of course." Wendy watched him with a look of concern.

Simeon propelled himself from his seat and into the small lobby and hit answer.

The moment he lifted the phone to his ear, he heard the sirens.

"Zeb. What's going on?"

There was a beat of silence.

"Zeb!"

"You need to get to the hospital." Zeb's voice was rough. "Abigail was in an accident."

"Abigail . . ." The room twisted around him, like he'd been swept up in a cyclone. "What happened?"

Zeb shouted something in the background, then came back on the phone. "I have to go. They're taking her to Brampton Memorial. I'll meet you there."

"Zeb." But the sirens cut off and everything went silent.

Simeon held the phone away from his ear. *Call ended.*

He staggered toward his office and fumbled through his desk for his keys.

"Simeon?"

His head jerked up. "Oh. Wendy. I'm sorry. I have to go."

"Is everything all right?" She stood, moving toward him.

He choked on his answer. "I don't know."

Rain pummeled the windshield, making it nearly impossible for Simeon to see. But he pressed his foot harder to the accelerator.

He had to get to his wife.

Oh, please Lord. Abigail. Please let her be okay.

The prayer barely made sense, but Simeon had repeated it a hundred times already. And he'd repeat it a hundred more times. A thousand times. He just needed her to be all right.

He growled as he hit a red light on the outskirts of Brampton. While he was stopped, he dialed Zeb again. But his brother hadn't answered a single one of his calls.

Because he didn't want to give Simeon bad news over the phone?

Simeon's stomach turned over, and he dry heaved once before getting himself under control. Letting his mind go to the worst case scenario wasn't going to help anything.

The light turned green, and Simeon gunned it through the mid-sized town, screeching into the hospital parking lot and leaving his vehicle in the first spot he came to.

He threw his door open and sprinted through the downpour, dodging a car that nearly ran him down.

Inside the hospital doors, he drew up short. Where would she be?

It only took a moment for his eyes to fall on Zeb. And for his heart to stop.

His strong, stoic, tough-as-they-come brother stood facing the far wall, his head braced on his arm.

Simeon weaved through the maze of chairs in the waiting room, apologizing as he tripped over a small girl's feet.

"What's going on? Where is she?" He grabbed his brother's arm.

Immediately, Zeb straightened, clearing his throat. A line of red rimmed his eyes, and Simeon's pulse accelerated straight past panic. "Zeb?"

"Abigail's in surgery now. They said she'll be all right."

"Oh, thank you, Lord." Simeon's knees gave out, and he grabbed his brother's arm. "What is she in surgery for?" *Please not a head injury.*

"She has a broken clavicle. A few broken ribs. A punctured lung."

Simeon forced himself to breathe. The thought of his wife going through all of that . . .

But it could have been so much worse.

"Thank you, Lord," he repeated.

And then he remembered. Abigail was supposed to drive Carly to the dress shop.

"Was Carly—"

Zeb gave a short shake of his head before Simeon had finished the question. "She didn't make it."

The words sucked the air right out of Simeon's lungs. They couldn't be true. This couldn't be happening. Zeb and Carly had been together since high school. They were having a baby.

Simeon's insides heaved. "The baby?" he whispered.

Zeb shook his head. "I'm going to get some coffee. I'll find a nurse to get you an update on Abigail."

"Zeb." Simeon tightened his grip on his brother's arm, but Zeb shrugged easily out of it and strode away from him.

Simeon gazed helplessly around the waiting room. All these years of helping others through their tragedies.

And he had no idea how to face his own.

Chapter 12

"Abigail?"

Where was that voice coming from? It sounded so far away. But so loud.

She tried to open her eyes, but they were too heavy.

"Abigail."

The voice sounded urgent, and she felt like she should respond. Tell whoever it was that she wanted to sleep a little longer.

She managed to pry her lids open a slit.

"Abigail! I'm here, sweetheart." That loud voice again.

Her eyes refused to focus properly, but she was pretty sure that was a man standing over her. She couldn't tell if he was laughing or crying.

Did she know him?

She tried to place his face, but her eyelids refused to cooperate any longer.

"You rest. I'll be here when you wake up." Lips touched her forehead, and she caught a fresh, earthy scent. She wanted to ask the man why he was kissing her.

But she was so tired.

She would figure it out when she woke up.

Simeon stared at the words of his Bible, blurred in front of him. He blinked to clear his vision, then glanced at the time. 10 p.m. He felt like he'd lived a dozen lifetimes today.

There was the before.

Planning the trip to Ecuador.

Counseling patients.

Then there was the call.

The ride here. The praying and pleading.

The shock of learning Carly hadn't made it.

The waiting. Talking to Dad and his siblings, who had gathered to be with them.

The relief of the doctor finally telling him that Abigail was out of surgery and would be fine.

And then more waiting at her bedside.

The rejoicing when she'd opened her eyes.

And more waiting when they'd closed again.

Simeon shifted his gaze back to his Bible. He'd always found his greatest comfort in the Psalms, and he directed his clients to them often. He'd been reading through them for the past hour, and his eyes fell now on Psalm 46. Exhaustion swirled the words together on the page, and he wasn't sure they were getting through to him anymore. Until he came to verse 10: "Be still and know that I am God."

Simeon looked at Abigail's still form, blinking hard against the sudden moisture that sprang to his eyes.

Be still.

That was what he needed to do. Be still and trust in the Lord.

He closed his Bible and reached a hand to hold Abigail's, lowering his head carefully onto the bed next to her and letting his eyes close. He would be still and wait. Wait on Abigail. And wait on the Lord.

He drifted in a half-sleep until a low moan brought his head up. "Abigail?"

Her eyes were open wide, and she swiveled her head around the room.

"It's okay, sweetheart. You're safe. You're in the hospital." Simeon stroked her hand.

"I don't—" Her voice was raspy, and Simeon stood and filled a paper cup with water, dropping a straw into it. He held it in front of her mouth. She hesitated a moment but then took a long drink.

He set it on the table, then just looked at her, his heart filling with all the things he had to tell her. "Oh, Abigail. I thought I'd lost you." He reached to brush her hair off her forehead. "I don't know what—"

She flinched as his hand made contact with her skin.

"I'm sorry. Did that hurt?" He peered at the spot, looking for any sign of a bruise or swelling.

She shook her head. "No."

"Oh. Good." He wrapped his hand around hers. "Do you remember what happened?" he asked gently.

She shook her head again, pulling her hand out of his. Simeon tried not to be hurt. This was a lot for her to process.

"You were driving to the dress shop, and it was raining. Zeb says it looks like you swerved and skidded out. The car went over the side—" His voice gave out, and it took a minute before he could finish. "Honey, I'm so sorry to tell you, but Carly didn't make it."

Abigail blinked at him. "Who's Carly?"

Simeon sat on the chair at Abigail's bedside, a hard thump echoing up at him as his Bible fell to the floor. He tried not to panic.

83

She was probably still confused from the anesthetic. It wasn't that uncommon.

"She's Zeb's wife, remember? You two were on your way to pick out bridesmaid dresses for Lydia and Liam's wedding."

Abigail turned away from him to look at the ceiling. "I don't know who you're talking about."

"Abigail." Simeon stood again and took her hand. "Look at me."

She did.

"Do you know me?" He tried to keep his voice calm and soothing through his rising unease.

She studied him with a bland expression, then shook her head and pulled her hand out of his. "No. Should I?"

Simeon pressed his fists to his head and turned away from her, forcing himself to keep his composure.

It was just the effects of the anesthesia. It was temporary. He turned back to her, pressing the call button on her bed.

"What are you doing?" she asked.

"It's okay. I'm going to have the doctor come in and take a look at you."

Abigail yawned and closed her eyes. "I thought you were the doctor."

"No." Simeon swallowed around the fear clogging his throat. "I'm your husband."

But Abigail's only response was the deep breath he recognized as her real sleep.

Chapter 13

Abigail could feel herself waking up again, but she didn't want to.

Every time she opened her eyes, people told her all kinds of things she didn't understand, asked her questions she couldn't answer, took her for scans or blood work or other tests she didn't want.

"Abigail?" A man whispered her name. She'd gotten used to the voice now. It was low and soothing and made her feel safe.

But she kept her eyes closed. Because as much as she liked his voice, the things he said didn't make sense. How could he be her husband if she didn't know him? He'd even had to tell her his name: Simeon.

"Abigail?" A hand stroked her shoulder. "It's time to wake up, sweetheart. There are some people here to see you."

Maybe this time when she opened her eyes, she'd remember him.

She cracked them open to find Simeon smiling down at her, though his forehead was creased into little lines of worry. Stubble that hadn't been there earlier covered his cheeks, and dark purple circles rimmed his eyes. She was sorry for causing him so much trouble. But he still felt like as much of a stranger as the last time she'd opened her eyes. She moved her arm a little, groaning as pain throbbed through her ribs.

Simeon pulled his hand away. "How's the pain?"

"It's okay," she murmured, though she couldn't find a part of her body that didn't ache, and something immobilized her left arm.

Simeon took a hand out of his pocket as if he were going to reach for hers but then tucked it back in. "Are you up for visitors? Everyone's been waiting anxiously to see you." Simeon moved to open the curtains, and what looked like midday light streamed in.

Abigail wanted to ask who *everyone* was, but she supposed it didn't matter. She nodded.

"Great. I'll be right back." Simeon's smile was warm, and Abigail decided she liked it.

He left the room, and Abigail turned her head to the window. She must not be on the ground floor, since she couldn't see the immediate surroundings from here. But she could see the sky—a bright, shining blue, and in the distance, low, rolling mountains. Was this where she lived?

She strained to remember. But her brain landed on nothing.

The door to her room opened, and she swiveled her head as Simeon led a whole parade of people into the room.

The first one—a red-haired woman with a scarred face—started crying the moment she saw Abigail, then flew across the room.

"Ava," someone called as a pair of thin but surprisingly strong arms closed around Abigail.

She groaned against the slice of pain that shot through her ribs.

"I'm so sorry." The woman let go and took a step backwards. "Did I hurt you?"

"She has broken ribs, a punctured lung, and a broken clavicle." Simeon stepped between her and the rest of the group. "So maybe no hugs for now."

The others—there were so many of them—took up every square foot of the room. Some greeted her, some smiled, some cried.

And she didn't recognize a single one.

An older gentleman who looked a lot like Simeon, except with white hair and a rounder form, stepped up next to the bed and gave her hand a quick, gentle squeeze. "Hello, dear." Something about his fatherly tone grabbed at Abigail's heart.

"Hi," she whispered back.

Behind the older man, Simeon let out a breath and clapped a hand to the man's shoulder.

"You remember him?" Simeon asked.

Abigail's eyes went from Simeon to the man and back again. She shook her head.

Simeon's expression fell so quickly that she wanted to take it back. She may not know him, but she didn't like the idea of disappointing him.

Across the room, she heard a sob, and her eyes went to a dark-haired woman who had buried her face in the shirt of the man next to her. This man also looked a lot like Simeon—and much closer to his age—although he was taller and maybe a bit broader.

"I'm sorry," Abigail whispered. Whoever these people were, she didn't want to hurt them.

"You have nothing to be sorry about." The older gentleman squeezed her hand. "I'm Abe. Or Pastor Calvano. Or Dad. Whichever you want to call me."

"Dad?"

"He's my dad," Simeon clarified. "Your father-in-law."

Abigail nodded because it seemed like the right thing to do. Simeon's smile told her it had been a good choice.

"And this is our family. My brother Joseph and his wife Ava." The woman with the scarred face waved at her, then swiped the tears from her cheeks. "Asher and his wife Ireland." The dark-haired woman who had buried her face in her husband's shirt turned to her with a wobbly smile.

"My sister Grace and her husband Levi. They flew in from Wisconsin to see you. And my other sister Lydia and her fiancé Liam," Simeon continued. Two nearly identical-looking dark-haired women and the men with them smiled at her.

"Hmm hmm." A throat cleared from over by the window.

"I was getting to you," Simeon said, and the whole group laughed softly. "My youngest brother Benjamin. Who has never been good at waiting his turn."

"That's because I'm always last," Benjamin said, but he sent Abigail a playful grin, and she decided she liked him.

"Zeb said he'd try to come by later," Simeon said. "He's . . ." His voice trailed off, and even Benjamin's face went somber.

Abigail tried to shift her position in the hospital bed but winced as her ribs protested.

"We should let you rest." The man holding her hand—she wasn't sure she could bring herself to call a stranger Dad—let go. "Before we leave, I thought we could say a prayer, if you don't mind."

Abigail shrugged. She didn't have a strong feeling about it one way or the other.

The others all folded their hands and ducked their heads, so Abigail did the same.

"Lord of all," Pastor Calvano prayed. "We thank you for preserving and protecting Abigail's life through the accident. We ask that you would bring her healing now. Give her your peace as she recovers, and let her remember, Lord, that she has a family who loves her and will always be here for her and walk with her through every hardship. Please pour out your comfort and peace on Zeb, Lord. Through his sorrow, let him also rejoice that Carly and their baby are now at your side in glory. Amen."

Abigail lifted her head. All around the room, people were hugging and wiping tears off their faces.

Unexpected tears pricked her own eyes.

Was this really her family? Did they really love her like they so obviously loved one another?

"We'll be back soon." Pastor Calvano squeezed her hand one more time, then the others were parading past her bed again, squeezing her arm and telling her they'd be praying for her.

And then it was just her and Simeon in the room again.

"You don't have to stay," she said.

He looked like he could fall asleep standing right there.

But he smiled wearily and sat in the chair at her bedside. "I'm not going anywhere."

Chapter 14

Simeon stared at the vending machine dispensing coffee into his paper cup. He didn't know how much longer he could take this. Why hadn't Abigail's memories come back yet? It'd been two days, and the effects of the anesthesia should have worn off by now.

They'd taken her for yet another neurological test, and then Simeon was supposed to have yet another meeting with the doctor to discuss the results.

"Coffee's done." Dad pulled the cup off the vending machine and handed it to Simeon.

"Oh. Thanks." Simeon lifted it to his lips. The scorching liquid burned its way down his throat, but it was better than the burning that had been there since Abigail had opened her eyes and not recognized him.

"Mr. Calvano?" A nurse popped into the waiting room. "Dr. Dorn is ready for you."

He nodded tightly, his gut twisting.

"Do you want me to come with you?" Dad asked.

Simeon didn't hesitate. "Yes."

The nurse led them to the end of the hallway, then ushered them into a small office. Dr. Dorn sat at his desk, studying a computer screen, but he stood and shook their hands, then directed them to the two stiff chairs on the other side of his desk.

Simeon sat on the very edge of his. "What did you find?"

Dr. Dorn folded his hands on the desk in front of him. "We've done a CT scan and an MRI. There are no signs of swelling or bleeding. No fractures. No brain trauma of any kind. We also did a functional MRI to test her brain function. Everything looks normal."

"That's good, right?" Dad patted Simeon's shoulder.

But Simeon couldn't answer, and Dr. Dorn kept talking as if Dad hadn't interrupted. "Does she have a history of depression or emotional stress?"

"Depression?" Dad dropped his hand from Simeon's shoulder and leaned forward in his seat. "What would that—"

But Simeon nodded dully. He knew where the doctor was going with this. "She's—we've—lost a number of pregnancies over the past couple of years. It caused her significant emotional stress and depression." Why had he not found some way to help her? He'd tried so hard . . . but he should have tried harder.

"I still don't understand," Dad interjected. "What does that have to do with the accident?"

"We've done a number of neurological evaluations," Dr. Dorn explained calmly.

Simeon could sense Dad's impatience for the doctor to make his point, but for his own part, Simeon wished the doctor would stop talking altogether.

"Her procedural memory is intact," the doctor continued. "But retrieval of long-term memories seems to be compromised."

Simeon's stomach roiled.

"What does that mean? Simeon?" Dad turned to him.

"It means," Dr. Dorn explained when Simeon couldn't speak. "She seems to have generalized amnesia."

"It could still be the effects of the anesthesia." The words shot out of Simeon's mouth. He had to believe it. Because if what Dr. Dorn was saying was true . . .

Dr. Dorn kept the same bland expression. "I would have expected it to resolve itself by now, if that were the case. Given that, and the fact that depression and trauma are risk factors for—"

"Generalized amnesia is very rare," Simeon argued.

"First case I've seen in thirty years of practicing medicine," Dr. Dorn agreed.

Simeon nodded grimly. He didn't want to mention the one case he'd seen while completing his clinical hours. He'd only worked with the amnesic and his wife for a few months before their marriage fell apart and they stopped coming to counseling.

"But she'll get her memories back, right?" Dad asked.

"There's no way to know," Simeon said quietly. "Some people get them back after a few days. Other people . . ." He couldn't finish the thought.

"I'd like to keep her under observation a couple more days," the doctor said. "But if all goes well, you should be able to take her home before the end of the week."

Simeon nodded numbly. He could take her home—to a life she didn't remember anymore.

Chapter 15

Abigail stared straight up, tracing the perpendicular lines of the ceiling tiles with her eyes.

Was it weird that this hospital room was the only home she remembered?

It wasn't so bad, really.

The doctors and nurses were nice. The food was fine. The view of the mountains was beautiful.

But now they said it was time for her to go *home*.

Wherever that was.

"Ready for this?" Simeon bustled into the room, followed by a nurse pushing an empty wheelchair. For her, Abigail realized.

She nodded mutely, in spite of the lump of apprehension snaking around her stomach.

Staying here didn't seem to be an option. And she had nowhere else to go, aside from with Simeon.

His family had been regular visitors while she'd been here, but when she'd asked why her own family hadn't come at all, Simeon had told her that her parents died when she was a little girl and she didn't have any other family. She felt like the knowledge should have made her sad, but she supposed it was hard to miss what you didn't remember.

"Can you get in the wheelchair yourself, or do you want me to help you?" Simeon asked.

"I can do it." Abigail slid her feet over the side of the bed. She braced her right hand against the edge of the mattress, careful not to jounce her left arm. She'd learned the hard way that moving that arm caused the pain in her screwed-together collarbone to flare. But as she pressed her weight into the bed, pressure exploded in her ribs, and she couldn't help crying out.

"I've got you." Simeon stepped forward, wrapping his arm around her and pulling her gently to her feet. Carefully, he turned her, then supported her weight as she lowered herself into the wheelchair.

"Thank you," she panted as Simeon let go and gathered the bag of clothing and toiletries his sister Lydia had brought earlier in the week. He walked alongside as the nurse pushed her out the door and down the hall.

Her apprehension grew as they approached the doors. She was going to a home she didn't remember to live with a man she didn't remember—not just to live with him, to be his *wife*.

She didn't even know *how* to be a wife.

"I already pulled our vehicle up." Simeon pointed to a black SUV.

The nurse steered her to it, and Simeon opened the passenger door, then set down her bag and helped her up out of the wheelchair and into the vehicle. He leaned across her to buckle the seatbelt, and that fresh, earthy scent she'd already come to associate with him lingered even as he moved away.

For some reason, it made her feel more comfortable about going home. Like she'd be safe and cared for with him.

Simeon closed her door and turned to say something to the nurse. Abigail studied him as he talked. She could see why she'd been attracted to him in the first place. He was tall—though not quite as tall as his brothers—and fit. His dark hair was short—but not too short—and dark, contrasting with the bright blue of his eyes. If she had to guess, the eyes were probably what had gotten her first. Not their color, but their kindness.

Then again, what did she know? Maybe she wasn't the type of woman who cared about kind eyes.

She dropped her head back onto the seat. This was all so confusing. Simeon had explained to her about the amnesia. He'd said there was no way to determine what had caused it—or whether she'd ever get better.

So what was she supposed to do, just go through life without knowing who she even was?

Simeon's door opened, and Abigail jumped. She hadn't noticed him walking around the vehicle.

"This is Brampton." Simeon gestured out the window as he pulled away from the hospital. "We live in River Falls, which is about an hour away."

Abigail nodded, watching the scenery, trying to pick out some-thing—just one thing—that felt familiar.

Simeon pointed out a few landmarks along the way—a place they appar-ently liked to hike, a restaurant they'd gone to a few times, the spot they'd once run out of gas and had to call his brother Zeb to rescue them—but mostly he was silent, and Abigail was grateful.

"And this is River Falls," Simeon said after a while.

Abigail sat up, peering out the window.

Simeon slowed the vehicle as he turned onto a street lined with quaint buildings. "My office is a couple of blocks that way." He pointed in the opposite direction. Abigail nodded. He'd mentioned he was a Christian counselor. "That's Joseph's vet clinic." Simeon pointed to a sign that read River Falls Veterinary. "And there's Daisy's Pie Shop. We've spent probably hundreds of hours in there."

Okay, she liked pie. That was good to know.

"That's Ava's photography studio. Henderson's Art Gallery. The Book Den. You work there."

"I work?" It hadn't really occurred to her to wonder what she did.

"Part-time. Ruth—" He seemed to catch himself. "She's your boss. Anyway, she says to take as long as you need to recover."

Abigail nodded, although she wondered how she was supposed to go back to a job she didn't know how to do.

Simeon kept pointing out the sights, looking at her hopefully with each one, as if expecting something would jar her memory. "And there's Founder's Park," he said as they crossed a bridge. "We'll have to take a walk there. You love the flowers, and they should be in full bloom now."

"Mmm." Abigail peered toward the riverfront park. It did look pretty, but it didn't fire any spark of recognition.

They drove in silence for a few more minutes, until Simeon pulled the vehicle into the driveway of a modest two-story house, its blue paint cheerful without being overly bright.

"And this is our home." He turned to look at her with an eager smile.

"It looks nice," she said politely.

Simeon's smile didn't falter, but his eyes skipped away. "It is," he said softly. "Sit tight for a second, and I'll come help you out."

Abigail obeyed, mostly because she was still examining the house. Had she picked out the wicker chairs on the porch? Had she planted the flowers that lined the walkway? Had she hung the wind chimes that tinkled in the breeze?

It was like she wasn't connected to anything—like she might float away.

Simeon pulled her door open. "Ready?" He held out a hand to her.

She nodded and took it, its solidity making her feel at least a little anchored to something solid.

Simeon helped her out of the vehicle, then wrapped an arm behind her back and ushered her toward the front door. She was a little woozy after spending so many days in bed, and she found herself leaning into him despite the ache in her ribs.

He held her as he unlocked the front door, then led her inside. Together, they stood in the small entryway as she gazed around the space. To the left was a comfortable looking living room, to the right a stairway leading up.

"It's nice," she said again.

"Do you want a tour, or do you want to rest first?" If Simeon was disappointed by her reaction, he didn't let on.

"Maybe rest." Suddenly the thought of seeing the whole house—of searching each room for some hint of who she was—seemed overwhelming. "If that's okay."

"Of course." Simeon turned them toward the stairs. "I'll take you up to the bedroom." He kept his arm firmly around her as they climbed the stairs, and Abigail thought briefly that it might not be the end of the world to be stuck with him forever. It was clear that he was kind and caring.

He led her past what looked like a spare room, an office, and a bathroom before they reached the last room off the hallway. "This is our room."

The doorway wasn't wide enough to fit them side by side, and he dropped his arm from around her back to gesture her inside.

She stepped through the door but then froze.

He'd said *our* room. As in both of theirs. But there was only one bed.

She supposed that made sense, given that they were apparently husband and wife.

She ran her right hand over her left, rubbing at the wedding ring that proved she was indeed married, whether she remembered her husband or not.

"This is the closet." Simeon's voice came from the other side of the room, but Abigail couldn't take her eyes off that bed. She reminded herself that Simeon had slept in the chair next to her bed every night in the hospital. It was practically the same thing.

"Abigail?" Simeon's voice drew closer, and she forced her eyes to him.

His gaze tracked to the bed, his expression sinking for a moment. But by the time he turned to her, he'd put on a gentle smile. "I'll sleep in my office for now. Until . . ." His eyes dropped from hers, and the blank space he'd left hung heavy with the possibility. Until she got her memories back? Or until . . . What was the alternative?

"It's your bed," Abigail protested. "I'm the one who should sleep somewhere else."

"Abigail." Simeon wheezed as if she'd knocked the wind out of him. "It's your bed too."

"Oh. Right. I just meant—" But she had no idea what she meant. No idea what anything meant right now.

The heaviness of exhaustion descended on her, and she looked for somewhere to sit down.

"Sorry. You wanted to rest." Simeon took her good arm, leading her toward the bed. "I'll wake you for dinner."

He pulled the blankets down, then eased her onto the bed and tucked them around her.

"Oh." She couldn't help the sigh. "Much more comfortable than the hospital bed."

Simeon chuckled, lifting a hand as if to brush the hair off of her face. But he dropped it before it reached her. "Sleep well. I love you."

It wasn't the first time he'd said it since the accident—or even since she'd woken up this morning.

And she knew she should say it back. After all, she was his wife. She must love him, right?

But her lips remained closed.

Because she didn't know.

Chapter 16

Simeon allowed himself one last glance at his wife before he closed the bedroom door with a soft click. A sigh seeped out of him, pulling all his energy with it. He forced his feet to carry him down the hallway but paused outside his office to stare down his recliner. Apparently, it was going to be his bed for the foreseeable future. At least it would be more comfortable than that hospital chair. He could still feel the cricks in his back after a week of sleeping in it, but it had been a small price to pay to be near his wife. Of course, he'd been looking forward to sleeping in his own bed again. To curling up close to Abigail and holding her.

But it had only taken one look at her face as she'd stared at that bed to know that wasn't going to happen. It should have occurred to him sooner, really.

For all intents and purposes, he was a stranger to her. Of course she didn't want to sleep in the same bed as him.

So he'd sleep in the recliner. For now. Until she got her memories back.

And he'd do everything possible to make sure that happened.

A surge of energy propelled him down the stairs. He needed to find all their pictures. And go to the grocery store. And make her favorite meal. Anything he could do to remind her of the past might help trigger her memories. So he was going to do it all.

Two hours later, he'd gathered every picture in the house onto the dining room table and was just putting the finishing touches on the enchiladas when the doorbell rang. Simeon gave the enchilada sauce a quick stir, then turned the burner off so it wouldn't get overdone.

He hurried toward the door before whoever was there could ring again. Knowing his family, it was probably one of his siblings coming to check on Abigail even though he'd told them to give her the day to get settled in. He couldn't be mad, though—not when he was so grateful for the love and support they'd shown her all week.

In fact, now that they were here, maybe he'd invite them to stay for dinner. The more people who shared memories with Abigail, the better.

He pulled the door open. "Zeb."

Though Zeb was four years younger than Simeon's thirty-eight, he looked like he'd aged a decade in the past five days. Lines marred his forehead, and thick smudges edged his eyes. He was in uniform, which Simeon guessed meant he hadn't taken any time off.

Simeon stepped back from the door. "Come in." He'd been trying to get ahold of his brother, but Zeb had been ignoring his calls and hadn't stopped by the hospital.

Not that Simeon didn't understand.

Zeb wasn't one to talk about his feelings on the best of days, but this . . .

It would have been too much for anyone. Even Simeon. If their situations had been reversed . . . He could barely handle thinking about it.

Zeb stepped inside, rolling and unrolling what looked like a stack of papers.

"How are you doing?" Simeon asked.

Zeb shrugged. "I'm fine."

Simeon nodded. If Zeb were a client, he'd probably push harder against the obvious lie, but he knew Zeb well enough to know that was all he was going to get right now. His better course of action was to convince his brother to stay—to show him they were there for him.

"Come sit down. I made enchiladas. I was just going to wake Abigail up, and—"

"I can't stay," Zeb interrupted. "I just came by to— Uh." He cleared his throat as if he were uncomfortable. "To give you this." He held the rolled up papers out to Simeon.

"What's this?" Simeon took them.

"I'm sorry, man. They found it in the car after . . ." Zeb cleared his throat again. "I wasn't sure what else to . . ."

Simeon eyed him. Zeb wasn't a loquacious man, but he didn't usually struggle to say what needed to be said.

Simeon unrolled the thin stack of papers.

Law Office of Zelensky and Baker.

Simeon blinked at the letterhead. What was this?

His eyes flicked to Zeb's grim expression and then back to the paper.

His gaze skimmed to a heading above a block of text. *Petition for Divorce.* Abigail's name stood out in bold on a line beneath that. Under it was a little "vs." And then Simeon's name.

"Oh." All the air left him, as if someone had popped his lungs.

He took a step backwards, looking for something to lean against. But there was nothing.

"I didn't realize you two were . . ." Zeb's voice sounded far away.

Simeon couldn't stop staring at the stupid piece of paper. "I— We're not. There must be some . . ." His mouth was too dry to finish the sentence.

He kept reading. The date on the paper was May 8. The day of the accident. Had she had these drawn up that morning?

He shook his head. Of course she had. They hadn't just magically appeared in her car.

"Are you okay?" Zeb stepped closer.

Simeon laughed ironically and rubbed a hand over his hair. "I have no idea."

Zeb shifted. "She didn't say anything about them?"

Simeon shook his head. "She doesn't remember anything."

"Yeah. Dad told me."

Before Simeon had time to consider whether it was a good idea, he lifted the papers in front of him and tore them down the middle, once and then again. And again.

Zeb eyed him. "You're not going to tell her?"

Simeon shook his head. "What good could it possibly do? She doesn't even remember me, let alone this." He shook the scraps of paper. "If I asked her why she wanted to get a—" He choked, unable to say the word. "She was in such a depression before the accident. That's all this was about." He waved the papers again.

Zeb pressed his lips together in that look Simeon knew meant he disagreed, but he nodded. "If you think that's best."

"I do." Simeon balled the fluttering papers in his hand. "Do me a favor and don't mention this to anyone else either, okay?"

This time Zeb's disapproving look was accompanied by a grunt.

"What?" Simeon asked, in spite of himself.

"Not telling us about Abigail's miscarriages didn't go so well. And now you want to keep more secrets."

"It's not a secret." Simeon rubbed wearily at his face. "I just don't want anyone looking at Abigail with resentment, wondering why she wanted—" Man alive, he was never going to be able to say that word. "If she's going to get her memories back, she needs everyone's full support and love."

"So you think she'll get them back?" Zeb asked.

Simeon's sigh cut the edges of his lungs like glass. "I hope so."

"But then won't she remember . . ." Zeb gestured at Simeon's hand, fisted around the remnants of the papers.

Simeon stared at the crumpled mess. "Yes. And we can deal with that then." Hopefully by then he'd know how to convince her that she'd been wrong to give up on their marriage. He'd remind her of how perfect they were together.

But that would only work if she got her memories back. If not . . . He couldn't let himself go there.

"I guess I should go." Zeb's voice startled Simeon out of his thoughts. "I have to finish up a couple of things for the funeral."

A fist slammed against Simeon's solar plexus. The funeral.

His brother still had to bury his wife.

"Is there anything I can do?" he asked.

Zeb shook his head. "Nah. Thanks." He turned to the door.

Simeon followed him. "Listen, I know you're not big into talking, but anytime you need to . . ."

"Yeah, I know, man. Thanks." Zeb trod across the porch and down the steps, his movements purposeful as always. It wasn't until he got into his police cruiser that his shoulders slumped and he ran both hands over his face.

Simeon closed the door so as not to intrude on his brother's grief.

He ran up the stairs and buried the crumpled papers deep in his office trash can.

Then he took a shaky breath and went to wake Abigail for dinner.

Chapter 17

Abigail tried to shake the groggy feeling from her nap as Simeon helped her down the stairs.

"Do you recognize the smell?" he asked, stopping at the bottom of the steps.

Abigail pulled in as deep a breath as she could without sending pain shooting through her ribs. Something savory with a hint of spice hit her nose. Simeon had said he'd made her favorite meal—but he hadn't said what it was. She inhaled again. But she didn't have a clue.

"I'm sorry." She couldn't meet his eyes because she didn't want to see his disappointment.

He shifted so he was standing right in front of her, and she had no choice but to look at him. "You have nothing to be sorry for. Come on, I'll show you."

He led her past the living room and down a short hallway into a cozy kitchen with white cabinets and a gray countertop. He pointed to the stove, where a pan held a bubbly green sauce. "It's enchiladas verdes."

She nodded. It did smell pretty good.

"Come on. Sit down, and I'll finish getting everything ready." Simeon hurried to the dining room table and pulled out a chair for her.

Abigail sat slowly, her eyes going to the stacks of framed pictures and colorful boxes on the table. "What's this?"

"Our life," Simeon said. "Or at least pictures of it. I have more on my computer too. And my phone. I thought we could look at them while we eat. Hopefully it will trigger your memories." He hurried back to the kitchen, and Abigail reached for the nearest framed photo. It looked like her and Simeon, though it must have been a few years ago, since Simeon didn't have any flecks of silver in his hair. They were both smiling, and it looked like they were somewhere tropical. A vacation?

Abigail ran her finger over her own image. How could that woman be her? How could she not remember being that woman?

"That's one of my favorite pictures." Simeon returned, setting a platter of what looked like tacos covered in a green sauce on the table. "I have a copy at work. It's from shortly after we met. In Ecuador."

She gaped at him. "We met in Ecuador?"

He nodded, a strange expression crossing his face. "On a mission trip. Man alive, I fell hard and fast for you." His smile seemed nostalgic, and Abigail reminded herself that this was probably as hard for him as it was for her.

"Did I fall hard and fast for you too?"

Simeon hesitated, seeming to consider the question. "I like to think so," he said quietly. "At any rate, I proposed to you after three months and you said yes. So I'd say that's pretty fast." He scooped an enchilada onto her plate. "Should we give thanks?"

Abigail nodded. After dozens of meals with him and his family in the hospital, she knew they never ate without first thanking God. It'd made her wonder if she'd had such a strong faith as well. Apparently she had, if she and Simeon had met on a mission trip.

"Dear Lord," Simeon started to pray, and Abigail ducked her head. "Thank you that Abigail is at last home." He cut off and cleared his throat, and Abigail found herself blinking back tears at the emotion in his voice.

They must have had such a wonderful relationship if he cared about her that deeply, even now, when she didn't remember him.

"Please continue to watch over her and help her to recover and remember," Simeon continued. "To know that I love her no matter what. And so do you. Amen."

"Amen," Abigail whispered, keeping her head down. Every time he said something about how much he loved her, the guilt over not being able to say it back stabbed a little deeper.

"Dig in," Simeon said, picking up his own fork.

Abigail obeyed. She was starving, and Simeon had said this was her favorite, so she cut off a large bite.

But the moment it was in her mouth, she realized it was a mistake. Something tasted like dish soap.

She grabbed the glass of water in front of her plate and downed a big gulp.

"What's wrong?" Simeon stared at her. "Did I mess it up?" He stuck a bite in his mouth.

Abigail shook her head.

"I think it's okay," Simeon said after he swallowed.

"No. It's good," she said. "I just took too big of a bite."

"Ah." Simeon seemed to accept her explanation. He stuck another bite in his mouth, and Abigail cut herself a much smaller piece. She managed to eat a few more before she set her fork down.

"You don't like it?" Disappointment trickled through Simeon's words.

"I'm just not very hungry." She didn't know why she felt compelled to lie. Only that she was desperate to erase the disappointment from his expression.

"Well, how about dessert then? I picked up a French silk pie from Daisy's." He sped over to the kitchen and was back a few seconds later with a decadent-looking piece of pie. Abigail's mouth watered. She had a feeling she wasn't going to have to pretend to like this. But she took a small first bite, just in case.

The moment it hit her tongue, she moaned, and Simeon chuckled. She liked the way his eyes crinkled when he smiled.

"Should we look at the pictures?" He dug into his own slice of pie but pulled a small striped box closer. "These are all from Ecuador. You made fun of me for getting so many printed when they're all on my computer, but I'm glad to have them now."

He spent the next hour showing her pictures—of Ecuador, of their wedding, of events with his family, of remodeling the kitchen of this house.

As she looked at the pictures and listened to his stories, Abigail couldn't help feeling like she was reading a book or watching a movie. It was a good movie, and she liked the characters. But she still couldn't convince herself that it was about her.

Chapter 18

Simeon eased the door of their bedroom open, careful not to wake Abigail. He should have thought to grab his suit and tie out of the closet before he'd gone to sleep last night, but it hadn't occurred to him then.

His heart crunched, seeing her sleeping on his side of the bed. Over the past months, it seemed she'd crept farther and farther to her side, until some nights he wondered how she managed not to fall out of bed.

He shuffled closer, nearly reaching to brush the hair off her cheek but stopping himself at the last second. She needed sleep. And he needed to get ready. He stepped into the small walk-in closet and pulled the door closed behind him before flipping on the light. Slowly, he pulled on his darkest suit.

Each piece weighed heavier on him, and by the time he'd cinched the tie, he wasn't sure how he was going to get through this day. He leaned his forearm on a shelf and rested his head against it, closing his eyes.

Give us all strength, Lord, especially Zeb. Help us to be there for him. And help him to know that you are with him. Give him comfort in knowing that Carly is with you. Amen.

Slowly, he pulled the closet door open, flipping off the light at the same time.

Abigail stirred, opening her eyes and sitting up. Her hair was mussed, and she looked slightly confused—and completely beautiful. Simeon's heart squeezed once again in gratitude. If things had been different, he

108

might be the one burying his wife today. The thought drove him to her side, but he stopped short of pulling her into a hug. She wasn't ready for that yet.

"Sorry I woke you," he whispered. "I needed my suit."

She looked him up and down. "You look nice."

"Oh." He hadn't expected the compliment. "Carly's funeral is today."

"Right." She seemed completely unaffected by the news. He supposed, in some small way, it was a blessing that she didn't remember Carly. He didn't want to imagine what she'd be going through right now otherwise. The accident hadn't been her fault, but Simeon had counseled enough people in similar situations to know she wouldn't necessarily see it that way.

"I wasn't sure if you wanted to come along?" Honestly, he wasn't sure how he was going to get through this without her at his side.

But she shook her head. "No thanks. I don't even know the dead woman so—"

Simeon felt himself wince, and she fell silent.

"Sorry," she whispered. "That's why I shouldn't come. I don't want to say something stupid like that and upset everyone."

"It's not stupid." Simeon forced his face back to neutral. "And no one will be upset."

Abigail shook her head again. "I'd rather stay here. If that's okay?"

"Of course." Simeon glanced around the room. He should have thought to have someone come stay with her. "Will you be okay by yourself?" He'd barely left her side since the accident, and the thought of leaving her alone now sent a small wave of panic through him. But he couldn't just not go to Carly's funeral.

"I assume I've been alone before?" Abigail's tone was light, almost laughing, and Simeon relaxed a little.

"You have. But maybe don't leave the house for now. In case you don't remember your way around town."

She nodded her agreement, and Simeon stood watching her, the need to wrap her in his arms nearly overpowering him.

"Go," she said, waving him away. "I'll be fine. I'll be right here when you get home."

Simeon nodded and swallowed. "See you soon. I love you."

He didn't wait for her to say it back because he knew she wouldn't. For now, it was enough to know that she heard him.

Ten minutes later, he pulled into the parking lot of Beautiful Savior. Instead of getting out of his vehicle, he stared up at the old brick building, the cross on its steeple pointing straight to the sky. So many important moments in his family's life had taken place here. His and Abigail's wedding. Asher and Ireland's. Joseph's and Ava's. Zeb and Carly's. His fingers clenched the steering wheel.

They'd said goodbye to Mama here.

And now they'd say goodbye to Carly.

Simeon shook his head but forced himself to get out of the vehicle and cross the parking lot. The moment he entered the lobby, his family descended on him.

"How's Abigail?" at least five voices asked at once.

"She's okay. Getting settled at home." He scanned the space where several groups talked in low whispers. "Where's Zeb?"

"In with Dad," Grace answered quietly.

Simeon nodded. "How is he? Really?" Grace and Zeb had always been close.

Grace sighed. "Same as any of us would be in that situation, I guess." She glanced up at Levi, who stood at her other side. Levi wrapped an arm around her shoulders, and Simeon was hit with a longing to have his wife at his side.

"God will get him through this," Grace added firmly. "And we'll all be here to help."

"Except Judah," Simeon muttered. Grace gave him a look, and he shrugged. Maybe now wasn't the time to bring up their estranged brother, but every time the family gathered for something like this, it was hard not to notice his absence.

"Hey, man, you been up to the front yet?" Benjamin asked in a low voice.

"Not yet." Simeon swallowed. "You?"

Benjamin shook his head, and they started toward the casket together.

"She used to babysit me," Benjamin whispered as they reached it. Simeon nodded and clapped a hand on his brother's shoulder.

"Don't tell Zeb," Benjamin leaned closer as he whispered again, "but I had a crush on her until I was like thirteen."

Simeon laughed quietly. "Weren't you thirteen when they got married?"

"What do you think cured my crush?"

Simeon's snort was way too loud, but he patted Benjamin's back. Trust his youngest brother to know exactly what to say.

But Simeon's laugh died as Zeb stepped up to the casket. Simeon moved to one side and Benjamin to the other, and the rest of the family closed in behind Zeb.

Zeb placed both hands on his wife's casket and bowed his head.

Simeon reached to clutch his brother's shoulder. After a moment, Zeb nodded and turned to sit down. They all followed, cramming into the first two pews as Dad made his way to the front of the church.

"This is not an easy day," Dad began the service. "When I stood up here nine years ago, asking Zeb and Carly to pledge their lives to one another, pledge to love each other until death parted them, I never imagined it would be so soon." He cleared his throat.

"But though it's never easy to say goodbye to those we love, we know that this goodbye is only for a little while. And though we mourn our loss, we can also rejoice at Carly's gain. The first time I met her, Carly was only ten years old, and I can so clearly remember her saying to me at Sunday school, 'Let us rejoice today and be glad.' And if she were here today, she would be telling us those exact same words. Because she knew that to live is Christ and to die is gain."

All down the pew, Simeon's siblings were wiping their eyes but also smiling—even Zeb.

Something released in Simeon. Grace was right. God was going to see Zeb through this. And he would see Abigail through it too.

⟨∾⟩

Abigail sighed, staring at yet another photo that meant nothing to her. She'd been trying to finish off the stack they hadn't gotten to last night. But without Simeon here to give the pictures context, they might as well have been images of strangers. One of whom happened to have her face.

She pushed back from the table, getting up carefully. As long as she didn't make any sudden movements, her ribs seemed to be okay right now.

She'd already toured the whole house twice this morning, hoping to find something, anything, that would jog her memories. But aside from the things that had happened at the hospital, her mind seemed to be a giant blank. It felt like she had just woken up in this life one day—as if she'd been born as a thirty-two-year-old with no history. Except all the evidence said she *did* have a history.

The house had grown stuffy, and she moved to the dining room windows. It took a lot of grunting and plenty of pain to open them, but it was worth it for the fresh breeze that swept through the screen, carrying with it a floral scent—possibly from the giant white blossoms on the tree in the middle of the backyard.

She made her way to the front of the house, taking a moment to psych herself up for the effort before she opened the living room window as well. The sound of laughter and joyful shrieking carried in on the wind, and Abigail tilted her head. Where was it coming from?

She eyed the empty sidewalk and the inviting blue sky. Simeon had said not to leave the house—but she'd been cooped up inside for so long. A little walk was just what she needed. With the way her ribs felt, she wouldn't be able to go far enough to get lost, anyway.

Now, all she had to do was find some shoes. She'd noticed a coat closet under the stairs, and she pulled that open. Sure enough, there was a pair of pink tennis shoes. She picked them up, making note that she apparently liked pink.

Outside, she paused to listen. The laughter and shrieking sounded like they were coming from down the street to her left. She set off in that direction, not sure why she was drawn to the sounds.

It was only a couple of blocks before she spotted a school playground full of children.

She stopped, watching groups playing kickball and hopscotch and four square. It had never even occurred to her to ask if she and Simeon had children, but she supposed he would have mentioned it if they did. Plus, there would probably be a children's bedroom and toys and car seats and whatever else went with having kids.

She let out a long breath. Thank goodness that was one thing they didn't have to worry about. It was bad enough she'd forgotten her husband, but she couldn't even imagine how terrible it would be to forget her own children.

A loud bell rang, and the kids all scattered toward the school's doors. Abigail watched until the playground was empty, then turned and walked back home, relieved when she spotted the house without any trouble. She took off her shoes and returned them to the closet. As she was about to close it, a basket on the top shelf caught her eye. Something fluffy draped over the side, and Abigail studied it for a minute. There was something about it that made her want to pull it down and hold it.

Needles rammed into her ribs as she reached for the basket, but she kept going. She managed to grip the edge, and it started to fall forward. Her ribs wrenched as she tried and failed to catch it, but it landed on the floor in front of her with a soft thud.

She stood over it, breathing heavily, pressing her hand tight to her ribs until the pain subsided a little. Then she crouched to dig through its contents. The fluffy item seemed to be a hand-knit blanket, and it wasn't until she'd lifted it out of the basket that she realized it was only half finished.

It was still connected to a thick skein of yarn with two knitting needles shoved through it. Abigail ran a hand over the blanket. Had she made it? It seemed impossible, and yet . . .

She carried the blanket and yarn and knitting needles to the couch in the living room. Spreading the blanket across her lap in spite of the heat, she slowly withdrew the needles from the yarn.

Her fingers seemed to know automatically how to grip them. And then she was winding yarn around the needles, pulling them back and forth. She didn't stop until she'd finished a whole row. And then she sat staring at it. How had she done that? She didn't remember ever learning how to knit. And yet, this most recent row looked just like all the rest.

Abigail shrugged and started another row. She watched her hands move back and forth, listened to the needles click together, and let her mind go blank.

She didn't know how long she'd been working when the sound of a vehicle in the driveway drew her eyes up from the blanket. She watched the front door, her stomach swimming, though she couldn't identify why.

Footsteps sounded on the front porch, and then the door opened, and Simeon was standing there, staring at her. His eyes were a little red, and his hair was windblown, but her gaze was drawn to his mouth, which he opened and closed and opened again, as if he wanted to say something but couldn't get the words out.

"What are you doing?" he finally managed. His eyes locked on the blanket in her lap.

She glanced down. "Knitting. I think?" She looked back up at him. "I just picked it up and started doing it." She bit her lip, not quite brave enough to ask the question that had been growing in her mind as she'd worked on the blanket.

"That's . . ." Simeon walked slowly across the room and sat heavily on the other side of the couch, rubbing both hands over his face.

The hope that had been building in Abigail fell a little. She'd expected Simeon to be more excited, if this meant what she thought it meant. "You don't think it means I'm getting my memories back?"

Simeon lowered his hands. He looked exhausted, but he managed a gentle smile that she had already figured out meant he was trying to soften the blow. "It might." He slid a little closer to her on the couch, although there was still a whole cushion between them. "More likely, knitting is something stored in your procedural memory."

"And that's bad?"

Simeon laughed a little. "No. It's good. Procedural memory is basically what people sometimes call muscle memory. It's why you can remember a skill, like riding a bike, even if you haven't done it for years." He gestured to the blanket on her lap. "Or knitting. But unfortunately, it doesn't have much to do with your long-term or autobiographical memories."

"Oh." She smoothed a hand over the even stitches, swallowing down the disappointment.

"It doesn't mean you won't get your memories back." Simeon slid closer again, and now there was only half a cushion between them. "We're not going to give up, okay?"

She nodded but couldn't find her voice to answer.

Simeon leaned back until his head rested on the top of the couch and closed his eyes.

"How was the funeral?" she asked quietly.

"Hard." Simeon opened his eyes and met hers. "But good. Dad's sermon was a good reminder that our hope isn't in this world but in the next."

Abigail nodded. She wasn't quite sure she understood what that meant, but Simeon looked too tired to explain.

"Do you want to take a nap?" she asked. "I can go somewhere else."

"A nap sounds nice." Simeon tipped himself to the side until he was lying down with his head on the far end of the couch, his legs bent so that his feet stopped just short of touching her.

She started to get up, but Simeon mumbled, "Please stay."

She hesitated. But she didn't have anything else to do. And he was looking at her with such a sharp ache that she could feel it right through her own middle.

She sat back and started knitting again, and within a few minutes, his soft snores joined the clacking of her needles.

Chapter 19

"You're sure you feel up to this?" Simeon parked the vehicle in Dad's driveway but turned to Abigail. He'd asked five times already, but he wasn't sure she understood how *much* spending the entire day with his family could be. They'd come to see her in ones and twos all week, but she hadn't been with all of them at once since the hospital. And they'd been pretty subdued there. Of course, they'd likely be fairly subdued today as well, even if they were celebrating Benjamin's graduation from culinary school. It had only been a week since they'd gathered to bury Carly.

"Simeon, I'm fine. I only feel bad that we didn't go to the ceremony yesterday."

"Benjamin understands." Simeon had wanted to go, but the school was six hours away, and there was no way Abigail could have sat in the vehicle that long with her broken ribs. And he hadn't been willing to leave her for a full day. "He'll be glad to see you. Everyone will."

Benjamin hadn't even wanted to have a party at all, but the rest of them had insisted, and Simeon was glad. They needed to be there for each other now more than ever.

He got out of the vehicle and went to open Abigail's door, holding out a hand to help her down. She didn't hesitate anymore to take his hand for things like this, and he cherished the warmth of her fingers in his, even if it only lasted a few moments. She pulled her hand back as they started toward the house, and he contented himself with breathing in the floral scent of her hair that drifted to him on the light breeze.

"This is a beautiful place." Abigail's gaze traveled from the ranch-style house to the yard that sloped behind it, all the way down to the meandering Serenity River. He had to remind himself that it was like she was seeing it for the first time.

He chuckled, and she gave him a quizzical look. "That's funny?"

"No. I was just remembering the first time I brought you here. I asked if you liked the view, and you hadn't even noticed it because you were so scared of meeting my mama. You were convinced she was going to hate you."

Abigail frowned. "Did she?"

"Of course not." Simeon laughed. "Don't get me wrong. She definitely had her . . . opinions about things. And people. But after she met you, she pulled me aside and said, 'I can't find anything to not like about her.'"

Abigail's laugh was loud and surprising—and it made Simeon rejoice. He couldn't remember the last time he'd heard a genuine laugh like that from her. Long before the accident, that much he was sure of.

"That sounds like high praise." Abigail was still laughing.

"Trust me. From Mama, it was. Just ask Grace. She had a time of it convincing Mama that Levi was a good guy."

Abigail's forehead wrinkled. "Levi's the football player, right?"

Simeon nodded. He appreciated the way Abigail was working so hard to relearn who was who in his family.

They reached the front door, and he paused. "Just to warn you—there will probably be a lot of hugs. I mean, I can try to stop them, but . . ."

She shook her head. "It's fine. As long as they don't squeeze too hard."

"I'll warn them." Simeon opened the door, expecting the usual wall of sound. Instead, only a low murmur of voices reached them. Simeon grimaced at the reminder of how much things had changed.

"Are you okay?" Abigail touched a hand to his forearm. It was enough to catapult Simeon's heart right up to his throat. It was the first time she'd touched him since they'd gotten home from the hospital, aside from letting him help her in and out of vehicles or chairs.

"I'm okay," he managed around a quick breath.

She watched him for another moment, then let her hand fall from his arm and passed in front of him to enter the house. She paused at the wall of pictures on the living room wall.

"We took this one a couple years ago," Simeon murmured, pointing to what looked like the newest family picture. "It was the first one we took without Mama." He wondered how long it would be before they'd be able to bear taking one without Carly.

"Everyone looks so happy." Abigail reached toward her own image in the photo, and Simeon nodded. That had been right before their first pregnancy.

"Come on." He dared to take her elbow and steer her through the living room toward the low voices coming from the kitchen. She glanced at him but didn't pull away, and Simeon gave thanks for the small sign of progress.

The moment they reached the kitchen, the talking stopped and a swarm of people descended on Abigail, just as Simeon had known they would.

"Don't hug her too tight," he called loudly enough for people in the next county to hear. "She still has broken ribs."

Abigail shot him a grateful—and amused—look, and he couldn't help but smile to see that she at least tried to return his family's hugs.

Simeon scanned the gathered group. "Where's Zeb?" he asked Joseph in a low voice.

Joseph frowned. "Working, I think. He went to the graduation ceremony yesterday. But he didn't think he'd make it today." He shook his head. "I don't know how he keeps going like this. If it were me . . ."

Simeon nodded. He knew exactly how his brother's sentence was going to end. Because even though he counseled other people through their grief all the time, if it were him, he'd be falling apart.

"How's Abigail?" Joseph asked.

"She's . . . healing." Simeon's eyes followed his wife, whom Grace was shepherding toward the other side of the room. "Her ribs are still pretty sore, but . . ."

"What about her memories? Anything yet?"

Simeon sighed. "Not really. She remembers how to knit, but skills like that use a different kind of memory, so . . ."

"Well, if anyone can help her, I'm sure you can, right?"

Simeon swallowed. He'd thought that more than once too. But so far, nothing he'd tried had worked. Photos. Food. Family. He'd surrounded her with memories, but she looked at every one of them as if it belonged to someone else—not to her.

Simeon went to congratulate Benjamin, then moved toward his wife, now seated at the dining room table with Grace. He pulled out a chair next to her. "Doing okay?"

Abigail smiled, seeming completely relaxed despite the large group. "I'm good."

Simeon's heart lightened, and instinctively, he reached for her hand on the table between them, though he stopped himself at the last second.

Lydia pulled out the chair next to Grace. "Did y'all decide how long you're staying?"

"Probably until Thursday or Friday." Grace sighed. "I hate to leave, but our friends have already been taking care of things at the B and B for us for two weeks."

"I was wondering." Lydia bit her lip. "Do you want to go dress shopping before you leave?"

"Y'all decided not to postpone the wedding then?" Grace threw her arms around Lydia.

"Postpone the wedding?" This was the first Simeon had heard mention of that.

Lydia extracted herself from Grace's arms. "We considered it. But Dad convinced us that postponing joy wasn't the best way to deal with grief. And Zeb said Carly would have wanted us to go forward with it. You know her favorite verse."

"Let us rejoice today and be glad," Simeon recited with his sisters.

"Yeah, so—" Lydia let out a breath. "We really have to get going on the dresses. But if you don't have time . . ."

Grace shoved Lydia's arm. "Of course I have time. Wednesday?"

"Great." Lydia turned to Abigail. "Does that work for you?"

"For me?" Abigail looked startled.

"Unless you're not feeling up to it," Lydia rushed to add.

"I'm in the wedding?" Abigail spoke slowly, as if trying to wrap her head around the words.

"Oh my goodness." Lydia slapped her forehead. "I forgot that you forgot. Yes, you're in the wedding. Unless you don't want to be." Lydia broke off, shooting Simeon a helpless look.

"I— Um—" Abigail looked to Simeon too, her expression uncertain.

He pictured walking down the aisle with her in the same church where they'd been married. "I think you should do it."

Hopefully she would have her memories back by then. But if not, it might be just the sort of powerful trigger her mind needed.

Abigail still looked uncertain, but she nodded. "Okay. I'll do it."

"Great." Lydia reached across the table and squeezed her hand. "I'll pick you up at ten o'clock."

A wolf whistle pierced the room, and Grace laughed. "That's my husband."

Although the whistle probably hadn't been necessary, given that it wasn't as loud in here as usual, the touch of normalcy eased Simeon's heart a little.

"Food's ready," Levi announced with a sheepish grin.

They all folded their hands, and Dad led them in prayer. Then Simeon helped Abigail up, and they filled their plates, then returned to the table. Grace and Levi and Asher and Ireland joined them.

"You don't have any food." Levi pointed at the empty spot in front of Ireland. She looked at his heaping plate and grimaced, her face taking on a pasty tinge.

"She gets her morning sickness at lunchtime," Asher answered for his wife.

Simeon stiffened, his fingers tightening on his fork.

"You're expecting?" Unlike the last time she'd found out, Abigail seemed delighted. "I bet you're the one I was knitting the blanket for. When are you due? I'll make sure to have it done in time."

"That's sweet." Ireland smiled at Abigail. "I'm due at the end of November. But it could have been for Ava. She's due in January. Or Car—" She broke off. Asher wrapped an arm around her.

Simeon's stomach rolled over on itself, and he set his fork down. The blanket hadn't been for any of them. Abigail had started it when she'd learned she was pregnant the first time.

He could still remember the day she'd come home with the yarn, telling him buoyantly that she was going to learn to knit. He'd been doubtful at first; knitting had seemed so staid and still—so un-Abigail-like. But she'd spent hours watching videos, until she'd mastered the craft. She'd only gotten a few rows of the blanket done before the miscarriage. She'd started on it again with the second pregnancy. The third time, she'd said she wasn't going to work on it until after the first trimester. But the baby hadn't made it that long.

"Aren't you hungry?" Abigail nodded to his nearly full plate.

"Oh. Yeah." He picked up his fork and stuffed a bite of cheesy potatoes into his mouth, ignoring the roll of nausea.

When he'd come home from Carly's funeral the other day to find Abigail working on the blanket, it had slammed into him like a fist to the stomach—she didn't remember their babies.

He'd considered telling her. But he couldn't bear to do that. The one blessing of all of this was that all the pain she'd been in—the depression that had clung to her for so long—had finally lifted. His own heart still ached to think of what they'd lost, but at least she didn't feel that pain anymore.

He knew that if—when—she got her memories back, she'd have to deal with it all over again. But he'd be there for her through all of it.

In the meantime, it was his job to make sure she was safe and protected. To shield her from pain so her brain felt safe enough to remember.

Chapter 20

"Was Simeon planning to go somewhere while we were out?" Lydia asked as she pulled into Abigail's empty driveway.

"No." Abigail frowned. In fact, it had taken all of her persuasive skills to convince Simeon that he didn't need to come dress shopping with her and her sisters-in-law.

"Do you want me to hang out with you until he gets home?" Lydia asked.

"That's okay. I'll be fine." The truth was, she wouldn't mind having a little time to herself. A little time away from Simeon's unrelenting attempts to help her remember, from the constant feeling that she was letting him down when she couldn't.

"You're sure?" Lydia frowned the same way Simeon did when he was worried.

"Positive. Thanks for driving me. I love the dresses we picked out."

They'd all agreed on a soft green that the other women had said was Carly's favorite color.

"All right." Lydia leaned over and gave her a hug, which Abigail returned, making sure to cover her groan as her ribs pulled with the movement. The pain was lessening day by day, but there was definitely still a constant ache.

She got out of the car and made her way to the house. It was starting to feel more like her home—or at least less like a stranger's home—although she still couldn't remember picking out a single item in it.

Inside, she set her purse on the small table next to the stairs, pausing to stare at herself in the mirror. She had almost gotten used to connecting the image there with herself.

She wondered what other people saw when they looked at their reflections. Was it their whole identity—their whole past—or did they only see the surface, the way she was forced to?

Abigail shook aside the question—it didn't do any good to dwell on it—and made her way to the living room. She'd made more progress on the baby blanket for Ireland, and even though her sister-in-law wasn't due for months yet, she wanted to get it done so she could make one for Ava too.

She turned on the TV for background noise but after a couple of minutes of searching for something to watch flipped it right back off.

Now the house was too quiet.

She pulled out her phone to text Simeon and find out when he'd be home but then put it away. He'd spent nearly every moment since the accident at her side. He deserved a break.

She set the baby blanket down and moved to the cabinet next to the TV, where she'd noticed a collection of DVDs. She squatted and ran her fingers along their spines, wondering which one might be her favorite.

But she didn't recognize a single title.

She grabbed one at random and pulled it out—but her eye caught on the DVD next to it. *Simeon and Abigail Calvano.*

She dropped the other DVD and slid this one out.

She rubbed her fingers across the image on the cover. It was the same picture of her and Simeon from their wedding day that sat on her dresser upstairs. And yet, it might as well have been a picture of two actors.

Without considering whether she really wanted to, Abigail opened the case and popped out the DVD. It took her a few tries to figure out how to work the DVD player, but once she did, she dropped back onto the couch and watched.

The video started with messages from all of the Calvanos, directed to them. There was one from Grace, who looked uncomfortable with Levi hovering next to her—from what Abigail had gathered talking to the other women while shopping today, Levi had only come along to their wedding so that Grace's mama would stop trying to fix her up with someone else. And then there was a message from Joseph and Benjamin—both apparently as goofy then as they were now. Next it was Asher's turn, and though he didn't say much, Abigail could tell his words wishing them well were sincere. And then Zeb came on the screen, his arm wrapped around a woman Abigail knew to be Carly from pictures she'd seen.

They looked happy, and a stab of remorse went through Abigail. On the way to the dress shop today, Lydia had grown silent as they'd driven past a section of road where the guardrail was damaged. She'd squeezed Abigail's hand and told her that it was the location of the accident.

But as hard as she'd tried to remember something, *anything*, about that spot, about what had happened there, Abigail couldn't.

She couldn't even remember the person who had died right next to her.

"We have one rule in our marriage," Carly was saying on the screen. "Always say 'I love you.' Even when you're mad or even when you're tired or even when one of you is just running out to the grocery store. Because you never know when it's going to be your last chance to say it."

Abigail's stomach rolled over. But she couldn't tell if it was because Carly wouldn't ever have another chance to tell Zeb she loved him or if it was because Simeon seemed to be following that advice religious-ly—and it tore at her every time he said those words. Because she didn't know when—*if*—she'd ever be able to say them to him again.

The video cut away from Zeb and Carly to Pastor Calvano, who was smiling as always. "Well, you two, I've been praying for y'all for a very long time."

Abigail sat forward. According to Simeon, they had only met a few months before they'd gotten engaged—and they'd gotten married less than six months after that.

"Simeon, I've of course been praying for you since before you were born. And, Abigail, I've been praying for you since before I ever knew you—before Simeon knew you. I prayed that God would bless him with a wife who was godly and who would walk together with him in faith. Who he could encourage and who would in turn encourage him. Who he could love with his whole heart and who would love him back without reserve. And watching the two of you together over the past few months, I see that God has answered that prayer even more richly than I could have imagined. I want you to know that as you start your life together, I will continue to pray for you. And I trust God will answer these prayers in even greater ways than I could imagine as well."

The screen faded, and Abigail reached to turn off the video. She couldn't watch anymore of this. Because she didn't know how to be that woman Pastor Calvano—everyone—seemed to think she was.

The front door opened, and Simeon rushed inside. "I'm so sorry I wasn't here when you got home. Liam needed a hand with a plumbing issue and it took longer than we expected and then Lydia showed up and I realized that meant you were here by yourself and—" He broke off, finally taking a breath. "Are you okay?"

"Of course." Her smile felt wavery, but she worked hard to hold it in place. She picked up the blanket she'd abandoned and started knitting, hoping he wouldn't notice the extra clacking from her shaky hands.

"What are you—" His eyes went to the TV, and he froze.

Abigail glanced at the screen. Apparently she'd only paused it.

"Our wedding video." He sounded surprised but delighted. "I wasn't sure if you would want to . . . Let's watch it together."

"Oh. Um." She tried to come up with an excuse, but he was looking at her with such hope. "Okay."

"Great." In two strides, Simeon was settling onto the couch—not close enough to touch but definitely close enough for her to get a drift of that fresh scent she hadn't been able to place.

Simeon pressed play, then looked at her with a wide smile. Abigail tried her hardest to return it.

Because she may not know how to be the woman they all thought she was.

But she could sure try.

Chapter 21

There. Everything was just right. Simeon swept the box he'd wrapped earlier off the table and placed it on the tray with the waffles, fruit, and orange juice. He had the perfect birthday planned for Abigail. Beginning with breakfast in bed. He picked up the tray and carried it carefully up the stairs, ignoring the ache in his lower back from two weeks of sleeping in his recliner. If things remained like this much longer, he might have to invest in a second mattress.

He banished the thought.

Being pessimistic wouldn't help anything. God could restore Abigail's memories. Simeon fully believed that.

Besides, Abigail seemed to be trying hard to remember. Finding her watching their wedding video the other day had reassured him of that. They'd watched it three more times since then, and though Abigail still hadn't recalled anything, it didn't mean she never would. And the activities he had planned for today might help too.

He eased the bedroom door open.

Abigail was sleeping diagonally across the bed, her head on her side, her feet on his. A slight smile played with her lips, and Simeon longed to know what she was dreaming about. Could it be him?

He crossed the room and set the tray on the nightstand, then sat carefully on his side of the bed. Abigail stirred but didn't open her eyes. The sweet tang of her fruity shampoo reached him, and it was all he could do not to lie down next to her and bury his face in her hair. He contented himself with brushing a strand off her cheek.

"Abigail," he whispered. "Happy birthday."

She opened her eyes and blinked a couple of times, as if trying to figure out what she was seeing, but her smile didn't falter. "I smell something."

Simeon laughed. "Well, I showered, so I'll assume it's not me. Could be the waffles though. Or the strawberries."

Her eyes widened as he reached for the tray and set it carefully between them.

"You did this for me?"

"I do it every year."

"Oh." Her eyes dropped, and her smile flagged for a second, but then she leaned forward and took a big breath right over the top of the food. "Yep. This is what I smelled." Her smile returned. "Thank you."

"You're welcome." Simeon pointed to the gift. "You can open that before or after you eat. It's up to you."

He was about to say that she usually chose presents first, when she said, "I think I'll eat first. Otherwise the food will be taunting me."

Simeon nodded and forced himself to hold his smile in place. She used to say it was the present that would taunt her. But that didn't matter.

"Aren't you going to eat?" Abigail glanced at him with a dot of whipped cream on her lip. Simeon stared at it. He used to kiss those lips.

"What? Do I have something . . ." She picked up the napkin Simeon had folded into an origami heart and swiped at her lips. "Did I get it?"

"Yeah." Simeon swallowed. "I left my plate downstairs. I'll be right back."

He hurried down the steps and made himself a plate, still fighting the desire to kiss the whipped cream off her lips. Maybe later today, if all went well . . .

He jogged back up the stairs, and Abigail slid the tray over to give him more room in the bed.

"Just to double-check, I'm thirty-three now, right?" she asked.

"That's right."

"And you're . . ."

"Thirty-eight."

She raised an eyebrow, sliding a bite of waffle into her mouth, her tongue darting out to lick off the extra whipped cream.

"It's okay if you tease me about being older." Simeon cut off a piece of his own waffle. "The worst was when we first met because you were still in your twenties, and you loved to make fun of me for being in my thirties."

"Sorry about that," Abigail murmured.

"Nothing to be sorry about. Your playfulness is one of the things I love about you." He let himself meet her eyes, but she looked away.

"So, um—" She cleared her throat. "When's your birthday?"

"January 10."

She nodded, and they finished their breakfast silently.

The moment she was done, Simeon pointed at the present. "Okay, open it now." He rubbed his hands together. He'd picked it out months ago, and he'd been eagerly waiting to give it to her ever since.

She pulled the paper off slowly, as if afraid of what she might find inside.

"Oh." She blinked at it. "Is it a jewelry box?"

"Yes. Open it." Simeon tried not to let his disappointment that she'd barely noticed the hand-painted pink river dolphins on the cover seep into his words. Why would she remember that dolphins were her favorite animal?

She lifted the lid, and it started to play "Spring" from Vivaldi's The Four Seasons, which had been their wedding processional song. Abigail had claimed to never have heard it before they went through the playlist of potential wedding songs, but the moment it came on, she'd said, "That's the one. That's how being with you makes me feel."

"It's pretty," Abigail said now. "Thank you."

"I'm glad you like it." Simeon ignored the fact that she hadn't actually said she liked it. "That song played for our wedding, and you've loved dolphins ever since we saw river dolphins in Ecuador."

Abigail nodded, but her smile looked forced and far away.

"I'll let you get dressed." Simeon stood and gathered the tray. "Wear something you can shop in, walk in, and eat in."

"Why?" Abigail's brow lowered.

"You'll see." Simeon headed for the door.

He was pulling it closed behind him when she called, "Hey, Simeon."

He turned. "What's up?"

"Thank you for breakfast. And for the gift. I really do love it."

Simeon smiled. He wasn't so sure about that. But he loved her for saying it anyway. "You're welcome."

Abigail was going to topple over pretty soon. They'd already taken a long hike, had a picnic, and gone shopping downtown—which had included a stop at the Book Den, where a spunky but sweet older woman named Ruth, who was apparently her boss, had asked when she was coming back to work. Simeon had jumped in to answer that it would be a while yet, but Abigail planned to have a conversation with him about that later. The idea of having something to do besides trying to remember all day every day was more than appealing.

"It's not too far to walk." Simeon smiled at her as he pulled into a parking spot at Founder's Park. "You look tired."

Abigail nodded but pushed her lips into a smile.

It had been a nice day, but she was exhausted, not only from all the activity but from the feeling that this was all one long test.

Every time they got to a new location, Simeon would ask what she wanted to do, where she wanted to go, what she liked. She could tell when her answers differed from what the woman she'd started to think of as "Past Abigail" would say by the way his eyes narrowed just the slightest bit, even as his smile remained fixed. But the way his eyes widened in delight when she got an answer "right" almost made the headache that had started at the back of her skull worth it.

Simeon turned off the vehicle and came around to open her door. She had discovered that he always did that. He held out a hand, and she took it even though the pain in her ribs had faded to a dull ache over the past few days.

"This way." Simeon tugged her down a walking path that led toward bright patches of flowers. A couple pushing a stroller approached from the other direction, and Abigail slipped her hand out of Simeon's so they could walk single file to let the family pass.

She tucked her hands into her pockets before she fell back into step with him. It wasn't that she didn't like the feel of his hand around hers—it was actually quite nice—but it still felt odd, holding hands with a man she'd just met.

You didn't just meet him, she reminded herself. *You only feel like you did.*

Still, she didn't take her hands out of her pockets.

"Let's start over there." Simeon pointed to a trellis covered in climbing roses.

They walked under the trellis into a fragrant garden. Roses of every hue lined winding cobblestone paths.

"What do you think?" Simeon asked.

Abigail glanced at him out of the corner of her eye, trying to decide how to answer. Did Past Abigail like roses or not?

Simeon's hopeful expression did nothing but make her stomach flip. She wanted to get this one right.

"They're nice," she said slowly, still watching his expression. It didn't change, and she wondered if that was a skill he'd learned as a counselor.

"Nice?" Simeon asked, his tone neutral.

"Maybe a little too . . . perfect for me."

Simeon's mouth opened and closed, and he shook his head.

Abigail's heart snagged. It had been the wrong answer. Again. "I'm sorry. I didn't—"

Simeon grabbed her hand. "Don't be sorry. It's just, that's exactly what you said the first time I bought you roses." He still looked stunned, and Abigail could tell he thought this was a sign that she remembered. But no matter how hard she tried, she couldn't recall the first time he'd bought her flowers. It was only a lucky coincidence that she'd said the same thing twice.

"Come on, let's go to the butterfly garden. Your favorite flower is in there." Simeon led her out of the rose garden and into one that looked wild and carefree. Abigail could tell immediately why she'd liked it better.

"Did I really complain about you buying me roses?" she asked as they strolled the crushed gravel paths.

Simeon chuckled. "I wouldn't say complained. More like your enthusiasm was a little too over the top. Eventually, you admitted that you found them a little too perfect." Simeon stopped walking and gestured to the pinks and blues and oranges and yellows all around them. "What do you think about the flowers in this garden? Are there any you like?"

The way he was looking at her, Abigail could hear what he hadn't spoken. He wanted her to identify the right flower as her favorite.

Another test.

She chewed her lip, turning in a slow circle to take in all the blooms, waiting for some sort of sign—a flash of recognition or a jump of her stomach or a quickening of her pulse—to tell her which it was.

But there was nothing.

"These are nice," she said as they reached a patch of tall flowers with bright purple petals and a brown center.

"They are." Simeon's voice was steady and neutral, not stunned the way it had been when she'd made that comment about the roses.

"But I like these too." She pointed to a section of bright yellow flowers with a ring of red in the middle.

Simeon nodded, and Abigail searched desperately for another variety that might be her favorite. "Or those." She waved a hand at a patch of blue, bell-shaped flowers. "Or maybe—" She spun again.

"Abigail. Hey." Simeon reached for her, but she took a step backwards.

"What? Did I still not get the right ones? How about these?" She reached for one of the huge, creamy peach blooms next to her, plucking it straight off the plant. She held it up and stared at it a moment. The flower was bigger than her hand, with veins of deep red running along the center of the petals.

"Excuse me." An older lady bustled toward them from behind Simeon. "You can't pick the flowers. They're not—"

"Ugh." Abigail chucked the flower at the ground and turned to flee.

"Abigail." Simeon's voice lifted above the older woman's, who was calling, "Miss. Come back here, please."

Abigail didn't look over her shoulder. Ignoring the growing ache in her ribs as her breath came in gasps, she kept running.

She came to a large gazebo. The people relaxing inside it were all staring at her, and she veered down a side path, though she didn't know where it led. Not that it really mattered.

Because wherever she went, she would still end up here: in a life she didn't remember.

"Abigail, stop." Simeon's voice was right behind her, and she wondered if he'd been right there the whole time she was running.

She stopped, grasping her ribs as she struggled to catch her breath. "I'm sorry," she managed to wheeze.

"You didn't do anything wrong." Simeon looked like he was going to reach for her hand but rubbed the back of his neck instead. "Come on. Let's go home." He touched a hand to her back just long enough to steer her toward the path that led to the parking lot.

"Which one was it?" Abigail asked quietly.

"Which what?" Simeon didn't sound angry or hurt or upset that she'd ruined the birthday he'd taken so much care to plan.

"Which flower was my favorite?"

"Oh." Simeon hesitated. "The last one. The one you picked. Hibiscus."

Abigail nodded, wishing she hadn't tossed it to the ground.

Chapter 22

A shriek shot Simeon up from his recliner.

What was that? Abigail?

He sprinted to the hallway, registering the open bedroom door just as sharp, staccato beeps pierced his ears. The smoke alarm.

"Abigail!"

"Help! Simeon!" The voice came from downstairs, and he hurtled toward it.

A thin, smoky haze hung in the air at the bottom of the steps, and Simeon's stomach dropped.

"Abigail!" He raced toward the kitchen. The smoke was thicker in here, and flames climbed from a pot on the stovetop, reaching for the range hood. Abigail was at the sink, filling a bowl with water, her eyes wide as she stared over her shoulder at the fire.

"Don't!" Simeon careened toward her and knocked the bowl out of her hand.

It landed in the sink with a loud clang, and Abigail screamed. "We have to put it out."

Simeon lunged for the cupboard where they kept the pots, shoving things out of the way to grab the lid he needed.

"Be careful," Abigail yelled as he moved close enough to slam the lid onto the pot. Immediately, the flames disappeared, and Simeon turned the burner off. He watched the pot a second longer to make sure it wasn't going to flare up again.

Then he turned and without thinking crossed the room and pulled Abigail into his arms. "You're all right," he murmured, though he didn't know whether he was trying to comfort her or himself. "You're all right."

She was trembling, but he felt her head bob against his chest. He tightened his arms, suddenly realizing it was the first time he'd held his wife in weeks. He never wanted to let go, even though the smoke still lingered in the air and the alarm kept up its shrill, persistent rhythm.

He tried not to think about what could have happened if he'd gotten down here a minute later and she'd thrown that water on the grease fire.

"Do you think we could make that noise stop?" Abigail asked after a few minutes.

Simeon nodded, his chin brushing the top of her head. But he held on for another minute before making himself let go. "I'll be right back. Why don't you go sit in the living room? It's probably not as smoky in there."

"I have to clean this up." Abigail gestured toward the scorched cook-top. Above it, the range hood appeared to be melted on the edges. And the pot was definitely done for.

"It's still too hot." He took her hand and pulled her gently toward the living room. "I'll take care of it later." He led her to the couch and made sure she sat. "I'll be right back."

He moved through the house, opening every window he could to let the smoke out. Then he grabbed a towel and stood under the smoke alarm, fanning at the smoke until the beeping stopped. He fanned another few minutes to make sure it wouldn't start up again, but most of the haze of smoke seemed to have dissipated.

He returned to the living room and dropped onto the couch next to Abigail, who had set her knitting in her lap but wasn't doing anything with it.

"That's one way to wake a guy up," he said.

Abigail giggled, and he turned his head toward her with a grin. He didn't ever want to go through anything like that again, but he couldn't regret making her laugh.

"I'm sorry," she said, her smile fading.

He sat up and leaned toward her, letting his hand fall on the couch a few inches from her knee. "It was an accident. What were you doing?"

She sighed and looked away. "I wanted to make breakfast for you. To make up for ruining my birthday yesterday."

"Abigail." Simeon lifted his hand to her knee, not removing it until she looked in his direction. "You didn't ruin your birthday. If anything, I'm the one who should be apologizing. I didn't mean to overwhelm you."

He'd spent half the night thinking about it. And he'd concluded that as much as he wanted to be the one to help her, maybe he was too close to the situation. Maybe they needed to bring in someone else.

"You didn't—" Abigail started, but he jumped in.

"I did. And I've been thinking—" He folded his hands in his lap so he couldn't accidentally wrap them around hers. "Maybe we should see a counselor." He caught his breath, unwilling to exhale. He'd suggested counseling to her a hundred times before the accident, and she'd always refused. But maybe now . . .

Her forehead crinkled. "I thought *you* were a counselor."

Simeon let out a breath on a small laugh. That wasn't a *no*. "I am. But even counselors need counseling sometimes. I just really want to . . . help you. But I think sometimes I'm getting in the way instead of . . ."

Abigail's hand fell on top of his. "You're not getting in the way," she said quietly.

He swallowed, letting himself free his thumb to rub it over the back of her hand. "So what do you think about counseling?"

"Do you think it will help me get my memories back?"

Simeon sighed but met her eyes. He wasn't going to lie. "I don't know. But I think it will help us cope better."

Abigail nodded. "Then I think we should do it."

"Good." He grinned at her. "I love you."

She winced and stood, her hand skipping out of his. "I'm going to go put the food away."

Simeon blinked at his empty hand, then stood as well, once again brushing off the hurt of not hearing her say the words. "I'll help you."

Abigail's smile was small but genuine, and he followed her to the kitchen. She moved immediately to the table, which had been set for two, with a bowl of cut fruit, a pitcher of orange juice, and full mugs of coffee.

Simeon eyed the spread, his heart lightening. She'd gone through all of that effort for him. She picked up the bowl of fruit and carried it toward the fridge, but Simeon intercepted her, plucking the bowl out of her hands. "I'm starving." He turned her back to the table. "Let's eat."

"There's only fruit," Abigail protested.

"I'll get us some cereal. Go sit down." He gave her a gentle nudge, and she obeyed.

Simeon grabbed a box of cereal, some bowls and spoons, and the milk. "There." He set them on the table. "Breakfast is served."

They were quiet for a moment as they passed cereal and milk and fruit back and forth. Then Simeon gave thanks for the meal—and for Abigail's safety—and they dug in.

"Out of curiosity, what were you making?" Simeon gestured over his shoulder at the stove.

"I was trying to make donuts." Abigail paused with a spoonful of cereal halfway to her mouth. "I thought it would be kind of like knitting. What did you call it—procedural memory?"

He nodded.

"But I guess cooking doesn't work that way," Abigail added.

Simeon took a bite of cereal, thinking. "It should," he finally said.

"Then how come—"

"Well." Simeon couldn't help the laugh. "You were always a terrible cook."

Abigail blinked at him a moment. Then her laugh joined his, which only made him laugh harder.

Every time one of them would get their laughter under control, they'd look at each other and start in all over again.

By the time their laughs eventually trickled off, Abigail was grabbing her ribs. "Just so you know, laughing like that with broken ribs is not a good idea."

"Sorry." But he wasn't. After the fear and tension of the morning—of the last several weeks—it had been exactly what they needed.

Chapter 23

Abigail fidgeted with the strap of her purse, readjusting herself on the waiting room chair. When she'd agreed to go to counseling, she'd figured it would take a few weeks to get an appointment, but it turned out that Simeon had a counselor friend in Brampton who had managed to fit them in with only a day's notice.

"There's nothing to be nervous about," Simeon whispered with a soothing smile.

Abigail tried to mimic the expression. But her eyes darted around the space. It was modern looking, with white walls and sleek black chairs. A tree she was pretty sure was fake stood in the corner. She got up to look. "It's real," she said in surprise.

"It is." A woman's laugh made Abigail spin around.

"Don't worry. I had to check it too when I first moved into the space. I'm still considering redecorating, but the tree stays either way."

"Everlee." Simeon stood and directed his smile to the blonde woman, who appeared to be in her early fifties. "Thanks for seeing us so quickly. This is my wife, Abigail."

"It's so nice to meet you." Everlee glided across the room, holding out a hand to Abigail with an open smile. "Let's go have a seat in my office. Can I get y'all some coffee?"

They declined, and Everlee led them into a spacious office with soft gray walls, a comfy looking couch and chairs, and a breathtaking view of the mountains outside.

Simeon's fingers brushed Abigail's back as he stood aside to let her take a seat. It wasn't the first time his touch had caused a tingle to travel up her spine.

She chose a spot on the couch, and Simeon sat next to her, seeming completely relaxed.

Of course he was. He'd been here before. He knew Everlee. He knew how counseling worked.

She didn't.

And even if she did, she wouldn't remember.

She sighed, and both Simeon and Everlee focused their attention on her.

"Sorry." She ducked her head.

"There's nothing to be sorry about." Everlee's tone was light and gentle. "Do you want to tell us what you were thinking?"

"Oh. Um." Abigail licked her lips, letting her eyes go to the window. "I was just thinking that Simeon has the advantage here, since he already knows you and I don't. And even if I did, I wouldn't remember."

"Abigail, there's no advantage or disadvantage." Simeon shifted on the couch, and she could tell he was looking at her, though she couldn't bring her eyes to his. "This isn't you against me or me against you. This is you and me together." A note of sadness had crept into his voice, and Abigail accidentally sighed again. She hadn't meant to hurt him.

"Does it bother you that Simeon remembers things that you don't?" Everlee asked.

Abigail pressed her lips together before she could blurt the response that had instantly sprung to mind. But when neither Simeon nor Everlee said anything for a full minute, she let herself say it. "Not as much as it bothers him." Though she hadn't spoken loudly, the words seemed to crack around the room, and she winced. "I'm sorry."

"You don't have to be sorry," Everlee assured her again.

But one glance at Simeon's stricken expression told Abigail otherwise.

"It's not that I don't wish I remembered," she tried to explain. "It's just that I don't feel like this other woman he seems to think I am. And every time I do something differently than she would or pick a different favorite than she would have, I feel like, I don't know . . . I'm disappointing him."

"Abigail." Simeon's voice was quiet, strained, like he was trying too hard to remain calm. "There is no other woman. She *is* you."

Abigail shook her head, brushing aside the hair that fell in her face. "But that's what I'm saying. She *feels* like someone else. Someone I can't live up to. You have all these memories of her, but I can't be her because I don't remember her."

"I don't— I can't—" Simeon fumbled to a stop, rubbing a hand over his jaw. "I'm not trying to make you feel like you have to be someone else," he finally said. "I'm just trying to help you remember yourself."

"And what if she never does?" Everlee's question was quiet, but it made Abigail jump. She'd almost forgotten the counselor was in the room. Simeon seemed to have the same reaction.

His brow scrunched, and he turned to Everlee. "I'm not ready to give up, if that's what you're asking."

"It's not." Everlee fixed him with a hard look that surprised Abigail. Were counselors allowed to do that? "I'm asking what if she doesn't get her memories back?" Everlee repeated. "Will you still love her?"

Simeon let out a hard breath. "Of course I will, but—" He broke off and stared toward a painting on the far side of the room. Abigail looked at it too. It was abstract swirls of color, and Abigail wondered if it was supposed to represent how she felt inside.

"Maybe it's time—" Everlee's voice gentled. "For the two of you to stop trying to fix Abigail's memory."

Simeon started to protest, but Everlee raised a hand to stop him. "I'm not saying she won't get her memories back. I'm saying instead of trying to snatch back the past, maybe it's time to look to the future. Get to know each other again, as you are now."

Abigail nodded slowly. She did want to get to know Simeon better. But did he want to know her—the new her?

He was still staring at that painting, but he turned to her. "I think that's a good idea. What about you?"

"Me too," she whispered.

"Good." Everlee jotted a note as she spoke. "Try to approach it as if you've just met. You don't know anything about each other yet. Start dating again, that kind of thing."

"Does that mean—" Abigail's words came out too quietly, and she cleared her throat and tried again. "Well, when people just start dating, they don't usually say, 'I love you,' do they?"

Simeon turned to her, his eyes incredulous. "You don't want me to tell you I love you?" He gave a choked laugh and shook his head.

Abigail bit her lip and turned to Everlee, who nodded for her to answer. "It's a lot of pressure," she said slowly. "I can feel him waiting for me—or well, *her*—to say it back. But I don't know him well enough to know if . . ."

The anguish in Simeon's eyes made her stop.

"Simeon?" Everlee asked. "How do you feel about that?"

Simeon was still staring at Abigail. "I can stop saying it," he said slowly. "But I can't stop doing it. I could never stop loving you, Abigail, no matter what."

Unexpected tears tickled the edges of her eyelashes, and she sniffed. She wanted to ask him why—why he would keep loving her when she had so little to give him in return—but she just nodded.

"Is there anything else you think would help you feel like you were both starting fresh, like you'd just met?" Everlee asked.

Simeon shook his head, but Abigail took a breath. He gave her a wary look.

She had to turn away, or she wouldn't be able to say this. "If we were just starting to date, I wouldn't be wearing this." She spun the wedding ring on her finger, watching the sunlight that streamed in from the window spark off its teardrop-shaped diamond. It was a beautiful ring, but—

The couch shifted as Simeon stood and strode to the window.

Abigail could only stare helplessly after him. She'd never seen him lose his composure before—not even in the hospital when she'd said she didn't recognize him.

"What is it about wearing the ring that's hard for you?" Everlee asked.

"It's just—" Abigail kept her eyes on Simeon. Though his back was to her, she guessed from the angle of his elbows that he was pressing his fingertips into his eyes or maybe pinching the bridge of his nose. She couldn't say anything else. He didn't deserve this from the woman he knew as his wife—even if she didn't know herself that way.

He cleared his throat and turned back toward them. "Sorry. Go on." He didn't move back to the couch, but he nodded, as if he wanted to know what she was going to say.

"It's just," she began again, shifting her gaze back to the ring. "Sometimes it feels like I woke up one day to some kind of arranged marriage. One that I didn't have a choice in."

At Simeon's quiet sound of protest, she lifted her eyes to him. "I mean, I know I did have a choice. Or *she* did. And I know she is me, but . . ." She shook her head helplessly. None of this was making any sense. And it was multiplying the pain in Simeon's eyes. Maybe she was being selfish. Maybe she should just accept that she was his wife, let him teach her who she was supposed to be. Eventually, maybe she would even *become* that woman again. "I'm sorry. I shouldn't have— I can keep wearing it."

"No." Simeon shook his head and moved back to the couch. He sat slowly, then held out a hand, palm up. "I don't want you to feel like that. You should take off the ring. For now."

"You're sure?"

He nodded stiffly, and she slid the ring off her finger, setting it carefully into his hand.

He stared at her for a moment, then closed his fingers around it and brought his eyes to hers. "I intend to give this back to you someday."

Abigail swallowed and nodded. She may not be ready to be his wife yet, but she really did hope she would be one day.

Chapter 24

Simeon downed the last gulp of his coffee, then headed for the stairs to check on Abigail. She'd said she'd be down in a minute—twenty minutes ago.

He reached the top of the stairs just as she emerged from the bedroom at the end of the hall, and he caught his breath. She was wearing the light pink floral sundress she'd bought on their honeymoon—and that he hadn't even known she still owned. She smoothed her hands up and down the fabric that he remembered feeling silky and soft.

"Sorry." Her smile wavered. "I wasn't sure what to wear."

He shook his head. "You look wonderful." He wanted to say more, to take her hand in his or even brush a kiss over her lips, but he held back. He was supposed to be acting as if they were just getting to know each other.

When Everlee had suggested it, Simeon's first reaction had been to wish they hadn't gone to counseling after all. But now that he'd had a couple of days to think about it, he could see the wisdom in it. Were he counseling another couple in a similar situation, he probably would have given the same advice. But that didn't make it any easier to implement in his own relationship.

His gaze went to Abigail's ringless finger, and he couldn't help thinking of those divorce papers he'd torn up. If she hadn't gotten in that accident, would they have ended up in this exact same spot, her finger no longer wearing the symbol of their unending love?

Maybe.

But the difference now was that she was actually willing to work on things, to give them another chance. He had to be grateful for that. And for the fact that she was willing to go to church with him this morning.

That had been another of Everlee's suggestions—one that Simeon was much more on board with. He and Abigail had always shared their faith—it had been the cornerstone of their relationship, at least until the past year, and he couldn't imagine losing that.

He stood aside to let her head down the stairs first, her flowery scent breezing past him and beckoning him down after her. But he gave her a little space before following.

"You probably have time to eat a quick breakfast before we leave." Simeon trailed her into the kitchen. "There's coffee."

"Thanks, but I'm too nervous to eat." Abigail pressed a hand to her stomach.

Simeon stepped closer, wanting to enfold her in his arms and reassure her but contenting himself with a smile. "There's nothing to be nervous about, I promise."

But a fistful of nerves walloped him. What if she didn't like the service? What if she said she was never going back? What if she was never willing to wear his ring again?

He worked to shove the worries aside. "Let me at least pour you a cup of coffee." He filled a travel mug and started to add sugar like he always did, then stopped. Maybe she'd only been drinking her coffee with sugar because that was how he'd been making it.

"Sugar?" he asked.

She made a face. "Do people actually drink it without sugar?"

He let out a breath and a small laugh. It was good to know some things hadn't changed.

He added another scoop, then stirred it, popped a lid on top, and passed it to her.

"Thank you." Her fingers brushed his as she took it, and it sent him back to the first time that had happened when he'd passed her a glass of chicha de piña, an Ecuadorian pineapple drink. The spark of her touch had caught him by surprise that day—and it was just as powerful now.

"You're welcome." He watched her take a sip and nod her approval, then led her out to their vehicle.

The drive was short and mostly silent, and Simeon used the time to pray. *If it is your will, Lord, please let her get her memories back. And if that's not your will—* His hand tightened on the steering wheel. The thought that she might never remember who he was to her—who she was to him—was too much to take. *If that's not your will, then help me to be the husband she needs me to be, even if that means acting like I'm not yet her husband. If she doesn't remember the love we once shared, then lead her to fall in love with me again.*

He let out a careful breath as he pulled into the parking lot of Beautiful Savior. He was going to need all the help God had to give him on that one. He'd always been completely baffled by what had made her fall in love with him in the first place.

"There are Lydia and Liam." Abigail pointed to the pair, who were just approaching the church, and Simeon's heart eased. He was grateful for how quickly she had grown close to his family again.

"And Benjamin." Simeon pointed to his youngest brother, who was unfolding himself from his tiny car.

"What's he driving?" Abigail asked with a laugh.

Simeon rolled his eyes. "That's his Gremlin. Don't let him hear you laughing at it. He loves that thing."

"Got it."

He pulled into a parking spot and got out to open her door. She only hesitated a second before sliding out of the vehicle. She looked up at the big brick building that had always felt like a second home to Simeon.

"There's nothing to be worried about," he reassured her again as they started toward the church. He nearly slipped his hand into hers as he had done a hundred times before as they walked into church but remembered just in time not to. He also resisted pointing out that they had been married here.

Inside, he led her to the pew where Benjamin, Lydia and Liam, Ava and Joseph, and Asher and Ireland already sat. The others all slid over, sending smiles and greetings to Abigail. Ava leaned over to hug her, and though Abigail looked surprised, she returned the gesture.

Simeon's heart expanded.

As Ava and Abigail chatted, Simeon glanced around the church, frowning when he didn't spot Zeb. He'd tried to call his brother several times over the past few weeks, but even when Zeb did answer—which wasn't often—their conversations were brief and superficial, with Zeb insisting he was fine.

Which was an obvious lie. Because how could he be, without his wife?

Simeon let his eyes go to his own wife, once again overcome with gratitude that she'd survived. He may not want to start their relationship over from scratch—but at least he had the opportunity. Which was more than Zeb had.

Abigail's eyes lifted to his, and she offered a soft smile. He had the overwhelming desire to wrap an arm around her shoulders and pull her in tight to his side, to reassure himself that she was really here and she was really his, but he clasped his hands in his lap.

"Good morning," a voice sounded through the sanctuary.

Abigail's eyes went to the front of the church, but a second later she leaned toward him, eyes wide. "That's not your dad."

Simeon chuckled. "That's Pastor Cooper. He works with Dad. He's the youth pastor."

"Ah." Abigail settled back into the pew, her arm lightly brushing his, her sweet scent making him lightheaded in the best way.

It took all of his concentration to focus on the service. Every once in a while, he let himself look at Abigail, who seemed to be listening intently to everything Pastor Cooper was saying. Simeon desperately wanted to ask if she remembered any of this, but he remained silent as Pastor Cooper stepped into the pulpit to deliver his sermon.

"How do y'all feel about storms?" Pastor Cooper asked. Simeon winced, glancing at Abigail. She had always hated storms, and after what had happened during the last storm . . .

But she appeared completely unperturbed.

"I never thought I was afraid of them," Pastor Cooper continued. "Until a couple of years ago, when we had a powerful storm roll through the youth camp. We were caught out in it, the thunder crashing right on top of us, lightning threatening to catch us, trees snapping under the force of the wind. And the rain—let's just say I wouldn't have minded having an ark. I can't speak for the other chaperones—" He glanced toward Asher and Ireland, who Simeon knew had been on that trip. "But I was scared—a lot more scared than I could let on to the kids. I had no idea what was going to happen to us or how long the storm was going to last or how we were going to get to safety."

Simeon felt Abigail shift, and he glanced in her direction. Tension crinkled her forehead, and he wondered if the description of the storm had caused it.

"When we finally reached the cabin," Pastor Cooper continued, and Simeon saw Abigail let out a breath. "It felt like we had reached dry land after being stranded in the middle of the ocean. Kind of like I imagine the disciples must have felt when they were in the middle of a storm with Jesus." He flipped open his Bible and read: "A furious squall came up, and the waves broke over the boat, so that it was nearly swamped. Jesus was in the stern, sleeping on a cushion. The disciples woke him and said to him, 'Teacher, don't you care if we drown?'"

Pastor Cooper looked up from the Bible. "These guys were not wimps. Many of them were seasoned fishermen. They'd seen their share of storms. But not like this. The wind howled through the sails, threatening to shred the masts to pieces. The waves relentlessly crashed up over the boat, threatening to overturn it. It was all the disciples could do to hold on for dear life. And what did Jesus do? He slept." Pastor Cooper shook his head with a laugh. "I'm a pretty sound sleeper—once the youth camp kids decorated me in shaving cream while I slept, and I never realized it until morning." He paused as the congregation chuckled, and Simeon's heart swelled to hear Abigail's light laugh join in.

"But y'all," Pastor Cooper continued. "Even I couldn't have slept through that storm. So why did Jesus? Was it because he didn't know what was going on? Was it because he didn't care? Or was it because he was giving the disciples an opportunity to trust him?"

The words struck Simeon. An opportunity to trust him.

Was that what God was giving him right now?

"Well, eventually," Pastor Cooper said. "It occurred to the disciples that they'd seen Jesus do some pretty amazing stuff. They wondered if he could do something about the storm. So they woke him up with their plaintive cry, 'Jesus, don't you care?' Instead of answering them, Jesus got up and spoke to the wind and the waves, 'Quiet! Be still!'" Pastor Cooper paused, and Simeon held his breath, even though he knew what was coming next.

"And the storm instantly stopped." Pastor Cooper snapped his fingers. "It didn't slowly wind down. It didn't get a little better. It calmed completely."

Pastor Cooper scanned the congregation. "I don't even have to ask if there are any storms in your life right now. We all have them. Illness. Financial stress. Trouble at work. Relationship struggles."

The air slowly seeped out of Simeon. His relationship with his wife had been floundering even before her accident. But now—now that relationship had been thrown into the middle of a roiling sea. His eyes went again to her ringless finger.

"Those storms can seem like they last forever," Pastor Cooper said. "It can feel like they're going to pull us under. We cry out for God to calm the storm, but it seems to rage on. Where is God? Doesn't he care?"

Simeon knew the answer was that he did care. That he was right there. But sometimes it felt like . . .

"Listen to his words," Pastor Cooper said. "'Quiet! Be still' He speaks those words to you. 'Quiet! Be still!' Even when the storms rage on. Even when everything around you threatens to overturn the boat. 'Quiet! Be still!'"

He paused, seeming to search the congregation. "But how? How can you be still when you have to figure out how to calm the storm? When you have to find a way to fix everything?"

Heaviness settled on Simeon's shoulders. That was just it. He should know how to fix this.

Pastor Cooper shook his head. "Take a lesson from the disciples. It's not about *you*. It's not about how *you're* going to repair the sails and bail out the water and keep the boat afloat. It's about who's in the boat with you. *Jesus is* right there. He gives you his peace. The storm outside of you may still rage. You may still be ill or dealing with financial problems. Your relationships may not be suddenly restored. But you can still have peace in the storm. Because you know Jesus—the one who has power even over the wind and the waves. He has all things, even the storms of this life, in his hands. He has promised us there is no storm so big it can pull us away from him. He has already taken care of the biggest threats. He has freed us from our sin, defeated the devil, won for us a place at his side in eternity. Whatever the storms we face in this world, none of that is going to change. That promise is secure. So 'Be still.' You have God's peace, even in the storm. Amen."

Simeon pushed to his feet as Pastor Cooper asked the congregation to stand.

That sermon—

It was like every single word had been intended just for him. It wasn't about finding a way to fix everything. It was about trusting that God was in control, even in this storm.

He let his eyes go to Abigail, who had bowed her head with the rest of the congregation for prayer. She looked up, as if she felt his eyes on her. He offered a smile, and she gave him a tentative one in return. The weight that had pressed on him since the moment she'd woken up and not remembered him lifted a little.

He opened the hymnal to the next song, "Be Still My Soul," and held it between them. But he had to stop singing as his eyes came to the second verse: "Be still, my soul, your God will undertake to guide the future as he has the past." Simeon blinked at the words, then cleared his throat so he could keep singing. God had guided him and Abigail to this point. And he would guide them to whatever came next. Whether she had her memories or not.

Chapter 25

Abigail surveyed the clothes in her closet. She should dress up for work, right?

She pressed a hand to her stomach, trying to decide if that was what the flip-flop of nerves was about—or if it was about seeing Simeon.

He'd been quiet ever since their appointment with Everlee the other day, but then yesterday, after church, something had seemed to shift between them. In a good way, she was pretty sure.

They'd gone to his dad's for lunch and then they'd taken a walk around their neighborhood, and he'd made a delicious dinner and they'd watched a movie—and not once had he mentioned what they used to do or asked if she remembered something.

She knew it was hard for him, acting as if they weren't married—she had seen his eyes go to her ring finger more than once—but she was so grateful that he was willing to try. It gave her hope that maybe they could start over, like Everlee had suggested.

She lifted a peach short-sleeved dress off a hanger and pulled it on, then ran a brush through her hair. She surveyed the results in the mirror. Based on what Ruth had been wearing when she and Simeon stopped at the Book Den on her birthday, the outfit looked work-ready. She ran a hand along her bare collarbone, which thankfully no longer caused her pain—not even the dull ache she still felt in her ribs most of the time. But her neckline looked bare. She glanced at the two jewelry boxes on the dresser—the new

156

one Simeon had given her, and the old, slightly worn one that she hadn't been able to bring herself to open yet. It felt too private.

She ran her fingers lightly over the top of both.

"Abigail?" Simeon's voice traveled up the stairs. "Are you ready?"

Abigail pulled her hand back and turned from the jewelry box. She'd go without a necklace.

"Coming." She sucked in a quick breath and forced her feet toward the stairs.

Simeon stood at the bottom, and the way his face lit up when he saw her made her heart do a funny little jump-step.

"You look beautiful."

"Oh. Thanks." She started down the steps toward him. "I wasn't sure if this was appropriate for work."

"It's perfect." Simeon stepped aside to let her pass. She headed for the kitchen, where he already had a cup of coffee waiting for her. "Thank you." She took a sip, glancing around the room.

"What do you need?" Simeon asked.

Abigail bit her lip. She didn't like this feeling of not knowing her own routines. "Am I supposed to bring a lunch or something?"

"You can." Simeon hesitated, but then said in a rush, "But I was thinking—do you want to go to lunch with me? You know, like a date?"

Abigail felt her lips lifting at the sweet nervousness in his tone. "I'd like that."

His return smile brought a wash of warmth to her cheeks, and she wondered if this was how she'd felt the first time he'd asked her out. But it didn't matter. She would focus on enjoying the feeling now.

"I suppose we'll have to get you a new car one of these days," Simeon said as they made their way to the SUV parked in the driveway.

"If I even remember how to drive," Abigail said wryly.

"I suspect it will be much like knitting," Simeon said. "You'll probably still have the procedural memory to do it. And if not, I'll teach you. We can have driving dates."

He opened her door for her, and a fresh batch of nerves took over as she watched him round the vehicle.

He got in, took one look at her, and asked, "What's wrong?"

"Nothing." Abigail tried to swallow. "What if I mess everything up? Or I hate it? Or—"

"Abigail." Simeon's fingers landed, light as a bird, on her hand. "You're not going to mess everything up. And if you hate it, you'll quit and find another job. Whatever *you* want to do." He held eye contact with her until she nodded.

He lifted his hand off hers and started the vehicle. She wrapped her own hands around each other, but it wasn't as comforting as his touch.

"Do you want me to come in with you?" Simeon asked a few minutes later, as he pulled into the parking lot behind the store. Sunlight blinked off the river at the far side of the lot, and couples and families already strolled along the riverwalk. The whole scene had a quaint, peaceful air that made Abigail feel at home.

"That's okay." She hoped her smile looked confident. "I'll be fine." She opened the door and got out slowly, careful not to turn too quickly and strain her ribs.

"Don't forget, you promised the doctor you wouldn't lift anything heavy." Simeon leaned across her seat, his brow lowered into lines of worry.

"I won't," Abigail promised. She reached to close the door.

"Abigail, wait. I—" Simeon cut off, his eyes fixed on hers. Finally, he blinked and looked away. "I'll see you at lunch. Twelve o'clock?"

She nodded and closed the door, glancing back to return his wave before she stepped into the building.

Simeon let out a long breath as Abigail disappeared into the bookstore. "Please bless her day, Lord," he whispered.

He backed out of the parking spot and headed for his office, trying to sneak a peek in the front window of the store as he passed. But he didn't catch a glimpse of Abigail.

She'll be all right, he reminded himself. Ruth would take good care of her. And he'd see her in a few hours for lunch. Anticipation loosened the tightness in his chest, and he opened his window, letting himself pull in a breath of the fresh—if humid—air. Bright flowers bloomed in large decorative planters in front of the various storefronts, and sounds of birds and laughter hung in the air.

Simeon let his tension release a little more. Maybe Abigail's accident wasn't about what they'd lost. Maybe it was about what they'd gained—a new beginning.

He pulled up to his office and jumped out of the vehicle, glad suddenly to be back at work. He'd spoken to many of his clients on the phone over the last few weeks, but it was always better to sit with them in person. He'd only lined up a few appointments for today, since he had plenty of administrative stuff to catch up on, but it would be good to get back into a routine.

Three hours later, as he ushered a couple out the door, Simeon had to rethink that. It wasn't that he didn't want to be here or that he didn't care about his clients. It was just that he'd spent an hour this morning refereeing a couple's argument over the division of chores.

The issue wasn't trivial, Simeon knew that. The majority of couples he saw started out with arguments like this—seemingly small things that reflected bigger underlying issues.

He blew out a breath, reminding himself that Jesus cared about even the smallest of problems—and it was his job to do that too.

Fortunately, it was time to pick Abigail up for lunch. He'd texted earlier to ask how things were going, and she'd replied with a cheerful, if brief, "great."

He remembered when she'd first gotten the job at the bookstore and he'd picked her up for lunch and she'd spent the whole time telling him about the books she'd discovered or the weird requests customers had made. He tried to push those memories away so he could go into today's lunch with no preconceived expectations of her.

He moved to his desk to grab his keys and wallet, trying to decide if they had time to go to the new pizza place outside of town or if they should stick to Murf's. Probably Murf's. Maybe he'd ask if she wanted to go to the pizza place Friday night.

It seemed so odd to be planning dates with her again, after her months of reluctance to leave the house for anything but work.

See, a new beginning.

He turned and strode out of the room, pausing to lock the door between his office and the lobby as an extra line of security for the sensitive records inside.

The exterior door chimed, and a woman's voice sang, "Hello, hello."

Simeon's shoulders tensed at the interruption, but he forced a smile as he turned. "Hi, Wendy."

She was on his list of clients to contact tomorrow to set up an appointment, so at least this would save him the phone call.

"I saw your vehicle and thought I'd see if you have time to talk."

"Oh. I'm sorry, I'm on my way out for lunch, and I'm already booked for the afternoon. Does Friday work for you?"

Wendy bit her lip. "Actually, I really need to do this right now. Before I lose my nerve."

"Lose your nerve?"

"Remember how I was telling you there was a guy I liked, last time I was here?"

Simeon nodded. "It was someone who'd been in your life for a while, right? Did you decide to tell him how you felt?"

Wendy licked her lips. "Sort of. I mean, I'm telling him right now."

"Over lunch?" Simeon smiled. Seemed he wasn't the only one with a lunch date. "You've considered the risks?"

Wendy shook her head. "Not over lunch. *Right now*, right now."

Simeon glanced around the lobby and then out the window, in case the guy was waiting for her outside, but there was no one. A rock slid from his heart to his stomach.

She meant—

"It was you," she confirmed, then gave a self-conscious laugh. "I feel pretty stupid about it now."

"It's nothing to feel stupid about," Simeon said gently. It certainly wasn't the first time it had happened. It was easy for some people to mistake the care of their counselor for more, especially if they'd lacked genuine, caring relationships in the past.

"Embarrassed then." Wendy covered her face.

"No need to be embarrassed either," Simeon reassured. "We can work through this. It might even help us pinpoint some of your relationship issues."

"You're not going to fire me then?" Wendy's eyes went wide and hopeful.

"Fire you? Of course not." Simeon shook his head. He'd only had to dismiss one client ever—and get a restraining order.

Fortunately, he couldn't foresee that happening with Wendy.

"So Friday, then?" he asked. "How about eleven o'clock?"

"Oh, that would be great." Wendy nodded, and Simeon quickly put the appointment into his phone, then led Wendy to the door. He was already late for his lunch with Abigail.

"I have to tell you," Wendy said as Simeon locked the door behind them. "I'm so relieved." She touched a hand to his arm, but Simeon brushed it off and moved toward his vehicle.

"It's nothing to worry about," he said as he opened his door.

"Okay, then I won't worry." She waved, then moved to her own black SUV, right next to his. Simeon motioned for her to back out first.

He waited until she'd driven away to pull out of his own spot.

He'd told her not to worry.

But that didn't mean he wouldn't.

He had his hands full trying to figure out how to make his wife fall in love with him. The last thing he needed was a client who already had.

Chapter 26

Abigail tore the receipt off the register and tucked it into the bag, then passed the package to the little girl who had come in with her grandmother for a girls' day out, as they'd told Abigail while she rang up their purchase.

"Y'all enjoy the rest of your day," she said.

"We will." The little girl tugged her grandmother toward the door. "We're getting pie next."

Abigail waved as her own stomach gave a quiet rumble. She checked the time on the register. 12:30.

Surprised, she looked to the door. Simeon should be here by now. He wouldn't stand her up on their first lunch date, would he? She pushed the doubt aside. He'd probably gotten caught up with his work, the same way she had.

"Well, how'd it go?" Ruth bustled up from the back of the store, where she'd been helping another customer find a book about Greece.

"I did it." Abigail grinned. It had been her first solo checkout with no supervision.

"I had no doubts." Ruth patted her hand, and Abigail couldn't help feeling proud of her achievement. So far, relearning the job had been pretty easy. She wasn't sure if it was because the job—or at least this part of it—was easy or because she still retained some procedural memory of how to do it. Spending the morning with Ruth had been nice. Her boss hadn't once asked her if she remembered something; instead, she'd acted as if Abigail were a brand-new employee. Abigail wondered if Simeon had called and asked her to do that or if Ruth had done it instinctively. Either way, Abigail appreciated the lack of expectations.

She fingered the spot on her hand where her wedding ring had left a pale band. Taking the ring off had had the same effect, like she was freed from the suffocating halo of expectations Simeon had for who she was supposed to be.

The cheerful bell over the front door chimed, and Abigail looked up to greet the new customer. The flutter that rippled through her when she spotted Simeon was unexpected but not unpleasant.

"Welcome to the Book Den," she greeted him with a grin.

He smiled back and weaved through the tables of books to the counter she stood behind. "Sorry I'm late. You look right at home here."

"Thanks. I *feel* right at home." She wondered if, on some level, some part of her did remember this place and that was why it had been so easy to step right back into it. But if that were the case, shouldn't she feel the same way about her actual home?

"Are we still on for lunch?" Simeon glanced at his watch. "I have an appointment at 1:30, but I think there's still time for Murf's."

Abigail looked to Ruth to make sure it would be okay.

"Go, go." Ruth shooed her out from behind the counter.

Abigail obeyed, pulling in a breath of Simeon's earthy scent as she fell in next to him. They reached a spot where the tables were too close together to walk side by side, and Simeon gestured for her to go first, his hand brushing her arm as she slipped past. The sensation of the touch lasted well after the contact ended.

Outside, Simeon helped her into the SUV, then steered out of the parking lot. "So you had a good morning?"

"I did." That sense of achievement stole over her again. "Did you?"

"It was fine." Something in his tone rang just a little too practiced, and Abigail turned to him. He was looking out the windshield, but Abigail got the odd feeling he was seeing something else.

"Did you catch up on a lot of work?"

"Huh?" He pulled his gaze to her. "Oh. Yeah."

She wondered if he'd always been so taciturn about his work. But then, she supposed it made sense. Counselors had to keep things confidential. Maybe she wasn't even supposed to ask.

It only took a few minutes to get to Murf's. Simeon turned off the vehicle, and Abigail waited for him to come around to open her door as he always did, but he just sat there, once again staring out the windshield.

"Is everything all right?" Abigail touched his arm, and he jumped, then looked at the spot where her fingers rested.

"Of course." He lifted his eyes to hers. "Sorry about that. Just thinking about something I should have left at the office. I'm all yours."

"It's okay if you don't have time for lunch. We can get it to go. I know your job is important."

"Not as important as you." He opened his car door and slid out. As they started across the parking lot, she found herself hoping he'd take her hand.

But he didn't, and she reminded herself that she'd been the one who wanted to start their relationship over. She doubted that they'd held hands on their first date.

They went inside to order, then brought their food out to a table under the pergola on the side of the building.

"So tell me all about your morning." Simeon dug into his burger and fries and listened attentively as she told him about her training. Apparently, he'd been successful in putting aside whatever had been bothering him because she really did feel like he was all hers. She could see why he made a good counselor.

By the time she'd wound down, their food was already gone.

"I can't believe I spent the whole time talking," she apologized. "I didn't even let you get in a word."

Simeon's smile spread through her. "I like listening to you. I only wish we had all day. How about a couple of milkshakes for the road?"

"Oh my goodness," Abigail groaned. "I already don't fit into half the clothes in my closet."

Simeon's eyes traveled over her dress. "You look incredible, Abigail."

She saw the sincerity in his eyes and tried not to think about the fact that since he was her husband, he must already know what she looked like underneath it.

"A milkshake sounds good," she squeaked.

"I'll be right back." He gathered up their garbage and headed back into the building. Abigail let herself admire him as he walked away. He moved with a natural grace and power that suggested he'd once been an athlete. Maybe a runner? Or a football player? She'd have to ask him.

A few minutes later, he returned, carrying two huge plastic cups and an even bigger smile, directed straight at her. Abigail's heartbeat stepped up its pace, and her lips lifted in response. It seemed she quite liked dating her husband. She should congratulate Past Abigail on her good taste in men.

A little giggle escaped, and Simeon tipped his head to the side, giving her a quizzical look. "What's so funny? Did I get ketchup on my shirt?"

He glanced down toward his buttons, and she giggled again. "No. Nothing's funny. I'm just . . . having a good day."

Simeon's eyes crinkled as his smile widened. "Good." He passed her one of the cups, and they each took a long pull on their straws.

"It's good, isn't it?" Simeon lowered his cup.

Abigail took another sip, then nodded. For the first time since the accident, it felt like maybe *good* was the perfect word to describe everything.

Chapter 27

Simeon could not stop staring at his wife. The last couple of weeks had been incredible. They'd gone on dates, taken long walks, and talked and talked and talked.

And somehow, every single day, he fell more and more in love with her.

"It's beautiful here." Abigail brushed a piece of wind-blown hair off her cheek as she gazed over the panorama of River Falls below the pizza place's patio.

"Yes, it is."

"Simeon." Abigail sounded exasperated, but her cheeks took on a warm glow. "You're not even looking at the view."

"I have the best view in the house."

Abigail shook her head. "You're impossible."

"Thanks." He grinned and instinctively reached across the table. It wasn't until his hand was halfway to hers that he realized what he was doing. He paused with his hand in midair.

"How was everything tonight?" A bubbly waitress popped up next to them, holding out the check. Simeon had no choice but to divert his hand and take it.

"It was delicious." Abigail smiled graciously at the waitress, and Simeon was grateful she'd beaten him to answering. His own response might not have been as civil, given that the woman had interrupted his first attempt to hold hands with his wife in weeks.

He pulled out his credit card, then contemplated reaching for Abigail's hand again as they waited for the waitress to bring it back. But she had tucked her hands into her lap—intentionally avoiding his hand or not, he couldn't tell.

"So, you liked it?" Simeon asked.

"It was delicious." Abigail smiled. "Do I have any pizza sauce on my face?"

Simeon shook his head, almost wishing she did so he'd have an excuse to touch her.

The waitress brought the credit card back, and Simeon slid out his chair, reluctant to end the date.

"Should we get some pie on the way home?"

Abigail groaned. "You really don't want me to fit into any of my clothes anymore, do you?" Her cheeks flushed. "I mean—" She blew a breath that fluttered her hair. "Pie sounds good."

Simeon chuckled to himself, wishing he could tell her how attracted he was to every single one of her curves. Instead, he silently moved to her side of the table. She stood as well, and they walked side by side around the restaurant.

Abigail's hand brushed against his, and Simeon moved his arm out of the way. But her fingers brushed his again. Simeon glanced her way, and she offered a soft smile.

Well then. What was he waiting for?

Simeon slid his fingers between hers, his breath catching as hers tightened around them. He never wanted to let go again.

But too soon they were standing next to their vehicle, and he couldn't figure out how to get them both into it without letting go.

He lifted their hands between them, the wedding ring he still wore standing out against the ridges of their knuckles. "If I let go now, can I have this hand back when I get in?"

Abigail laughed. "I guess you'll have to wait and see."

"Or we could stand here all night so I don't have to risk it." He took a step closer so that their bent arms were the only things separating them. His gaze went to her lips, their smile beckoning.

He took a step backwards and let out a breath. He had to take this slowly. Like he'd just met her.

With his free hand, he reached past her to open the passenger door, then lifted her hand to his lips, dusting a quick kiss across the back of it. Reluctantly, he let go. As soon as Abigail was settled in her seat, he rushed around to his side of the vehicle and jumped in.

Before he could even ask if he could hold her hand again, she was holding hers out to him.

They drove hand in hand to Daisy's, but when they got there, Simeon spotted a familiar figure through the pie shop's big windows. He'd only had one appointment with Wendy since she'd confessed her feelings for him—and it had been fine. They'd discussed the fact that one of the reasons she'd likely developed feelings for him was that she knew he was unavailable. But that didn't mean he wanted to run into her in public. Besides, he didn't really feel like sharing Abigail with anyone else right now. "How about getting our pie to go?"

"That sounds nice." The smile in her voice sent Simeon's heart flying.

He pulled up to the drive-through, waiting for Abigail to scan the menu. Last time they were here, she'd said she was going to try a different kind every time until she found her new favorite.

"I think I'll try pecan today," she said.

Simeon bit his tongue before he could tell her that she'd once said she didn't understand desserts with nuts in them. He ordered himself a piece of chocolate cream pie that he could trade with her if she didn't like the pecans.

When they got home, they walked side by side to the front door, and Simeon almost wished he were dropping her off, since that would make it natural to kiss her goodnight. Instead, he unlocked the door and waited for her to enter in front of him.

"Do you want to eat our pie under the stars?" Maybe it was corny, but it sounded more romantic than the same kitchen table they ate at every day.

"Outside?" Abigail sounded surprised.

"Well, I mean, I could tape some stars on the ceiling in here, but yeah, I was thinking outside."

Her laugh traveled all the way through him. "Sure. Let's eat under the stars."

"Okay. Hold on one second. I'll be right back." He handed her the bag of pie and raced up the stairs, heading straight for the bedroom. The trunk at the bottom of the bed held extra blankets, and he chose two large ones, then ran back downstairs.

"Abigail?" He looked around the empty entry area.

"In here." Her voice came from the kitchen. "Just getting us some drinks." She'd placed a pitcher of sweet tea and two glasses on the tray that he'd used to bring her breakfast in bed. She scooped the slices of pie out of their clamshell containers and put them on plates, then added those to the tray.

"Good idea." He moved to pick up the tray, letting her open the patio door.

He led her to the middle of the yard, then set the tray down to spread one of the blankets on the ground, setting the other one to the side in case they got cold.

He grabbed her hand, relishing the easy way her fingers instantly wrapped around his, and pulled her to the middle of the blanket. "Sit."

She did, and he lowered himself next to her. He reached to the side and lifted the tray, relocating it between them, not only for easy access to the tea and pie but as a barrier to keep himself from wrapping her in his arms as his whole body screamed for him to do.

Slowly, he reminded himself, pouring them each a glass of tea. He held his glass up. "To new beginnings."

Abigail clinked her glass to his, and they each took a drink, then picked up their slices of pie. Simeon watched Abigail take the first bite of hers, trying not to hope she'd hate it. It didn't matter if she felt the same way about pecan pie as she used to.

She chewed slowly, swallowed, then took a long drink of tea.

"How is it?" he asked.

"It's . . . okay." She stabbed another forkful, making a face as she pushed it into her mouth.

Simeon chuckled. "Really?"

She shook her head and took another long drink of tea. "Definitely not my favorite. Whose idea was it to make a pie entirely of nuts?"

Simeon's heart jumped at the familiar words, but he was careful to keep his expression neutral.

"Here." He took the plate out of her hands and held his out to her. "Try this one instead."

She gave him a wary look. "This is yours."

He shook his head. "Now it's yours."

"Simeon—"

171

"Just try it." He scooped up a giant bite of the pecan pie and stuffed it in his mouth. "This one's mine now."

She shook her head but slid her fork into the chocolate cream pie. The way she closed her eyes when it hit her tongue pulled a joyful laugh from Simeon.

"This one is definitely a contender," Abigail said, cutting off another piece.

"Good. Because I really wanted this pecan pie." Simeon polished off the rest of it in four bites. Abigail was still working on his slice of chocolate pie, and watching her lick her lips to get a dollop of the silky filling was driving him crazy with the desire to kiss her, so he lay back on the blanket. It took a moment for his eyes to adjust so he could pick out the stars starting to appear in the dark canopy above.

Next to him, he heard Abigail set her plate on the tray. Shuffling indicated that she had lain down too, but he didn't let himself turn to look at her—because if he did, he might be tempted to shove that tray out of the way and cozy up next to her.

He did allow himself to reach around the tray to seek her hand, though.

She curled her fingers in his, and he closed his eyes, thanking God for this moment.

"Oh, I see one." The surprised delight in Abigail's voice made Simeon open his eyes. "And another. And another. Oh wait, that one's a plane."

Simeon chuckled and squeezed her hand tighter. "There will be more soon, don't worry."

They watched the sky silently for a while, until Abigail asked, "Do we do this often?"

"We've never done this before," Simeon answered honestly. They'd certainly admired the stars together when they'd happened to be outside at night, but they'd never just lain on a blanket and looked up at the sky together, though Simeon couldn't for the life of him imagine why.

The soft darkness, the low serenade of crickets, the light floral scent of the magnolias—everything about being out here with her was perfect.

Abigail's hand jerked out of his suddenly, and she smacked at her neck.

"Sorry. Bug." She scratched at the spot, but then moved her hand to slap her leg.

That was probably why they didn't do this more often. Although mosquitoes generally left him alone, they ate Abigail alive.

He should suggest that they go inside.

His eyes fell on the extra blanket next to them. "Hold on. I have an idea."

He started to pull the blanket over them, but the tray was in the way—and if he covered it with the blanket, chances were good that one or both of them would end up drenched in sweet tea.

Not letting himself consider whether or not it was a good idea, he picked up the tray and moved it to his far side, then lay back and pulled the blanket up to their chins, making sure to leave the same amount of space between them as if the tray were still there.

But when he reached for Abigail's hand, she was closer than he'd expected. Simeon swallowed. The evening was way too warm for this blanket, and her body heat radiated toward him. But there was no way he was going to move a muscle.

"Can I ask you something?" Abigail's voice joined the melody of the night.

"Of course."

"What made you decide to become a counselor?"

"Oh." Simeon blinked up at the stars.

Abigail was the only one he'd ever told the full reason he'd become a counselor. To others, he always said it was because he liked helping people work through their problems by guiding them with God's Word. Which was true. But the deeper reason was much harder.

"You don't have to tell me if you don't want to," Abigail said softly. "I just thought—"

"No." Simeon squeezed her hand. "I want to tell you." He turned his head to find her watching him, her chin peeking out from under the blanket.

"When I was seventeen," he started, "I had this friend, Steve, who was going through a hard time."

Abigail nodded, her gaze too full of compassion. He turned his eyes starward again. "I tried to be there for him, tried to listen to him, you know? But sometimes it all got to be a little . . . much. Anyway, one night I ignored his call. I figured I'd see him the next day at school." Simeon broke off, the stars above him seeming to blink on and off. Why hadn't he taken that stupid call?

Abigail's hand touched his arm under the blanket, and he realized she was waiting for him to finish the story.

He let out a breath. "He didn't come to school the next day." He swallowed. "Because he took his own life that night."

Abigail's gasp broke through the quiet of the night. "Oh, Simeon. I'm so sorry."

Simeon shook his head, the hard dirt under the blanket pressing against his skull. "Me too. Anyway, it made me realize that I never wanted to be in a situation like that again, where I didn't know how to help someone who was struggling like that." He refused to mention that not knowing how to help *her* had given him some of those same feelings all over again. But at least now it felt like they were moving forward from that.

Or at least they had been, until he'd totally subdued the mood of their date.

"I'm sorry." He turned to her with a rueful smile. "I didn't mean to ruin our date with that story."

"You didn't ruin it." Abigail's hand rubbed his arm, leaving a trail of heat behind. "If anything, I feel . . ." She glanced away, as if searching for what to say. "Closer to you." Her eyes came to his, and Simeon swallowed. His pulse pounded against his throat the way it had the first time he'd kissed her.

"Abigail," he said hoarsely.

He rolled onto his side just in time to spot a giant mosquito feasting on her cheek. He brought his hand up to shoo it away, but another immediately took its place.

"Come on." He sat up quickly but reluctantly, pulling her up with him. "Let's get you inside before the mosquitoes carry you away."

He stood, then held out his hands to her. She took them, and he tugged her easily to her feet. There were only a few inches between them now.

His eyes locked on hers. Did she want to kiss him as badly as he wanted to kiss her?

Her hand shot into the space between them, swatting at yet another mosquito.

Simeon released a breath.

Kissing while being swarmed by mosquitoes wasn't exactly romantic.

"Go inside." He gave her a gentle push toward the house. "I'll clean up and be right in."

"I can help." She slapped a hand to the back of her neck.

"I don't think you can. Mosquitoes have always found you delicious. Not that I blame them."

Okay, maybe that had been too far.

But Abigail laughed and took off for the house.

Simeon gathered the blankets and tray as quickly as he could and followed, hoping against hope that he'd find her waiting inside to pick up where they'd left off.

It took a little juggling to get the door open with his full hands, but when he finally managed, she was nowhere in sight.

"Abigail?" he called.

When there was no answer, he set the tray and blankets on the table, then headed for the front of the house. But the living room was empty, and the lights above the stairway were on. His heart folded in on itself. She must have gone to bed.

Because she'd sensed that he wanted to kiss her and she wasn't ready?

He went back to the kitchen, grabbed a glass of water, and turned off the lights. He may as well go to bed too, though there was no way he'd be able to sleep with the electrical charge from being so close to her still coursing through him.

He made his way up the stairs, sighing as he spotted the closed bedroom door.

"Hey." Abigail popped her head out just as he reached his office.

"Hey." He tried not to sound disappointed. If she wasn't ready to kiss him yet, she wasn't ready. He wasn't going to make her feel bad about it.

She opened the door farther, and he caught sight of the sleep shirt and leggings that hugged the curve of her hips.

"I just wanted to say thanks." She slid her bare toes back and forth across the floor. "I don't think I've ever had such a special date. I mean, that I remember."

Simeon chuckled. "Me neither."

"Really?" She looked doubtful, but he nodded. They'd certainly had fancier dates and more adventurous dates and even more romantic dates. But somehow, tonight had felt more special than any of those.

"Well." Abigail watched her toe sliding along a crack in the floorboards. "I think I'm going to get some sleep. See you in the morning."

That was right. He'd wake up in the morning and get to see her again. "See you in the morning. Sleep well."

She nodded and closed the door, and Simeon stood staring at it, allowing himself to imagine the day when he'd sleep next to her again.

For weeks, he had been afraid it might never happen.

But now— Now he had hope.

Chapter 28

Abigail woke to a silent house, and her heart fell. Had she missed Simeon?

She turned her head to check the time. It was only 7:30. He didn't usually leave for the office until almost eight on days she didn't work. But maybe he'd wanted to escape early this morning, after the way she'd run away from him last night.

She sighed and flopped onto her back to stare up at the ceiling.

The whole evening had been . . . perfect. Dinner. Holding hands. Lying side by side on the blanket. Watching the stars. Listening to him talk.

And the way he'd looked at her—like he wanted to kiss her.

In that moment, she had wanted nothing more.

But then the stupid bugs had interrupted.

When she'd gotten inside, she'd stood in the dining room, watching him through the patio door, the desire to kiss him so overpowering that it felt like it came from somewhere outside herself. Like it was some sort of memory stored in her heart that her head didn't share.

And that had made her wonder—when he looked at her like that, was it *her* he was seeing, *her* he wanted to kiss? Or was it *past her*?

She didn't know why it mattered so much. After all, he was obviously right when he said she was the same person as Past Abigail. Even if she couldn't remember.

But somehow the idea that he might want to kiss a memory more than he wanted to kiss her had gotten in her head, and she'd freaked out and retreated to bed.

Still, the way he'd looked at her when he said goodnight—it hadn't felt like he was looking at a memory. And she believed he'd been sincere when he said their date was the most special he'd been on.

So take that, Past Abigail.

She rolled her eyes at herself and pulled the blanket up over her head.

A sound from downstairs made her bolt upright and bounce out of bed. Maybe she hadn't missed him after all.

She was halfway to the stairs when she realized she was still in her pajamas and her hair was probably a tangled mess. Not to mention she hadn't even brushed her teeth yet. But somehow the need to see him outweighed all of that.

She ran lightly down the steps.

Simeon sat at the dining room table, reading his Bible and sipping a mug of coffee. Abigail hesitated, letting herself enjoy the play of concentration on his face, the way he ran a finger over his temple as if he were thinking.

After a minute, he closed the Bible and slid his chair back. He startled but smiled as his eyes lifted to her. "I was trying to be quiet so I wouldn't wake you up on your day off. Guess I didn't succeed."

"That's okay. I have plenty to do today."

"Oh yeah?" Simeon raised an eyebrow. "What do you have planned?"

"That's for me to know." She gave him what she hoped was a mysterious—and maybe slightly flirtatious—smile. "And you to find out."

"Hmm." He raised an eyebrow. "I'm not sure if I should be curious or alarmed." But he looked pleased. "Maybe I should stay home to find out."

Abigail shook her head. "Nope. It's a surprise."

"Just please tell me you're not going to attempt to cook again." He gazed at the new range hood Liam had helped him put in last week.

Abigail laughed. "I think I've learned my lesson."

"Good." Simeon moved closer to set his empty coffee cup on the counter. It would only take a step or two for Abigail to tuck herself into his arms.

Remembering her unbrushed teeth, she took a step backwards.

Simeon's smile faltered a little. "I guess I should get to work then. Have a good day." He touched his hand to hers on his way past, the tingle he left behind cementing her desire to kiss him.

Tonight. She'd definitely kiss him tonight.

The moment she heard the front door close, Abigail pulled out her phone and texted Benjamin. *Are we still on for today?*

She held her breath as she waited for his reply, hoping he hadn't changed his mind about giving her a cooking lesson. She'd lain awake in bed last night, trying to figure out what she could do to show Simeon how she felt, when the idea had come to her. She'd felt strange texting Benjamin to ask if he'd help, but fortunately, his response had been an instant and enthusiastic yes.

I'll be there at 1:00, his text came through now. *Do you want me to stop at the store on the way, or should we go together?*

Let's go together, she texted back. If she was going to do this for Simeon, she wanted to do all of it.

She ran upstairs to brush her teeth and shower, letting her mind play through the various scenarios for her first kiss with Simeon later.

She barely managed to keep herself busy with a book and her knitting until one o'clock. When Benjamin arrived, she was more than ready to go.

She opened the door before he could knock, and he stepped back with a surprised laugh. "Well, hello."

"You have to tell me. Is this weird?" It wasn't the greeting she intended, but it was what came out.

"Is what weird?" Benjamin snorted. "You accosting me at the door? A little, but—"

Abigail couldn't help joining in his easy laughter. "I meant me asking you to help with this."

"Of course not." Though he couldn't be much older than his early twenties, Benjamin's eyes crinkled with his smile, just like Simeon's did. "This is what family's for, right?"

Abigail nodded slowly. From what she'd seen of the Calvanos, she had to believe that was true.

"Come on. Let's go to the store." He gestured toward his little Gremlin in the driveway, and Abigail wanted to ask how they were going to fit groceries in it. But she remembered Simeon's warning about making fun of Benjamin's car, so she kept her mouth shut. If worse came to worst, she supposed she could always pile the bags on her lap.

"So how's the new job?" she asked as Benjamin steered the car out of the driveway. It was a good thing that she apparently wasn't claustrophobic, since the car was somehow even smaller on the inside than it looked on the outside.

"It's good. Really good, actually."

They spent the drive talking about his new position as head chef at Ireland's brother's restaurant, The Depot. It fascinated Abigail that someone so young could know so much about cooking when her first foray—at least that she remembered—had almost burned down the house.

"So what do you want to make?" Benjamin asked as they walked across the parking lot at the store.

Abigail bit her lip. She'd been thinking about that. As far as she could tell, Simeon wasn't terribly picky, but she wanted to make something he would really love.

"Do you have any suggestions?" she asked Benjamin.

"Let's see." Benjamin looked thoughtful. "Simeon's always been a meat and potatoes guy. How about bacon-wrapped pesto pork tenderloin with twice baked potatoes?"

"Whoa." Abigail rubbed her head. "I don't even know what half of those words mean."

Benjamin chuckled. "Don't worry. It's not as complicated as it sounds. You can handle it."

"If you say so," Abigail murmured.

Inside the store, Benjamin grabbed a cart and led her up and down the aisles, picking out groceries with a practiced hand.

They were standing in the produce section, Benjamin explaining to her how to pick out fresh basil, when he suddenly stiffened and fell silent.

"What's wrong?" Abigail looked over her shoulder, but all she saw was people browsing a grocery store.

She turned back to Benjamin, who was still gaping at something—or maybe someone.

She followed the line of his gaze again.

Oh.

A young woman who looked close to his age had just started unloading her cart at the checkout.

"Who's that?" Abigail grinned at him.

"What?" Benjamin shook his head and dragged his eyes back to the basil. "No one. So anyway, you don't want the stuff with wilty leaves." He shuffled through bunches of basil, finally holding one up. "You want ones that are crisp, like this."

"Crisp. Got it." Abigail nodded as he stuffed the bunch into a plastic bag. "What's her name?"

"Whose name?" Benjamin's eyes darted to the checkouts again.

Abigail rolled her eyes. "You're not really going to play dumb, are you?"

"Summer," Benjamin said, his eyes coming back to Abigail. "Her name is Summer."

"And you like her."

"What?" Benjamin shook his head as if Abigail were crazy. "No. I just— I mean, we used to . . . But . . ."

Abigail studied him. "But you still have feelings for her." She was proud of her deduction, even if it had been pretty obvious.

"No," Benjamin said firmly, turning his back to the checkout. "She's not . . . Come on, we need some scallions." He moved farther into the produce section, and Abigail followed, deciding to let the topic drop for now, though she had to bite her tongue every time she spotted Benjamin glancing up from the scallions toward the checkouts.

He was stalling, she could tell.

Finally, he seemed satisfied, and they went to pay for their purchases, Summer nowhere in sight.

With everything bagged and loaded into the cart, they headed for the parking lot, where Benjamin miraculously fit it all into the Gremlin's miniscule backseat.

"Abigail, hi," a woman called just as Benjamin was about to return the cart to the store.

"Who is that?" Abigail murmured out the side of her mouth, trying not to move her lips.

Benjamin shrugged. "No idea," he murmured back.

Abigail pushed a smile to her lips. Obviously she'd met this woman before, even if she didn't remember. She had no idea how the woman hadn't heard that she had amnesia. One thing Abigail had learned very quickly about River Falls—word traveled quickly in a small town.

"I'm sorry." She used her politest voice as the woman reached them. "You'll have to remind me of your name. I had an accident and—"

"Oh yes, I know all about your amnesia," the woman said. "Don't worry. I wouldn't expect you to remember my name. You and I have only met once. But I know Simeon well. I'm Wendy." The woman held out a hand, which Abigail dutifully shook.

"Oh. Okay." She wasn't really sure how else to respond to that.

"And you're Simeon's brother." Wendy tapped her lip. "Let me see. Benjamin, right?"

Benjamin raised an eyebrow at Abigail but nodded and also shook Wendy's outstretched hand. "Nice to meet you."

"Oh, you too. You too. Anyway—" Wendy gestured toward the store. "Better get to my shopping. Are y'all done with the cart?"

Abigail nodded, and Wendy took it. "Perfect timing then. See y'all later."

She headed toward the store, and Benjamin shook his head. "That was weird."

"Yeah." Abigail spent most of the drive wondering how Simeon knew Wendy, but the moment they got home, Benjamin dove into her cooking lesson, and she was too busy to give Wendy another thought.

He taught her how to make the pesto, how to prepare the meat, how to bake and then scoop out the potatoes.

They talked as they worked—about Benjamin's job, Lydia and Liam's upcoming wedding, the rest of the Calvanos—but every time Abigail tried to turn the conversation back to Summer, her talkative brother-in-law grew silent—which only confirmed Abigail's suspicions.

By the time everything was prepared, Abigail was pretty sure her brain was going to explode, but the scents wafting around the kitchen made it all worth it.

"I have to get to work." Benjamin cast a satisfied eye over the messy kitchen. "Make sure you put the pork in the oven about thirty minutes before you want to eat. The potatoes can go in one more time for about twenty minutes.

Abigail nodded. "I think I've got it."

"I think you do too." Benjamin headed toward the door. "We should do this again sometime. It was fun."

"It was. Thanks again."

"You're welcome." He stepped forward and hugged her.

Abigail grunted at the slight pang in her ribs but squeezed him back.

And then he was gone.

She checked the time. She had one hour until Simeon got home. Just enough time to change and get everything on the table. And to decide whether she should kiss him right when he walked in the door—or wait until after dinner.

Chapter 29

Simeon rolled his shoulders as he steered toward home, trying to release the tension of the day. It had been a rough one, with a couple who was trying to work through infidelity and a teenager struggling with anxiety and depression. The hardest part had been the fear he'd seen in the mother's eyes.

It was one of the things about becoming a parent that had always terrified him. But it wasn't enough to make him give up on the idea of children altogether. It was way too soon to mention adoption to Abigail—first they had to continue to redevelop their relationship, but after that . . .

Simeon pushed away thoughts of the last time they'd talked about it, right before the accident. She'd said she couldn't adopt.

But that had been the depression and fear talking, he was sure of it. Now that those had improved, she would be eager to adopt.

Unless she doesn't want kids anymore.

He ignored the worry. She still liked chocolate pie. She'd still want kids.

Simeon snorted at his own logic and tried to turn his thoughts in another direction. They landed where they'd been landing all day—that non-kiss last night.

Her lips had been so close he could almost taste them—he wondered if they still had the faint strawberry flavor of her lip gloss—and then she'd run away.

Be still, he reminded himself as he pulled into their driveway. He needed to be still and let things unfold in God's timing.

He turned off the car and took a moment to leave the problems of the day out here—something Dad had taught him to do early in his career.

A savory scent drifted through the air, and Simeon pulled in an appreciative breath as he made his way to the front door. One of the neighbors was making something tasty.

He went through a mental inventory of the food in their pantry, trying to figure out what he could make for dinner. He'd never minded being the one to do all the cooking—he kind of enjoyed it, actually—but maybe he'd see if Abigail wanted to join him in the kitchen tonight. As much as he loved their dates, they needed some ordinary, everyday things to connect over as well.

He opened the door, and the cooking scents intensified.

Frowning, he stepped inside. "Abigail?"

"In here." Her voice came from the kitchen, and Simeon followed it, still trying to figure out why the delicious smells were growing stronger. Had Abigail ordered takeout from somewhere?

He reached the kitchen, and his feet stopped working. Abigail stood in front of the open oven, and she was sliding out a pan covered in what looked like twice baked potatoes.

She turned to set it on the counter, her eyes lighting as they fell on him. "Hi." Her smile was bright, her cheeks glowing with the heat of the oven. "One second. I think—" She turned back to the oven and pulled another pan out, frowning at it. "I think this is done, right?"

Simeon's mouth watered as his eyes fell on what looked like some kind of meat wrapped in bacon. "What's going on? Who made all this?" He managed to pry his feet off the floor and cross the room.

"I did." She gave him a proud smile and spun to turn the oven off. "Well, Benjamin helped, but . . ."

"You did this?" Simeon asked incredulously.

Abigail laughed. "Don't look so surprised. It turns out I'm a fast learner when it comes to cooking."

Simeon shook his head. "It's not that." He took another step closer. "It's— You did this for me?"

Abigail nodded and bit her lip, looking suddenly shy. "You've done so much for me, and I just wanted to . . . I don't know, do something for you."

Simeon swallowed. "Abigail, that's—" His eyes fell on her collarbone, and his heart skipped.

Abigail lifted a hand to her neckline, fingering the delicate gold necklace that rested there. "I'm sorry. Should I not have—"

Simeon shook his head, gently hooking a finger under the chain. "I gave this to you for our anniversary last year," he said quietly. "You definitely should wear it."

His eyes went to her lips, which spread into a soft smile. He tried to swallow, but he didn't remember how.

"Abigail." He let the chain fall and moved his hand to brush her hair off her cheek, relishing the feel of her skin under his fingers. "I know we haven't been dating again all that long, but—" He ran a finger down the line of her jaw. "Would it be okay if I kissed you?"

Abigail startled, and his hand fell from her face. "I'm sorry." Simeon cleared his throat and took a step backwards. "I didn't mean to— I wasn't trying to rush you." His stupid heart was throwing a tantrum, slamming itself around his chest.

"No, it's not that." Abigail was giving him the strangest look, as if she were dazed. "Have you ever said those words before?"

Simeon's heart stopped its tantrum, stilling completely. "Why do you ask?"

"I don't know exactly." Abigail shook her head, as if trying to work out what she meant. "I just got the weirdest feeling of déjà vu when you said that."

Simeon nearly shot right up through the ceiling. "I said something along those lines the first time I wanted to kiss you." He had to work hard to keep his voice steady, to not give away the hope surging through him.

Abigail nodded, and he waited, not daring to take a breath, as if that might scare away the fragile memory.

"And what did I answer?" Abigail asked after a moment.

"You said—" Simeon lifted his hand to her cheek again, letting his palm cup it tenderly. "'I've been waiting for you to ask that.'"

Abigail laughed, her cheekbone lifting under his hand. "That was a good answer."

Simeon tilted his head but waited. "Is that a yes?"

"It's a yes," she whispered.

Simeon resisted the desire to rush in and take her lips in his. He wanted to savor this moment.

He brought his other hand to her neck and let it slide under her hair. Her eyelids fell closed, her lashes dusting her cheeks, and she lifted her face toward him. Letting his own eyes close, he lowered his lips onto hers.

They were as soft as he remembered, as warm, as perfect. Her arms circled his neck, and he pulled her closer, keeping the kiss light, unhurried, undemanding. It had been worth every moment of the wait.

After a moment, he pulled back, wanting to make sure she was still okay with this.

She opened her eyes, her hands sliding from his neck to his biceps and resting there. "Did I— Was that— I mean, did I kiss like . . ."

Simeon rubbed a thumb across her cheekbones with a chuckle. "You kiss like *you*, Abigail. It was perfect."

"Okay. Good." She bit her lip, and he couldn't resist leaning forward and pressing his lips there again.

She responded instantly, her lips yielding easily. He had no idea how much time went by before she pulled back with a gasped, "I almost forgot about the food."

"Right. The food," he murmured, bending to touch his lips to hers again.

"Simeon." She pushed a gentle hand to his chest but deepened the kiss before pulling back again. "Benjamin would kill me if we didn't eat this."

"He never has to know." Simeon slid a wayward piece of hair behind her ear.

She laughed but shook her head and turned to the counter.

"All right," Simeon grumbled. "I'll eat, but on one condition." He caught her hand and pulled her back into his chest.

"What's that?" Abigail sounded as breathless as he felt.

"We kiss some more after dinner," he said into her hair.

"I think I can live with that." She turned and popped a light kiss onto his lips before moving to the counter to grab the meat. Simeon eyed it. Everything looked delicious, but he was pretty sure this was going to be the fastest meal he'd ever eaten.

Chapter 30

Abigail turned up the volume of Lydia's new album, combing out her wet hair and singing along to her sister-in-law's soulful tune about trusting God even in the storm. After spending her day off hiking with Ireland, she'd desperately needed a shower before tonight's date with Simeon.

He hadn't told her where he was taking her, but it didn't matter. As long as she got to be with him, she'd be content. Snugging her robe tight around herself, she made the short trip from the bathroom to the bedroom.

Of course, not knowing where they were going did make it harder to get dressed.

She pulled out her phone and sent him a quick text: *Can I at least have a wardrobe hint?*

She moved to the closet, skimming through her clothes as she waited for a response. On the other side of the space, Simeon's shirts hung all neat and tidy, and on an impulse, she grabbed one and buried her face in it, pulling in the faint trace of his warm, masculine scent.

For the past week, she hadn't been able to get enough of that scent. Hadn't been able to get enough of his arms around her. Hadn't been able to get enough of his kisses.

She wondered if this was what their relationship had always been like—kisses at breakfast, kisses when they said goodbye, kisses when they returned home, kisses as they snuggled on the couch to watch a movie.

Something Ireland had said when Abigail had mentioned that Simeon was taking her out tonight had made her think maybe not.

"It's so good to see you two happy again," Ireland had said.

When Abigail had asked what she meant, Ireland had stammered a couple of times before saying, "I mean, after the accident and everything. It's been hard on all of us." But her flustered look, combined with the way she'd quickly changed the subject, had made Abigail question whether she'd been referring to something else.

Her phone dinged with a text, and Abigail pushed aside the thought. Whatever things may have been like in the past, it didn't matter. What mattered was the state of their relationship right now. And that was pretty great.

She turned on her phone, the smile that tugged at her lips when she spotted Simeon's text further confirmation that she had nothing from the past to worry about.

You'll look beautiful whatever you wear, the text read. *But jeans would probably be good. Can't wait to see you.*

Can't wait to see you either, she texted in response. She added a little heart emoji after the words but then deleted it before she hit send. As much as she loved being with him and kissing him, she wasn't sure if she was quite ready to say she loved *him* yet, even in an emoji.

But if things kept going the way they were, she could see how it might not be too long . . .

She shook her head and pulled a soft blue sleeveless shirt off a hanger. She'd asked Simeon not to pressure her into saying she loved him—and she wasn't going to pressure herself either.

She slipped into the shirt, then moved to the dresser to find a pair of jeans. But the first pair she pulled out of the drawer refused to budge when it hit her hips, and though the second pair made it farther, she had to decide between zipping it and breathing. She pulled it back off with a dismayed grunt. Apparently, Past Abigail hadn't wanted to admit her clothes didn't fit anymore. She glanced at the time. She still had an hour before Simeon would be home. She might as well go through all these jeans and get rid of the ones that didn't fit.

The next pair she tried on was snug but tolerable. She left them on and bent to pull out the remaining pairs. Something smooth and shiny caught her eye as she lifted the jeans out. It looked like— Was that a laptop?

She set the jeans aside and reached for it.

Sure enough. It was a computer.

But what was it doing in her dresser drawer?

She carried it to the bed and sat, ignoring the way the jeans dug into her waist. She opened the laptop and pressed the power button, but nothing happened. It must be dead.

She set the computer on the bed and moved back to the dresser, but there was no cord in the drawer.

Oh well, she should finish getting ready anyway. She tried on the last couple pairs of jeans, grateful when the final one hugged her hips without squeezing too tight.

She still needed to put on some makeup and do something with her hair, which was probably air drying into a fuzzy mop.

Her eyes went to the computer again.

Maybe there was a cord in the drawer of her nightstand. She moved to check, but all she found there was some lip balm and hand lotion. She scanned the room, but there were no other obvious places to store a computer cord.

Wait. Obvious places.

Simeon's office? He kept a laptop in there. Maybe it was the same kind.

She strode down the hall and into his office. His laptop sat on the desk, an unplugged cord gathered next to it. She hurried across the room and scooped it up, glancing at the recliner Simeon had slept in every night since she'd come home. He hadn't complained once, but she couldn't imagine the old thing was nearly as comfortable as the bed.

She pushed the guilt aside—it had been Simeon's idea—and rushed back to the bedroom.

She plugged the laptop in, then plopped onto the bed and waited impatiently for it to load, though she couldn't explain why she felt so compelled to see what it held.

When it had finished loading, she glanced at the icons on the screen. It looked much like the computer they used at work—web browser, email, word processing software. Her eyes went to the bottom of the screen. It looked like she'd left her email and some kind of document open. She clicked on the email program first and scrolled through a list of hundreds of unopened emails—but they all appeared to be ads.

She clicked over to the document instead.

The cursor blinked at the top of a blank page, and for a second Abigail thought that was all there was to the document. But then her eyes fell to the page numbers. Apparently, this was page 176 of 176. She scrolled up, past pages and pages full of words, until she reached the beginning.

It read, "*Title to Come* by Abigail Calvano."

Abigail stared at the words.

Title? As in . . .

Had she been writing a book?

She scrolled to the next page, which started, "Chapter One."

Apparently she had.

Her eyes went to the text.

There are things, it began, *that a person can never forget, no matter how hard they try. No matter how much they want to.*

She snorted. If she had written this, that was some twisted irony. She kept reading.

But maybe, maybe if I get the words out—if I put the memories on the page—maybe I'll finally be able to let them go.

Abigail stared at the screen, her pulse throbbing against her skull so hard that she couldn't think.

Was this— Had she written down her memories? Was her entire past in the pages of this book?

Her hand trembled as she tried to scroll again, sending the mouse on a wild chase across the page.

She had to calm down. Simeon had shown her hundreds—probably thousands—of pictures of her past, and none of those had brought her memories back. This book—or whatever it was—might not either.

But she kept reading, trying to take in what it said about her child-hood in an affluent political family.

That made no sense.

Simeon had told her that her parents died when she was ten, and she'd grown up in the foster system.

Could he have lied to her about that? And if so, why?

As the pages went by, the book made less and less sense. And yet, it gave her that same sort of déjà vu feeling she'd gotten when Simeon had asked if he could kiss her. It was a vague feeling, and it didn't help her conjure up anything beyond the words on the page, but it was strong enough to make her wonder if it could be real.

"There you are."

The sound of Simeon's voice made her jump and look up.

"What are you—" Simeon stopped halfway across the room, then rushed to her side. "What's wrong?"

"What is this?" She passed the computer to him as he sat next to her.

He scanned the open document. "I'd forgotten all about this. It's your book. It's good, isn't it?" He looked proud.

"I . . . It's . . . Is it true?"

"True?" Simeon stared at her blankly. "That you wrote it? Of course."

"I mean, is the book true? About me?"

"About you?" Simeon's brow wrinkled, and he looked back at the screen. "Oh, you mean like is this a memoir?" He chuckled. "No. It's a novel."

A novel.

She tried to understand. "But it says *I*."

Simeon shrugged. "Lots of novels are written in first person."

Abigail nodded. "I guess so, but . . ." She shook her head, but she couldn't push away the feeling.

"But?" Simeon asked gently, setting the computer aside and moving closer to grasp her hands in his.

"But it feels . . . familiar."

"That's good." Simeon's brow smoothed. "You wrote it, so the fact that it feels familiar is really good."

"No, I mean—" She pulled her hands out of his to run her fingers through her hair. "It feels . . . *Real*."

Simeon still seemed unperturbed. "That's because you're a talented writer. You made it feel real to me too."

Abigail shook her head and stood, pacing to the window. She stared out at the still leaves of the magnolia. "Not real like a good story. Real like . . . memories." She could only whisper the last word.

"Abigail, listen to me." The bed creaked as Simeon stood, and his footsteps moved toward her. His hands fell gently on her arms, and he turned her to face him.

"I can only imagine how disconcerting it is not to have those empty spaces in your past filled in. But the book is *fiction,* not memories."

She bit her lip, trying to convince herself that he was right. He had to be, didn't he?

"How can you be so sure?" she asked.

He rubbed his hands up and down her arms. "Have you read all of it?"

She shook her head. "Just the beginning."

"Trust me, if you read the rest of it, you'll see that it can't possibly be anything but made up."

"Why?" She felt her own brow crunch. "Are there aliens or something?"

Simeon's laugh was rich and deep, and it made her laugh too. She was being ridiculous about this whole thing.

"No," he finally said. "No aliens. But the things your main character does—they're not things you could ever have done."

"Well, now I'm curious." Abigail glanced toward the laptop.

Simeon stepped to the side to block her view. "You can read more of it later. For now, are you ready to go?"

"Go? Oh. Our date." She clapped her hands to her half-dry hair. "I'm so sorry. I was in the middle of getting ready when I found the computer. Why was it in the dresser anyway?" She launched herself out of Simeon's grasp and grabbed a brush off the dresser. She was going to have to settle for a ponytail tonight.

"I'm not sure." Simeon came up behind her and dropped a kiss onto her neck that made her stop brushing.

She spun and let her lips dust across his. "I just need five minutes to finish getting ready."

"You look perfect just the way you are." Simeon brought his mouth back to hers. "I can think of another way to spend those five minutes."

She laughed but pushed him away gently. "Don't you want to change too?"

He glanced down at his dress shirt and slacks. "Yeah. I guess I should." He wrapped an arm around her waist and pulled her close for another kiss, then released her and moved to the closet to grab a change of clothes.

"See you in three minutes," he said as he left the room. A second later, the bathroom door clicked shut, and Abigail found herself making her way back to the computer.

She picked it up but then set it right back down. She was supposed to be preparing for a date in the present—not figuring out if she lived in a fictional past.

Simeon dropped into the recliner. His date with Abigail tonight hadn't gone exactly as planned, and he blamed himself. He'd bought them tickets to see Shakespeare's *The Comedy of Errors* at an outdoor theater near Brampton. He'd been prepared for the mosquitoes, with plenty of bug spray. But what he hadn't been prepared for was the way all of the mistaken identities in the play would capture Abigail's imagination.

"How do you know I don't have a secret identity I never told you about?" she'd asked on the way home. "And that's what my book is about."

He hadn't meant to outright laugh at that, but the idea was so preposterous. Still, his reaction had hurt her, and he knew the only reason for such a ridiculous question was that she needed *something* to fill in the gaping hole that was her memory of everything before the accident.

He'd apologized, and she'd accepted it, but that didn't change the fact that she'd gone straight to bed when they got home. She was probably in there, reading more of the book, right now.

Well, good. That was good.

She'd read it and see that it couldn't be true. She'd never been the daughter of a state senator like her protagonist. Never gone to nursing school like her protagonist. And certainly never gotten involved in a car theft ring like her protagonist.

Simeon shook his head against the back of his chair. He had no doubt that Abigail had always kept some secrets—she'd never been willing to talk about her time in foster care. But to think that she had an entirely different identity as a car thief—that would strain the credulity of even the most gullible person.

He closed his eyes. He might as well take advantage of some extra sleep.

But an hour later, he was still wide awake. With a resigned sigh, he got up and moved to his desk. If he couldn't sleep, he might as well get some work done. But his laptop battery was almost dead—he thought of the cord he'd seen snaking from Abigail's computer—so he gave up on that too. After he closed the computer, he just sat there for a few minutes, before opening his drawer and pulling out a notebook and a pen.

He opened to the first page and let his pen hover there for a moment. Was this a good idea?

He shook his head. He'd run it past Everlee before deciding whether to show it to Abigail. But if she wanted a book about her past, he could give her a book about her past—about *their* past.

He'd just finished writing about the first day they'd met in Ecuador—when he'd told her not to touch a glass dolphin figurine in the market, as if she were a child, and she'd thrown him a defiant look, picked it up, and moved it two feet down the shelf, then turned and flounced away—when a strange sound caught his ears. He stopped writing and listened. There it was again—a muted shout. He shoved his chair back and took off for Abigail's room. The door was closed, and no light shone through the crack at the bottom.

Maybe he'd been imagining things. Or maybe it had been from outside. Sometimes the neighbor's dog barked at night.

He started to shuffle away, but the sound broke through again, more like a whimper than a shout this time. He turned and pushed the bedroom door open. Abigail had kicked all the blankets off but lay curled up in the center of the bed, her arms wrapped around herself, as if she were scared. She made that whimpering sound again.

Simeon crossed quickly to the bed and touched a gentle hand to her shoulder. "Abigail, wake up."

He had to repeat it twice before she opened her eyes, blinking up at him. "Simeon, what—"

"Shh. You were having a bad dream." He reached for the covers and pulled them over her.

She clutched at them. "There was a man." Her words came in short, gasping bursts. "He was holding my arm so tight, and I was telling him to let me go. But he said there was nowhere for me to go."

Simeon dropped onto the bed next to her, gathering her closer so that her head was in his lap. "Shh," he soothed, running a palm over her damp hair. "It was just a dream."

Her head shook back and forth against his leg. "I called the man Garrick. Just like in the book." She shuddered. "I think— I think it was a memory."

"Sweetheart, listen to me," Simeon said firmly. "It wasn't a memory." He said the words slowly and clearly. "It was a dream. You read the book earlier, and your mind took all those ideas and threw them together into a dream. It's like that time you had a dream that I turned into Spider-Man after we watched the movie."

"I don't remember that," she whispered.

"I know you don't." Simeon brushed her hair back from her cheek. "But I do. Okay?"

She didn't say anything, and he sighed. "This is normal. It's called confabulation. Your brain is inventing false memories to fill in the gaps. And it's using whatever it can to do it."

"It doesn't feel like false memories," Abigail insisted. "It feels like . . . Like that déjà vu feeling I got when we kissed. Was that con- con- whatever?"

"Confabulation," Simeon said quietly. "And I don't know." The words tore at his ribs on their way out. When she'd mentioned the déjà vu the other day, he'd allowed himself to hope that maybe somewhere, on some level, she did remember.

But if she thought she also remembered being a car thief . . .

"You should go back to sleep." Gently, he slid her head back to her pillow. "Do you want me to stay with you?"

"No. I think I'm okay." Abigail curled her arm around the blankets.

Simeon brushed a kiss over her forehead, trying to swallow his disappointment.

He was halfway to the door when Abigail called his name.

He stopped.

"Did I really dream you were Spider-Man?" she asked.

"Yeah. You did."

"That's silly." She yawned. "You'd make a much better Batman."

Simeon chuckled. "Goodnight, Abigail. I lo— Sleep well."

"You too," she murmured.

Simeon watched her for a moment, then made himself close the door.

Chapter 31

Abigail readjusted herself on the stool at the kitchen counter and stared at the blinking cursor. She'd just finished reading her book for the eighth time in a week, and she wondered, as she did every time, what came next?

She'd searched the computer, hoping to find notes or an outline or something that would give her a clue to what she'd been thinking. But there seemed to be nothing. Because the whole story was already in her head? Because she had lived through it?

She gnawed at her lip. After a few days of her incessant questioning, Simeon had suggested that she stop reading and obsessing over the story. So Abigail had stopped bringing it up to him. But that didn't mean she was ready to let it go. Not when every time she read it, it felt more like a memory than it had before.

She supposed Simeon could be right. It could be confabulation, or whatever it was that he'd called it. That was probably the logical answer—otherwise, how had she ended up here, in River Falls, with Simeon?

She saw now why he'd said the book couldn't be her memories. He didn't want to believe she could have been a car thief. Neither did she. Not really. But what if . . .

She shook her head, reading the last page again.

I felt invincible, like we owned the world, as Garrick revved the Jag's engine. He'd said he lifted it from some unscrupulous lawyer. But I didn't care at this point.

The thrill. That was what I was in this for.

He's going to ruin your life, *a little voice in the back of my head yelled. But I pretended I couldn't hear it over the scream of the tires on the road.*

Abigail touched her fingers to the keyboard, closing her eyes, trying to picture the next part of the story. Whether it was her memoir or just a story she'd made up, shouldn't she be able to figure out what came next?

But there was nothing.

With a sigh, she closed the computer. She was going to be late to meet Simeon at work so they could head over to Everlee's office together. They'd finally bought a new car to replace the totaled one a few days ago, and it turned out that she did remember how to drive. Simeon had made her drive around and around town to prove it.

She ran upstairs and tucked the laptop into the dresser drawer so Simeon wouldn't know she'd been reading it. Then she charged back down the stairs, grabbed the keys, and ran out the door.

Thankfully, she didn't have to think very hard about what to do as her body seemed to take over. She turned up the volume on the Christian radio station Ruth always had on at the bookstore and that Abigail had come to enjoy—not least because they played a couple of Lydia's songs.

She was making a left turn into the downtown area when the sound of a siren made her jump. Her eyes flicked to the rearview mirror, though she was sure she hadn't been speeding.

But the lights were right behind her, and when Abigail slowed and pulled to the shoulder to let the officer pass, the patrol car pulled up behind her.

She gripped the wheel tightly. Now what?

She had no idea if she'd ever been pulled over before, but if she had, she didn't remember what to do.

She watched in the mirror as the police car's door opened. The moment the officer stepped out, her chest caved in. She'd only seen Simeon's brother Zeb a couple of times, from a distance, but the brothers all looked enough alike that it couldn't be anyone else.

From what she understood, the accident hadn't been her fault—but she'd also been the one driving. And she'd survived, while his wife hadn't.

Sweat slicked her palms, but still she couldn't release her grip on the steering wheel. Zeb reached the side of the car and made a motion for her to roll down the window.

Right.

She pried her fingers off the wheel and pressed the window button.

"Abigail?" Zeb sounded completely taken aback.

"Yes," Abigail said meekly. "Was I speeding?"

"Uh. No." Zeb rubbed a hand over his hair the same way Simeon did when he was uncomfortable. "You don't have a license plate. Did you— Is this a new car?"

"Oh. Yeah." She looked away, hoping he wasn't thinking about what had happened to her old one. "Simeon said he did all the paperwork, but—"

"No, I mean, it's okay. Just had to make sure the vehicle wasn't stolen. Been a rash of car thefts in the area lately."

"Oh. Um. No. Not stolen." A shaky laugh slipped out. Oh goodness, did that make her sound guilty?

"Well, okay." Zeb tapped the car. "I'll let you get on your way then." He stepped away from the vehicle.

"Zeb. Wait." Abigail closed her eyes. She didn't know what she thought she was going to say. There were no words. But she couldn't just not say anything.

She opened her eyes to find him standing still but staring at his police car.

"I'm sorry." The words felt so very inadequate, but they were all she had. "About your wife."

Zeb shook his head but then turned and met her eyes. "It's not your fault. Carly wouldn't want you to blame yourself." He strode back to his car, leaving Abigail to blink back the sting of tears.

The rest of the drive to Simeon's office was blurry as she kept swiping at her eyes. She hadn't even realized she'd been burdened by guilt over Carly's death until Zeb had set her free from it.

She pulled into a parking spot and gave her eyes a more thorough drying, then took a breath and headed for Simeon's building. His office door was closed, so she took a seat in the reception area. She'd been here a couple of times with Simeon, and he'd told her that she'd helped decorate it—which might explain why she felt more at home in the comfy blue chairs than in the stark whites of Everlee's lobby.

She thumbed absently through a magazine but set it down again as the door to Simeon's office opened.

A dark-haired woman stepped out, and though Abigail couldn't recall ever using the word ravishing, it was the first word that popped into her head. Thick curls spilled over the woman's shoulders, her low-cut blouse and clingy skirt emphasizing a figure Abigail had thought existed only on dolls.

"Abigail." The woman headed in her direction with a wide smile. "Wendy. We met at the store, remember?" the woman said just as the memory clicked into place. No wonder it had taken a moment—Abigail was pretty sure Wendy hadn't been dressed like *this* at the store.

Abigail's eyes went from Wendy to Simeon, and she tried to decide whether his frown was meant for her or for the other woman.

"When was this?" he asked.

"Oh, a couple of weeks ago," Wendy said breezily. "Abigail was there with some other guy." She giggled as if she had given away some big secret.

"Benjamin," Abigail murmured.

Simeon nodded. "We should get going."

"Oh, right." Wendy turned and sashayed toward the door. "See you next week." She waved, and the door chime tinkled as it opened then swung shut behind her.

Simeon let out an audible breath. "Sorry about that. Her session was supposed to be done fifteen minutes ago."

Abigail wanted to ask why Wendy was seeing him, what they talked about, but it was none of her business.

"It's okay," she said instead. "I just got here a minute ago. I had a little encounter on the way over."

"An encounter?" Simeon was staring toward the parking lot, and Abigail followed his gaze to where Wendy was getting into a black SUV.

Something in Abigail's chest jerked. Should she be worried about her husband spending time alone with a woman who looked like that?

Of course not. Simeon was a loving husband. He would never—

Well, how did she know what he would never do, when she could only remember back two months?

She shook the question off. She may not remember very far back—but in the time she did remember, he had never once shown anything but complete devotion to her.

"Abigail?"

She turned to find Simeon studying her. "What kind of encounter?"

She told him about getting pulled over by Zeb, her composure slipping a little as she recounted his comment about not blaming herself. Simeon pulled her into his arms and stroked her hair. "I'm glad the two of you talked. Though I wish he would have chosen a better forum."

Abigail laughed into his shirt, letting his now-familiar scent comfort her. He dropped a kiss onto the top of her head, and she knew without a doubt—there was no way this man was cheating on her.

∾

Simeon washed his hands, then stood letting them drip into the sink. He shouldn't be so shaken up by learning that Abigail had met Wendy at the store. It was a small town—people ran into each other all the time. It wasn't like Wendy had sought Abigail out. They'd probably struck up a conversation in the checkout line or something.

He was only agitated because he hadn't made a lot of progress with Wendy over the last couple of weeks. And she'd chosen today's session to casually mention that she was aware Abigail had started divorce proceedings before the accident. Simeon had calmly—he hoped—explained that the session was not about him or his relationship but about her, and she'd seemed to move on from there. But the way she'd run up to Abigail in the waiting area—Simeon had nearly had a heart attack at the prospect of Wendy mentioning the divorce to his wife.

He shook off his hands and grabbed a paper towel. Wendy may not have gotten past her feelings for him yet, but she wasn't malicious. It was his job to help her, and he was going to do that.

He tossed the paper towel in the trash and strode back to the lobby of Everlee's office. Everlee and Abigail were already involved in an animated conversation. Or rather, Abigail was animated. Everlee was listening with the same calm, neutral expression he used with his own clients.

"I don't know how to explain it." Abigail's words reached him halfway across the lobby. "It's like, when I'm reading it, it feels so *real*. Like I've *been* there, done those things."

Simeon accidentally let an impatient sound escape his throat. Both Everlee and Abigail turned toward him, Everlee's expression surprised, Abigail's annoyed.

"Why don't we step inside and talk some more." Everlee directed them into her office. Simeon suppressed a weary sigh. He knew Abigail wanted a past—but imagining that the things in that book could be her past was a waste of time. He'd suggested that she stop rereading it—but he suspected that the book was the reason she'd gone to bed early every night this week. And the reason the progress they'd been making on their relationship had pretty much stalled. Why every time he kissed her, she seemed distracted and far away, as if she was comparing his kisses to those of some fictional character.

They both sat on the couch, though there was a much wider gap between them than there had been last week, when he'd wrapped his arm around her shoulder and she'd pressed herself into his side.

"Abigail mentioned to me that she found a book she was writing," Everlee said as she settled into the chair across from them. "You know she was writing a book?"

Simeon nodded. "I had read some of it, yes." He didn't mention how he'd come across it on her computer. "It's very good. Very realistic feeling," he added pointedly.

Abigail threw her hands in the air. "Why can't you admit that it *could* be true?"

"For one, you *told* me it was a novel," Simeon answered evenly. "For two, if you really were a car thief, don't you think you'd be in prison? And for three, I *know* you, Abigail. The woman in that story is *not you*."

Abigail crossed her arms and shook her head. "Then why does it feel like it is?" she asked quietly.

"I told you." Simeon rubbed a hand over his rough cheeks. "Your brain doesn't like having gaps. It's trying to fill them in."

Abigail turned to Everlee. "Isn't there any chance it's true?"

Everlee considered. "I suppose it's possible."

Simeon started to interrupt, but Everlee held up a hand. "But it's unlikely. It's much more likely, as Simeon said, that your brain wants something—anything—to fill in those gaps. And since the story is written in your voice, it makes sense that it would feel like memories."

Abigail shook her head, refusing to look at either of them. Simeon's heart softened. As frustrating as this was for him, it had to be a thousand times more so for her. He reached for her hand, and she let him take it, though she didn't lace her fingers through his.

"Simeon, you seem upset about Abigail's feelings about the book. Why?" Everlee asked.

Simeon sighed. It was exactly the question he would have asked in her place—but it was really annoying to be the one on the receiving end of it.

"I'm not upset," he finally said. "I'm . . . frustrated, I guess. We agreed to stop trying to force the memories and to start our relationship over again from the beginning. And it was going so well. We were spending time together, getting to know each other again. Kissing—a lot." He squeezed Abigail's hand, and she ducked her head, but he saw the soft smile that hovered on her lips. "But it feels like once you found that book, that was the only thing you could think about. Instead of moving forward. I want to keep moving forward, Abigail."

She looked up, meeting his eyes. "Me too."

He let out what may have been the world's biggest breath. "Good." He leaned forward to set a soft kiss on her lips.

"Wow, I *am* good," Everlee said from her chair, and they all laughed.

The three of them talked for a while longer, Simeon allowing himself to slide closer to Abigail every few minutes, until he was near enough to wrap an arm around her.

"Daisy's?" he asked as they walked to their vehicle after the session was over. The sun kissed the top of the mountains to the west, and Simeon let his heart release the stresses of the day. Talking to Everlee had been good for them.

"Absolutely." Abigail wiggled her fingers in between his. "I'm sorry I spent so much time obsessing over the book," she said as they neared downtown River Falls. "I know you're probably right that it's just a story I made up. Anyway—" She sighed. "The way my heart almost beat a hole in my chest when Zeb pulled me over before, I'm pretty sure I couldn't be a car thief."

Simeon chuckled and lifted her knuckles to his lips. "That's what I'm saying."

Chapter 32

"Wow. There are a lot of people here." Abigail clung to Simeon's hand as they wove through the crowds surging into Founder's Park as dusk fell around them.

Simeon turned to grin at her. "Yeah, tickets sold out weeks ago. Good thing we're family."

"I guess so." Abigail had been listening to Lydia's songs, but this was her first time seeing her in concert—that she remembered—and she'd had no idea that her sister-in-law was so famous.

"There's Joseph." Simeon pointed to his brother, who was waving both arms over his head from the front row of seats that had been set up in the grassy area in front of the stage. It took a little more weaving and jostling, but they finally made their way to the section the entire Calvano family had already claimed.

"Abigail." Ava wrapped her in a hug, followed by Ireland, whose baby bump was just starting to show.

"Look at you." Abigail couldn't help gushing. "I have your blanket almost done. And then I'll start on yours," she promised Ava.

Would she someday be knitting one for her own baby?

The question flashed briefly through her mind, but she didn't let herself dwell on it. She was content with where things were in her relationship with Simeon right now. It was way too soon to think about children.

"Do you want anything to drink?" Simeon's breath whispered over her shoulder, and Abigail shook her head but let herself lean back into him. Both Ava and Ireland grinned at them.

"Good evening." From the stage, a man Abigail didn't recognize called out to the crowd.

"That's Harrison Bemis," Simeon whispered as they took their seats. "He organizes Builders for the Kingdom projects. If Liam had waited any longer to ask Lydia out, I'm pretty sure Harrison would have asked her."

Abigail nodded, glancing down the row. She spotted Liam's teenage daughter Mia but not Liam. "Where is he?" she asked.

"Managing the lighting, I'm sure. Or sneaking a last-minute kiss." Simeon snuck his own kiss onto Abigail's lips, and she laughed, resting her head on his shoulder.

She hadn't looked at the laptop once all week, and putting it away was the best thing she could have done. With some distance from the story, she could see that it had been absurd to think it could be her memoir. And that had allowed her to accept that she might never know her past. To focus on moving forward.

With Simeon.

She impulsively lifted her head to kiss his cheek.

He turned to her with a surprised smile. "What was that for?"

She shrugged. "I'm just happy."

"Good." His look said that if there weren't hundreds of people around them right now, he'd pull her in for one of those deep kisses that left her feeling lightheaded and safely anchored all at once.

Around them, the crowd broke out in wild cheers, and Abigail turned to see her sister-in-law gliding onto the stage. The music started, and Lydia's resonant alto launched into a ballad.

As the concert continued, Abigail couldn't decide if she was glowing more from the music or from Simeon's arm around her, but she supposed it didn't matter. She would just let herself soak up this night.

At the end of the first set, Ireland stood to slide past them. "Sorry. Need to use the restroom."

"I'll go with you." Abigail pushed to her feet as well. "Be right back." She squeezed Simeon's shoulder on her way past.

"I'll miss you." Simeon gave her a goofy, lopsided grin.

"Aw, you two are so adorable," Ireland said as they started toward the restrooms.

All Abigail could do was grin and nod.

Fortunately, they made it to the restroom ahead of the crowd, but by the time Abigail had washed her hands, the small room had filled, and there was nowhere left to stand.

She'd have to wait for Ireland outside.

She stepped out the door and moved away from the building to leave room for the line that had formed. Bugs flitted in the lights above, but fortunately they'd left her alone so far. She let her gaze go higher, to the stars sparkling against the dark backdrop of the sky, a smile tickling her lips as she thought of the night she and Simeon had lain out under them.

Something solid bumped against her, and Abigail took an involuntary step backwards, bringing her gaze back to earth.

"Oh, Abigail. I'm so sorry. I didn't see you." Wendy stood in front of her, smoothing the cropped tank top she wore along with a pair of denim shorts that showed off her legs.

"That's okay," Abigail mumbled. She scanned the crowd for Ireland.

"Hey, I just wanted to tell you." Wendy grasped her arm as if they were best friends. "I'm so glad you decided not to go through with the divorce. I mean, that day you came in to get the papers, someone could have knocked me over with a feather. And then with the amnesia and all. And seeing you at the store with another man. I mean, I didn't know what all to think." She finally paused to take a breath, and Abigail thought of a thousand things she could say.

But her whole body seemed to have gone numb—including her tongue.

"There you are." Ireland materialized at their side. "I thought you'd gone back to our seats, but Simeon said you never came back." She turned to Wendy. "I'm Ireland."

"Wendy. Nice to meet you."

"You too. I'm sorry to interrupt your conversation, but we'd better get back before Simeon sends out a search party. I barely stopped him the way it is." She laughed and took Abigail's arm.

"Of course. Enjoy the rest of the concert." Wendy waved and disappeared toward the stage. Abigail's eyes followed her, but the crowd had already closed in around her.

"I don't think I've ever met her before," Ireland said, steering them back toward their seats. "How do you know her?"

"I don't, really." Abigail pressed a hand to her swirling stomach, the word *divorce* still tumbling through her head.

⚜

"How about some pie before we head home?" Simeon glanced to the passenger seat, where Abigail was staring out the side window. He shifted the car into reverse and waited for a young family to cross behind them.

"Do you mind if we go home?" Abigail asked, studying the family. "I have a headache."

"Of course. Let's go home and get you some aspirin." A headache might explain why she'd been so quiet for the second half of the concert, though

Simeon had an uneasy feeling there was more to it than that. She'd gone to the restroom completely cheerful and cuddly and returned subdued and distant. And no matter how hard he had tried, he couldn't account for the change. In his experience, headaches didn't strike that quickly.

"Is something else wrong?" he asked.

"No," she answered too quickly. "It was a really nice concert. Lydia is an incredible singer."

"She is." Simeon stuffed down his frustration. He didn't want to talk about the concert. He wanted to talk about her—them. About why it was that every time their relationship seemed to be moving forward, she decided to throw things into reverse.

She'd finally let go of her crazy notion that her book could reflect her real life—and now something else was holding her back.

It had been two months since the accident. The first time they'd met, they'd been engaged within three months. Shouldn't it be faster for her to fall in love with him the second time around?

Simeon's thoughts went to the email he'd gotten earlier today, confirming their trip to Ecuador. Tomorrow was the last day he could cancel and get any money back. He'd been holding off—at first because he'd hoped she'd get her memories back in time and they could use the trip to celebrate, and later because he'd hoped their relationship might be at a point where it made sense to take a trip together.

Earlier today, he'd thought they were there. He'd planned to ask her over pie.

But now . . .

He sighed. Maybe it was best to cancel the trip rather than lose the money. They could always go someday in the future.

Assuming she stayed with him.

He pulled into their driveway and turned off the vehicle. Abigail had closed her eyes somewhere along the drive, and she didn't open them now. He reached to wake her, but she spoke before his hand made contact.

"Were we getting divorced?" Her whisper snapped around the vehicle, and Simeon yanked his hand back.

"What?"

"Were we getting divorced?" She turned her head to him, opening her eyes. In the faint glow that reached them from the porch light, he could see the doubt in them.

Something hot and sickly pooled in his stomach. "Why would you ask that?"

Abigail lowered her gaze to her hands, which were playing with a pen in the console between them. Simeon should wrap those hands in his, reassure her, but he couldn't seem to move.

"I ran into Wendy at the concert."

"Wendy," Simeon repeated dumbly.

Abigail nodded. "She said we were getting divorced. Before the accident."

Simeon's fists clenched. This time Wendy had gone too far. Talking to him about things that were none of her business was one thing. But talking to his wife—that crossed a line.

"I'm so sorry she said that to you." His voice was hard with anger, and he worked to gentle it. Abigail wasn't the one he was angry with. "She has some . . . issues. I'll talk to her."

Abigail nodded, but her pleading eyes met his. "But were we? Getting divorced?"

Carefully, Simeon took her hands in his. "No," he said firmly. "We most definitely were *not* getting divorced. Come on." He released her hands. "Let's get you inside so you can take some aspirin and go to bed."

Abigail nodded and opened her door. Simeon took her hand as they walked to the house. Inside, he sent her upstairs, promising to be up in a minute with the medicine.

He moved to the kitchen to get it, trying to ignore the bite of his conscience. He hadn't lied to Abigail. She may have had the divorce papers drawn up, but she had never given them to him.

Because she was in an accident and got amnesia.

All right. Maybe that was a technicality. But even if she had presented them to him, he would have refused to sign them. He would have fought for their marriage to his dying breath.

Just like he was doing now.

He palmed the medicine and grabbed a glass of water, then headed upstairs.

He knocked on the bedroom door, and she called for him to come in. She'd already changed from her ruffled sleeveless shirt into an oversized t-shirt that Simeon recognized as one that used to be his. Seeing her in it did something crazy to his brain.

"Let's go to Ecuador," he blurted.

"What?" Abigail looked at him as if he'd spoken a foreign language.

"I was going to surprise you for our anniversary. I'd actually bought the tickets the day of the accident. I keep meaning to cancel them, but I just can't bring myself to do it. Because I still want to go with you."

She looked doubtful. "Simeon, I don't think— I mean, my memories probably won't—"

"It's not about getting your memories back. It's about making new ones. Away from all of this." He waved a hand around. "Just you and me."

He crossed the room to pass her the water and medicine. Once she'd swallowed the pills, he took the glass from her and set it on the table, then held his hands out to her.

She set hers in them. "You really think this is a good idea?"

"I do." He held his breath until a grin broke over Abigail's face.

"Well, then, I guess I could handle a little vacation. If I have to."

"Good." Simeon pulled her to him, then dropped his head, letting his lips search out hers.

This trip would be exactly what they needed.

Chapter 33

"Are you all packed for your trip?" Lydia asked from the front seat of her car.

The other women had all graciously agreed to move up the date of their dress fitting to accommodate Simeon and Abigail's trip to Ecuador.

Abigail's stomach flipped. She still wasn't sure if she'd been crazy to say yes to Simeon's proposal that they go—and yet there was a part of her that really wanted to see this mysterious place where she'd fallen in love with him.

"Not quite yet," Abigail answered from the backseat—she, Ireland, and Mia had let Ava take the front seat since her morning sickness also gave her car sickness. "It's still five days away, so there are a lot of things I can't pack yet."

"Cómo van tus lecciones de español?" Mia asked.

Abigail scrunched her nose, thinking. *Cómo* meant how. And *español* meant Spanish, so . . .

"Pretty good?" When she'd asked Simeon if she spoke Spanish, he'd said she had picked some up on their first trip to Ecuador—but apparently she hadn't known it well enough to retain it in her procedural memory because she didn't remember a lick of it.

Simeon, on the other hand, was fairly fluent. He'd been teaching her useful phrases like, *Dónde está el baño?* And *Cuánto cuesta?* Plus, he'd downloaded an app on her phone that she'd been using to practice. But her favorite way to study was the Spanish movies they'd been watching together. Not because of the content—she had no idea what was going on most of the time—but because it gave her an excuse to snuggle close to Simeon. To enjoy the feel of his arms around her.

To convince herself a little more each day that there was no way they had been getting divorced before the accident.

She didn't know what Wendy might have against her, but Abigail wasn't going to let the other woman come between her and Simeon.

Anyway, if Simeon were interested in Wendy, he could have easily run off with her—and Abigail would have been none the wiser. Instead, he'd stayed by her side—even when she'd tried to push him away.

"Yoohoo, Abigail." Ireland waved a hand in front of her face. "We're here."

"Oh. Sorry." Abigail unbuckled her seatbelt and jumped out of the car.

"It's okay." Lydia gave her a squeeze as they made their way to the boutique's door. "We've all gotten lost in thoughts of our men before."

"Ew, stop. Your man is my dad," Mia protested.

The women were still laughing as they entered the store.

"That's what I like to see." Gloria, the cheerful shop owner, scurried toward them. "A group of ladies loving life. Come on, I have your dresses all ready."

As Abigail trailed behind the other women, she turned Gloria's words over in her head. *Loving life.*

Yes, she supposed that was a fair assessment of how she felt right now. She still had no idea what her life had been before, but it seemed to matter less and less each day. Whatever her life had been, she was loving *this* life, right now.

Gloria escorted them into the dressing rooms, and there was shuffling and rustling as they all changed.

Abigail emerged first, examining herself in the oversized mirrors. The dress fit perfectly, emphasizing her curves in a way that was flattering. Ava came out next, looking slightly pale from the drive but still glowing with the way the dress's soft green tones set off her red hair. She rarely wore makeup to cover the scars on her face that Abigail had learned were from a fire, but they didn't detract from her natural beauty at all.

Ireland stepped out of her dressing room, running a hand over the spot where the dress pulled taut over her growing baby bump. "I think mine is going to need to be let out some more," she said with a chuckle.

"Lydia, are you coming out?" Ava called. "We're dying to see the dress."

"Almost ready," Lydia responded, and a second later, her dressing room door opened. Gloria emerged first with a wide smile. "It's perfect."

When Lydia stepped out, they all gasped, then hurried toward her, echoing Gloria's sentiments.

Tears streamed down Lydia's face, and she brushed them away with a laugh. "I don't even know why I'm crying."

"Because you're happy." Ava wiped at her own wet cheeks. "I blame the baby for my tears."

"Oh, come on." Ireland nudged Ava. "You cried so much at your own wedding, and there was no baby to blame it on then."

Ava sniffed with a laugh. "That's true. I don't know how you stayed so calm and collected for yours. I think I cried more than you did, and I was just the photographer."

A pang went through Abigail. She'd been at those weddings too. But she had no memory of them. She couldn't even remember her own wedding.

"And you." Ava pointed at Abigail. "Joseph told me you drove his mama nuts because you were so calm about the wedding day and all the planning. You told her you didn't really care about all the hoopla." Ava laughed. "I always thought that was very brave of you because she definitely *did* care about the hoopla."

"I just wanted to marry Simeon," Abigail said simply.

The other women froze, staring at her.

"Is that—" Lydia lifted up the floofy skirt of her dress and bustled closer. "Do you remember that?"

"I—" Abigail stammered. She hadn't really thought about it before she'd said it. Somehow she'd just known it was true. She'd felt it. But did that make it a memory?

She searched her brain for even the slightest detail from her wedding day. But there was nothing.

"I don't know," she finally answered.

"It's a memory of your heart," Ava said, and the others nodded.

Abigail forced herself to nod along, even though she wasn't sure there was such a thing as a memory of the heart.

Still, she couldn't help but hope there was.

Chapter 34

Simeon finished his email to Pastor Mateo, confirming details for his and Abigail's arrival in Baños de Agua Santa. He couldn't wait to reintroduce Abigail to everything they had fallen in love with in Ecuador. Including each other. Only a few more days . . .

But first he had to get through the next appointment. He'd been dreading it all week. But he had to tell Wendy that she'd crossed a line, mentioning the divorce to Abigail. Guilt gnawed at him yet again for not telling Abigail the full truth about that. But it would only hurt her, make her have questions and doubts where she was starting to have trust and certainty. Not only in him but in their life together.

The chime over the exterior door clanged. It had never sounded so ominous.

Simeon shook his head at himself. He was overreacting. He'd had harder talks than this with plenty of clients.

He pushed to his feet and strode to the door. Might as well get this over with.

"That was speedy. I didn't even have time to sit down." Wendy sounded bright and cheerful, and she hit him with her wide smile.

When Simeon didn't return it, her expression faltered. "What's wrong? Are you mad at me?"

"Come have a seat." Simeon stepped back as she entered the room so she couldn't "inadvertently" brush into him.

"Okay." Her voice wobbled a little, and Simeon made himself soften his expression. He wasn't trying to upset her.

"I understand that you spoke to my wife at the concert last week," he said as he sat.

"Oh, yeah. I ran into her at the— Is that not allowed?" Wendy crossed one leg over the other, causing her slim skirt to ride up her leg.

Simeon averted his eyes. "You upset her," he said evenly.

"I did? I'm so sorry. I didn't mean—"

"You told her we were getting divorced."

Wendy shook her head. "I said I was glad you *weren't* getting divorced." Her eyes widened. "Is that why she seemed so surprised? She didn't remember?"

"I'd prefer if you stayed out of my private life," Simeon replied. "That includes not talking to my wife."

"Of course." Wendy leaned forward. "Why didn't you tell her? Are you afraid she would go through with it?"

Simeon's hands tightened, and his neck knotted. "Did you do those journal exercises we talked about?"

Wendy shook her head. "How can you be so blind? She was going to *divorce* you. And now she doesn't even remember you."

Simeon stood. "I think you should go."

Wendy blinked up at him. "I still have forty minutes."

"I won't charge you. I think it'd be best if you found a new counselor."

"Wait. What?" Wendy jumped to her feet. "You're firing me?"

Simeon made himself nod. He hated to give up on a client, but it was clear that he wasn't helping her. "I can get you the names of some other counselors."

"No. Please. You can't. You're the only one who can help me. I just know it."

Please, Simeon, pick up the phone. You're the only one who understands. That had been Steve's message the night he'd taken his own life.

It's not the same, he told himself.

But it sure *felt* the same.

A tear trickled down Wendy's cheek. "I'm such a horrible person. Why do I always do this?"

Simeon sighed. Based on what she'd told him about her childhood, this kind of behavior wasn't surprising.

"You're not a horrible person," he said. "You're confused and you're hurting and you think I'm the one who can help you. But I'm not."

"Yes. You are, Simeon. I know you are."

He couldn't tell if she lunged or fell forward, but suddenly she was much too close, and he had to catch her arms to keep her from running into him.

The next thing he knew, a pair of lips—hot and wet—pressed to his, and hands clutched at his shoulders.

Simeon reared back, shoving her arms away and jerking out of her grasp.

"I— What—" He was breathing too heavily to get more than a word out at a time. It didn't matter. His brain wasn't working anyway.

"Oh, I shouldn't have done that." Wendy took a step backwards. "I'm sorry. I didn't mean to— I think maybe—"

"You. Need. To. Leave." Simeon kept his voice calm, his words measured.

"Okay. Yes. I'll leave." Wendy took a step backwards, running her fingers over her lips. "I'll see you when you get back from your trip?"

"I'll send you the names of a couple of counselors I'd recommend." He marched to the door.

"No one else will be able to help me," she wailed, not following.

"They will." Simeon opened his office door and waited for her to cross the room—much too slowly—and step into the reception area.

He followed her out, jumping as his eyes fell on Zeb, sitting against the back wall. How much of that had his brother heard?

Wendy stopped at the exterior door, tears streaming down her cheeks.

Simeon darted a glance at Zeb. "Goodbye, Wendy."

She nodded mutely and slid through the door.

When she was gone, Simeon let out a long, slow breath, counting to ten before he turned to face his brother.

"Rough one?" Zeb asked.

Simeon snorted. "You could say that. What's up?"

Zeb stared at his hands, which were running up and down a crease in his pants. "I was wondering if you had a minute to talk?"

"For you, bro? Yeah, I've got a minute."

Chapter 35

"Are you sure we didn't forget anything?" Abigail opened her purse as Simeon pulled out of the driveway, though she couldn't have said what she was looking for.

"Hmm?" Simeon pulled onto the street, and Abigail frowned. He'd seemed distracted the last few days, and he hadn't even packed until yesterday. She'd tried to tell herself he was just preoccupied by all the things he had to arrange at work to be able to take almost two weeks off, but a not-so-tiny part of her wondered if he was having second thoughts about the trip.

"We can cancel the trip if you have too much work to do," she offered, just in case.

"What?" Simeon's head jerked toward her. "We're going." He linked his fingers into hers. "And yes, I'm sure we didn't forget anything. Anyway, all I need is you, and I'll be content."

Abigail relaxed a little into her seat. That sounded more like the Simeon she'd grown used to. "Well, you might want your passport too; otherwise, you won't be coming with me."

"My passport." Simeon braked hard enough that Abigail braced herself against the dashboard.

"Relax." She readjusted in her seat so she could grip his hand better. "I packed it."

"You're wonderful, did you know that?" Simeon's smile erased the lines of worry that had furrowed his brow for the past few days. "I don't know what I would do without you."

The words seemed to carry more weight than the lighthearted conversation warranted, but Abigail soaked them up. This man really did love her, there was no question about that. And she was starting to think she might—

"Zeb came to talk the other day, did I tell you that?"

"No." Abigail turned to him. "How's he doing?"

Simeon sighed. "He's not sleeping. Having a hard time focusing. All the usual symptoms of grief."

They spent the rest of the drive to the airport talking about Zeb and his grief, about Benjamin and Summer—whom the young Calvano still refused to talk about—about Joseph and Ava and Asher and Ireland and their babies, about Lydia and Liam's wedding, which would be only a week after they returned.

The farther they got from River Falls, the more Simeon seemed to relax.

At the airport, Abigail let him take the lead, since she had no recollection of how getting on a flight worked. It wasn't until they'd boarded the plane and settled into their seats that the turbo-powered butterflies kicked in.

"Am I afraid to fly?" she asked Simeon.

He looked at her with a raised brow. "I don't know. *Are* you?"

She gave a shaky laugh. "I think I might be."

Just then, the plane started to move, and Abigail grabbed Simeon's arm. "Is it too late to get off?"

He chuckled but slid as close to her as he could with the armrest between them. "It's okay. I'm right here with you."

Abigail knew there was nothing he could do to keep the plane in the air, any more than she could. But still, she somehow felt better, just knowing he was with her.

The plane started its descent, and Simeon turned off the book he'd been listening to. He and Abigail had spent the first few hours of the flight talking. Then they'd watched a movie, and she'd fallen asleep on his shoulder somewhere in the middle of it.

Simeon glanced at her now, reveling in the chance to just be with her—without the distractions and problems of home. He told himself for the hundredth time that he wasn't running away from his issues with Wendy. He was just giving them some distance—giving Wendy some time and space to find a new counselor.

He pressed a fist to his lips, wishing he could forget that he'd ever felt her lips there. He'd called Everlee almost immediately after it had happened, both so there'd be a record of it and to ask her to take over Wendy's counseling.

You have to tell Abigail. The thought hadn't left him alone for the past four days. But he thrust it aside. There was no way he was going to ruin their trip by telling Abigail something like that. Besides, it was a work problem—one he'd already dealt with. He had full confidence that by the time he and Abigail returned to River Falls, the separation, along with Everlee's capable counseling, would help Wendy move past her feelings for him.

The plane gave a sharp jolt, and Abigail's eyes sprang open. "What's happening?"

"Just some turbulence." Simeon brushed her hair off her cheek as she sat upright. "We're landing now."

Abigail's eyes widened. "We're here? How long did I sleep?"

Simeon chuckled. "A few hours at least."

"I'm so sorry. Were you bored?"

"Nope," Simeon answered honestly. "I had my book to listen to. Plus, I like watching you sleep."

The plane gave another jump, and Abigail clutched his arm.

"It's completely normal," he assured her. "Look out the window. We're coming in to Quito."

Abigail turned toward the window, and Simeon leaned closer to look over her shoulder, letting himself soak in the flowery scent of her hair.

"I didn't realize there would be so many mountains. How are we going to land this thing?"

Simeon chuckled and dropped a kiss onto her shoulder. "Don't worry. *We* don't have to land it. We just have to sit here and enjoy the view."

"If you say so." But Abigail leaned back into him, and Simeon nuzzled his face into her hair.

"This is amazing," Abigail breathed as they passed over the crinkled hills and canyons. "I've never seen anything like this before. I mean—" She sat up, but Simeon pulled her back to him.

"It's okay. I know what you mean. And I'm a little jealous of you, getting to experience all of this for the first time again."

They watched the ground draw closer, and then the plane bumped to a relatively smooth landing. They disembarked and managed to locate their luggage through the jostling crowds. Then Simeon led Abigail through the airport to the shuttle that would carry them south to Baños, a small city nestled in a valley of the Andes, at the edge of the Amazon rainforest.

For the next three hours, Simeon savored every delighted expression from Abigail as she took in the volcanic peaks surrounding them with rough rock formations and lush greenery.

"It's like a different world," she marveled as they passed through the thick mists of the cloud forest north of Baños.

Simeon pulled her in closer. "It changed my world."

He could only thank God for knowing exactly what—exactly *who*—he needed when he'd brought Abigail into his life.

The sun soon fell, but still Abigail watched the scenery go by, seeming eager to soak it all in. When the driver announced that they had arrived in Baños, Simeon was almost disappointed. He could have sat snuggled here with her all night.

"Baños?" Abigail turned to Simeon with a wrinkled nose. "I thought that meant bathroom."

From up front, the driver broke into loud chortles. "Baños de Agua Santa," Simeon clarified. "Baths of Sacred Water. It's named for its hot springs."

"Ah. That sounds much nicer."

The driver wound through the streets lined by brightly painted storefronts and apartments, past a large church and countless signs for llapingachos, the fried potato patties he and Abigail had devoured the first time they were here. At last, he pulled up to the address Simeon had given him.

Pastor Mateo's house was as welcoming as Simeon remembered. Warm light spilled from the small building, highlighting the cheerful yellow paint.

The driver got out to unload their luggage, and Simeon opened the door and stepped outside. Cool, damp air embraced him, and the last of his worries seemed to fall away. He turned to help Abigail out of the van.

"Oh. I thought it would be hot." She wrapped her arms around herself.

Simeon pulled her into his arms, running his hands up and down her soft skin to warm her. "It's winter here right now. Still warmer than winter at home though. It gets into the sixties during the day." He turned to tip the driver, then picked up their bags. "Come on. We'd better get inside. I'm sure Pastor Mateo and his wife can't wait another minute to see you."

"Me?" Abigail looked startled.

"Oh yes." Simeon grinned. "You were always their favorite."

As if to prove his point, the front door burst open, and a couple in their mid-sixties rushed out. Simeon barely had time to say, "They're going to hug you," before Pastor Mateo's wife Linda had thrown her arms around Abigail.

⌒⌒⌒

"It's so good to see you, cariña," the woman with the long white braid whispered as she stroked Abigail's back.

"You too," Abigail whispered back, though she didn't know why. Something about the woman's fragrance—a mix of flowers and cooking scents—gave her that déjà vu feeling she'd gotten a few times since the accident. She tried to ignore it. After the debacle with the book she had thought was real, she'd learned not to trust the feeling.

The woman loosened her hold and held Abigail back at arm's length, seeming to inspect her. "How are you? You're good?" She spoke with a faint accent, barely enough for Abigail to pick up.

"I'm— Yes, I'm good." Abigail looked to Simeon, who met her gaze with a wide grin.

"I probably should have warned you about Linda sooner," he said with a laugh.

232

"What? Warned her?" Linda let go of Abigail and swatted playfully at Simeon. "I've never harmed a fly."

"No." Simeon's grin grew. "But you sure could hug one to death."

The man Abigail assumed must be Pastor Mateo guffawed.

"Oh, you." Linda pulled Simeon into an equally fierce hug.

"See what I mean?" Simeon said over her head. But the way he returned the hug, Abigail could tell there was genuine affection there.

"Forgive our exuberant greeting." Pastor Mateo's accent was thicker than his wife's, giving his voice a musical quality. "We're just so happy to see you that we got carried away." He held out a hand. "I'm Pastor Mateo. And that's my wife Linda."

"Abigail," she said as she shook his hand—and then realized he already knew that. Just because *she* had forgotten them didn't mean they'd forgotten her.

"Come on." Linda's colorful skirt swirled around her ankles as she spun toward the house. "Let's get you settled. And then I made locro de papa."

She swished in front of them, and Abigail turned to Simeon. "Something potato, right?"

He grinned. "Yep. Potato soup." He gestured for her to follow Linda, and she heard him and Pastor Mateo fall into step behind them.

Linda ushered her through the door, and Abigail stepped into the small but welcoming space.

"The bedrooms are upstairs." Linda gestured to a narrow stairway to the right of the door.

Abigail nodded, relieved the woman had said *bedrooms*. As in, more than one. She'd been wondering what the sleeping arrangements for their trip would be.

"Go on up," Linda urged. "Your bedroom is the first one on the left."

Abigail nodded, admiring the photos that hung on the stairway wall as she climbed. At the top, she turned to the room on the left. It was simple—just a bed and a small dresser—but painted a soothing shade of blue.

"There's an air mattress in the closet." Linda bustled into the room, followed by Simeon with their luggage. "I'm sorry we don't have another room to offer you, but our granddaughter is coming in a few days to be here for vacation Bible school next week."

"It's no problem," Simeon assured Linda, even while shooting Abigail a questioning look.

"Oh." Realization hit Abigail. The air mattress was for Simeon. They were going to share a room.

She swallowed but nodded. She should probably say they didn't need to get the air mattress out—that she and Simeon could share the bed. They *were* married, after all. And it would save Linda a lot of work.

But something held her back.

"Here it is," Linda puffed as she pulled a rolled up bundle out of the closet. "We'll set it up later. But first—" She hurried to Abigail and took her arm. "Let's get you some soup. You must be starving."

"Famished," Abigail admitted as Linda led her to the stairs.

Halfway down, a picture caught her eye, and she stopped, squinting at it. A group of children posed in front of a small, squat building, all of them grinning widely. On one side of the group stood Pastor Mateo and Linda. And on the other side—

"Is that us?" She raised a hand, letting it hover over the glass.

"Yes, it is." Linda grinned. "I love that picture."

"Who are all the kids?"

"Students from vacation Bible school. You wouldn't believe it, but Marco is in high school now. Hard to believe he was that little when he was in VBS." She pointed to one of the boys.

Simeon came up behind Abigail and rested a hand on her shoulder. "He had such a crush on you. I think he was pretty devastated when you chose me over him."

They all laughed and continued down the stairs, where Linda plied them with heaping bowls of a rich, creamy-looking soup that smelled incredible. They bowed their heads, and Pastor Mateo gave thanks for the meal before they dug in. It tasted even better than it smelled, and Abigail was content to eat and let the conversation swirl around her. But she couldn't get that picture out of her head.

"So we helped with VBS?" she asked during a lull in the conversation.

"Oh, yes." Linda passed her more bread. "You were wonderful with the children. I told Mateo it was perfect timing that you were coming during VBS this year, but he reminded me you're here on vacation, not to work. And he's right, of course."

"Oh, we should help." Abigail didn't know why the idea appealed to her so much, but it did.

"Really?" Simeon paused with his spoon halfway to his mouth, sending her a look she couldn't quite define.

"Oh. Um— I mean, unless you made other plans." She should have asked him before volunteering their vacation away.

"No. I mean, yes. I mean, if VBS is next week, we can do all the touristy things this week and then help next week. If you're sure you want to."

She nodded. "It sounds fun."

Simeon's smile swept all the way through her before he turned to Linda and Mateo. "Sign us up."

"Consider yourselves hired." Pastor Mateo smiled gratefully. "One of our regular volunteers couldn't help this year—and she usually does the work of at least two people. So you are an answer to our prayers."

Abigail warmed at the words. She hadn't been trying to answer anyone's prayer—but somehow God had used her to do that anyway.

They spent the rest of the meal discussing the needs for VBS, deciding that Simeon would help with the Bible stories and games, and Abigail would help with songs and snacks.

She tried to cover her yawns as the conversation continued, but the long day of traveling was catching up with her, and she finally excused herself to go to bed.

"I'd better set up the air mattress." Simeon got up too, resting a hand on her back as they climbed the stairs.

In their room, he unrolled the air mattress and got the pump set up while Abigail got ready for bed in the bathroom. By the time she returned to the bedroom, the air mattress was full, and Simeon was rummaging through his luggage. "I'm going to get ready for bed." He closed the distance between them. "In case you're asleep by the time I get back, goodnight." He caught her lips in a long, lingering kiss.

Tired as she was, Abigail would be willing to keep kissing him all night. When he finally pulled away, he led her to the bed and pulled the covers down, tucking them around her and then bending to kiss her forehead. "Goodnight."

"Simeon?"

He paused, halfway between standing and bending over her. "Yeah?"

It would be easy. Just tell him that he didn't have to sleep on the uncomfortable-looking air mattress. They could share the bed.

"I'm glad we came," she said instead.

Simeon smiled and turned out the light. "Me too."

Chapter 36

Simeon rolled over to check the time, wincing as the air mattress creaked. It was still dark, and his phone said it was only five in the morning, but he couldn't lie in this uncomfortable contraption any longer. After sleeping on it the past few nights, he wasn't sure his back would ever recover.

Carefully, he pushed himself off the mattress, cringing every time it creaked or groaned or—somehow—growled. In the bed, Abigail rolled over but didn't seem to awaken.

Simeon tiptoed to her side, a powerful surge of love for his wife hitting him as he watched her sleep. Aside from the air mattress, everything about the past few days had been perfect. They'd biked to the area's many waterfalls, soaked in the hot springs, shopped at the markets, and taken a day trip to the Amazon. They'd talked, they'd laughed, they'd kissed. Every day, he could feel them growing closer together. Every day, he hoped it would be the magical day when she said she loved him again.

Be still, he reminded himself. *Be patient.*

He blew her a quiet kiss, then tiptoed out of the room and down the stairs. It was still dark, but Simeon had become comfortable enough with the layout of the house to maneuver through the living room toward the small kitchen.

"Hola, señor."

Simeon jumped at the small voice that came out of the dark.

"Mariana. What are you doing here in the dark?" He could just make out the silhouette of Mateo and Linda's granddaughter at the kitchen table.

"Coloring." The girl held up a crayon as if for proof.

"In the dark?"

She shrugged. "I can see. Where's Abigail? I made a picture for her."

Simeon's heart squeezed. He'd been worried, when Mariana had first arrived, that some part of Abigail might still find it difficult to be around children, even if she didn't remember all they'd been through. But Mariana and Abigail had become fast friends. Every time he saw them together, Simeon was reminded yet again of what a wonderful mother his wife would make.

"She's still sleeping," he said to Mariana. "Like you should probably be too."

"You're awake," Mariana pointed out.

"Well, yes, but I'm—"

"A grown-up." Mariana sighed. "That's what grown-ups always say."

"For your information—" Simeon pulled out a chair and sat across from her. "I was going to say I'm weird."

Mariana giggled and held out a crayon to him. "Want to color with me?"

"I thought you'd never ask." Simeon took the crayon and paper she passed him and set to work.

Mariana was nothing if not a chatterbox, and by the time Pastor Mateo and Linda came down for coffee, Simeon had learned all about her school, her favorite animals, and her baby brother.

"Well, look at you two early birds." Pastor Mateo grinned at them. "Are you excited for VBS today?"

"Yes," Simeon and Mariana answered in unison, then laughed and gave each other a fist bump.

"I'd better go wake Abigail up." Simeon pushed back from the table and filled two mugs of coffee to take upstairs. He'd been completely taken by surprise when she'd suggested they help with VBS—but in the best way. It was where they'd made their first connections, after all.

He pushed the bedroom door open to find Abigail lying in the middle of the air mattress, eyes wide open.

"What are you doing?" he asked.

She struggled to turn to her side. "This thing is horribly uncomfortable."

Simeon laughed. "Tell me about it. So why are you lying there instead of in the perfectly comfortable bed?"

Abigail shrugged and ducked her head so that her hair covered her cheeks—but not before Simeon spotted the blush that had arisen there. "I woke up and you were gone, and I missed you so . . ."

It really didn't matter what the next part of that sentence was. Simeon hurried across the room, only remembering at the last second that he was carrying two full mugs of coffee. Carefully, he set them on the floor. Then he lowered himself to sit on the edge of the air mattress. The movement made Abigail roll toward him, and he bent to catch her lips in a kiss. "You missed me, huh?"

"Maybe a little." But she pulled him closer for another kiss. "Where did you go?"

"I couldn't sleep, so I went downstairs and colored with Mariana."

Abigail laughed. "I didn't know you colored."

"Oh, yes." Simeon put on a serious expression. "I'm a very well-known crayon artist." He kissed her one more time, then begrudgingly got to his feet, suddenly wishing they had the day to themselves. "We'd better get ready for VBS."

"I almost forgot." Abigail tried to push upright but fell back onto the mattress. "Seriously." She giggled, rolling to the edge of the mattress to try again. "This thing is terrible. No wonder your back has been hurting."

Simeon turned to her. He'd thought he'd done a good job hiding the back pain that had plagued him for the past few days. Apparently not.

"You can't keep sleeping on this," Abigail announced as she made it to her feet.

"It's only another week." Simeon bent to pick up their coffees, careful not to groan as his back twinged in the process. "I'll be fine."

"No, you won't," Abigail said firmly. "You shouldn't be the one who always has to make sacrifices."

"It's not a big deal. I would sacrifice a lot more than a good night's sleep for you."

"I know you would." Abigail took a sip from her mug. "But I have a better idea."

"Abigail." Was she asking him to share the bed?

"No arguments," she insisted. "From now on, _I_ sleep on the air mattress."

Simeon swallowed his disappointment along with his coffee. It was okay that she wasn't ready. "There's no way I'm going to agree to that." He kissed her lightly. "But thank you for offering." He moved to his suitcase and grabbed some clothes. "I'm going to go get ready."

"We're not done with this conversation," Abigail called behind him.

Chapter 37

"El pegamento." Abigail nodded toward the glue in the center of the table. It wasn't a word she'd practiced before they'd come, but she'd picked it up quickly helping with vacation Bible school all week.

How could it already be the last day? The week had been exhausting but wonderful, and she had no idea what she'd do without these little people in her life once she and Simeon returned home.

A wave of giggles went through the children, and Abigail lifted her head to see what was going on.

Mariana pointed over Abigail's shoulder. She followed the girl's finger to discover that Simeon had taken some of the googly eyes they were using to make puppets and stuck them on his eyelids.

"Simeon." But her reprimand came out as more of a laugh. She'd seen such a light side of him this week, and it had only fueled her growing feelings for him. That déjà vu sensation she'd been experiencing more frequently all week hit her hard in the chest.

"Qué?" Simeon asked, raising his hands to his sides innocently. "No te gustan mis ojos?" He shook his head in a circle, making the googly eyes go wild.

"Oh no. Me gustan mucho." Abigail reached for a pair of googly eyes, pressing them against her own lids. "Te gustan *mis* ojos?"

There was no answer for a moment, and Abigail started to pull the googly eyes off but then a pair of hands stopped her. "Sí." Simeon's voice was soft. "Y tus labios." His lips pressed to hers.

"Oooo," the children shrieked.

Abigail pulled back, pretty sure her face was redder than the crayon Mariana was holding, but she couldn't help laughing.

"Okay, todos," Pastor Mateo called. "Ha llegado el momento de la gran final."

"It's time for the grand finale?" Abigail ran her translation past Simeon.

He nodded. "Muy bien."

"Thanks. What grand finale?" She didn't remember planning that.

Simeon grinned and took her hand. "Come on. You'll see."

Mariana grabbed her other hand, and together they led her out to the small lot behind the church.

In the center of the space were two big bins, filled with what looked like large, colorful eggs.

Abigail squinted at them. "Are those water balloons?" She glanced at the sky. Though it was sunny and probably in the low sixties, it wasn't exactly what she'd call water balloon weather.

"Better." Simeon smirked. "Shaving cream balloons."

"What are—"

But before she could finish the question, Pastor Mateo's booming voice rang over the group in rapid Spanish. From what Abigail gathered between her own pitiful translation and Simeon's explanation, he was giving the rules of some game. But what game and what those rules meant still wasn't clear to her by the time he stopped talking.

Apparently, the children had all gotten it though, because they took off for the bins of balloons.

"Come on." Simeon grabbed her arm and pulled her along with the children. "We're on the blue team."

Before she could ask what that meant, a balloon hit her side and burst, covering her in shaving cream.

Simeon chortled. "Come on." He kept pulling until they reached a bin of blue balloons. He handed one to her. She still didn't know what she was supposed to do with it. But she did know what she *wanted* to do with it.

She took a dozen steps backwards, then called, "Simeon."

He looked up from loading his arms with balloons.

Without hesitation, Abigail lobbed her balloon at him.

Simeon's eyes went bigger than the balloons in his arms as it arced through the air toward him. He stepped to the side at the last second, and the balloon grazed off his shoulder, not breaking.

"Ha!" he crowed. "Nice try."

Abigail eyed the balloons still clutched in his arms. With a grin, she started jogging toward him. He watched her, a smile playing on his lips.

She kept running, judging the distance. Five yards to go. Four. Three. Two.

"Abigail, what—"

She ran right into him, shrieking as several balloons popped between them. Sticky shaving cream coated the front of her shirt and dripped onto her legs, but it was totally worth it to see Simeon's incredulous expression—and to hear his rich, warm, carefree laugh.

"We're supposed to be on the same team." But the words came around his laughs, and he scooped a blob of shaving cream off his shirt, plopping it onto her nose.

"Hey!" But she couldn't stop laughing. Impulsively, she leaned forward to kiss him, then tilted her head to transfer the shaving cream to his cheek.

"We should probably—" A hailstorm of shaving cream balloons pelted them from all sides, and Abigail turned to find they'd been surrounded by laughing children, all tossing balloons at them.

Her heart filled fuller than the biggest balloon.

She couldn't imagine a more perfect moment.

Thank you, Lord, for bringing me here. She hadn't planned on praying, but the words just came, and she thought of Pastor Mateo's sermon from last Sunday. She couldn't remember the exact verse he'd preached on, but she did remember that it had been about being rooted in Christ and overflowing with thankfulness.

That was exactly how she felt right now—like she was overflowing with thankfulness.

The children ran out of balloons fairly quickly, and everyone was still laughing as they worked together to clean up. Then Pastor Mateo called them all together for a closing prayer.

Abigail closed her eyes and tucked her hand into Simeon's as Mateo began. "Gracias, Dios, por todo lo que nos has enseñado esta semana."

"Thank you, God, for everything you have taught us this week." Simeon whispered the translation to her.

Abigail nodded. She had understood most of that.

"Gracias por nuevos amig—" There was a pause and then a thud and several screams.

Abigail's eyes jumped open.

Pastor Mateo no longer stood in front of the group, and Abigail's gaze followed the scramble of children to where Pastor Mateo lay slumped on the ground.

Before she could process what she was doing, Abigail was dodging through the children to get to Mateo. She dropped to her knees at his side. "Help me roll him over," she said to Simeon, who had followed her.

"Are you sure we should move him?" he asked.

"Yes." Abigail couldn't have said why she was certain—but she was.

Simeon's face settled into a grim look, but he gripped Mateo's shoulder and rolled him onto his back.

"Pastor Mateo, can you hear me?" Abigail pressed two fingers to the older man's wrist, watching his chest for signs that he was breathing. There was nothing.

"Call 911." She barked the words as she centered her hands on Pastor Mateo's chest and began compressions. "And get the AED." Pastor Mateo had been so proud when he'd pointed it out earlier this week. He'd purchased it with a grant, and the church was one of the few places in the city that had one.

Simeon scrambled to his feet. "Is it a heart attack?"

"I think it's sudden cardiac arrest."

Simeon blinked at her. "How do you—"

"Go," she shouted. There was so little time.

With one more look at her hands compressing Pastor Mateo's chest, Simeon turned and sprinted toward the church.

"I've got emergency services on the line." Linda spoke calmly and crouched on the other side of Pastor Mateo to take his hand.

Abigail kept compressing, vaguely registering that next to her, Linda was whispering, the word Dios standing out from the others Abigail couldn't translate. The woman must be praying.

Please help him. Abigail prayed too. *Help me know what to do.*

Simeon skidded back to their side, holding out the defibrillator.

"Open it and turn it on," Abigail instructed.

Simeon did what she asked, and voice prompts from the machine instructed them to prepare the pads. As Simeon did that, Abigail pulled up Pastor Mateo's shirt.

She took the pads from Simeon and placed them on Pastor Mateo's chest, where the diagram on the machine showed to put them.

"Are you sure that's right?" Simeon asked.

Abigail nodded. For some reason, she *was* sure.

"Stay clear," she said, just as the machine said the same thing.

"Press the shock button," the robotic AED voice said.

"Clear," Abigail said again, making sure no one was near enough to touch Pastor Mateo. Then she pressed the shock button.

She kept her eyes on Pastor Mateo even as emergency workers descended on the yard. One dropped to the ground next to her.

"Le diste una descarga?" he asked.

Abigail stared at him. She hadn't understood a single one of those words.

"Yes," Simeon said from behind her. "You shocked him."

"Oh. Yes."

The paramedic reached for Pastor Mateo's wrist. "It worked? Fue efectivo?"

"I don't know," Abigail whispered, her eyes trained on Pastor Mateo's pale face.

"Tiene pulso," the EMT said after what felt like half a lifetime.

"He has a pulse," Simeon translated.

Abigail sagged backwards into her husband's solid legs.

"Bien." The EMT grabbed his bag and pulled out a clear plastic mask, fitting it over Pastor Mateo's nose and mouth. "Cuidaremos de él."

"Come on, they're going to take care of him." Simeon pulled her to her feet. Her legs shook as she tried to walk, but he wrapped an arm firmly around her back and led her to a bench near the church door. "Man alive, Abigail." He kissed the top of her head. "You were amazing. How did you do all of that?"

She could only shake her head and watch the paramedics working on Pastor Mateo.

Within a short time, they had him loaded on a stretcher and were wheeling him out of the yard.

Simeon got up and strode to Linda. "You go with him. We'll stay until all the children are picked up and then meet you there with Mariana." He looked to Abigail as if to make sure that was okay with her, and she nodded.

Mariana climbed into her lap, and Abigail wrapped her arms around the tearful girl. Abigail smoothed the girl's hair and tried to figure out what she'd just done.

Chapter 38

"Oh, look at this!"

Simeon let Abigail pull him toward yet another stall in the market. They'd spent hours at the hospital with Linda last night, before she'd insisted they go back to the house. Abigail had gone upstairs to tuck Mariana in and then never come back down. When Simeon had finally gone up to check on them, he'd found Abigail sprawled on Mariana's bed, her arm wrapped protectively around the little girl. Simeon's heart had both rejoiced and broken at the image.

Mariana's parents had come this morning, and they'd all gone over to the hospital together. Pastor Mateo was doing much better—so well, in fact, that he'd refused to let Simeon and Abigail spend their last full day in Ecuador at the hospital.

When Abigail had protested, the pastor had taken her hand in his. "God put you in the right place at the right time to save my life," he'd said. "Now he's giving you the opportunity to spend your last day in our beautiful city with your husband. Please take it."

As they'd walked out of the hospital hand in hand, Abigail had turned to Simeon. "Do you think God really brought us here so I could save Pastor Mateo's life?"

"I think," Simeon had said, "God's ways are so much higher than our ways, his plans so beyond our searching out, that we can't begin to fathom them. But yes, I do think he put you in the right place at the right time to save Pastor Mateo's life. It's no coincidence that we happened to be here right when he needed you—or that you knew what to do."

Though he still couldn't figure out *how* she'd known. She'd never taken a first aid class, to his knowledge. But the way she'd responded instantly and instinctively—it had to have been procedural memory. But procedural memory of *what*? From *when*?

"Are you coming?" Abigail's voice pulled Simeon out of the questions swimming laps in his head.

She had moved to a table a few steps away, and Simeon joined her just as she reached for a glass dolphin.

"Be careful." The words came out unintentionally, and Abigail froze, her fingers inches from the figure.

"What did you say?" She gave him an odd look.

"Sorry." Simeon offered an apologetic smile. That was how he'd gotten in trouble the first time he'd met her too. "I didn't mean—"

"No." Abigail seemed to shake herself. "I just got this feeling . . ."

Now it was Simeon's turn to freeze. "What kind of feeling?"

"Nothing." Abigail pulled her hand away from the dolphin. "I've just been getting these déjà vu feelings sometimes."

Simeon blinked at her. "You have? Why haven't you said anything?"

She shrugged. "I figured they didn't mean anything. I had the same feeling about my book, right?"

"Abigail." Simeon reached past her to pick up the figurine. "It was a dolphin," he said slowly. "The first time we met, you were reaching for a dolphin a lot like this one, and I told you not to touch it."

Instead of reflecting the growing excitement he felt at what this meant, Abigail frowned, crossing her arms in front of her. "So how am I supposed to know what's a real memory and what's not?"

Simeon set the dolphin down and slid his hands up and down her arms, waiting for her to meet his eyes. "You ask me."

Slowly Abigail nodded. "I can do that."

"Good." Simeon pulled her into a kiss that earned them a few whistles from the crowds bustling around them.

"Come on." He swept the dolphin off the table.

"What are you doing?"

"Buying you an anniversary present." He bit his tongue. He hadn't meant to tell her what today was. He didn't want her to feel any sort of pressure based on the date. He tugged her toward the vendors, hoping maybe she hadn't noticed.

But her feet didn't move.

"It's our anniversary?" She looked stricken. "I'm so sorry. I didn't get you— I didn't realize."

"I know you didn't." He tugged her gently until she stepped into the curve of his arm. "I didn't say anything."

"Why not?"

He kissed her head. "Because this day is perfect just the way it is. Now come on. Let's buy the dolphin and then get some espumilla." They'd eaten so much of the meringue dessert served in a waffle cone over the past week and a half—but there was always room for more.

Twenty minutes later, with their dolphin wrapped up and their espumillas in hand, Simeon steered them down a side street.

"Where are we going?"

"You'll see." The farther they went, the fewer people there were on the streets.

"Are we lost?" Abigail asked after fifteen minutes. But she didn't sound worried. Instead, she sounded completely content.

"Nope. We're here." He pulled her into a small courtyard between buildings. A simple round fountain bubbled in the middle of the space, its splashes creating the perfect musical backdrop.

"Wow. This is beautiful." Abigail let go of his hand and moved to the fountain, trailing her fingers in the water.

"We found it on accident one night when we were wandering around the town." Simeon watched her, trying to tell if she was getting that déjà vu feeling again. Of all the places in the city, this was the one he most wanted her to remember. It was where he'd first told her he loved her. But there was no sign of recognition on her face.

Simeon quashed his disappointment. She didn't have to remember.

They could create a new perfect memory. He strode to her side and caught her in his arms.

"Oh." She gasped and then his lips were on hers. Her arms slid around his neck, and he kissed her like he might never get another chance to kiss her again.

When the kiss finally ended, they stood forehead to forehead, their breath coming in short gasps.

"What was that for?" Abigail asked with a shaky laugh.

"I love you, Abigail." The words tumbled out before he could remind himself not to say them. "I know I'm not supposed to say that right now, but I need you to know. I love you with everything in me. And I'm not talking about the old you or past Abigail or however you think about yourself before the accident. I'm talking about *you* you."

Abigail made a sound that may have been the word "oh," or it may have been only a breath.

"I'm not asking you to say it back to me," Simeon whispered. "I just need you to know. Nothing has changed, except that I love you even more now than the first time we came here."

Abigail nodded, and Simeon pulled her tight to him for a hug.

"Come on." He kissed her temple. "Let's go check on Pastor Mateo."

Why hadn't she told him she loved him?

Abigail lay in bed, staring up at the ceiling, jumping as a sudden flash of lightning illuminated the room, accompanied by a sharp crack of thunder that echoed off the mountains.

She pulled the blankets tighter to herself, her stomach swirling.

She *did* love him. She knew that beyond a shadow of a doubt. But after he'd made that beautiful proclamation of his love—not to mention kissed her in a way that left no uncertainty—she still hadn't been able to say it back to him.

She'd had plenty of opportunities.

At the fountain.

On the way to check on Pastor Mateo.

As they'd packed.

And yet she'd remained silent.

She heard the bathroom door open, and her heart quickened. She could tell him now.

The bedroom door opened quietly, and Simeon tiptoed in. She waited until the creaking of the air mattress stopped.

"Simeon?" she whispered.

"I thought you were asleep," he whispered back.

"No." A series of flashes lit the room as thunder shook the house. Abigail let out a small, involuntary scream.

Across the room, Simeon chuckled.

"Are you laughing at me?" Abigail tried to sound indignant, but it was hard when she felt so foolish.

"No." Simeon's chuckles still rumbled. "Maybe. But only because a month after we got married, I was woken from a dead sleep in the middle of the night by a body landing on top of me. That was how I learned you were afraid of storms."

"You're making that up," Abigail accused, though she was laughing at the image he painted.

"I promise you I'm not." Simeon's laugh grew. "I thought we were under attack or the ceiling was falling or something."

Thunder shook the house again, and a torrent of rain unleashed against the window.

Abigail tucked herself under the blanket. "So I've always been afraid of storms?"

"Yeah. You have. I learned to hold you whenever it stormed at night—both to comfort you and to ensure my own safety." Simeon's laughter had petered out, and he sounded wistful.

"Will you—" Abigail swallowed roughly, her heart thundering louder than the storm. "Will you hold me now?"

A sharp exhale came from Simeon's direction, followed by a series of creaks from the air mattress. His footsteps crossed the floor, and then he was peeling back the blankets.

Abigail rolled away to make room for him, holding her breath as the mattress rocked with the solidness of his form. And then his arms came around her, pulling her back tight to his chest, and she let out a breath.

Thunder rattled the windows. But she had never felt safer.

"Simeon?"

"Hmm." He nuzzled his face into her hair.

"Did we ever talk about having kids?" The question had been rolling around her head all week during VBS.

The room flashed with bright blue light, and a loud roll of thunder echoed around the space. Simeon tightened his arms around her but didn't say anything.

"Simeon?" she finally asked.

"Yeah," he answered, his voice so low that the rain pelting the window nearly drowned it out. "We talked about it."

"Oh." Abigail waited, but when he didn't add anything else, she asked, "What did we decide?"

She told herself that the answer didn't matter. Just because she'd started to think she may want to be a mom someday didn't mean she'd be good at it anyway.

Simeon let out a long breath that lifted her hair off her neck. He loosened his hold on her enough to find her hand and take it in his. "We decided to try." His voice was hoarse. "Two years ago."

"Two years ago?" Abigail was no mathematician, but surely they should have a baby by now, if that was the case. Unless . . .

"Are we unable to . . ."

His sigh was weighted, and it made her heart ache for him. What had he been through that she didn't remember?

"It took a few months," he said at last, "but you got pregnant."

"I did?" She let go of his hand to roll over and face him. None of this was making sense.

"We lost the baby, sweetie." In the dark, Simeon's eyes shone with sorrow. "At about two months."

"Oh." Abigail swallowed hard against the sudden ache in her own throat. "And we never . . ."

"We did," Simeon whispered. "Two more times. We lost them both too."

Abigail pressed a hand to her stomach, nausea overtaking her. "Did I do something wrong? Did I—"

Simeon pulled her tight to him, crushing her arm between their ribs. "You didn't do anything wrong," he said into her hair. "Not a single thing. It just happened. I need you to know that, okay?"

She nodded against his chest, but tears cascaded from her face onto his shirt.

He held her tighter as the tears erupted into a sob.

"It's okay." He slid his hand up and down her back. "It's okay." But she felt him shudder too and she wrapped her arms around his back, holding him tight.

She couldn't understand it—where these tears were coming from. How could she grieve for babies she didn't even remember conceiving, let alone losing?

And yet, something deep within her ached for what could have been.

"Why didn't you tell me sooner?" she whispered into Simeon's chest.

She wasn't sure he heard her at first, but then he slid a hand over her cheek, wiping away the tears. "It was so hard to go through the first time. I thought I could protect you from reliving it."

"And just carry that burden yourself forever?"

He shrugged. "For you, yes, I would carry any burden."

"Well." Abigail reached up to touch his cheek. "Maybe we should share the burden."

"Maybe we should." He brought his lips to hers in a feather-light kiss.

"Simeon?" She ran a hand over his stubble-roughened cheeks. "Can I tell you something?"

"Of course. Anything."

"I love you."

Simeon let out a choked breath. And then his lips were on hers again.

When he pulled away, he tucked her against his chest and stroked her hair. She listened to his heart beating over the sounds of the storm and let herself fall asleep in his arms.

Chapter 39

Simeon didn't want to open his eyes. They'd been home for almost a week now, and it still felt like a dream, waking up with Abigail in his arms every morning. Sometimes he worried it was.

But he could feel her against him, solid and soft and perfect. Her breath warmed a spot in the middle of his chest, and her arm draped over his side.

He cracked one eye open to verify. The sun had already risen, its golden light giving the room a magical glow that enhanced the feeling of being in a dream. He slid a hand over her cheek, and she opened her eyes with a sleepy smile.

"Good morning," he murmured. "You're really here."

"Where else would I be?" She snuggled closer to him.

Simeon swallowed and kissed her hair. He'd waited so long for her to feel that way. Like there was no question that she belonged with him.

"I should get ready for work." The words were less than halfhearted, directed more to himself than to her.

"Do you have to go?" She laced her fingers through his, and Simeon suddenly thought that maybe he'd never go to work again. If this was a dream, maybe he could just spend all day with her.

But his phone pealed, bringing him rudely back to reality. "I'm afraid I do. But I'll be home early for Lydia and Liam's rehearsal."

"Oh my goodness, I completely forgot." Abigail kicked the covers back. "I promised Lydia I'd help finish making the centerpieces today."

She sat upright, but Simeon caught her arm and pulled her back to him.

"Simeon," she protested with a laugh.

"Don't worry. I'll let you go. But first—" He propped himself onto an elbow and leaned to kiss her. "I love you."

She smiled up at him, her eyes wide and sincere. "I love you too."

Every time she said it, it set his heart afire.

"Good." With a groan of regret, he rolled away from her and pushed out of bed. His phone had stopped ringing, and he checked his notifications. But it wasn't the missed call that caught his eye. He clicked on the text from Pastor Mateo. It was a picture of the older man and his wife—at home.

He showed the picture to Abigail.

"Thank the Lord," she whispered, and Simeon's heart filled again. Watching her grow again in her faith over the past couple of months had grown his own faith too.

She loved him. She loved God. Everything was perfect.

He thought of the ring he'd placed in the top drawer of his desk.

"Is it really 8:30 already?" Abigail rushed past him to the closet. "I told Lydia I'd meet her at nine."

Simeon got up slowly. He'd let her get ready for now. But maybe tonight he'd put that ring back on her finger.

Abigail hummed along to the music on the radio as she pointed her car toward home, a giddy joy flipping through her middle.

They'd easily finished the centerpieces this morning, and everything was perfect for Lydia and Liam's wedding tomorrow.

Just like everything was perfect for Simeon and Abigail too. Everything about their trip to Ecuador, everything about the past week at home together—it was all perfect.

She may not remember Past Abigail's relationship with Simeon, but she dared to think that their relationship now was even better than it had been before the accident.

She turned onto their street, her heart jumping to see a black SUV in their driveway. Maybe Simeon had beaten her home.

But as she got closer, she realized it wasn't quite the right style to be Simeon's vehicle. She tried to recall where she might have seen it before but drew a blank.

She slowed to pull into the driveway, peering into the other vehicle, but there didn't appear to be anyone inside.

Abigail got out of her car slowly, still trying to figure out whose vehicle it could be.

"Over here," a woman's voice called from the direction of the porch, and Abigail hurried around the SUV to the walk that led to the house.

Her steps faltered as she spotted the woman sitting on the wicker chair under the front window.

But Wendy waved as if they were old friends and pushed to her feet. "It's such a beautiful day, I thought I might as well sit out here and wait for you."

"Wait for *me*?" Abigail asked warily, climbing the porch steps.

"To give you this." Wendy held out a manila envelope.

"What is it?" Abigail loosened the sealed flap.

"A copy of your divorce papers. My boss was going through her files, and when I explained to her about your accident, she realized you might have lost the papers, so she asked me to— Are you okay?"

Abigail groped for the porch railing, but her vision had gone all wavery, and she couldn't find it. "Yeah. I'm— Thank you." She stepped toward what she was pretty sure was the front door.

"You don't look so good. Maybe you should sit." Wendy hurried toward her and grabbed her arm, but Abigail jerked herself out of the other woman's grip.

"I get it. You don't want to see me." Wendy's voice sounded far away, even though she was still much too close. "For what it's worth, I'm sorry about the kiss."

Abigail whirled on the other woman, her vision suddenly going laser sharp. "What kiss?"

Wendy covered her mouth, her eyes opening wide. "He didn't tell you?"

"What kiss?" Abigail demanded again. Her whole body had gone numb.

"It was one time," Wendy said. "And it was my fault, really."

"He kissed you." Abigail didn't even know if she was asking or telling at this point, but Wendy nodded slowly.

"When?" The word blasted right past the numbness.

Wendy touched her lips, as if reliving the kiss. "A couple of weeks ago?"

"A couple of . . ." Abigail grabbed for the door handle, fumbling it open. She was going to be sick.

"Abigail, wait. I—"

But Abigail slammed the door behind her and sprinted upstairs to the bathroom. Tears mingled with the vomit as she heaved over the toilet.

When she had nothing left in her, she rinsed her mouth and washed her face and walked numbly into the bedroom. She dropped to the edge of the bed and finished opening the envelope Wendy had given her, barely able to grab the papers with her trembling fingers.

Once she had them out, she could only stare at the words.

Petition for Divorce. Her name. Simeon's name.

Her eyes tracked to the bottom of the form. The date was the date of the accident. And the signature—that was hers.

She blinked at it.

None of this made any sense. She and Simeon were in love. They had been before the accident, and they were now.

Weren't they?

She wrapped her arms around herself and rocked forward.

They were getting divorced. Simeon was kissing other women.

Most of her life was missing. And what was left of it was a lie.

Chapter 40

Simeon shut down his computer and grabbed his keys out of his desk drawer, whistling a little as he headed for the door.

It had been a good day. He'd managed to at least touch base with most of his clients this week and had even called Everlee to make sure Wendy had followed up on the referral. She had—and Everlee seemed optimistic about working with her, which had been a huge weight off Simeon's shoulders. He hated the idea that he had given up on a client, but in this case it had been for the best—the fact that he hadn't heard from Wendy once since he'd gotten back was proof enough of that.

And now he was on his way home to Abigail. He'd been thinking about it all day and had decided for certain—tonight was the night he'd ask her to wear her wedding ring again. After Lydia and Liam's rehearsal dinner.

If he could wait that long.

He spent the drive planning what he'd say—how he'd tell her that getting to know her all over again had only made him fall more deeply in love with her. How he would continue to love and cherish her all their days. How she made him want to be the best husband he could be.

By the time he got home, he knew—he couldn't wait until after the rehearsal. He had to ask her right now.

He practically flew into the house, calling her name.

When she didn't answer, he headed straight for the stairs, bounding up them two at a time. At the top, he darted into his office and grabbed the ring, tucking it firmly into his pocket.

"Abigail." He couldn't make his feet—or his heart—slow down as he catapulted for the bedroom. She was probably getting ready—

"Abigail?"

She was sitting at the edge of the bed, staring right at the door, her eyes puffy, her expression stony.

"Abigail, what is it?"

Something had happened.

Something bad.

But she didn't have any family, and if anything had happened to his family, someone would have called him.

He crossed the room and wrapped his hands around her shoulders, his heart pounding in all the wrong ways.

Abigail shrugged out of his grip, then picked up an envelope that rested on the bed next to her.

Silently, she passed it to him.

"What is this?"

She shook her head, not looking at him.

Dread collected in his stomach as he reached into the envelope.

The moment his eyes fell on the letterhead, he knew what it was. "Abigail."

"You said we weren't getting divorced." Her words were quiet, but somehow they seemed to reverberate off the walls.

"We weren't," he said firmly.

"Then what's that?" She struck at the papers in his hands and met his eyes, the heartbreak in hers thrashing at his chest.

"You had them drawn up on the day of the accident. That morning, I guess. I didn't know anything about them until Zeb found a copy in the car after . . . I never would have signed them, Abigail. That's why I said we weren't getting divorced when you asked. Because we *weren't*. I wouldn't have signed them," he repeated. "I would have fought for our marriage. Even when you couldn't.'"

Her brows lowered, creasing her forehead into lines that he wanted to smooth away. Instead, he lowered himself carefully onto the edge of the bed next to her. He braced his elbows on his knees, staring at the floor. He'd so badly wanted to shield her from this. But he should have told her.

"Losing the babies was so hard on you," he started. "You were depressed, and no matter what I did, I couldn't reach you. I felt so . . ." He exhaled sharply as the feelings hit him again. "So helpless— I knew I was losing you, and you just kept pushing me away. But I didn't know you were going to file those—" He broke off, shaking his head. He still couldn't believe it. "I should have told you when you asked. But everything was still so new to you—*I* was still so new to you—and I didn't want you to think that maybe we didn't belong together. Because we do." He reached for her hands, but she tugged them away.

"Do we?"

He jerked upright, turning toward her. "How can you even ask that?" he said hoarsely.

She refused to look at him. "You kissed another woman." The flat words conflicted with her contorted expression.

"What?" The dread that had been collecting in his stomach imploded. "Why would you—"

"She came over today." The defeat in Abigail's voice was too familiar—too much like it had been before the accident. "She brought those."

264

Abigail pointed to the papers Simeon had tossed onto the bed. "Along with the little announcement that you two kissed a couple of weeks ago."

"Wendy came here?" Simeon's whole body went cold, then hot. How dare she—

"You kissed her a couple of *weeks* ago, Simeon." Abigail looked up, her eyes brimming. "So don't tell me the problems were only before the accident."

"Man alive, Abigail." Simeon stood, needing to do something with all the pent-up energy that suddenly surged through him. "After everything, do you really think I would—" He stopped. This wasn't her fault. He should have told her the moment it happened. "*We* didn't kiss," he said. "She kissed me. I pushed her away and told her to find another counselor. Which she did. I just spoke to her counselor today, and it sounded like she was doing well. I never thought she would—"

"Why didn't you tell me?" Abigail cut off his explanation.

He scrubbed his hands over his face. "It was a work thing. I didn't—"

"A work thing?" Abigail's laugh was incredulous. "Another woman kisses you, and you call it a *work thing*?" Her lip lifted in a sneer.

"Abigail, she was a client. She got confused and thought she had feelings for me. I promise you, I had no feelings for her. I fired her. You can ask Everlee. I called her to document everything."

"But you didn't tell *me*." The ache in her voice nearly destroyed him.

He rushed to the bed and dropped to his knees in front of her, wrapping his hands around hers tight enough that she couldn't pull away. "You have to believe me when I say I would never do anything to hurt you. I love you. You believe that, right?"

She didn't respond, and Simeon dropped his head to their joined hands in her lap. "I'm so—"

The blast of his phone cut him off.

He kept one hand wrapped around hers as he pulled the phone out of his pocket with the other.

The screen showed Asher's name, and Simeon was about to ignore the call when Abigail said, "They're probably wondering where we are."

The rehearsal.

Simeon's eyes flicked to the time. 5:15. They were supposed to be there fifteen minutes ago.

He swiped to answer the phone. "We're on our way," he said before Asher could get a word out.

"Everything okay?" Asher asked. In the background, Simeon could hear talking and laughter.

He glanced at his hand still locked around Abigail's. "Yeah." He swallowed. "Everything's good." As he hung up, he prayed that was true.

Chapter 41

"Abigail?"

Abigail startled to find Ava standing over her, her matching green dress shimmering in the lights of the church conference room that they'd transformed into a dressing room to get ready for Lydia and Liam's wedding.

"Ready for pictures?" Ava asked, holding up her camera.

"Pictures?" Abigail tried to shake herself out of her thoughts.

"I already did the guys." Ava fiddled with some buttons on the camera. "We'll do the girls now and then everyone together after the ceremony."

"Right. Okay." Abigail pushed wearily to her feet.

She'd barely slept last night. Her thoughts—of the divorce papers, of Simeon's pleas for her to understand why he hadn't told her about the kiss with Wendy, of walking down the aisle next to him for the rehearsal but feeling like he was miles away—had refused to let her rest.

Though she'd stayed far on her side of the bed, rather than snuggling into Simeon's warm arms as she had every night since they'd gotten home, she was pretty sure he hadn't slept much either.

Part of her had longed to roll closer to him, to tell him that she understood, to ask him to hold her again. But every time she started to, she pictured Wendy standing in front of her, touching her lips as she talked about Simeon's kiss.

"Are you okay?" Ava lowered her camera and peered at her.

Between the rehearsal last night and getting ready this morning, she'd been asked the same question more than once by every one of her sisters-in-law.

The truth was, she had no idea if she was okay.

But she answered the same way she had every time. "Of course."

This was Lydia's day, and she wasn't going to ruin it. She swiped a smile onto her face and stood.

The moment her eyes fell on Lydia, she felt her smile become real. Her sister-in-law was glowing from the inside out, her dark hair falling over the shoulders of her elegant bridal gown.

Grace helped her finish fastening the veil, and then Lydia made a slow, graceful turn.

"Wow, you're gorgeous." Ireland pressed her hands to her cheeks, her own dress protruding adorably over her baby bump. "I love the way the light catches on the beadwork."

"Amazing," Abigail agreed, a genuine surge of joy for Lydia filling her.

"I'll make sure the coast is clear." Mia pulled the door open just wide enough to slide her slim body through. A few seconds later, she popped back into the room. "All clear. Uncle Simeon is standing guard so my dad doesn't try to sneak out to see you."

The other women all laughed, but Abigail swallowed and gripped the back of the nearest chair. If Simeon was in the hallway, there would be no way to avoid him.

They'd taken separate vehicles this morning, since the women needed more time to get ready than the guys, so other than a quick greeting, they hadn't really spoken much today.

"Come on." Mia stood at the door and waved them each through, as if directing a crew of spies.

Abigail's heart ramped up as if she really were a spy as she stepped into the hallway. But it hit the brakes as her eyes fell on not Simeon but Joseph. He snuck a kiss from his wife and gave the rest of them a thumbs-up as they passed.

"Where's Simeon?" She didn't realize she'd spoken the words out loud until Joseph answered.

"He had some sort of wardrobe malfunction."

Abigail stopped. "What kind of malfunction? Does he need help?"

Joseph smiled gently, and Abigail wondered if he knew about the divorce papers—about everything. "Nah. He's fine. It was just a button that came off, but it turns out that he has mad sewing skills."

"He does?" Abigail blinked at Joseph. Was this yet another thing she didn't know about Simeon?

"No." Joseph laughed. "But Liam's mom does. It's all under control." He waved after the other women. "You'd better go before my wife comes back and carries you away."

Abigail hesitated a second, then hurried after the other women.

Pictures took longer than they intended, and when they finally finished, they had to scramble into the hallway to line up for the processional. Abigail squinted toward the lobby, but she already knew she wouldn't find what she was looking for. The groomsmen were lining up in the front of the church and meeting the bridesmaids halfway down the aisle—so she wouldn't see Simeon until they were in the church.

The music swelled, and Ava started to walk toward the sanctuary door, just as Pastor Calvano had instructed last night.

But Lydia called "Hold on" from her spot at the back of the line.

They all spun toward her, and Lydia laugh-cried. "I just wanted to tell you all how thankful I am for you. I never could have imagined having a family like this. And—well—just thank you." She wiped her eyes, and

Abigail swiped at her own tears. She knew exactly how Lydia felt. Being part of this family was like . . . like knowing you always had a place you belonged.

But apparently she'd been ready to give that all up once.

If it hadn't been for the accident, maybe she and Simeon would be divorced already. Her tears came harder, and she gulped to get them under control. Ireland had already entered the church, and Abigail was next.

She crossed slowly through the lobby, and then she was standing in the doorway to the sanctuary, gazing down the aisle toward Simeon. His eyes met hers, and her breath caught. That déjà vu feeling slammed into her more powerfully than it ever had before, and she couldn't move.

She had done this before—walking down the aisle toward Simeon. Not just last night for the rehearsal, but years ago—for their wedding. She couldn't picture it, couldn't remember any details. But she could *feel* it. Like her heart remembered.

"Abigail, you have to go," Grace whispered from behind her, giving her a gentle nudge.

"Hmm? Oh."

Simeon was almost to the spot in the aisle where they were supposed to meet, his gaze meeting hers in concern.

Abigail started forward, slowly at first but then picking up speed until she was at his side.

He gave her a tentative but tender smile and tucked her hand against his arm, leading her toward the front of the church.

"Are you okay?" he leaned close to whisper, his fresh scent reinforcing that feeling of déjà vu.

She managed to nod. "I just got that feeling again," she murmured. "Was it real?"

"Oh, it was real." Simeon pulled her in closer, his voice thick with emotion.

They'd reached the front of the church, but Simeon didn't release her arm. Instead he turned her toward him and kissed her forehead. "I love you," he whispered.

"Excuse me," Levi whispered from right behind them, and Abigail startled. She'd forgotten they weren't alone.

"I think you're supposed to keep going." Levi gestured with his head for Simeon to make his way to the other groomsmen.

Simeon gave Abigail a look that made her heart quiver, then let go and turned toward the groomsmen. Abigail made her way to the line of bridesmaids, Grace and then Mia close behind her.

The moment she was in position, Abigail's eyes strayed across the church to Simeon. His gaze was locked on hers.

She was barely aware of the change in the music, barely aware of the rustle that went through the church as everyone stood, barely aware of anything or anyone but Simeon, until Liam stepped toward the aisle with an audible "wow" as Lydia approached on Pastor Calvano's arm.

Abigail laughed along with the rest of the congregation, her eyes traveling from Lydia, radiant in her flowing dress, to Liam, beaming as he took her arm. Abigail looked again to Simeon, whose face shone with joy for his friend and his sister.

As Pastor Calvano stepped into place to begin the ceremony, Abigail forced her attention to her friends. Today was about them, not about her and Simeon.

"The passage Liam and Lydia have chosen for their wedding day is 1 Corinthians 13:4-8," Pastor Calvano said. He opened the Bible in his hands and read: "Love is patient, love is kind. It does not envy, it does not boast, it is not proud. It does not dishonor others, it is not self-seeking, it is not easily angered, it keeps no record of wrongs. Love does not delight in evil but rejoices with the truth. It always protects, always trusts, always hopes, always perseveres. Love never fails."

Pastor Calvano looked from Liam to Lydia. "You know, I must have preached a hundred wedding sermons on these verses over the years. Which doesn't mean I'm old—just seasoned." The congregation chuckled, and Abigail's heart warmed. Pastor Calvano had such a way of setting people at ease.

"The thing that amazes me," Pastor Calvano continued, "is that every single time I preach on these verses, God shows me something new about them. This time, it's how unnatural all these attributes of love are. Patience. Kindness. Forgiveness. Humility. Trust. Hope. Those words go against everything in our sinful human nature. Every part of us wants to rebel against them. So how can these verses tell us everything love is—everything we know we're not—and then go on to say, 'Love never fails'? I can see it in my own life. I'm sure you can see it in yours. Love fails all the time."

Abigail's heart crunched, her eyes skipping to Simeon, whose Adam's apple bobbed with a swallow. Was that what had happened to them? Their love had failed?

"So how can Paul tell the Corinthians that love never fails?" Pastor Calvano's question pulled Abigail's gaze back to him. "How can *I* tell *you*—" He looked at Lydia and Liam. "That love never fails?"

His somber expression transformed into a smile. "You already know the answer. Because there is One love that never fails—God's love. The One who is the very definition of love sent his only Son into this world to live in perfect love for us. To *die* in perfect love for us. To forgive our sins. To forgive us for all the times our love *has* failed. All the times it *will* fail, including in our marriages. And to give us the strength to forgive one another—to *love* one another—even through those failures."

Pastor Calvano's eyes traveled down the row of groomsmen and then the bridesmaids, and Abigail felt as if they rested right on her. "These verses show us that love isn't passive. It isn't something we fall into and out of on a whim. It's not something that just happens to us. Love is active. It takes work. It takes patience and kindness. It takes forgiveness and perseverance. It takes trust and hope."

Pastor Calvano faced Lydia and Liam, but Abigail felt herself leaning in to catch every last word.

"I'm not saying it's always going to be easy." Pastor Calvano chuckled wryly. "Sometimes it's going to seem downright impossible. But it's not. Because God *is* love. And his perfect love will always be there to sustain us, to grow us, to love us—with a love that never fails. Amen."

As Pastor Calvano directed Lydia and Liam to exchange rings, Abigail's eyes sought out Simeon. He was already watching her, his gaze full of earnestness and longing.

Full of love.

Abigail pressed a hand to her chest as she realized: All those things Pastor Calvano had said about love—Simeon had shown every one of them to her. He'd been patient and kind. He'd put her needs ahead of his own, even when it hurt him. And, oh, how had it never occurred to her how much it must have hurt him to receive those divorce papers after the accident? Yet his only concern had been to protect her.

Applause broke out in the church, and Abigail realized that Pastor Calvano had introduced Lydia and Liam as husband and wife.

They started down the aisle, and Abigail waited impatiently for her turn to walk with Simeon.

When they were finally standing face to face, she threw her arms around him. He let out a surprised breath and then his arms were holding her tight.

When he finally let go and they started down the aisle, Abigail couldn't stop smiling. Love didn't just happen. Love took work.

And she wanted to do the work—with Simeon.

Chapter 42

"Dance with me?" Simeon stood and held out a hand to Abigail, who sat at one of the dozens of picnic tables that had been set up in Liam's spacious backyard, with its view over the Serenity River. Abigail looked up with a smile, her features soft in the muted lights that draped the trees.

She set her hand in his and let him pull her to her feet, stepping close enough that he could wrap an arm around her. He led her to the open grassy area that had been set aside as a makeshift dance floor. Some of Lydia's friends in the country music industry were playing a soft ballad, and Simeon wrapped his arms around his wife.

He had no idea whether it had been the church or the wedding ceremony or Dad's sermon, but something had completely transformed Abigail this afternoon. She hadn't stopped smiling once since they'd walked out of the church together. She'd stood close to him through the pictures, held his hand tight on the short drive from the church, kissed him when they'd arrived here.

And now that they were on the dance floor, she nuzzled in close to him and rested her cheek on his chest. He wondered if she could hear his heart, beating her name.

Simeon closed his eyes, pressing his hands to her back and letting himself savor this moment as it mingled with memories of their own wedding day.

"Simeon?" Abigail murmured into his chest.

"Mmm hmm." He rested his cheek on top of her head, letting himself drift away on the sweet scent.

"Thank you." Abigail pulled back enough that Simeon had to move his head.

"You're welcome. For what?"

"For . . ." She licked her lips and swallowed. "For loving me like those verses your dad was talking about today."

"Oh." The word was more of a gasp, and Simeon crushed her to him, cupping the back of her head in his hand. "I've failed so many times. But I want to love you like that. Always."

"I want to love you like that too." She wiggled free of his grasp and brought her gaze to his. "Do you think— Would it be okay if I put my wedding ring back on?"

Simeon's laugh was so loud that people around them stopped dancing to stare, but he didn't care. "Yes, I think that would be very okay." He reached into the pocket of his dress pants.

"You have it with you?" Abigail's eyes widened.

"I was going to ask you to wear it last night, but . . ." He didn't want to dwell on that. "It felt foolish to bring it along today, but I couldn't help myself."

"Good thing." Abigail laughed and held her hand out to him.

Filled with awe, he took it into his and slid the ring onto her finger, the same way he had on their wedding day.

Applause broke out around them, and it took Simeon a moment to realize it was for them.

"Kiss her, you fool," Liam called.

Simeon grinned and slid his hands across Abigail's cheeks, bringing his lips tenderly to hers as the sounds of laughter and applause swirled around them.

When they pulled apart, Lydia was at the microphone. Guitar chords accompanied her warm, rich voice, floating on the night.

When we promised forever, how could we have known
All the years would bring us, how the time would flow?
There'd be fights and forgiveness, questions and fears
Hopes and promises, so many doubts and all those tears
There'd be heartache and hurt, mixed with laughter and joy
But through it all, we've found this love that nothing can destroy
Because one thing we knew then,
And we know it still today
Our love is built on something much stronger than clay
It's built on the One who made us all the way back when,
You for me and me for you,
Oh yes, he made us—one flesh out of two.

Simeon pulled Abigail close, and they spent most of the rest of the night on the dance floor, taking only occasional breaks to talk to friends and family. They were among the last to leave, and by the time they said goodnight to Liam and Lydia and headed home, it was well after midnight.

But any tiredness Simeon felt disappeared the moment they stepped through the door of their house and Abigail spun to kiss him the same way she used to when they were first married.

Simeon returned the kiss, letting his hands explore her hair, her shoulders, her arms, her waist.

After a few minutes, Abigail pulled away, her cheeks adorably pink. "Have we ever talked about trying again?" she asked.

Simeon blinked, trying to figure out the context of the question.

"Sorry. Kids." Abigail bit her lip. "Have we ever talked about trying to have kids again?"

"Oh. *Oh*." Simeon's sigh felt too heavy for the joyous evening they'd had. He hated the thought of telling her anything that could hurt her. But he wasn't going to keep things from her anymore. Instead, he would be there for her, whatever happened. He took her hand in his. "Shortly before the accident, you were supposed to go to the doctor. For some testing," he said gently. "Because of the miscarriages."

For the first time in hours, Abigail's smile dipped, and Simeon hated himself for it. She gripped his hand tighter. "What did the tests show?"

Simeon shook his head. "You canceled the appointment. You said you didn't want to try to get pregnant anymore."

She seemed to be weighing the information. "Did we talk about adoption?"

"We did. We went to a meeting, filled out all the paperwork. But then you said you couldn't do it."

Abigail's forehead creased. "Why not?"

"I don't know." Simeon still hadn't figured that out. "I had a feeling it was related to your depression. But by then you weren't—we weren't—talking much."

"Okay." Abigail looked thoughtful. "We should definitely talk more about that." She tugged his hand, pulling him toward the stairs. "Tomorrow."

Chapter 43

Abigail surveyed the kitchen. It was a disaster. But the roast baking in the oven smelled delicious, the cheesecake looked perfect, and she'd only had to call Benjamin twice to ask what the recipe meant.

Overall, she was pretty sure this meal was going to be a success. Perfect for the one-month anniversary of putting her wedding ring back on. She may not remember the first month of their marriage, but she was pretty sure even that couldn't have been this perfect.

She checked the time again.

Simeon had promised to be home from the office early tonight. Which gave her maybe an hour to finish getting everything ready.

The mess would have to wait.

First she had to get *herself* ready. She brushed off the basil and Parmesan that clung to her shirt and hurried to the bedroom. She'd splurged and bought a new dress—a white halter style with a flared skirt and open back—for the occasion.

She quickly pulled off her dirty clothes and grabbed the dress, pulling it on and tugging it down, then moved to the mirror to examine herself. The dress hugged the curves that Simeon seemed to love so much, and she couldn't help grinning as her eyes caught on the ring glinting from her finger.

She moved to the bathroom to put on a little makeup, but her phone rang before she had a chance to blend the foundation she had dotted onto her cheeks.

She scooped it off the counter, careful not to smear it with the makeup still coating her fingers.

Her heart leapt right up to the ceiling at the words that lit up the screen: Hope for Tomorrow.

It hadn't taken her and Simeon long after she'd put her ring back on to decide they wanted to move forward with adoption. After all they'd been through, neither of them was ready to deal with the potential heartbreak of another pregnancy loss. Plus, they both loved the idea of becoming a family for a child who otherwise might not have one. They'd submitted their paperwork three weeks ago and had been waiting for a call about starting the home study process.

Abigail's fingers shook as she swiped to answer, putting the phone on speaker so she wouldn't get makeup on the screen.

"Hello?" Did she sound too eager?

She probably did—but she didn't care.

"Is this Abigail Calvano?" The woman on the other end of the line didn't sound nearly as enthusiastic—but Abigail supposed this was fairly routine for her.

"Yes, this is Abigail." She rubbed at the foundation on her face, just to give her hands something to do.

"This is Janice Stark. I'm a caseworker at Hope for Tomorrow."

"Yes." Abigail tried to keep the impatience out of her voice. Who cared about pleasantries when they were waiting to start their family?

"And your maiden name is Harris?" Janice continued in that same monotone.

"Um. Yes." Not that she remembered it. But that was what Simeon had told her.

"I see." Janice's tone shifted, and something about it raised goosebumps on Abigail's arm.

"Is something wrong?"

"As part of our standard procedure, we run a criminal background check on all applicants." Janice was back to monotone-speak. "It's the law."

"Of course." A consent form had been one of the papers they'd signed.

"Yours came back with some information you failed to disclose on your application."

"I don't understand." Abigail dropped her hands from her half-blended face and picked up the phone, holding it in front of her as if that would make everything clearer. "What kind of information?" Had she gotten a speeding ticket? Maybe jaywalked—she and Simeon had been joking about that the other day when they'd crossed the street.

"It looks like you were arrested about . . . let's see . . . six, no seven, years ago?"

"I— What?" Abigail's voice squeaked, and her hands were shaking as hard as her head. "There must be some—"

Janice's monotone turned steel-hard. "It looks like the charges were dropped in return for your testimony, but this is still a very serious matter that should have been disclosed on your application."

"Charges? What kind of— I don't under—"

"Grand theft auto." Janice paused, then shot the word at her. "Manslaughter."

"But I never— This has to be a—"

Abigail's lungs seized as a barrage of images assaulted her.

Riding in a car that wasn't hers.

A man—not Simeon—kissing her hard and then laughing.

Police sirens.

A scream.

And then the crash.

No. No. No.

She gasped, but the air was too heavy. It refused to make it all the way to her lungs.

More images pummeled her.

Her childhood.

Her parents.

Nursing school.

Meeting Garrick.

No. No. No.

It was all from her book. It was just a story.

"Abigail?" The voice came from far away. "We'll need to set up a meeting to—"

Abigail pressed her finger to the red circle on her phone screen. Janice's voice disappeared.

But the room was loud. So loud with memories.

The jail. The courtroom. Her parents banishing her.

Meeting Simeon.

Their babies. Oh, their babies.

And Carly. Carly was gone, and Abigail hadn't even said goodbye.

She braced herself on the counter. The world was sliding out from under her, and there was nothing she could do to stop it.

What was she going to tell Simeon?

She'd been so upset with him for not telling her about the divorce and Wendy—but he'd kept all of that to himself to protect her.

She'd lied to him—about everything—only to protect *herself.*

She lifted her head and blinked at her reflection, wiping at the tears sliding down her cheeks, streaking the half-finished makeup.

Maybe she didn't have to tell him anything. He'd said himself that the fact that she hadn't gotten her memories back by now meant chances were good that she never would. He'd said it with such *compassion*—as if it were a sad thing that she'd never remember her past.

Because he didn't know what her past was.

She pressed her fingers to her lips as a sob ripped through her. Once he knew, he would send her away, just like her parents had.

Unless—

Unless she left first.

Chapter 44

Simeon barely had the patience to turn off his vehicle before he shot toward the house. The clock had moved way too slowly today as he'd imagined this moment—coming home to his wife. He couldn't wait to hold her, to kiss her, to show her in every way how much he loved her.

Man alive! He'd left the flowers in the vehicle. He sprinted back down the walk and grabbed the bouquet of peach hibiscus off the passenger seat, then darted back to the house.

He pushed the door open. "I'm home," he called, a wave of thankfulness washing over him.

Things had been hard—harder than Simeon had ever anticipated, even after all his years of counseling troubled couples—but God had brought them through it. And now they were looking forward to their future. To starting a family.

A persistent beeping returned his greeting. Not piercing enough to be the smoke alarm, thankfully. The oven timer?

"Abigail?" he called up the stairs as he headed for the kitchen. "I think whatever you have in the oven is done." The savory scent of garlic—maybe a little burnt—hit him as he reached the kitchen. Abigail must not have heard the timer going off.

He set the flowers on the table and hurried to the oven to jab at the annoying alarm. The burnt smell intensified as he pulled the oven door down, and Simeon coughed. He switched the oven off, then reached for a pair of oven mitts and pulled out what looked like a blackened roast. He set it on the counter and waved the smoke away. It didn't look salvageable, but his heart sang anyway at Abigail's thoughtfulness in making it.

And was that cheesecake on the other side of the counter?

It looked perfect.

He swept the flowers off the table and headed for the stairs, grinning at the thought of finding Abigail still getting ready.

"Hey, the roast got a little burnt, but I think— What are you doing?" He stopped in the bedroom doorway.

Abigail had her back to him and was stuffing clothes into a small suitcase open on the bed.

"Are we taking another trip?" He could get on board with that. "Give me ten minutes to pack."

But Abigail shook her head, and then her whole body followed suit with a shudder.

Simeon crossed the room in less than a heartbeat.

Abigail tried to skirt out of his reach, but he grabbed her elbow and spun her toward him. Her face was wet and splotchy, streaked with what might have been makeup.

But it was her eyes that made Simeon feel like someone had stabbed a dull knife into his chest and was slowly ripping his heart away from the sinews.

Her eyes were empty.

Hopeless.

Like they'd been before the accident.

"What is it? What's wrong?" He stepped closer, and the flowers rustled in his hand. "Here. These are for you." He held them out, as if their fragile petals could fix whatever was wrong.

"Thanks." Abigail sniffed but didn't take them.

Simeon tossed the bouquet on the bed and pulled her to him. But she pushed away and stuffed a pair of jeans into the suitcase. It knocked the breath out of him harder than the time he'd fallen out of the giant oak in Liam's backyard.

"Abigail. What's going on? Why are you packing?"

She shook her head, tears pelting her cheeks. "I have to go."

"Go? Go where? Why? Did Wendy get to you again?" Everlee had called him the other day to say that Wendy wanted him to know she was sorry—and that she wasn't calling him herself because she wasn't going to interfere in his life anymore. But maybe that had been a ploy.

Abigail's only response was to shake her head and reach for a pile of socks.

"Abigail, stop!" Simeon grabbed her arm again. "Tell me what's going on."

"I can't stay here." Abigail's voice wobbled with each word.

"What do you mean, you can't stay here? Where? River Falls?"

She slid her wedding ring off her finger.

The whole room rocked like the deck of a ship as she held it out to him.

He shook his head, balling his fists so she couldn't slip it into his hands. "Why are you doing this?" His voice sounded strangled, like someone had cut off his oxygen supply. He was pretty sure someone had.

"The adoption agency called." She moved to her dresser and set the ring on top of it.

"This is about the adoption?" Relief coursed through Simeon. "I told you, if you changed your mind, we don't have to—"

"I didn't change my mind." She wiped at her cheeks, sounding suddenly matter-of-fact. "They did. Because of me."

Simeon stared at her. They hadn't even done the home study yet. "What do you mean? Because of your amnesia? They said that wouldn't—"

She shook her head, her expression going grim. "Because of my background check."

Simeon let out an involuntary laugh. This was absurd. "Your background check? What could have possibly—"

"My arrest record." She didn't say it with a hint of a smile, but Simeon laughed again. There was no way that was right.

"There's obviously been some kind of mix up. I'll call Zeb. Someone must have stolen your identity or something."

"It's not a mistake." Abigail's voice was way too even, way too calm.

Why wasn't she upset that someone had used her name to commit crimes?

"Of course it's a mistake. You never—"

"It's not a mistake," Abigail repeated. "I told you before the accident. I'm not who you think I am."

"Before the . . ." Simeon tried to bring some sense to the words. "Are you saying you remember?"

⁂

The look on Simeon's face would forever be seared in Abigail's memory. The hurt, the confusion, the longing.

She'd planned to be gone before he got home, so she'd never have to tell him all of this. But she'd found herself moving through tar as she'd collected her clothes and filled her suitcase.

It was probably better this way. Once he knew everything, he'd send her away and never come looking for her. Never wonder what had happened to her. Never wonder what he'd done wrong, when he'd been nothing but wonderful.

She choked back a sob, fighting for enough control to answer his question.

"I remember," she whispered. "I remember everything." She'd waited months to be able to say those words—and now that she could, all she wanted to do was forget again. Go back to being the person she'd thought she was. The person Simeon loved.

"Come sit down." Simeon dropped onto the bed, shoving her suitcase aside and patting the spot next to him. "Tell me what you remember."

That hope, that kindness in his eyes stabbed her right through the middle.

She retreated to the window, wrapping her arms around herself. Beyond the mountains, the sun dragged its light away from the town.

"I lied to you." Bile tried to escape with the words, but she forced it back down.

"About what?"

The question was simple, but Abigail laughed ironically. "Everything."

"Could you be more specific?" The strain in Simeon's voice nearly broke Abigail.

"Everything. From the moment we met. My past. My parents. My—" She swallowed and licked her lips. "My crimes."

She heard the bed creak, and she was so tempted to go over there and bury her head in his shoulder and let him tell her everything would be okay. Because he would do it. He would do anything for her.

She'd taken advantage of that once. But she wouldn't do it again.

So she made herself remain upright on shaky legs.

Simeon hadn't said a word, and she dared a glance at him. He was watching her, waiting.

She wondered if this was what his clients felt like—like he was someone they could pour their hearts out to, tell their worst secrets, and he would still look at them with compassion.

Only she wasn't a client.

She was his wife.

And once she told him all of this, he would hate her.

She rubbed at the sharp pain in her chest. It was too late to turn back now.

"Do you remember my book?" she asked.

Simeon's expression flipped to relief. "Abigail—" He stood and crossed the room, stopping close enough that his scent—it was sage, she remembered now—tried to lure her into his arms. "Is that what this is about? We've been over this. That book is—"

"A memoir," she said flatly, taking a step backwards. "Or maybe more of a confession. An attempt to leave it all behind for good. But now I see that's impossible."

Simeon shook his head. "It's a novel. You told me that."

"No. You said it, and I let you believe it. I'm sorry."

Simeon scrubbed his hands over his face, and she longed suddenly to feel the rough stubble of his cheeks under her fingertips. But she never would again. She already knew that.

"That doesn't make sense." Simeon's patience sounded stretched thin. "Think about it. The character in your book—"

"Me," she interrupted.

He shook his head but kept speaking. "Is the daughter of—"

"Illinois state senator Colin Harris," she said flatly.

"Exactly." Simeon looked relieved, as if he felt like he was making progress with his argument. "And your parents died a long time ago."

Abigail shook her head with a ferocity that made it ache. "They're not dead. They sent me away. So I couldn't ruin my dad's career. I figured that since I was dead to them, they may as well be dead to me too."

Simeon still didn't seem to grasp what she was saying. "Even if that's true—"

"It's true. You read the book, Simeon. I was a car thief. Or, well, my boyfriend Garrick was. He was part of a crew. I made some calls for them once in a while. Went with him to deliver the cars. I told myself it was all harmless. They were only stealing from really rich people, you know? And I figured their insurance would cover it, so they weren't really hurting anyone, and—" She had to stop. Listening to herself now, parroting back the lines Garrick had fed her, made her sick.

"But in the book," Simeon said slowly. "The narrator—"

"Me," Abigail corrected again.

Simeon shook off her comment. "She was a nurse and this Garrick guy—" He broke off, his eyes widening. "A nurse," he repeated.

Abigail nodded, even as her heart crumbled. He believed it now, she could see it in his eyes. "That's how I knew how to save Pastor Mateo. I was a nurse."

She cleared her throat, forcing herself to go on. "I met Garrick in nursing school. He was a student too. He was always driving these really nice cars, so one day I asked him about it, and he said it was a job perk." She dropped her head against the window. She'd been so naive. "By the time I realized what the job was, I was head over heels for him." She swallowed. "I knew it was wrong, but if I said anything, he'd leave me." Oh, how had she ever been so stupid?

"That's what happened in the book," Simeon said, turning away to pace the room. "It wasn't real." He shook his head as if trying to dislodge the possibility.

"There's more." Now that she'd started, she had to finish. "The part I hadn't written in the book yet. The reason for the manslaughter charge."

Simeon stopped pacing to stare at her. "Manslaughter?" His voice was too thin, his face too pale.

Once she told him the rest, there'd be no hope of salvaging their marriage. But she couldn't make him live in this lie anymore.

She ran a finger up and down the window pane, watching the smudge it left behind.

"We were supposed to deliver a Jaguar," she said, making sure to speak loudly enough that he'd hear her. Because there was no way she'd be able to repeat this. "Garrick was speeding like always, and suddenly there was this cop behind us. I told Garrick to pull over, but he wouldn't. He seemed to be exhilarated by the chase. We were going so fast." She clutched at the curtains. "We ran a red light and hit a car." She had to stop and take a few quick breaths. Finally, she managed to force the words out. "There was a passenger. A woman." She gasped for air but couldn't grab at any. "A pregnant woman."

Her legs folded under her, and she dropped to the ground, burying her face in the rough curtain, a flash of memory washing over her. When she'd lost the first baby, she'd sat right here in this spot and cried. Because she'd known it was her fault. It was what she deserved. She shoved the curtain harder against her face to stifle her sobs.

Strong arms wrapped around her back, and she tried to wiggle away. Simeon tightened his grip, but she turned and shoved against him.

His face registered surprise and hurt as he dropped his arms.

"Don't you see?" She was screaming now, and she probably sounded like a crazed lunatic. "It's my fault we lost our babies. I'm responsible for the death of that woman and her baby. That's why God took our babies away."

"Oh, Abigail." Simeon reached for her again, but she scooted backwards and jumped to her feet.

"Don't. I didn't finish yet."

Wariness cloaked Simeon's features as he stood but didn't move closer.

Good. At least he had the sense to know that he should be worried about what else she could possibly say.

"They arrested us." She could still feel the cold metal of the handcuffs biting into her skin. "I was facing years in prison. But my dad pressured the prosecutor to drop the charges in return for my testimony. I put the rest of the crew in prison, and I walked away scot-free. The moment the trial was over, my parents shipped me out of the country." She paused, waiting to see if he'd make the connection.

It only took a moment. "Ecuador?" he whispered.

She nodded numbly.

"But you told me . . ." Simeon looked so lost that she barely resisted going to him and wrapping her arms around him and telling him it was all a joke. That she hadn't really done any of these things.

"I know what I told you," she said instead. "That I went on mission trips every year. That serving God was my passion. But the truth is—" She licked her lips. "Up until that point, I'd barely stepped foot in a church, except at Christmas and Easter. But I thought maybe the trip wouldn't be such a bad thing. Maybe I could make up for some of what I'd done. Become a better person. And then I met you and—" She shook her head helplessly. She didn't need to tell him anything that would hurt him more.

"And what?" Simeon pressed.

"And I thought maybe it was a chance to start over. To become someone else. The kind of woman who would belong with a man like you."

"So it was all a lie? Right from the beginning?" His voice was flat, and she hated it. She would have much preferred anger. Then she could get angry back, and it wouldn't have to hurt so much.

"It was— I don't know what it was." She forced her voice to remain composed. "I wanted to tell you the truth, but I didn't know what I'd be coming back to, after Ecuador, and then you asked me to marry you, and it seemed like the perfect chance to start over. To be the woman you thought I was."

"Did you—" Simeon cut off, shaking his head, as if he couldn't bring himself to finish the sentence.

"Did I what?" she whispered.

"Did you ever really love me? Or was it all an act?" Torture clung to the words, and he refused to look at her.

"I remember our wedding day," she said softly. "Waiting in the church lobby, and then seeing your face. I was so in love with you." An unexpected sob escaped, but she forced herself to push the rest back down. "And I was so in awe that someone like you could be in love with someone like me." Another sob fought its way up her throat. "But you weren't in love with me. You were in love with this persona I created. And I wish—" She sniffled, choking back another sob. "I wish I could be her again. But I can't. I can't lie to you anymore."

Simeon shook his head, his expression warring between stunned and hurt and confused.

"I still have these." Abigail lifted the divorce papers off the dresser. She'd been planning to leave them for him to make things easier. "They're still valid. All you have to do is sign." She held them out to Simeon, wanting to beg him not to take them. Not to sign.

But he took a step forward and slid the papers out of her fingers.

Chapter 45

Simeon stared at the divorce papers that had somehow materialized in his hands. How was he supposed to comprehend what his wife was telling him? How was he supposed to make sense of the fact that she remembered a past he'd never known about? A past that meant she wasn't the woman he thought she was?

He glanced up from the papers to find her watching him. The tears had stopped falling, but her eyes held fear and anguish.

She really expected him to sign them.

Simeon's eyes went again to the papers.

And then he did the same thing he'd done the first time he'd seen them.

In one long, smooth action, he tore them in half from top to bottom.

"Simeon," Abigail gasped. "What are you—"

He dropped the papers onto the floor and stepped forward, pulling her into his arms, hard.

She fought for a second but then buried her face in his chest with a muffled sob. "You can't do this Simeon. You can't stay with me." But she clutched at the back of his shirt.

"I can and I will," he growled into her hair, clutching at her just as fiercely.

Her head shook back and forth against his chest. "You can't. You'll never be able to have a family. Because of me."

"*You're* my family." Simeon kissed the top of her head, then relinquished his hold just enough to look into her eyes. "I'd love to have children with you, and I still think it's worth talking with the adoption agency about that, if you want to. But the bottom line is, whether we have children or not, we're still a family. You and me." He wiped gently at the tears again slipping silently down her cheeks.

"But—" She tilted her head to the side, as if trying to figure him out. "Why?"

He laughed softly. "Because I love you."

"You can't," she said, pressing a hand weakly to his chest, as if to ward off the words. "Not anymore. Not now that you know."

He slid his hands down her cheeks to rest on her shoulders. "I'm sorry, but you don't get to set limits on my love. I told you the first time I said it, I told you on our wedding day, and I'm telling you now: nothing's going to change that. Ever."

"But I'm not who you thought I was," Abigail whispered.

Simeon let his eyes travel over all of her before bringing them back to hers, their openness sparking renewed hope deep in him. "You are." He bent forward, taking her lips in his, kissing her tenderly. "You are exactly the woman I thought you were. Kind. Loving. Thoughtful." He placed a new kiss on her lips with each word. "Funny. Open. Trusting."

"But, Simeon, the things I've done," she protested, turning her head so that his last kiss landed on her cheek.

"Are in the past," he said firmly. "You aren't captive to those things anymore. You're a new person now."

She shook her head. "You're the one who said old me and new me were the same person."

"They are." Simeon tucked a finger under her chin and turned her to look at him. "And they're both washed clean in the blood of Christ. Which means you're a new creation in him. Right?"

She seemed to consider the question, then nodded slowly. "Right."

"Right," Simeon repeated. He stepped away from her for a moment to scoop her ring off the dresser.

Then he dropped to one knee, grasping both of her hands in his, the same way he had five years ago.

"What are you doing?" Abigail laughed through her tears.

"I'm asking you to be my wife." Simeon stopped, suddenly choked up and needing to clear his throat before he could continue. "I'm asking you to renew our vows. Not because the old ones weren't good enough. But as a symbol of our fresh start—of the way God has renewed us and our relationship. Abigail Calvano, will you marry me again?"

"I will." Abigail dropped to the floor next to him and threw her arms around his neck.

"You didn't let me put the ring on your finger," Simeon protested with a laugh.

"Oh." Abigail let go and held her hand out, and Simeon slid the ring back onto it, then laced the fingers of his left hand between hers so that their wedding rings appeared to intertwine.

They both stared at their interlocked hands for a moment, and then Abigail looked up, her eyes shining.

"Of all the things I remember," she said. "You're my favorite."

He laughed. "And you're mine."

Chapter 46

"You have to hold still so I don't pull your hair."

Abigail let out a breath and tried to obey Grace's command. But it was impossible.

Butterflies were zooming around her stomach at Mach-10, under the white satin bodice of the wedding dress she'd last worn five years ago. She didn't remember being this nervous for her actual wedding, and this was just a vow renewal.

Except, it felt like more than "just" a vow renewal. It felt like a chance to start over, like a commitment to a new life together with Simeon.

"There." Grace slid one more bobby pin from her mouth into Abigail's hair. "I dare that veil to try to slip." She gave Abigail a quick hug, then stepped out of the way so Abigail could look at herself in the mirror they'd set up in the corner of the church conference room.

"Wow." Abigail stood and moved closer to her reflection.

Grace laughed. "I'll say. I think you look even more beautiful today than you did on your wedding day."

Abigail shook her head, sliding her hands down the smooth fabric of the simple dress. Fortunately, the dress shop where they'd gotten everything for Lydia's wedding had been able to alter Abigail's dress within their two-week timeline, and it slid easily over the new curves she'd developed since her wedding day.

But that wasn't what drew her attention.

It was the way wearing the dress made her feel—like the old her and the new her had finally become one person. One memory.

"Are you ready?" Ava bustled into the room, her baby belly finally starting to show under her simple peach dress. "I don't think Simeon can wait a moment longer."

"Almost." Abigail turned to her sisters-in-law. "But first, I just wanted to say—" She had to stop to blink. Grace had worked hard on her makeup, and she didn't want to ruin it. "I wanted to say thank you to y'all for—" Oh man, there went the first tear. "For being there for me and Simeon through all of this." It was all she managed to get out before the tears started to fall in earnest and arms surrounded her from all sides, crushing her in a group hug.

"Watch her dress," someone cried, and they all laughed, but no one let go.

"What are y'all doing?" A male voice from the other side of the room made them all shriek, and the other women formed a wall in front of Abigail.

"Joseph," Ava scolded, stepping toward her husband. "I told you I'd get her."

"Well, you're taking too long. It was either I came in here and dragged y'all out, or Simeon would."

"All right. All right. We're coming." Ava pushed Joseph playfully toward the door, then turned to Abigail. "Ready?"

"Absolutely." The butterflies in her stomach went still, and Abigail suddenly found she couldn't stop smiling.

She followed her sisters-in-law toward the lobby. Only Grace had been in their first wedding—Ava and Ireland hadn't been dating Joseph and Asher at the time, and no one had even known Lydia was part of the family then—but Abigail had wanted them all to be up there with her this time.

As Ava stepped into the sanctuary and started down the aisle toward Joseph, Zeb fell into place next to Abigail. She and Simeon had debated asking him to walk her down the aisle, as he had at their wedding, but he'd put an end to their debate by asking if they'd allow him to do it.

"You look happy," he whispered to Abigail as Ireland started down the aisle toward Asher, her rounded middle giving her a soft, maternal look.

"Thanks. I *am* happy. I only wish—" She swallowed back the words as Zeb shook his head.

"Me too," he said simply. "But she'd be happy for you."

Abigail nodded, once again failing to fight back her tears. She let them fall as they walked toward the sanctuary. Lydia was making her way down the aisle now, followed by Grace. Abigail smiled through her tears as she scanned the line of bridesmaids and groomsmen, all of them her family. A family that had blessed her in ways she couldn't even count.

The piano switched songs, to Vivaldi's "Spring," and from inside the church Abigail heard the sound of a hundred people getting to their feet.

"Are you ready?" Zeb asked.

"Absolutely." She gave him a quick hug before taking his arm. "I'm so ready."

As Zeb led her into the church, Abigail had to fight the urge to run straight to the end of the aisle, where Simeon stood with his eyes fixed on her, his smile reflecting such love that it took her breath away.

When they reached him, Zeb hugged each of them. The moment he stepped back, Simeon leaned forward and kissed her tenderly.

"Ah, Simeon," Pastor Calvano said from in front of them. "I think that part is supposed to come at the end." The guests all laughed.

"Sorry." Simeon grinned at her. "I couldn't wait. And technically, she's already my wife." He took her hand, and they turned to Pastor Calvano so he could begin the service.

He started with a prayer and a responsive reading, then turned to Simeon and Abigail for the sermon.

"When Simeon told me the verse he wanted me to preach on for your vow renewal," Pastor Calvano began, "my first reaction was, 'Son, I love you, but you haven't got a clue about romance.'" The congregation burst into laughter, and Abigail shot a curious glance at Simeon. He hadn't said anything about requesting that his dad preach on a specific verse.

He smiled back at her and squeezed her hand tighter.

"But the more I thought about it," Pastor Calvano continued, "the more I realized that this verse was perfect for you, Abigail, and all you've been through. And I had to admit that maybe my son knows what he's doing after all."

Simeon snorted quietly. "Thanks, Dad."

Abigail laughed and brought her eyes back to Pastor Calvano as he flipped open the Bible in his hands. "We read from Philippians: 'But one thing I do: Forgetting what is behind and straining toward what is ahead, I press on toward the goal to win the prize for which God has called me heavenward in Christ Jesus.'"

Pastor Calvano closed his Bible and looked up, smiling at them. "When I was a kid, there was this older man in our neighborhood who walked past our house every day—backwards. I would just watch him, waiting for him to fall, because he never looked at what was in front of him, only what was behind him." He shook his head. "Sure enough, one day, some kid left a roller skate in the middle of the sidewalk. It wasn't me," Pastor Calvano added with a chuckle. Abigail's laugh mingled with Simeon's and they smiled at each other in the way that made her heart know this man understood her absolutely.

"But I saw it," Pastor Calvano continued, "and I saw him getting closer to it, and I thought, 'I have to warn him.' So I ran to the door and shouted, 'Hey, mister.' Just in time to watch him fall." He paused for a moment, but then continued. "Don't worry, I went and checked and he was all right. And the next day, he was out there walking backwards again. And you know what I wish?" He paused. "I wish I had asked him why. What could possibly have led him to walk backwards instead of forward? And why did he keep doing it after he'd fallen once? Now, in the years since, I've Googled it, and apparently there are some benefits to walking backwards—it strengthens your calves and hamstrings, for one. And it's apparently good for balance. Some people even say it helps with short-term memory. I don't know. All I know is, walking backwards can make you stumble and fall."

He looked up. "That's what Paul is saying in these verses, right? He says we should forget what is behind. In other words, don't walk backwards. Don't spend your time looking at what is behind you, regretting all the mistakes you've made, dwelling on all the sins you've committed, thinking about all the things you wish you'd done differently." Pastor Calvano was wearing that warm smile he always wore when he preached, and his eyes rested on Abigail.

She swallowed. How was she supposed to not look back—not think about those things—now that she remembered?

"You're wondering how," Pastor Calvano said, and Abigail nodded with a smile. He seemed to have a knack for knowing what people were thinking.

"Paul says to *forget* what is behind," Pastor Calvano said. "But is that even possible?"

Abigail sighed. It had been for her. For a short time. It had been nice to shed all that baggage of her past sins. To forget what she had done and who she had been.

"I'm going to be honest," Pastor Calvano continued. "Short of developing amnesia—" He looked to Abigail with a fatherly smile. "It's pretty tough to forget some of these things, no matter how much we might want to. But that doesn't mean we have to walk backwards, looking at them every day, dwelling on them, letting their weight drag behind us. What Paul is saying here is, 'Turn around. Leave those things behind you. Let go of them.' By trusting that Jesus has taken them on himself. By crying out with David, 'Have mercy on me, O God, according to your unfailing love; according to your great compassion blot out my transgressions.' And trusting that he hears you. That he *does* have mercy on you. That his love and forgiveness are *limitless*. That means that your sins, whatever they are, are forgiven."

Pastor Calvano looked from Simeon to her and back again. "Instead of looking backwards, move forward. In your relationship with each other, yes. And also in your relationship with your Savior." He lifted his Bible and read again, "Straining toward what is ahead, I press on toward the goal to win the prize for which God has called me heavenward in Christ Jesus."

He closed the Bible and looked to the bridal party and then the congregation. "Let's make sure we understand this correctly. Paul isn't saying turn around and work hard to earn your salvation. No, he's saying, turn around and look at the prize that has *already been won* for you. Heaven is yours. Not because you deserve it. Not because you've turned your life around. Not because you try hard. Not because you're a good person. Heaven is yours because *he* has promised it to you. Go back again to those words of David: 'Have mercy on me, O God, according to your unfailing love, according to your great compassion blot out my transgressions.'"

He leaned toward them. "Did you hear that? God forgives you because of *his* unfailing love, not because of yours. He blots out your transgressions because of *his* great compassion, not because you've shown so much compassion for others. The reason Paul encourages us to press on isn't to *earn* our forgiveness. It's because we already *have* that forgiveness. Do you see the difference?"

Abigail found herself nodding. Simeon's arm came around her back, and he pulled her close to him. His eyes glistened, and he pressed a long kiss to the top of her head, breathing in deeply.

Abigail closed her eyes, unsure if she needed to laugh or cry—or both.

"This doesn't mean you have to literally forget everything you've ever done," Pastor Calvano said. "The peace isn't in the forgetting. It's in the *remembering*. Remembering Jesus and what he's done for you. Remembering the lengths he went to for you. Remembering the strength of his unfailing love. And when one of you forgets that, when one of you struggles, the other will be there to remind you. To encourage you. To focus your eyes—and your relationship—on him. So that together, you can walk forward. Amen."

Abigail smiled through her tears as the piano began to play and Lydia's and Grace's voices joined in singing "How Firm a Foundation." She leaned closer to Simeon to whisper, "Those were the perfect verses."

He smiled and held her close until the song ended, and then they repeated the same vows they'd made at their wedding. Though that whole part of the ceremony had seemed to pass in a blur five years ago, this time Abigail made sure to focus on every word as they promised to love, support, and cherish one another as long as they both lived. Simeon had already loved and supported and cherished her more than she ever could have imagined on their wedding day. And she was determined to do the same for him—with God's help.

As the ceremony ended, Pastor Calvano grinned at Simeon. "All right, son, I think this is the part you've been waiting for."

"Yes, sir." Simeon turned and gathered her to him, his lips coming to hers in a kiss that sparked applause and cheers and even a wolf whistle from the direction of the groomsmen.

Abigail laughed—and kept kissing her husband. After all, she wanted to make sure the memory would last.

Epilogue

Abigail clutched the baby blanket tight as she and Simeon stepped onto the hospital elevator. They'd just been here a couple of months ago to welcome Asher and Ireland's new bundle of joy, whom the couple had named Caroline Rose in honor of Carly. And now it was Joseph and Ava's turn.

Simeon pressed the button for the second floor, then wrapped an arm around her. "Are you okay?"

"I'm wonderful," she answered honestly, the anger and jealousy that had consumed her when she'd learned her sisters-in-law were expecting replaced by nothing but joy for them.

Over the past few months, she and Simeon had completed the adoption home study process, and after extensive interviews that had included painful questions about her past, they'd finally gotten word last week that they'd been approved to adopt. Their caseworker Janice had warned that it could be months or even years—or possibly never—before someone chose them.

As much as Abigail was ready to raise a family with Simeon, she was also willing to surrender the timing—and everything else—to the Lord. Looking back over her life, she could see his faithfulness in so many ways, and she was ready to trust this to him too.

She glanced at her wedding ring again, admiring not only its shine but also the way it reminded her of all their marriage had endured—and how God had strengthened and refined them through it. Every day, she remembered Pastor Calvano's—Dad's—sermon message about finding peace in remembering what Jesus had done for her. It didn't mean she had completely forgotten her past—but it did mean she didn't feel captive to it anymore.

The elevator door opened, and they stepped into a lobby already filled with Calvanos. Ireland was the first to notice them, and she descended on Abigail with a one-armed hug, her other arm cradling a sleeping Caroline Rose, wrapped in the blanket Abigail had made for her.

"Joseph was out a second ago to announce it's a boy," Ireland related happily. "Noah Paul. We can see him in a minute."

Abigail nodded. Noah was one of the names she and Simeon had considered for a boy before their first miscarriage, but she was glad Joseph and Ava had used it.

Behind them, the elevator opened again, and Zeb and Benjamin stepped out. The two men were laughing together, and Abigail's heart filled as Zeb stepped to Ireland's other side and gathered baby Caroline into his arms. Though Carly's death obviously still weighed on him, over the past months, he'd seemed to be coping better.

"I call dibs on holding Joseph and Ava's baby first," Benjamin announced loudly.

Simeon snorted. "You are such a textbook youngest child it's not even funny." But he grinned as he shoved his brother's arm.

"I'll take that as a compliment," Benjamin snickered. "Anyway, I may be younger than you, but I can kick your butt in football. Or do I need to remind you of our Christmas Day game?"

"Ah, no. I still remember." Simeon rubbed at the wrist he'd sprained in the game. Fortunately, he'd only had to wear a brace for a couple of weeks.

"Anyway, it wasn't my fault. I was distracted by my beautiful wife on the sidelines."

"Hey, don't blame me." Abigail laughed at the same time Benjamin made a retching sound.

"Excuses, excuses," he said, grinning at both of them.

Simeon shrugged. "Maybe you should find your own excuse one of these days."

"Yeah, how's Summer?" Abigail asked in a teasing tone. She'd finally managed to pry it out of him that he and Summer had been friends until the end of high school, when they'd dated briefly. But they'd broken up when he'd left for culinary school. Abigail had been encouraging him to ask her out again.

But Benjamin's brows lowered. "I don't want to talk about it."

"Uh oh. What happened?"

Before Benjamin could answer, a beaming Joseph strode into the room. "Y'all can come meet my son now."

"I'm first." Benjamin pushed past the rest of the crew to get to Joseph's side. The others gave half-hearted protests and laughs as they followed Joseph down the hall.

Abigail and Simeon fell to the back of the group, and Abigail allowed herself a brief moment of sadness that she and Simeon would never spend a night in one of these rooms, waiting for their own little one to be born. But she pushed the sorrow aside. God had a different plan for her and Simeon—and whatever it was, she trusted it was for their good.

By the time they stepped into Ava and Joseph's room, Benjamin had already staked his claim to Noah, standing with the baby cradled in his arms, making silly faces, though the baby's eyes were closed.

"You know he can't see you, right?" Asher called.

"That's okay." Benjamin made another face. "This way, the moment he wakes, he'll know I'm the funny uncle."

As if on cue, baby Noah opened his eyes, blinked at Benjamin, and let out a wail.

"Guess he doesn't like your jokes." An exhausted but radiant-looking Ava laughed.

Benjamin scowled good-naturedly and passed the baby to his dad.

Little Noah quieted and gripped Pastor Calvano's finger. "The Lord bless you, little one," Pastor Calvano murmured.

After a few minutes, he passed the baby to Lydia, who held him for a bit, then passed him on to Liam, who then turned to Abigail. In the middle of their handoff, Abigail's phone burst to life with a loud ring.

Noah startled, and Abigail winced, sure he was going to cry again, but instead, he waved a little fist. Liam eased his arms back, and Abigail nestled the baby closer, wrapping the new blanket around him.

Her phone peeled again, and she turned to Simeon. "It's in my purse. Can you turn it off?" She ran a finger over the baby's smooth cheek, and she was almost sure he smiled up at her.

The rush of awe nearly knocked her off her feet. This baby was perfect. And someday, maybe someone would give her and Simeon the gift of their own child.

"Ah, Abigail?" Simeon's voice sounded weird, and Abigail wondered at first if she was holding the baby wrong.

She glanced at Simeon, who was grasping her still-ringing phone.

"Hit the power button, and it'll stop," she said.

But instead of turning it off, Simeon shook the phone. "It's Janice."

"Janice?" The caseworker had said everything was squared away and she'd check in with them in a few months, unless . . .

Abigail met Simeon's eyes.

Unless she had news sooner.

"Answer it," she rasped, the air suddenly too thin and dry.

Simeon nodded tightly and hit the button to answer the call, then beckoned Abigail to follow him into the hallway.

She hurriedly passed baby Noah to Asher, then raced after Simeon. He had the phone pressed to his ear but lowered it and hit the speaker button, holding the phone between them.

"I know this is unusual, but it's kind of an emergency situation," Janice's voice echoed into the hallway. "We have a birth mom who thought she had a couple more months to decide, but she went into preterm labor last night."

"Preterm?" Simeon closed his eyes, and Abigail reached for his hand.

"Almost thirty-two weeks." Janice's voice was somber. "The baby was born at 1:30 this morning. She's three pounds, twelve ounces and sixteen inches. She's had some breathing problems and is on a ventilator right now, but the doctors think . . ."

Abigail missed the rest of Janice's sentence as Simeon dropped his arm to his side, muffling the phone against his leg.

"We can't," he whispered, his voice choked.

Abigail shook her head but stooped to peel the phone out of his hand.

" . . . Reviewed the files this morning," Janice was saying. "And she chose the two of you."

Tears overran Abigail's eyes and clogged her throat. They had been prepared to wait months or even years, and now God was answering their prayers, right here, right now, today?

"We can't," Simeon repeated.

"We can." Though Abigail was still crying, the words came out with a certainty she felt all the way to her soul.

"If something happens— If she doesn't—" Simeon shook his head. "I can't risk losing you again."

"You won't." Abigail stepped forward and threaded her arms around his shoulders. "No matter what happens. We'll get through it together."

"I understand if y'all need to talk about it," a voice interrupted, and Abigail startled. She'd forgotten that they were still on the phone with Janice. "It's an unusual situation. And obviously the baby will be in the NICU for a while."

Abigail stared at the phone. She'd noticed the sign for the NICU on their way to Ava and Joseph's room. "The NICU where?"

"Brampton Memorial," Janice answered.

Abigail grabbed Simeon's arm. "That's where we are right now."

"Is everything all right?" Janice sounded concerned.

"Yes. Great. Simeon's brother and his wife just had a baby." Abigail was still staring at the phone. This felt too good to be true.

"Well, no pressure, but I'm here right now too, if y'all wanted to come meet her," Janice said.

Abigail glanced at Simeon. He had been so patient with her all these months, never pushed her or pressured her as their relationship redeveloped. And she wasn't going to pressure him into this if he didn't think it was best for their family. It had to be something they both wanted.

"Can we pray about it and get back to you?" Simeon directed his question at the phone.

"Of course. I'll pray for you too. Just give me a call back whenever you're ready." Janice's name disappeared from the screen, but they couldn't seem to look away from it.

"We should, ah—" Simeon stammered.

Abigail nodded. "Let's ask everyone to pray with us."

Simeon's eyes met hers. "You're sure?"

She nodded. "They're our family. I want them to be part of this. Whatever we decide."

The tension in Simeon's face loosened a little. "Me too."

Every Calvano eye seemed to be on the door as they stepped back into the room.

"Well?" Benjamin asked first.

"They have a baby for us," Simeon choked out, and Abigail grasped his arm as the whole room erupted into cheers.

But Simeon held up his other hand. "There are some complications. She's a preemie—and she's having some breathing problems."

The room quieted, and everyone's gaze seemed to shift to Noah and Caroline, both healthy, strong babies.

"What are you going to do?" Zeb asked quietly.

"We thought we'd pray," Abigail said tentatively. "We were hoping y'all—"

Before she could finish her request, they were all folding their hands and bowing their heads. Tears pricked her eyes as she followed suit. How had she not realized before that this family would be at their side, rooting for them, praying for them, supporting them, no matter what happened?

"Dear Lord," Simeon started, but his voice cracked, and he went silent. Next to her, Abigail could feel him trembling, and she wrapped both of her arms around his, pressing herself close to his side.

"Dear Lord." She tried to take up the prayer, but she didn't get any farther than Simeon had before her voice was swallowed up by the enormity of the choice before them.

"Dear Lord—" This time it was Pastor Calvano's voice that lifted them in prayer. "We come before you on behalf of Simeon and Abigail. We thank you, Lord, for the love you have given them for one another. We thank you for their desire to raise a child together in you. We ask that you would give them wisdom and guidance as they decide whether to adopt this child. We ask that you would watch over your newborn babe and give her healing and health and, most of all, lead her to know you."

Simeon wrapped his arms around Abigail as Pastor Calvano continued his prayer, followed by everyone else in the room. By the time the whole family had finished praying for them, Abigail's face was drenched with tears, but her heart was buoyant with the love in the room.

Peace filled her as she realized—God had made this baby, whom they hadn't even met, for them. She belonged in this family, where she would be loved and cherished and told of God's love every day.

She pulled back to meet Simeon's eyes, praying he felt the same way. "What do you think?"

"I think," he said slowly, "that we should go meet our new daughter." A giant smile overran his face, and Abigail lunged to wrap her arms around him, a laugh-sob exploding out of her as the room burst into a chaos of congratulations.

Abigail groaned as the baby's cry interrupted her line of thought. She loved little Genevieve with all her heart; she just needed her to nap five more minutes so she could finally finish writing her book.

At first, Abigail had resisted Simeon's suggestion that she use the time she sat at Genevieve's side in the hospital to continue working on it. She'd even come close to deleting the whole thing. But as she'd reread it, as she'd remembered the pain of the guilt she'd been tormented by when she'd started writing it, she'd realized maybe it was a story she needed to finish. To share the hope that God had given her after all the pain.

She'd changed names and details so that it wouldn't cause problems for her parents—whom she'd finally reached out to a few weeks ago. They'd talked on the phone a couple of times since then, and though things had been stilted and awkward and difficult, Abigail was determined to keep trying. God had forgiven her for every awful sin she had committed. And with his help, she was learning to forgive her parents too.

"I've got her," Simeon called. "Keep writing."

"Thanks," Abigail murmured, already sucked back into the world of her book. She'd already incorporated the parts Simeon had written—she hadn't even known he was doing that until he'd presented them to her a few weeks ago. And now she was finishing up with the day they'd met Genevieve. The moment Abigail had laid eyes on her tiny, frail body attached to tubes and monitors, something strange had happened.

Her tears had dried, and her fears had eased, and her heart had grown a thousand times—because she had *known* without a doubt that this was her daughter, the child she would raise and discipline and laugh and cry with.

When Simeon had asked what they should name her, Abigail had answered instantly: "Genevieve." It was her favorite name from the list they'd made during their first pregnancy.

Simeon had laughed. "That's a big name for such a small girl."

But Abigail had been sure the name fit her. "It means God's blessing."

Simeon had pressed a kiss to Abigail's forehead as they'd both stood over the incubator. "Hello, Genevieve, we're your mom and dad."

There had been a few scares during Genevieve's first several weeks, but God had seen their little family through them, and after just under two months in the hospital, Genevieve had finally been able to come home three weeks ago.

Now that they were home, Abigail and Simeon were getting used to their new role as parents. And even though Abigail had never been more exhausted in her life, she'd also never been happier.

"Rejoice in all circumstances," she tapped on her computer. "The first time I heard that verse, I thought the person who wrote it must be crazy. But now I know, it's not craziness. It's faith. Faith that God is with us, regardless of our circumstances. That he doesn't change, even when we do. That nothing can separate us from his love."

She chewed her lip. How did she want to end this?

"Even when I forgot everything about my life," she typed, "God was there. And he surrounded me with everything I needed. With all the people who loved me. With a family."

Her vision blurred, smearing the words on the screen. But that was okay. Because they were written on her heart.

"Hey." Simeon popped into the room, Genevieve snuggled in his arms. "Someone wanted to see Mama."

The word filled Abigail's heart to overflowing, and she held out her arms to take the baby. "I just finished."

"You did?" Simeon threw his arms around both of them. "What are you going to call it?"

Abigail had given the question a lot of thought, and she kept coming back to one phrase. "I think, *Memories of the Heart*."

Simeon considered the title. "I like it. Can I read it?"

"Yes. But only if you promise me one thing."

"Anything."

She knew he meant it.

"Read the end first."

Simeon laughed. "Won't that ruin the story?"

Abigail shook her head. "Trust me, it's the best part. Because it brought us to where we are right now."

Simeon dusted a light kiss over her lips then pressed one to Genevieve's head. "I do like where we are right now."

"Me too." Abigail leaned back contentedly in the rocking chair, her baby in her arms and her husband next to her, and thanked God for all he'd brought her through. Even when she'd forgotten him, he'd never forsaken her. And she finally understood: he never would.

❧

Thank you for reading MEMORIES OF THE HEART! I hope you loved Simeon and Abigail's story! Find out if things will ever work out between Benjamin and Summer in the next River Falls book, WHISPERS OF TRUTH. And, of course, you'll also get to catch up with the rest of the Calvano family, including all those new little ones.

Also, be sure to sign up for my newsletter to get Asher and Ireland's story, REFLECTIONS OF LOVE, as a free gift.

Visit https://www.valeriembodden.com/freebook to sign up or use the QR code below.

A preview of WHISPERS OF TRUTH (River Falls Book 4)

Chapter 1

Summer peeled her fingers off the steering wheel, then swiped her palms over her cheeks, wiping the moisture they came away with on her t-shirt. She pulled down the sun visor and flipped up the mirror to assess the damage. Fortunately, she hadn't done her makeup yet, or her face would be a disaster. But she looked bad enough the way it was. A full night of crying had left her with puffy eyes and a red nose, and this fresh round of tears had created great pink splotches on her cheeks. She'd have to tell Mama it was a cold. Or allergies.

She supposed other women might turn to their mothers for comfort after a breakup. But she wasn't other girls. And Mama wasn't other mamas. If she knew Nick had dumped Summer, it would be just one more weapon in the arsenal of insults she could hurl at her daughter.

Taking a shaky breath and letting it out slowly, Summer opened the car door and made herself get out. Instantly, the July humidity sucked to her already sticky face. She let herself gaze into the distance for a moment, her eyes roving hungrily over the lush green mountain slopes that ringed the town of River Falls. They always looked so inviting, and more than once as a kid, she had dreamed of running away from Mama and living out there on her own. If it hadn't been for her brother TJ, maybe she would have.

She let out a long breath and moved resolutely to the trunk to unload the groceries, then hurried to the door. She might as well get this over with. She only had a couple of hours before she needed to be in costume and ready to entertain a roomful of giggling girls.

She probably should have saved the shopping for tomorrow and gone to church this morning, but the thought of showing up there all red-faced and puffy-eyed had been less than appealing. Especially knowing that Benjamin would be there, and he would be all sweet and concerned and wonderful—and she couldn't take that right now.

Besides, this way she wouldn't have to do Mama's shopping after the party, when she'd be completely worn out.

She tromped to the stoop and set one of the bags down to fish out her keys, then took another breath and forced herself to unlock the door and step through.

"Good morning, Mama." She didn't bother to try to sound cheerful—that would have made Mama suspicious—but she managed to keep the tears out of her voice.

From her chair in front of the TV, Mama grunted something in Summer's direction. Summer kept going until she reached the kitchen and deposited the packages. She made two more trips to the car, relieved that Mama never once glanced in her direction.

Summer made quick work of unpacking the groceries, then emptied the dishwasher and sorted through the refrigerator for leftovers that had gone bad. She held her breath as she opened the garbage can, hoping against hope that she wouldn't find—

She let the breath out. Sure enough, an empty bottle of whiskey nestled on a bed of beer bottles. Summer tossed the rotten food on top of the pile, her stomach churning. She never bought alcohol for Mama, but somehow it always found its way into the house. Summer suspected that Mama paid a neighbor to pick it up for her.

She did a quick search of the cupboards but didn't find any more. And even if she did find it, she wasn't sure what she would do. The last time she had dumped Mama's stash, her mother's wrath had been intense. Summer had learned to face the fact that if end stage liver disease wasn't enough to stop Mama's drinking, there was nothing she could do to stop it either.

"Bring me a sandwich," Mama called from the living room.

Summer bit back a reply of, *What's the magic word?* and started putting together a ham and cheese sandwich.

TJ was constantly asking her why she still came over here, why she took care of Mama when Mama had never worried about taking care of them. It was a question Summer had asked herself more than once. And she still didn't have a good answer.

She finished making the sandwich and poured Mama a glass of milk, then carried them both to the living room. "Here you are, Mama."

Mama's eyes flicked from her soap opera to Summer. She took the sandwich but waved the milk away. Summer sighed and set it on the TV tray that lived next to Mama's chair. "It's good for you."

Mama grunted. "I'm not thirsty. What's the matter with you, any-way?"

"Nothing."

"Then why's your face all splotchy and your eyes all puffy?"

Summer wished she could believe that was concern in Mama's voice.

"It must be allergies." She sniffed to make the statement convincing.

Mama snorted. "Yeah, and I have a touch of the flu." She turned toward Summer, her yellowed skin gaunt on her cheeks. "Your boyfriend dump you?"

Summer winced even though the comment was exactly what she'd been expecting. She sniffed back the fresh burst of tears that threatened. "He got a job offer in California."

A wave of humiliation rolled over her as she recalled her reaction to his announcement: "I can't move to California."

And his response: "I wasn't asking you to."

But that was nothing Mama needed to know.

"Yeah, well." Mama glanced at her, and Summer couldn't tell if it was her imagination or wishful thinking, but she could have sworn she saw a flash of sympathy in Mama's eyes. Before she could analyze it, it was gone, replaced by Mama's signature cynical expression. "It's like I always told you. A man will amuse himself with you until something better comes along and he realizes he doesn't really want you." Her eyes swung back to the TV.

Summer wondered for the eight-millionth time if Mama would have been like this even if Summer and TJ's father hadn't left the day Summer was born. "Took one look at you and that's the last I ever saw of him," was the way Mama told it, making it abundantly clear that it was some undesirable quality in the newborn baby that had chased him away.

Maybe *that* was why Summer was so driven to take care of Mama—she felt like she had to make it up to her.

"Do you need anything else before I go?" Summer picked up a throw pillow off the floor and tossed it on the worn couch Mama never used.

"What about the laundry?"

Summer checked the time. If she didn't get going, she wouldn't have enough time to get ready for the party. "I can start it. Do you think you can put it in the dryer later?"

"Yeah, sure. Maybe I'll have a dizzy spell and fall down the basement steps and then you won't have to worry about my laundry ever again." Mama's eyes remained glued to the TV the entire time she spoke.

"Don't talk like that." Summer grimaced. "I'll put the laundry in now and then I'll come back after my party to finish it."

"Isn't twenty-two a little old to still believe in fairy tales?" Mama rolled her eyes. "Aren't your tears plenty proof that there's no such thing as a happy ending?"

Summer ignored the questions—Mama was still absorbed in her TV show anyway—and marched to the bedroom to grab the laundry. But just because she hadn't answered out loud, didn't mean the thoughts weren't bouncing around in her head.

Did she believe in fairy tales and happy endings?

Yes, absolutely.

Just because she was unlikely to ever experience one didn't mean she should keep other girls from that dream.

She carried Mama's clothes down to the basement and dumped them into the washer, thinking, as she poured in the detergent, that at least it wouldn't be much of a stretch for her to play Cinderella today. Even if her Prince Charming was some high school kid she'd found through an online ad. He had only one qualification that had gotten him the job: he was the only one who applied.

There was another, a little voice reminded her. But she pushed it away. Benjamin Calvano had only been joking—that man didn't know how to be serious.

And anyway, if there was anyone she *didn't* need to play her Prince Charming right now, it was Benjamin. She could only imagine the havoc *that* would wreak on her heart. Aside from Nick, he was the only other guy she'd dated—and it had turned out that he hadn't wanted her either.

She closed the washer harder than she meant to and pulled her phone out of her pocket as she walked up the stairs. If she left right now, she should be—

She stopped in the middle of the steps, as her eyes fell on the text that had popped onto her screen.

Can't make it today. Sorry.

She didn't recognize the number, but a sick feeling in her stomach told her she already knew who it was from. She clicked over to the string of earlier texts to check. Sure enough, it was her Prince Charming.

She groaned.

She never should have agreed to Mrs. Feldman's request that she provide not only a princess but also a prince for this party. She was a solo act. She'd told Mrs. Feldman that. But the influential woman had insisted, and Summer knew this party had the potential to bring her a bunch more clients looking for princess parties. It seemed like her last chance to finally get her fledgling little business off the ground.

Which was why she couldn't afford for anything to go wrong.

She scanned the dingy stairway, as if a Prince Charming might suddenly materialize.

When none did, she fired back a quick text. *The party starts in two hours. I don't have time to find someone else.* She sent it, even though she already knew it would do no good. The kid hadn't exactly struck her as the reliable type.

She marched up the stairs, calling, "I'll be back in a few hours, Mama," on her way through the living room. Mercifully, Mama's only answer was a light snore.

When Summer got to her car, she checked her phone again, but her text remained unopened. She let out a breath, wracking her brain for a solution. She couldn't show up without a prince, not when she'd promised Mrs. Feldman. It would be the end of her business, for sure.

With a resigned sigh, she tapped her brother's name. TJ had taken his four-year-old son Max fishing after church, but Summer knew her nephew well enough to know he wouldn't last long before getting antsy anyway, and if they left right now, they could get back in time for the party.

Still, she hated to ask TJ to rescue her yet again. He already let her live with him and Max rent-free so that she wouldn't have to live with mama. Sure, she babysat Max while TJ was at work and covered as many other expenses as she could, but that came nowhere near to making it even.

But she didn't see what other choice she had right now. She sent a quick text asking him, then started the car and backed out of the driveway. If she didn't get going, there wouldn't be a princess party at all. Fortunately, the drive through downtown River Falls—where families mingled on the streets in front of the bookstore and the art shop and Daisy's pie shop, and where couples strolled the riverfront walkway, and where everyone's smile seemed to mock Summer's loneliness—took less than ten minutes. The instant she pulled into the driveway, she grabbed her phone and found a reply from TJ.

You know Benjamin offered to do it.

Summer made an annoyed sound. Her brother's obsession with getting the two of them back together was wearing on her. The first thing he'd said when she'd come home crying last night was, "Nick is an idiot. And so are you if you don't know who you should call now."

I'm sure he has to work, she texted back. *And I'd rather go princeless than ask him.*

Ouch, TJ replied. *You better hope I don't tell him that.*

TJ, was her only reply.

Yeah, I'm on it, his text came back a moment later. *Bring the Prince Charming costume with you and send me the address.*

Summer heaved a sigh of relief and sent a *Thank you, thank you, thank you* message.

Then she headed inside, stubbing her toe on one of Max's dinosaur toys. She hobbled toward her bedroom and opened the door of her small closet, smiling as she always did at the gem-colored ball gowns hanging there. It was her five-year-old self's dream come true. Her heart suddenly lighter at the thought of making another little girl's dreams come true, she grabbed the blue dress and prepared to transform into a princess.

Chapter 2

Benjamin pulled his arm back, pumping the football a few times as he waited for his brother Joseph to get open in the makeshift end zone of Dad's front yard. The moment he saw his opening, he let the ball fly, the satisfaction of a perfect spiral coursing through him with the same power as it had at the state championship game he'd led his team to three years in a row in high school.

Joseph caught the ball effortlessly, and Benjamin threw his arms in the air with a cheer. "And that's how the kids do it," he called to his older brothers Zeb and Simeon and his brother-in-law Liam.

"I'm not sure I still qualify as a kid," Asher muttered to him. "But I'll take the win anyway."

Together, the sweaty brothers jostled and laughed their way to the porch where Simeon, Joseph, Asher, and Liam all went instantly to their wives. Zeb, whose wife had died just over a year earlier, scooped Asher and Ireland's little girl, Caroline, off of Dad's lap and kissed her cheek.

Benjamin debated between claiming Ava and Joseph's six-month-old Noah or Simeon and Abigail's little Genevieve, born the same day in the same hospital.

"Ah, I think this guy needs a diaper change," Ava announced, and that decided that.

Benjamin reached for Genevieve, and Abigail handed her over with a smile. The little girl grinned at him, two teeth poking through her gums, and patted his face.

He listened as multiple conversations flew around him, soaking up the sounds of his siblings' chatter as he made faces at Genevieve. The little girl's giggles were contagious.

"So." Abigail looked up at him from the rocking chair. "How are things?"

"Good. Why?"

"Any news on the dating front?" Abigail smiled knowingly.

"Oh. That." Benjamin shrugged. He'd been planning to wait until he saw how things went before he brought it up with his family. Otherwise, they were likely to blow everything out of proportion. As the youngest and the only remaining unmarried sibling—although they hadn't seen Judah in so long that it was entirely possible he was married and had a family they knew nothing about—he was often the victim of unwanted matchmaking. "I have a date tonight." A Sunday night date might seem strange to some people, but Jasmine hadn't batted an eye when he'd mentioned that he had Sunday-Monday and Tuesday-Wednesday off on alternating weeks. As a realtor, her weekends were busy too.

"I know." Abigail grinned, and Benjamin didn't bother to ask how. River Falls was a small town, and he had a big family, so it was pretty much a given that nothing could be kept secret.

"Oh, who is it with?" Ava joined the conversation eagerly.

"Jasmine," Abigail answered for him.

"The real estate agent who sold you the house?" Ireland jumped into the conversation. "She's nice."

"She is," Abigail agreed. "Although I wish you would have asked Summer out. I still don't get what happened there. You're the most impulsive person I know, and you dragged your feet for months on that. And then it was too late."

Benjamin shrugged, even though his heart agreed with his sister-in-law one hundred percent. He had been an idiot not to ask Summer out before that Nick guy got to her.

He'd spent the last four months kicking himself for that. But now it was time to move on. Besides, it wouldn't be bad to have a fresh start with someone who had never broken his heart before.

"Where are you taking her?" Lydia joined the conversation too, and Benjamin rolled his eyes. So much for keeping this under wraps. "The Depot?"

Benjamin snorted. "So all of my coworkers can ogle us? No thanks. I was thinking that pizza place up on the ridge, but I should text her to see if she's okay with that."

He adjusted Genevieve so he could reach into his pocket, but his phone wasn't there. "Where is my . . ." He glanced around. "I must have left it in the house." He planted a big kiss on his niece's cheek and gave her back to Abigail, then traipsed into the house.

His phone was on the kitchen counter, and he swiped a cookie as he picked it up.

A string of texts from his friend TJ lit the screen, and he scrolled through them.

You busy? Summer needs a Prince Charming. 3pm to 5pm.

Benjamin grinned, his eyes flicking to the time. It was 2:15 now. And his date wasn't until 7.

You there? If you don't do it, I'm going to have to. But I think we'd both prefer if it was you. Benjamin stared at that one for a moment, trying to decide if *both* referred to TJ and Benjamin or to TJ and Summer.

Before he could figure it out, another text came through. *I guess you're busy. I'll go. But don't say I didn't give you your opportunity. She and Nick broke up last night, btw.*

Benjamin blinked at the words, his heart racing and breaking at the same time. He hated to think of anything hurting Summer, and yet . . . If she wasn't with Nick—

He stopped himself right there. He had a date with another woman tonight. And anyway, if he and Summer started dating again, chances were good that it would only destroy the friendship with her that he'd worked so hard to rebuild over the past year.

Still . . . Friends helped friends out.

I can do it, he texted TJ.

Three seconds later, TJ texted an address in the foothills on the outskirts of town. Benjamin was going to have to leave right now if he wanted to get there on time. He slid his phone into his pocket and made his way back through the house and out the door.

"So I guess she likes pizza?" Lydia asked with a laugh.

"Huh?" Benjamin halted. "Who likes pizza?"

"Jasmine." Lydia rolled her eyes.

"I don't know. I didn't get a chance to text her."

"Then what were you doing, and why are you grinning like a fool?" Abigail asked.

"Eating cookies." Benjamin grinned back easily. It wasn't a lie. "I gotta take off."

"Where are you going in such a hurry?" Joseph asked. "Don't tell me it's going to take you four hours to get ready for your date."

Everyone laughed, but Benjamin didn't care. "I have to do a favor for a friend first."

KEEP READING WHISPERS OF TRUTH

Also By Valerie M. Bodden

More River Falls Books

While the books in the River Falls series are linked, each is a complete romance featuring a different couple.

Pieces of Forever (Joseph & Ava)

Songs of Home (Lydia & Liam)

Memories of the Heart (Simeon & Abigail)

Whispers of Truth (Benjamin & Summer)

Promises of Mercy (Judah & Faith)

River Falls Christmas Romances

Wondering about some of the side characters in River Falls who aren't members of the Calvano family? Join them as they get their own happily-ever-afters in the River Falls Christmas Romances.

Christmas of Joy (Madison & Luke)

The Hope Springs Series

While the books in the Hope Springs series are linked, each is a complete romance featuring a different couple.

Not Until Forever (Sophie & Spencer)

Not Until This Moment (Jared & Peyton)

Not Until You (Nate & Violet)

Not Until Us (Dan & Jade)

Not Until Christmas Morning (Leah & Austin)

Not Until This Day (Tyler & Isabel)

Not Until Someday (Grace & Levi)

Not Until Now (Cam & Kayla)

Not Until Then (Bethany & James)

Not Until The End (Emma & Owen)

Want to know when my next book releases?

You can follow me on Amazon to be the first to know when my next book releases! Just visit amazon.com/author/valeriembodden and click the follow button.

Acknowledgements

Oh, this book. Writing it has done all kinds of things to my heart. It was both easy to write and hard to write. Easy because once I got to know Simeon and Abigail on the page, the words somehow just flowed. But hard—*so hard*—because of the things they had to deal with——which meant I had to deal with those things too. Some of them are things I've experienced in my own life, like Abigail's miscarriages and Simeon's struggle to "be still" and leave things in God's hand. And others I may not have personally dealt with (like a secret criminal history), but I still had to face them on some level. Because while I may never have been charged with a crime, I *am* guilty. There's an elephant on the other side of my teeter-totter too. And even though I know Jesus has lifted that elephant off, it can be hard not to walk backwards. Not to look back with regret on my sins. Not to think that there's no way God could possibly forgive *me*. Not to feel like I don't deserve to be loved by anyone, least of all by God.

But that's the beauty of the Gospel message: I don't deserve to be loved, but *God loves me anyway*. Because he *is* love. So my first and highest thanks is to him. For loving me. For saving me. And for giving me the gift of storytelling to share that beautiful promise with others. Because his love is not for only a select few. No, God loves *the world* so much that he sent his one and only Son to die for every single person, that all who believe may be with him in heaven.

330

And I thank him for blessing me with an incredible husband and four wonderful children, as well as the two babies who did not make it past the first trimester of pregnancy. Miscarriage is one of those topics that I think a lot of us have personal experience with, but we don't talk about often. That's part of why I wanted to share Abigail's story. The heartache is real—but so too are God's grace and comfort and healing.

As always, I am thankful for my parents, sister, in-laws, and extended family. You're all part of the reason I love writing supportive, encouraging families like the Calvanos.

And speaking of supportive and encouraging, I can't give enough thanks for my incredible advance reader team. You'll never know how much it means to me when your emails come flooding in, saying how much you loved Simeon or how much you related to Abigail or how much you hurt for Zeb or how much you were touched by Pastor Calvano's sermons. Special thanks to: Patty Bohuslav, Vickie, NJM, Lincoln Clark, Michelle M, Rhondia, Seyi, Sandy G, Connie Gandy, N Fudge, Jeanne Olynick, Diana A, Trista Heuer, Margaret N, Judith Barillas, Darla Knutzen, Joy Lacey, Vicki, Terri Camp, Maxine Barber, KBH, Pam Williams, Teresa Malouf, Deb Galloway, Trudy Cordle, Carol Witzenburger, Jan Gilmour, Becky C, JS, DS, Josie Bartelt, Ilona, Ginny Durr, Lisa Gallup, Thomas Morschhäuser, Ann Diener, Kathy Ann Meadows, Alison K, Bernie Cinkoske, Christine Gerber, Evelyn Foreman, Sandy H, Barbara J Miller, Joan Arning, and Carissa Anders.

And finally, thank *you*, dear reader, for spending time with the Calvanos. I hope that your time with them has been a blessing. And most of all, I hope that their story has reminded you that you don't have to get amnesia to let go of your past—because the peace comes in *remembering* what Jesus has done for you.

About the Author

Valerie M. Bodden has three great loves: Jesus, her family, and books. And chocolate (okay, four great loves). She is living out her happily ever after with her high-school-sweetheart-turned-husband and their four children. Her life wouldn't make a terribly exciting book, as it has a happy beginning and middle, and someday when she goes to her heavenly home, it will have a happy end.

She was born and raised in Wisconsin but recently moved with her family to Texas, where they're all getting used to the warm weather (she doesn't miss the snow even a little bit, though the rest of the family does) and saying y'all instead of you guys.

Valerie writes emotion-filled Christian fiction that weaves real-life problems, real-life people, and real-life faith. Her characters may (okay, will) experience some heartache along the way, but she will always give them a happy ending.

Feel free to stop by www.valeriembodden.com to say hi. She loves visitors! And while you're there, you can sign up for your free story.

Printed in Great Britain
by Amazon

46311400R00192